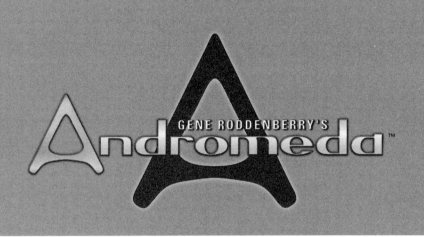

GENE RODDENBERRY'S

Andromeda™

WAYSTATION

GENE RODDENBERRY'S

Andromeda™

NOVELS FROM TOR BOOKS

DESTRUCTION OF ILLUSIONS
KEITH R. A. DeCANDIDO

THE BROKEN PLACES
ETHLIE ANN VARE WITH DANIEL MORRIS

WAYSTATION
STEVEN E. McDONALD

VISIT THE *ANDROMEDA* WEB SITE
AT WWW.ANDROMEDATV.COM

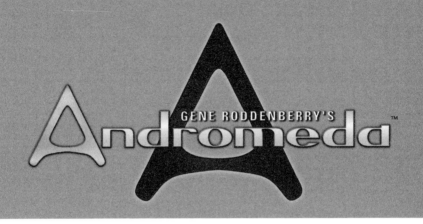

GENE RODDENBERRY'S

Andromeda™

WAYSTATION

STEVEN E. McDONALD

A TOM DOHERTY ASSOCIATES BOOK

NEW YORK

TOR®

GENE RODDENBERRY'S ANDROMEDA™: WAYSTATION

Copyright © 2004 by Tribune Entertainment, Inc., and Fireworks Entertainment, Inc.

Edited by James Frenkel

A Tor Book
Published by Tom Doherty Associates, LLC
175 Fifth Avenue
New York, NY 10010

www.tor.com

Tor® is a registered trademark of Tom Doherty Associates, LLC.

ISBN 0-765-30485-6

EAN 978-0765-30485-8

First Edition: May 2004

Printed in the United States of America

0 9 8 7 6 5 4 3 2 1

For Sylvia,
for loyalty and courage
rarely matched

ACKNOWLEDGMENTS

The theory is that writing keeps me sane—well, to a point. The truth is that I consequently drive everyone around me crazy.

This is by way of explaining why my editor, James Frenkel, has spent months studying certain arcana in preparation for the day when the book was set, and I could be safely—and deservedly—beset by ravening hounds of hell. Jim, I have only the best things to say about you for many reasons.

Thanks to my wife, Sylvia Lau-McDonald, for pitching in with notes, comments, and correction. Sometimes it isn't about writing, it's about rewriting—as our daughter Miriam, who just added sportswriter to her accomplishments, is finding out.

Mark Cantwell, Mutt to my Jeff. I can't say enough.

For ethereal support, thanks to Ashleen, Debra, Carol, and CJ.

In the virtual world, a shout-out to folks at *Sanity Assassins* (http://forums.delphiforums.com/sanityassassin), both my co-mods and various guests—some of them can be found hidden in these pages. Steff, Paul Jack, Mario, Jens, Micah, Harris, Ian, Kady Mae,

Kirk, Jard, Robert, Patty, Mary, and so on, and so on, you've been an incredible support.

Sixteen bars at 130 beats per minute to my fellow musicians in the Tapegerm Collective (http://www.tapegerm.com) for letting me take an extended leave of absence.

Thanks to Wendy Despain, manager of the official *Gene Rodden-berry's Andromeda* Web site, to various fan site owners, to Seth Howard for a long discussion about Trance's true nature, and to everyone who helped me acquire episodes.

Finally, thanks to Laura Bertram, for bringing some intriguing aspects to the character of Trance Gemini, and, more generally, to the cast and crew of the show.

—Steven E. McDonald
Tucson, Arizona

NOTE

This story takes place directly after
episode four of season three, "Cui Bono."

There comes a time during the history
of any civilization when the art of diplomacy
as expressed in the handshake, hug, and knife
in the back gives way to the art of diplomacy
as expressed in the use of massed cannon
and smart bombs.

—GENERAL KORDOS RIEKAN,
DIPLOMACY AND WAR: A PREDICTIVE PERSPECTIVE,
CY 9263

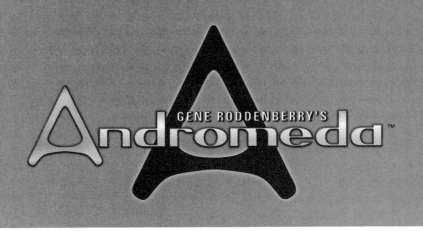

GENE RODDENBERRY'S

Andromeda™

WAYSTATION

ONE · BROAD HINTS AND DEEP MYSTERIES

Never shake hands with a razorpig.

—INFORMAL HIGH GUARD MOTTO,
CIRCA CY 5000

Nothing was clear. That scared her, as much as she could be scared.

Her name was Trance Gemini, at least for now. Her skin was gold, shading to pink in some areas, and her long red hair was caught into tight braids, some of which were woven into an ornate design that offset her sharply pointed ears. Depending upon mood or need, her face could seem soft and caring, or become a mask of cold determination. Even her shipmates, long used to her mercurial state, had no hope of predicting what she would do, say, or manifest next.

She was watching the stars, looking for the lines of force, and trying to divine individual characteristics. She was standing on the huge observation deck of the *Andromeda Ascendant*, a former Systems Commonwealth High Guard starship that was the epitome of the iron fist in the velvet glove—her outward beauty, composed in the main of curves with only a handful of straight lines, concealed an ability to destroy entire star systems. Prior to the fall of the old Commonwealth, the 1.4-kilometer-long *Andromeda Ascendant* had carried a complement of forty-seven hundred. Now it was occupied by only a handful of people. Trance had left her mark on the ship, however— the hydroponics gardens had flourished in her hands, and she had placed plants all over the ship. Andromeda was extremely pleased.

She was Trance Gemini. Once upon a time she had been younger, purple, and equipped with a prehensile tail. All those things were gone. Her tail, always a useful tool, had been shot away in a firefight. Her younger self had gone forward in time, and she had come backward to replace her, and temporal paradoxes be damned. She had come back from a terrible future, a time that had claimed all too many of the people she had known, as well as an increasing chunk of the universe.

She had said, time and again, that her agenda was to create the perfect possible future. Yet she had arrived amid chaos in a place where time was out of joint and almost limitless quantum possibilities radiated into the future. Faced with too many choices, she had narrowed them to one. In that instant she had locked down one reality, condemned a brilliant Perseid scientist to the fate he had already suffered, and saved a human she cared about from a horrible death.

She had made the choice out of friendship, for better or worse. She had easily admitted that later. She had also admitted that she had no idea as to the long-term consequences of her actions. It was almost the complete truth at the time. Within seconds she had felt her memory starting to blur and shift, leaving her feeling as though she were looking at her own existence through smoked glass.

It was not the first time she had been through that particular temporal nexus, but she was going to keep *that* piece of information to herself, at least for now. She had caused one man to sacrifice himself for the good of billions. A fair trade, perhaps . . . no, she was certain. Gaheris Rhade had been a trusted and admired first officer, and he had betrayed the ship and her crew when the Nietzscheans had revolted against the Commonwealth. He had murdered the captain, his friend, and been frozen in time as the *Andromeda Ascendant* moved inexorably toward the event horizon of a black hole. Three hundred years later the ship had been pulled free. Rhade had been devastated when he discovered what had happened since the Nietzscheans—*his* people—had brought down the Systems Commonwealth.

Imposing his will on the great starship, and taking on the salvage crew that had rescued her, he had set out to repair the damage and rebuild, by any means necessary, the Commonwealth.

He had failed, his efforts leading to exponentially worsening conditions. Trance had lived in a future of black despair and endless destruction. When the opportunity arose, she had marshaled her powers and ridden the probability stream until she reached the nexus she needed. Time and space were tangled in complex knots at that point, victims of an out-of-control tesseract machine that was folding space a bit too efficiently.

She had stepped out of her present and into her past. Her younger self had nervously changed places with her—she hadn't remembered being quite *that* shade of purple—and she had gone to speak with Rhade.

The conversation had not been a long one. When it was over, she had taken him through a spatio-temporal interface, leaving him on the *Andromeda Ascendant* just before his betrayal. She had left, but she knew what had happened then. Gaheris Rhade had, in defiance of temporal logic, shot his younger incarnation, taken his place, and reversed events by allowing himself to be killed by the man he had betrayed.

Everyone else believed that the mysterious tesseract generator was the sole source of the space-time distortions. Trance, however, knew the truth—that the tesseract generator was only one of the reasons space-time had suddenly begun tearing itself apart.

The universe had needed to realign itself following Rhade's final actions. She had not helped the healing process much by looping around once more, coming backward from a future that was only marginally less terrible. Her younger self was, if anything, even more nervous about changing places with her. There had been no choice other than to take the second journey into the nexus. There was far too much at stake for her to hesitate.

There was a price for her determination, however. With each decision she made, each step she took to set things right, she endured another mental upheaval as her memory realigned to each change in the timeline. The shifts felt like tidal currents pulling at her mind, and sometimes all she wanted was to be swept away. Keeping all the pieces in the proper places was no easy task, even for her.

There was so much to do, still. Sooner or later she was going to have to let more of the truth out, and bear the consequences.

Someday she would have to tell them all what she really was.

Still, things had changed. She hesitated to trust that the changes were all positive, but she could hope. She had put too much of herself into this to fail now.

Nothing was clear anymore. Nothing.

She bowed her head for a moment, and took a deep breath, trying to focus. She looked up again, centering herself, and letting her mind drift until the starfield was all she was aware of.

"Help me," she whispered. "Please. Help me."

Captain Dylan Hunt, the tall, towheaded commander of the Systems Commonwealth starship *Andromeda Ascendant*, strode out onto the expansive Command Deck. There was always pleasure in the moment of contemplation before his mind turned to command issues; *Andromeda* was a live being, and he could feel her pulse, her heartbeat.

Come to think of it, he could *literally* feel her pulse or heartbeat if he wanted to—all he had to do was reach out to *Andromeda*'s android avatar. Seamus Zelazny Harper, their sometimes-lunatic engineer, had built the avatar using old High Guard manuals found on a former High Guard station. He had started with a standard maintenance android as his template and by the time he was done he had created a perfect match for the idealized image that the ship's AI used. The avatar was slender and exotic, but the sylphlike appearance was deceptive. He had fought alongside her on several occasions, and always felt slow and clumsy in comparison.

To his right, standing at one of the bridge consoles, Andromeda—Rommie, as she preferred to be called—turned her head to look at him. Her face was still, and she said nothing, but it was enough to make him take a mental step backward to see what he was doing to pique her curiosity.

He was smiling, he realized. One of those big, beaming smiles, full of sunshine. Alarmed, he realized he was on the verge of becoming perky.

"Radiant joy and gleaming hope." Dylan turned to his left, still smiling. The words were bright, but in the dour, laconic drawl of Tyr Anasazi they had all the qualities of a dirge. "Have you seen the light of the Divine then, Dylan, and decided to follow the Way?"

As suggestions went, it was certainly not a bad one. Wayists were among the most peaceful beings in this brave new Systems Commonwealth that he had kick-started into existence. He had seen for himself that the Wayist path could tame even the ferocity of Magog. Well, one Magog, the Reverend Behemiel Far Traveler. Rev Bem had left their small company suddenly, driven by a need to find answers to unexpected questions. It was the best path for Rev to take, Dylan knew, but he still felt the loss on a spiritual level.

Tyr, of course, felt quite free to mock the Way. The religion encouraged a passivity that ran counter to everything in the Nietzschean culture's philosophy, where survival by any means was the ultimate goal. Bioengineered into existence by Drago Museveni, who had turned his own son into the first of the Homo sapiens invictus genus, Nietzscheans had inherited a drastic philosophy—they were to be the perfect, unconquerable people. It was the perception that their existence was threatened by Commonwealth policies toward the feral Magog that had caused the Nietzschean prides to unite in a revolution. Ultimately, the Commonwealth had fallen. With the onset of the Long Night, the Nietzschean prides had turned on each other. In Dylan's time they had been warriors, poets, artisans. That was no longer the case.

Tyr had indeed survived, outliving the rest of his pride, but it was not exactly a worthy achievement by Nietzschean standards. It had, instead, made his genetic line suspect—if the Kodiak Pride had fallen before their enemies, then it indicated weakness.

He had no time to retort to the Nietzschean, however. Beka Valentine was standing at the pilot's console, leaning slightly backward. Her full lips quirked slightly. "Tyr's got a point. A good point." She looked across Command, to where the slight and extremely rumpled figure of Seamus Harper was standing and staring into a mug of coffee. Inducted into the reconstituted High Guard or not, there was no chance that Harper was ever going to come close to any sort of uniform code.

Harper suddenly realized he was being looked at. "Huh?"

Oh, yes, a typical Harper moment. Normally he lived in overdrive, but there were moments when he underwent a complete disconnect.

Harper looked at each of them in turn, his face screwing up further and further in confusion. He finally looked back at Beka. "Wh*at*?"

Another Harper tic. Seamus Harper could turn any monosyllabic word into one containing two syllables or more. It was definitely not his most appreciated talent.

"You slipped something into Dylan's breakfast, didn't you?" Beka said. "I know you, Harper. It's that crazy engineer stuff you do."

Tyr turned to look at Harper. The big Nietzschean had the expression of a man regarding a bug he was contemplating crushing. In the Nietzschean's case that might be *exactly* the thing he had in mind.

"Hey, wait a freakin' minute!" Harper protested, his expression shifting between astonishment, disbelief, and annoyance in rapid succession. "Why would I do something like that?"

"Wouldn't be the first time," Beka said.

"Oh, come on, that was a freakin' *accident!*" Harper cried as Tyr, Rommie, and Dylan turned to look at Beka.

"Tyranian joy-juice," she said.

"So I didn't *know*, okay?" Dylan, Tyr, and Rommie looked back at Harper. Dylan wondered if this was what life had normally been like on the *Eureka Maru*, Beka's salvage ship. More sullenly, Harper added, "The guy in the store said it was like orange juice for humans. I thought it would be good with breakfast."

"It took us a week to get Trance back to normal," Beka said ruefully, looking at Dylan.

"You mean whatever passes for normal with Trance," Harper added.

"I believe I understand what has been behind my good mood of late," Tyr said quietly. Dylan's smile faded as he tensed. Tyr couldn't be taking this seriously, could he? Then again, Dylan couldn't remember *any* indication of a good mood on Tyr's part lately.

"Oh, no! Ohhh, no!" Harper said, holding up a hand as Tyr stepped off of the command riser and walked toward him. Dylan almost started to smile again at the contrast. Tyr was very tall, very dark, and extremely muscular. His expression was calm, but his gaze did not waver in the slightest, and the mass of long dreadlocks that hung halfway down his back only added to the image of a predator sizing up a snack.

Harper, on the other hand, was a wiry, rumpled man of average height. While it was not a good idea to underestimate Harper's ability in a fight, he was no match for Tyr.

Harper turned to Rommie. He was beginning to look desperate now. "Rom-doll, you see everything—"

Rommie's holographic avatar shimmered into view next to Harper, startling him. "We all know how good you are with my systems, Harper."

"He does have a way with women, doesn't he?" the android avatar said to the holographic avatar.

Screens lit up with the image of the ship's core AI. "That's one way of putting it."

"So," the android Rommie said, "I can't vouch for you, can I?"

Harper had now worked all the way through to slack-jawed astonishment. "I don't freakin' *believe* it. Rommie, if I'd been messing around with your circuits—"

"Perhaps you have a secret agenda," said Tyr.

Dylan could almost see Harper's brain suddenly going full blast, as though someone had thrown a switch. "Yeah, right, like *I* care, Tyr. That stuff's your department. Well, yours and Trance's."

"I have a secret agenda?" The sound of Trance's voice made everyone turn toward the Command Deck entrance. Dylan, knowing all too well what Trance was capable of, wondered how long she had been standing there. "And why are you trying to scare Harper?"

Tyr raised an eyebrow. "The spirit of fun," he said.

"Oh, sure," Harper said with a sneer. "Your idea of fun is blowing stuff up. Or shooting things. Or shooting them and *then* blowing them up."

"I think we've had enough fun for now," Dylan said. "We're back in the business of making new friends, and I want everybody ready to make the best possible impression when we reach Kantar. Even you, Mr. Harper."

Harper looked down at his rumpled clothes, then across at Beka. "This is just fine, right, Boss?"

"Oh, for a lot of things," Beka said. Harper had been her engineer on the *Eureka Maru* for years before they had encountered Dylan. As far as she cared, Harper could wear whatever he wanted, just as long as he got the job done and didn't scare the clients. "Just not for these diplomatic missions Dylan likes to bore us with."

"I don't think it'll be so boring," Trance interjected. Somehow, her baby-doll voice managed to fill the deck.

All levity was suddenly gone. Trance Gemini was an enigma, and every time there seemed a possibility of finding explanations for her, other questions arose. She was the most disingenuous person Dylan had ever known. She had signed up with Beka's crew on the *Eureka Maru*, but no one had known her background—no one had asked. In this day and age, even with the formation of a new Commonwealth, questions could get you killed.

"Well," Dylan said with a smile, "I do like to keep my crew entertained."

Trance did not return the smile. Her expression was deadly serious, and Dylan realized that she was not blinking. He had a momentary and unnerving feeling that he was suddenly trying to stare down a snake. He wasn't sure which bothered him more—the idea that Trance's objectives might always be obscure . . . or the idea that she might one day suddenly make complete sense to him.

Trance Gemini without the slightest attempt at obfuscation was not cause for comfort.

The background sounds of the bridge, all the beeps, hums, hisses, and the quiet pulse of the sublight engines took on an oppressive quality, everything seeming too loud.

Dylan wasn't willing to let the sounds close in on him, unnerving him further. "What is it, Trance?" He kept his tone just shy of full authority, shading it with concern.

She walked up to him, still unblinking. He was more than a third of a meter taller than she was, but if he had ever hoped to intimidate her with his stature he had failed long ago. Everyone else involved with the salvage of *Andromeda Ascendant* had become furious at Dylan's spirited defense of his ship against the trespassing salvage crew. Not Trance. Trance had teased him and led him on a merry chase.

When Trance announced that she was fed up with the attempts to track Dylan down and kill him, and that she was quitting the operation, Beka's Nightsider client, Gerentex, had cold-bloodedly shot Trance at point-blank range. Up until that point, Dylan had been treating the struggle almost as a game, even when dealing with Tyr's mercenary band.

Dylan had flown into a rage. While he had no intention of killing anyone, he certainly intended to deal out some pain. His mother came from a line of heavy-grav-adapted humans and as a result he was fast, light on his feet, and could punch at least twice as hard as any ordinary human. His High Guard training and Argosy Special Operations skills were a bonus. Except for Tyr, the mercenaries had not stood a chance.

Somehow, though, he had ended up with half of the trespassers as his crew. Trance should not have been among them—to all indications she was dead, and beyond any attempt to save her, even if they had known what species she was. He had been quite surprised to find her fully recovered, quite cheerful, and showing absolutely no sign that she had been shot.

"Life is filled with surprises," Trance said softly. Rommie heard, of course; the android's hearing was acute. Dylan noted Rommie's quizzical expression.

Dylan waited.

Finally, Trance said, "Lighthouse keepers."

Rommie was looking completely baffled now. "What? That wasn't exactly a complete sentence, Trance."

Trance's face screwed up as she gave all the appearance of struggling for words.

"Here we go again," Tyr muttered. "Mystery and confusion."

"When I get my flashes . . ." Trance started. She shook her head, glanced at Rommie, then fixed her gaze back on Dylan. "It's never precise, Dylan. Things come in jumbled and confused and . . . and I have to focus really hard to . . . to . . . I don't know!" She flapped her arms helplessly. Now she was back in little girl mode.

Dylan had grown too used to Trance's mercurial states to pay the shift any attention. "Lighthouse keepers," he prompted.

"Oh. Right." Trance squinted. "Watch out for the lighthouse keepers was the first thing." She wrinkled her nose. "A plague of lighthouse keepers was another. And cold." She shivered. Dylan didn't think that was an act. "Lots of cold."

"Whoah!" Harper exclaimed, his face lighting up. "If we're going someplace with lots of snow, I'm bringing a snowboard."

"I don't think it's that kind of cold place," Trance said, turning to look at him.

"Ooookay," Harper said, just a little too frantically. "Everybody who's in favor of turning the ship around and going somewhere else, raise your hands and say 'aye!'" He raised a hand. Everyone else ignored him. "I'm gonna say I told you so, guys, right before we get blown into itty-bitty pieces."

Tyr rolled his eyes, then glared at Harper. "Mr. Harper, I fail to find your defeatist commentary either amusing or relevant."

"Does this have anything to do with where we're going?" Dylan asked her. This latest performance from Trance made him wonder if they were on the verge of a colossal mistake.

"I don't know." Trance looked confused, as though she had lost track of an important thought. "Maybe." She frowned. "Not the cold part, though."

She was silent for a few moments longer.

Finally, she said, "Something's wrong, Dylan, that's all I know."

"All this," Tyr rumbled, "to say that we must stay alert."

"It's more than that, Tyr," Trance said urgently. "It's more than that."

"Or perhaps it is less than notable." Tyr shook his head and turned back to his fire control console, leaning on it. "I have heard more convincing mutterings from would-be fortune-tellers. At least their goal was to part the gullible from their money."

Dylan glanced at Beka, who was watching Trance with rapt attention. "Beka?"

Beka looked at him, and he could see the lines of concern in her face. Beka had been through too much to discount any possible warning sign. She was the best Slipstream pilot he had ever known, but her life had been difficult, with everything from a family rife with criminals to her own daily battle against her addiction to Flash, a powerful drug that could enhance a pilot's reactions tremendously—at the cost of destroying them physically.

Still, he trusted her to assess the things Trance had said and give him an appropriate response. Beka was his strong right hand.

"We know Trance's flashes," Beka said, finally.

"We know how much trouble we can get into as a result," Rommie said. Beka and Dylan looked around. Rommie had her arms folded across her chest, and a determined look on her face. "Although I will admit that she seems to be somewhat less chaotic since her . . . change."

Trance gave Dylan a look that said, in no uncertain terms, *I'm vindicated.*

"Besides, it isn't just the flashes," Beka continued. Directly to Trance, she said, "We always could count on you for happy accidents, Trance."

In her I'm-so-cute voice, Trance said, "I'm your good-luck charm."

"You are also quite annoying when you do that," Tyr grumbled.

"The voice of Mr. Happy," Harper said. "Keep this up, Tyr, and I *am* gonna slip something into your food."

"His nanobots would handle it," Trance said. Her face suddenly went blank. It was brief, but Dylan was startled. "Dylan, remember that."

"Tyr's nanobots?" Dylan said, baffled. Nietzscheans used a complex mixture of genetic and social engineering, along with a liberal dose of nanotechnology. As a result they were tough, fast, and smart, an amplified breed of humans now classified as Homo sapiens invictus.

"Just nanobots. All you have to do is remember the nanobots at the right time."

"Right. The nanobots."

"And the lighthouse keepers," Beka reminded him.

"And the plague of lighthouse keepers," Tyr added. "Whatever that is."

"Well," Beka said, "we can't just dismiss it out of hand. I just wish I knew where to look for ideas."

"That's my job," Rommie said.

The holographic avatar shimmered into life and said, primly, "Actually, it's mine."

The ship's interface lit up again. "I hope you two aren't going to start arguing."

"Never," said the holographic Rommie.

"Depends on the subject," the android responded.

"Just don't kill the messenger, okay?" Trance said. Everyone turned to look at her. "Figure of speech."

Tyr glowered at her. "If anyone could figure out a way to kill you, Trance, I might be tempted."

Dylan sighed. He hated it when Tyr got into a grumpy mood. Then again, Tyr's use of emotion as a tool of manipulation was just as fine-tuned as Trance's.

It was time to break the chain and get on with business. "Beka, how long until the next Slip point?"

Beka glanced at one of her consoles. "Just under five minutes."

"Good enough. Harper, go do whatever it is you're doing."

Harper bounded onto the Command Deck riser. "Sure thing, Boss." He headed for the bridge exit, chuckling to himself. "And what was I doing? Just being Seamus Zelazny Harper, freakin' *genius!*"

"And a model of modesty, too," Beka called after him.

"Trance?" Dylan said.

Trance hesitated for a moment. Then she said, "Got it." She followed Harper. Both of them had their favorite bolt holes on the ship—Harper's was Machine Shop 17, while Trance's was the hydroponics gardens.

Dylan waited for a few moments, until he was certain that Trance was gone, then turned to Beka. "Transit to Slipstream as soon as you can. I'll be in my quarters."

Beka glanced quickly at Rommie, who responded with a shrug that essentially said, *Hey, he's Dylan, he's designed to act weird.*

"Okay," Beka said after a moment. Dylan was almost always on the Command Deck when the *Andromeda Ascendant* transited to Slipstream. "I'll put it on shipwide when I'm ready to go."

"Thanks," he said, and left Command. He was aware of Rommie starting to follow him, and then changing her mind.

This was shaping up to be a hell of a day.

Dylan was comfortably settled into his office chair, his long legs propped up on his desk, when Rommie's holographic avatar shimmered into existence. Even though he knew where to find the various projectors that created the illusion of this slim young woman standing before him in a formal at-ease stance, he still marveled at the grace and cleverness of Vedran technology. It still tugged at his heart that his homeworld of Tarn-Vedra seemed to be utterly gone, somehow hidden by the Vedrans as the Commonwealth collapsed following the assassination of the Vedran Empress.

He and *Andromeda* had been frozen in time for more than three hundred standard years. Despite his initial bravado, he had understood the magnitude of his loss—*their* loss—and it had threatened to bring him to his knees. Somehow, between his motley crew and his ambition to re-create the Commonwealth he had known, he had contrived to stay sane.

Still. . . .

"I'm not quite as idealistic as I used to be, am I?" he asked Rommie.

She raised an eyebrow. "Actually, I think it's worse than that," she said. He sat back, knowing he had set himself up without thinking. "Your teeth have lost that Space Ranger Bob gleam. You'll have to do something about that."

He snorted, not quite laughing. "For a warship, you're full of mischief."

"For the captain of a warship," she noted, "you're remarkably relaxed."

He sighed. "I really wanted to hold on to the past, Rommie. I really tried."

"The present won't let you do that."

"It never does." He pushed away from the desk, putting his feet down on the deck. He nodded at his casual shirt. "It took me more than two years to stop clinging to the uniforms and the symbols."

She smiled. "I know. I was here. Speaking as one who cares, I was glad to see you finally hang up the uniform. You're still High Guard, whether you're in dress uniform or breeches and a sleeveless shirt."

"There's a picture I'm not sure I'd like to see." He sighed again and shook his head. "That really isn't the point, Rommie. I have to let go of the past. If I can't do that, how can I figure out the future?"

"By taking it one step at a time like the rest of the universe?" she suggested. "I prefer to leave the long-term planning to Trance. She seems to have an idea of where everything is going."

He sat upright, attentive, his musing pushed aside for the moment. "Our good-luck charm was struggling to find the right thing to say."

Rommie mused for a moment. Dylan wondered how many different things she was doing in that span of time. "Perhaps those mysterious powers of hers are starting to fail."

"I don't know," Dylan admitted. He looked around his quarters. They were sparsely decorated, with a few trophies and a handful of treasured items. This was one of the few places on the ship that Trance had not managed to make her presence known in the form of plants. "She's been subdued for a few months."

"She did derail history," Rommie said. With the exception of Beka and Trance, who had an unpleasant future to look forward to, they were all supposed to have gone out in a blaze of glory. Trance had given them a painfully graphic description of the coming catastrophe . . . and Dylan had used that, and Trance herself, to change the course of events.

Trance had seemed a lot less prone to her flashes since then.

"So she could have burned herself out," Dylan said.

"Or moved our track so far away from the one we were on that she can't get a grip on what comes next. All hypothesis, of course. Trance appears to operate on some kind of multiplexed quantum level that I don't really understand. I do my best work in shooting at things, not soothsaying and reading minds." She suddenly looked toward the ceiling. "Shipwide is on."

"Heads up, everybody," Beka said, her voice carrying through the entire length of the ship. Dylan braced himself automatically against his chair. "Transiting to Slipstream in five . . . four . . . three . . . two . . . one . . . now!"

White light suffused the ship and Dylan felt himself being shaken and stretched as the *Andromeda Ascendant* shot through the Slipstream portal she had opened and dove into the nest of cosmic strings that comprised the Slipstream itself.

The transitional sensations continued until Beka guided the huge ship's Slipstream runners into contact with the streams she needed. Reality reasserted itself.

Dylan took a deep breath, waiting for his nervous system to shake off the transitional effects. When he was ready, he said, "We need to find some answers, Rommie, and I don't think we have much time."

TWO • BY THE LIGHT OF A BURNING MOON

We have noticed that some people do not take kindly to personal visits.

— SYSTEMS COMMONWEALTH TAX INSPECTOR
JAGO PEARCE, ON WHY HIS STAFF REQUIRED
PERSONAL ARMOR, CY 9384

Trance's personal haven was *Andromeda*'s immense hydroponics gardens. When she had come aboard, she had been delighted with the wonderful variety of plant life—some of the species she had found had supposedly been extinct for centuries.

The hydroponics gardens served the dual purpose of providing the *Andromeda Ascendant* with fresh oxygen and a broad selection of vegetables. The ship was equipped with air recycling equipment that could more than meet the needs of a full crew, but the hydroponics provided an important element—air that didn't smell or taste machine-cleaned.

Trance had worked her way through the gardens during her first couple of months aboard the ship. During that time she had cleared the cluttered areas, allowing each plant its breathing space. She had pruned, transplanted, seeded, and nurtured, sometimes spending hours rooted to the spot as she contemplated a particularly difficult issue. Beka had once called her a wood sprite, but that had been back in her purple pixie days, when she had been disarmingly cute.

These days, she thought, she was probably more dryadlike.

"Never mess with a dryad," she said quietly, but she had already moved on from that thought. The vague flashes she had brought to Dylan were gnawing at the edge of her mind. She had hoped that some time in her gardens would help her clarify her thoughts.

The celestial landscape had helped far less than she had hoped, however, and she had an uncomfortable feeling that the gardens would offer no help either.

She picked up her pruning shears. Frowning, she leaned over one of her tiny bonsai trees, contemplating the crooked branches. After a few moments' regard, she turned to another of the tiny trees. Not there, either. She put the shears aside, sighing.

Stepping back, she focused on the trio of bonsai.

For some reason, the pattern was not coming clear to her. She turned to the left, and then to the right, reached out for the shears again, and promptly changed her mind.

She picked up one of the bonsai and held it out in front of her. Closing her eyes, she tried to clear her mind. Slowly, she walked forward, suddenly shifted left, then right, and proceeded to weave gracefully around one obstacle after another without once opening her eyes.

Time to stop. She opened her eyes again, and gently placed the bonsai on a stand. Surrounded by large-leaved plants, the little tree almost vanished from sight. No matter. She knew where it was. She always knew where things were, particularly living things.

She stepped away from the tree, assessing the change. She was pleased to see that the balance of energy had returned to equilibrium. The smallest things could make such significant changes. Move a plant, find harmony. Throw a switch, lock down the timeline. That sort of thing.

On the other hand, this more balanced garden of hers did not address the main issue—sorting out the muddy impressions tumbling through her mind. She desperately wanted to be able to tell Dylan something more useful, more pertinent. Something better than telling him the equivalent of *there's trouble on the way*.

She stepped back a little, so that she could sit cross-legged on the soft loam that bordered the access path. She rested her chin on her hands, letting her mind drift, caught up in the delicate traceries of the plant life around her. Once she placed herself in harmony with the plant energies, she could extend her awareness throughout the *Andromeda Ascendant*, and from there out into the celestial field. If she didn't mentally ping-pong from one probability path to another, she might pick up something useful—and there was a chance that she might be able to bring some sort of stability to her shifting memory.

She cleared the wandering thoughts away, and took deep breaths. She really did not need to—a point that everyone on the ship suspected, considering her propensity for getting over dying on a regular basis—but the technique helped her to relax and focus.

She was beginning to feel sunlight warmth when something touched her mental boundary. Annoyed, she snapped back out of her meditative state and looked around.

Her eyes widened with surprise. "What?"

A few yards away, a somewhat less mature voice also said, "What?"

Trance stared into the shocked purple face of her younger self. "What are *you* doing here?" she demanded.

Wide-eyed, the younger Trance was peering at her around a bush she had been pruning. She was wearing a rather garish multihued plush shorts and halter-top outfit that left her midriff bare. Her multicolored hair and accessories somehow managed to blend with the clothes.

The younger Trance's prehensile tail snapped up, flicking in agitation. "Who are—" she started, halting with a gasp. "You're *me*!" She frowned. "But what are you doing here?"

"What are *you* doing here?" She almost added *we changed places*, but stopped herself in time. Things were starting to get confusing again. She stood up, like a plant reaching for sunlight.

"I've always been here." The younger Trance's nose wrinkled slightly as she considered that statement. "Well, not always *here*, but always . . . here. Oh."

Trance struggled with her memory, trying to place this moment, but there was nothing there, no memory of this meeting. *I've stepped sideways.*

"Things are going to go badly," she said simply. She stepped toward the purple girl, holding out her right hand. Hesitantly, the younger Trance took it, holding on delicately. She felt a flush of solar warmth as the circuit was completed. Her skin first shaded to a burnished and translucent gold, then deepened and darkened, glittering as though thousands of tiny stars had come to life, and her eyes filled with amber swirls.

Suddenly she was seeing not only the surface world, but the patterns of energy that existed both beneath and above that surface. Her purple counterpart gasped softly, and she took that as an indication that she was seeing much the same. Together, they turned and started to slowly follow the path through the gardens. There was no destination in mind.

"How bad will it get?" the younger Trance asked. Then, before any answer could be given, the purple girl gave her older counterpart a shocked look. "Oh, no! What happened to our tail?" Her tail flipped around, close to her body, and she caught the end of it in her free hand. The tip vibrated rapidly, a sure sign of anxiety.

"There was a battle," she said, melancholy tingeing her voice. The younger woman responded with a sad-eyed look. "There was nothing anyone could do. I had to learn new ways of moving."

"Not to mention finding a whole new wardrobe." The younger version nodded at her older counterpart's snug red-gold leather outfit. "Not that we seem to have had *that* much of a problem."

Trance smiled. "This comes a lot later. When it starts getting to be practical."

"When it starts getting bad."

"When it starts getting bad." Trance shook her head. "I don't even know when it'll start for you. I used to, but everything's changed so much."

The purple girl gave her another startled look. "Following the probability tracks is becoming difficult?"

"I don't know," Trance admitted. "Everything *seems* okay . . . but this shouldn't be happening. I shouldn't be meeting you."

"I'm not the right younger you, am I?"

"I don't think so, no." Trance frowned, trying to grab hold of the threads of several ideas. Forming something coherent out of the bits and pieces she was getting was difficult. She contained the powers of both chaos and order, but she rarely had a choice as to which one would manifest at any given time. Chaos had the upper hand at the moment, and she was starting to feel that she would have had an easier time arguing with a battalion of lawyers. "I'm not even sure this is real."

"It seems real enough."

Trance looked down at their linked hands, seeing the swirls of energy there. "It looks real enough." She looked up. "Maybe this is just our mind trying to help me work things out."

"Our mind is like that," the other Trance said. She shrugged. "Still, if it seems real to us, then it is real."

Trance chuckled. "One of these days we're going to start getting our tenses mixed up."

"All of our grammar." The younger Trance flashed a mischievous grin. "Although it's really fun to get Tyr confused. He's so *glum* and full of himself."

In all seriousness, she said, "It's hard enough to keep the stories straight *now*. It isn't going to be easy holding everything together."

"We can't always warn them of what's coming," the younger woman said. "I know that. I've had that experience. Sometimes it doesn't help even if you do come up with a warning in time." The tip of her tail vibrated in sympathy with her frustration. "Sometimes the only thing I can give them is something they don't understand."

"It would be so much easier if Dylan or Beka . . . or even Tyr or Harper . . . could see things the way we do. Maybe they could put the pieces together for themselves." Trance pursed her lips, her expression both thoughtful and regretful. "If they could . . . if they could, they wouldn't have to walk through the fire."

"It isn't for them." The younger Trance knelt and touched the leaves of a small plant. Their consciousness was drawn into the plant, into the root system, and into the connective energy structure of the garden. In a flash, Trance built up a map in her mind. The cold, structured lines of the irrigation system snapped them both back to the present moment. "They couldn't deal with it. Most species suffer from single-line perception."

"I have to figure out why this is happening," Trance said.

Purple Trance crouched to inspect another plant, turning her head this way and that. After a few moments' consideration, she took out a small pair of clippers and made a couple of quick, judicious snips. "There. All better." She stood up again, putting the clippers away. "Something in our future is disrupting things."

"Upsetting the probabilities?" Trance mused for a moment. "If Harper's tesseract machine . . . no, I don't think it's that. This isn't crazy enough."

"For want of a nail," the younger woman said. "For want of a nail, the kingdom was lost. We have to find the nail, whatever it is."

"Or a needle in a haystack," Trance said unhappily. "I hate it when things get complicated. At least when they don't have to. I like my plans to stay simple."

"Me too." Purple Trance smiled, and flicked her tail from side to side.

It was time. Trance saw the acknowledgment in the purple girl's face as well, a slight moue of disappointment. There never was enough time, even when she had all the time she could want. It was simply a matter of what happened when. Racing the clock sometimes left her ragged and exhausted, even though many of her races were run only in her mind as she looked for the best possible solution to a crisis.

Their hands slipped apart, and Trance's enhanced viewpoint quickly faded away, leaving her feeling lost. Her purple counterpart had a blank look for a moment, then blinked twice as her reality reasserted itself. "Wow."

"Stay alert, and stay safe," Trance advised her younger counterpart. She wished she had some memory of this conversation, if indeed it had happened at all. "They need us. That's why we're here."

"I won't forget." The purple girl tilted her head, looking momentarily distracted. "So much to do . . ."

"I have to go," Trance said. She was reluctant to break the spell—

it was rare that she enjoyed such an idyll as this, a bubble of peace free-floating in the cosmos. No decisions, no directives, no destinations. "I'm still not completely clear, but I think I know more now."

"Good luck," the younger Trance said. She smiled sweetly, a genuine expression. There really had been a touch of true innocence before her change, she decided. "For the perfect possible future."

"Exactly." With that, Trance turned and began to walk back along the pathway. When she glanced back, the purple girl was gone.

Dylan Hunt, bold, bright-eyed captain of the lone surviving *Glorious Heritage*–class High Guard battleship, lay on his bed, staring at the ceiling and contemplating lies and evasions—mostly his own.

The truth was, simply put, that he still mourned everything that he had lost. A Commonwealth that had been a million worlds strong, not fifty, protected by a High Guard that more often acted with compassion than the swift cruelty they were capable of. His fiancée, Sara Riley, who had tried, and failed, to rescue him. He had even lost Terazed, the world she had brokered, where the old values still stood, and a traditional High Guard cadre trained and fought as they had for thousands of years.

Sara had meant that world to be the heart of a new Commonwealth. He had made the right moral choice in the end, as difficult as it had been. Sara's world, her hopes, had fallen to isolationist choices. He had felt the memory of her slipping through his fingers.

He had begun adapting to this dark time with frightening swiftness, learning from the all-too-severe lessons doled out to him. He had begun his quest with a kind of wide-eyed eagerness to revive the old ideals, something the old purple Trance had encouraged from the moment he had discovered her sitting up cheerfully when she was supposed to be stretched out lifeless.

"You're like the first candle of millions to come," she had said, and he could have sworn that he saw bright spirals of light glittering in her eyes. He had been fascinated with her. "It isn't going to be easy for you, but you can do it. It's like learning to make plants grow, y'know? Besides, you're tall, and you're kinda cute, and we'd better get going because I think there's going to be all kinds of pieces to pick up."

Rommie had shimmered into view, a quizzical look on her face. "Do you come with any kind of guidebook? You're quite confusing."

Trance had grinned. "Just stick with me. You won't have trouble following along."

"That," Rommie said dryly, "is precisely what I'm afraid of."

Within days his idealized view of existence had come under fire in the form of a corruption of High Guard rituals and values. He had not even begun to properly process his knowledge of the state of the Known Worlds before being plunged full-tilt into horror.

His own descent had begun then, slowly but steadily. The *Andromeda Ascendant* had ceased to be a tool to be used to benefit a new Commonwealth. Instead, she had become his own personal instrument of force. No doubt Tyr liked that idea a great deal—always field a force stronger than that of your opponent, and strike swiftly, preferably with a certain degree of subterfuge involved.

He sighed and sat up, rubbing at his eyes. He had hung up the High Guard uniform alright, and had no intention of adopting that of the new High Guard, but he still ached for his old idealism.

He was already sensing the corruption at the heart of the new Commonwealth. He had immediately resisted the political push to make him First Triumvir, but sometimes he wondered if he had made the right choice then. There were periodic reminders that the Commonwealth was moving on despite him—around him, even. Having to baby-sit Beka's Uncle Sid, the notorious Sid Profit, as he made a bid for Triumvir had been bad enough, but it was something that could be handled. Except, of course, that Sid wouldn't be easily handled. By the time the dust had settled, thousands were dead, Sid's business rivals had been destroyed, and Sid himself was sent on his way with the blessings of the Commonwealth.

There was a bright shimmer to one side of the bed. "You're thinking about Uncle Sid again," Rommie said.

"And you're wearing your psychiatrist hat again," Dylan said grumpily. "Lights."

The lights turned on, slowly increasing in intensity. Dylan blinked. Sleep seemed to be a difficult proposition lately.

"It's my psychotherapist's hat, actually," Rommie said primly. She tilted her head, as though regarding him. "You should be glad, as it's quite a bit cheaper. And you *were* thinking about Sid."

Dylan nodded slowly. "I was thinking about Sid." He sighed. "That bastard's the epitome of everything that went wrong with the Commonwealth, Rommie, old or new. It's people like Sid who see the first weakness and move in. After that it's a feeding frenzy."

"And never mind his effect on Beka," Rommie said.

Dylan didn't take the bait. Rommie was pushing a bit to see where he might be sensitive. "Beka's capable of handling his effect on her, Rommie." He pushed back the sheets and got out of bed. The artificial gravity field on the *Andromeda Ascendant* was set to a level comfortable for most, but for him, with a heavy-gravity genetic structure inherited from his mother, it seemed far too weak. He sometimes felt as though a careless step would send him flying into the ceiling. "I admit I don't understand why she's resisted the temptation to shove him out of an airlock."

Rommie raised an eyebrow. "Strong family ties, perhaps?"

"Of the noose around the neck variety." He shook his head. "If dealing with the Magog Worldship means accepting a Commonwealth where people like Sid are the norm . . ."

"You're afraid that we won't be able to handle the Worldship when it gets going again."

That was a thought he had wanted to keep buried as long as possible. A massive construct of huge, interlinked modules, the Magog Worldship was big enough to carry a small sun within its confines. It also had a monstrous deity—the Spirit of the Abyss. The Nova Bomb Beka had launched at the Worldship should have destroyed the craft completely. Instead, most of the energy from the artificial nova had been sucked away by the Spirit. The Worldship had been left dead in space, but would eventually get moving again. Time was running out.

Dylan had made the Worldship a pressing issue. It had sped things up a little bit here and there, but for the most part nobody really seemed to give a damn. So there were lots of Magog on the way. All you needed was bigger Gauss guns and a lot of smart bullets, that was the reigning philosophy, especially among the Nietzscheans.

It wasn't that easy. Andromeda knew that. She had been up against the Worldship twice. Both times she had failed. The second time she had almost been destroyed.

"It's coming," he said simply. "It's coming, and one day soon we're all going to wake up as Magog breakfast food."

"An engaging thought," Rommie said. "At least you couldn't be considered the single-serving size."

He gave her a dour look. "Thanks for the comfort. I'll sleep *so* much better now."

"You're welcome. I have some answers for you, by the way."

"The lighthouse keepers."

"Indeed." The hologram assumed a more formal position, looking at a point just over the top of his head. "Much of what I found is of a generic nature, of course—a lighthouse, essentially, is a lighthouse, intended to serve the purpose of warning sea craft away from treacherous coastal areas. These structures can be in the form of everything from the tall cylindrical buildings common to Earth and numerous other planets, with a rotating light of great intensity set on top, maintained by a lighthouse keeper, to the floating lights of Pen'hra, guided by a network of AIs, which not only provide warning of treacherous waters, but can, if needed, provide aid and rescue to water craft in difficulty."

"So that covers the lighthouses and lighthouse keepers," Dylan said.

"Not quite," Andromeda countered. "I found references also to several security organizations, as well as three vague references to a planetary defense system."

"Which planet?" Dylan was starting to get an idea of the direction Trance's flashes had taken, although he was still far from putting all the pieces of the puzzle together.

"That information seems to have gone missing," Andromeda said with a hint of annoyance in her voice. "Of the security organizations, all but one are defunct, and the lone company still operating is based on Kartob IV. That world is located in Triangulum, and is thus in the wrong galaxy to be of current concern."

"Which leaves the planetary defense system," Dylan mused.

"Or something else entirely."

"Meaning?"

"A name for an organization such as the Knights of Genetic Purity, perhaps, purpose unknown. We are entering the realm of speculation at this point, however."

Dylan padded across his quarters into his office area. He sat down in his chair and put his feet up on the desk. He regarded his toes idly, trying to keep his mind clear and open to see if anything might occur to him that had some kind of bearing on this situation.

"The phrase 'the plague of lighthouse keepers' seems somewhat easier to interpret," Andromeda said, following him into the office. "Again, there are multiple references, all with a common theme—the effect of the post of lighthouse keeper upon the individual granted that position."

"At a guess," Dylan said, leaning back and trying not to feel the weariness creeping through him, "issues of loneliness and stress."

"More than that, there are numerous recorded instances of lighthouse keepers falling prey to various forms of insanity. While some stories appear to be quite apocryphal, and ghost stories abound, other cases are quite well documented. The problem appears to have resulted from a tendency to select individuals who seemed capable of a solitary life."

"No wives, no children, no nearby towns to visit for a drunken night?" Dylan said.

"Precisely. As a result, many keepers cracked from the conditions. Alternative ideas were, as a result, mandated. These included automation of lighthouse systems, as well as the requirement that those hired as keepers have at least a companion, as well as an assistant."

"Insanity," Dylan said softly. His eyes took on the half-closed look that indicated that he was busy processing an idea. "Rommie, this should be starting to make sense by now, but it isn't. It's making even less sense than it did before."

"Maybe," the hologram said with no tinge of irony in her voice, "that is the point."

Trance was on her way back to her quarters, thinking back over her earlier encounter, when the cosmos shuddered and deposited her somewhere else.

This is beginning to get weird, even for me.

She unholstered her force lance, thumbing it on and setting it to fire effectors, the tiny but highly effective smart projectiles that could burn through almost any armor. The lance made a small whine as it came up to full power.

She was no longer on the *Andromeda Ascendant*. She looked around, carefully. She was standing in broken terrain of some kind, the wreckage of a city enduring a long and difficult war. She could hear the sounds of battle, well in the distance, and the sound of heavy weapons firing at steady intervals.

It was night, and the air was filled with dust. The smell of carnage that came to her made her feel ill, and momentarily weak. So much death, so needless. This was not the future she was seeking, so why was she here? She could feel no familiarity with this world, so it seemed unlikely that she had ever been here.

There were fires all around, lighting the destroyed buildings and smashed roads. A few of the fires threw infernal light across scatterings of bodies, both complete and otherwise, but she could neither see nor sense anything living, no matter where she looked.

The savage nature of the destruction gave her a strong desire to cry, but tears would not come. By this token, she knew that she had something to learn here. After she had found and dealt with whatever had called her here—whether this was real, or occurring in a corner of her mind—she could mourn.

There was another source of flickering light, less easily identified than the fires that lit this dying city. Hesitantly, she looked up into the sky.

This world had a moon, and it was burning.

She had no idea what kind of weapon might have caused this particular catastrophe. Nova Bombs worked specifically on suns. A point singularity bomb would either have ripped part of the moon away, punched a hole through it, or imploded it.

She looked away again. It didn't matter what kind of weapon had been used, at least not to her. What mattered was that someone had unleashed catastrophic destruction on a planetary scale. It might be Magog at work, or Nietzscheans, but someone was responsible.

Slowly, she walked through the ruins, keeping her awareness open and trying to avoid falling into a pit of depression.

She had been walking for more than two hours, listening to the weapons fire get closer, and then recede again, when she found Tyr, or rather he saw her.

"Girl," he said, from somewhere inside a pool of shadows, his voice husky and broken, "are you crazy?"

She was shocked by the sound of his voice. "Tyr?"

"It is indeed," he said, and she saw movement in the shadows, and the glint of light from something metallic—no doubt one of Tyr's beloved multibarreled guns.

She moved toward him. "I don't even know where we are."

"You are in a very, very bad place, Trance Gemini," Tyr said. As she moved closer, and crouched, Trance recognized something else in his voice. Weakness. "I don't know how you are here, but if you are something other than a figment of my imagination, you have made a terrible mistake."

She smiled. "And you always said *I* talked too much."

"I have too many words and too little time," he said.

Her vision adjusted to the darkness, and she gasped as she realized what he meant. Tyr was terribly changed. His leonine dreadlocks were gone, leaving him bald. There was a long, wide scar across the top of his head. He had an eye patch over his right eye, and more scars on his cheeks. One arm and one leg had been replaced with cybernetic prosthetics. Two fingers on the other hand were also prosthetic.

"Too many battles," he said after a moment. "With each one, I was that much older, that much slower, and eventually I became what I am, working my old trade, and earning the retirement benefits of that trade."

"You're a mercenary again?" she asked, struck with horror.

"Oh, yes." He coughed suddenly, then drew in breath with a wheeze. "In the end, it was all I could go back to."

She found a comfortable position next to him, listening while she looked him over.

Noticing her inspection, he said, "I am dying. I very much doubt that there is anything you can do."

She looked up, into his face. "Tyr . . ."

"One battle too many," he said. There was no note of complaint in his voice. "Are you here, then, to carry away my spirit as it relinquishes the body?"

She smiled. "I think that would be more Rev Bem's job."

"Ah. Yes." Tyr raised his eyebrows. "How is the good Reverend Behemiel Far Traveler?"

"I don't know," she admitted. "Well, I hope. Tyr, what happened?"

He frowned. "You know. You were there." He paused for a moment. "Trance, it is difficult to think. You were on *Andromeda*. . . ."

"I need to know, Tyr," she said. She was looking him over again. She saw the problem now—he had been hit by rounds from a Gauss gun, and at least two had penetrated his armor. He was bleeding profusely, and she could sense the internal damage the smart bullets had caused. An ordinary human would have been dead long ago. She looked up, into his eyes. "You're right, I can't help you here. I might still be able to help us all, but I need to *know*."

The wheezing was growing worse, and his eyes were starting to glaze. With an effort, he refocused. "I was a fool," he said. He was suddenly wracked by a coughing spasm, and blood foamed at his lips. Trance placed her hands on his shoulders, doing what she could to ease his pain. He was silent for a moment. "We were attacked. Dylan hesitated to take direct action, and I grew frustrated and angry with him. So I abandoned Command, and took out a Slipfighter, intending to deal a few blows." He closed his eyes, his face anguished. "I was a fool. I did nothing but get in the way. The *Andromeda Ascendant* was destroyed. I alone survived, barely . . . and it would seem that you, too, escaped."

"It only seems that way," she said softly. "What happened then?"

He coughed again, then settled down. "My Slipfighter was disabled, and I was cast adrift. Within an hour, I was taken prisoner. I was incarcerated and questioned, but my captors seemed little interested in any knowledge I might have had. I was merely imprisoned, not tortured or subjected to drugs or surgery. One day I was released, given papers and a menial job, and left alone." He stopped talking again. His breath was beginning to come in short gasps.

"Slowly," Trance said. "Take it slowly."

"You need to know, you said." He tried to push himself into a better position. Carefully, she helped him sit up. "Eventually I was able to get to a ship. I had the ambition of following my schemes, you see. I was too late. Olma, into whose care I gave my son, Tamerlane, betrayed me by handing him to the Sabra-Jaguar coalition. He leads them now as the Nietzschean messiah, the reincarnation of Drago Museveni." He lifted a hand, weakly. "The reincarnation of the Progenitor was supposed to *reunite* the prides! Instead, this is what we have wrought."

"This is a Nietzschean world?" she said, shocked.

"One of many left in flames," he said. "The prides will be reunited in death. There are few of us left. Before long there will be no more than two lone Nietzscheans, fighting over piles of rubble."

"Was there nothing you could do?"

He looked at her, sadly. "I was a pariah from the moment my pride was destroyed, girl, and more so once my bone blades were taken by those tunnel creatures." He held up his normal arm. Tyr had been abducted by a mysterious group of aliens and returned with his bone blades neatly removed—no evidence of surgery, even. There had never been an explanation as to why or how it had been done. "My fellow Nietzscheans thought me weak, and treated me as little more than a kludge."

"So you returned to being a mercenary," she said.

"With all else taken from me, and no will to die easily, it was all I had left." He coughed again, and more blood foamed at his lips. "The money is of no importance. I keep enough for food, shelter, and weapons. All else I give to the Way. The Reverend would be proud of me, I am sure."

Trance heard the note of sarcasm. "Rev Bem would say something about the Divine, and you would act grouchy but secretly be pleased."

He gave her a mournful look. "I could never have been that transparent."

"Not always," she said gently, "but as you learned, your heart changed."

"Yes, it did," he said. "But in the end, I forgot to follow it. I destroyed everything."

His eyes fluttered rapidly, and she felt him swiftly weakening. "Tyr . . ." She paused, fighting back tears. "Tyr, you were always my friend, no matter how obnoxious you could be. I won't allow this to happen."

"You cannot change what is," he said softly. "Not even you can do that."

"This hasn't happened yet," she told him. "This is not the perfect possible future that I know we can have."

"It is the one that we have," he said. "Enough debate. It seems my time is here."

"Yes," she said, "it is."

He took a breath. "I am Tyr Anasazi," he said, barely above a whisper, "out of Victoria . . ."

He fell silent, his breathing stilled, his eyes glassy. Trance felt his life flow away into the darkness. "You were Tyr Anasazi, out of Victoria by Barbarossa," she said, "and you were superior." Cannons boomed in the distance. "And I swear *this will not happen!*"

She looked up at the burning moon.

The cosmos shifted again, and she found herself on her knees in the middle of one of *Andromeda*'s corridors. She was weeping.

She looked down, and gasped.

Her hands were stained with blood.

THREE ▪ BUILDING FOR A BETTER FUTURE

A curious revelation: as we progress through life, we make this decision and that decision. Yet the choices we might have made remain with us, silent or not.

For each of us there is a multitude of echoes and reflections, unto infinity.

—CHARMA BESENCHI,
MIRRORS AND MIRACLES,
CY 9545

Trance stood, shaking. She and Tyr had often come into conflict over one thing or another, but seeing him as such a broken shell was heartrending. No matter what the others on the *Andromeda Ascendant* thought, she was not impervious to pain. Physical distress she could moderate to a great extent, but emotional pain was another matter entirely. She knew she was emotionally attached to these people—that had been part of the bargain from the outset.

She looked down at her bloodied hands again, trying to force her experience into a more understandable shape. This had been no matter of extending her mind along lines of probability. Somehow she had been there with Tyr as he died.

Doggedly, she pulled herself back to reality. She was running out of time to grab hold of events so that she could turn them to advantage.

She lifted her hands in front of her face. What she did now would be crucial to their survival. She had to make the right choices, in the right sequence. Her head began to swim with a sea of probabilities.

In a fraction of a second she was focused on the present reality again. She knew where to go first, and what needed to be done.

Tyr, she thought, *by dying you managed to tell me how we're going to live.*

In the blood on her hands, as she looked more deeply than any unaided human could, she saw a few of Tyr's nanobots.

She began running.

Rommie's holographic form materialized in the corridor that Trance had just vacated at a run. She looked around in an all-too-human way, although she didn't need to.

"Trance?"

There was no answer. She frowned, something else she didn't need to do. Had it concerned her, she might have blamed her programmers for the nonfunctional behavior. At that point one of her other selves would have reminded her that she had a more or less infinite capacity for learning—which, naturally, included behavioral elements.

She dematerialized again, reappearing a few meters away, past an intersection. She tried a few other nearby spots, but there was still no sign of Trance, or of the anomaly that had caught her attention.

She returned to the original location, still frowning. Daring to hope, she sent her consciousness rippling through the length and breadth of the ship. As she had expected, she could find absolutely no sign of Trance. It was baffling—Trance seemed to have to make an effort to make herself visible to the internal sensors, a point that could prove disastrous someday. Besides, that sort of ability had no place in an orderly universe. *Her* orderly universe.

Now she was starting to look annoyed. Not only that, but knowing she *looked* annoyed irritated her. Her android avatar was beginning to have a very bad influence on her.

She sighed heavily.

Realizing what she was doing at almost the same time as she was doing it, she closed her holographic eyes and put a hand over her face. While this made very little impression on her actual perceptions, she did manage to produce a momentary but interesting effect as the holographic fields went out of phase. Vedran technology had been brilliant, and often unsurpassed, but the Vedrans themselves had been pragmatic, prizing life and culture above machinery.

As an artificial intelligence, growing to readiness as the warrior heart of the *Andromeda Ascendant*, she had learned quickly where her place was with the Vedrans, and within the Systems Commonwealth. Born out of technology, she had become a person, and she was seen that way. The dark times that she and Dylan had emerged in were far less accepting—these days many people saw her as no more than an extension of antiquated technology, something to be erased if she became inconvenient. Fortunately Harper had provided a partial solution to the problem by building her android avatar.

"You look like you've got a headache."

Rommie switched her attention back into the outside world. She hadn't just been standing around brooding, of course, but all of the other processes were running in the background, under the control of the main AI.

She realigned her holographic fields to execute an instant 180-degree turn, causing Beka Valentine to take a step back, startled. "I *hate* it when you do that!"

"Sorry," Rommie said.

"No you're not." Beka folded her arms across her chest, giving Rommie a challenging look.

"Because I'm a machine?" She raised an eyebrow.

"No," Beka said with a grin. "Because you enjoy scaring the crap out of me by doing that."

"Oh."

"You don't?" Now Beka seemed concerned.

"Well . . ."

"You do?" There was a long moment of silence as the two stared at each other in confusion. "Rommie, *wars* have started over less than this. Yes or no?"

She frowned in a way that she knew made her look hopelessly helpless, which made Beka grin broadly. "I really never gave it any thought."

"A brain the size of a small moon, and you never gave it any thought," Beka said. "Rommie, sometimes you shock me."

Rommie smiled. "I'm not exactly one for practical jokes. I'm quite good at blowing up small moons, though."

"One of your more lovable qualities, I'd say. Some moons deserve it."

"Not to mention some planets."

"Let's start small."

"Your Uncle Sid?" Rommie suggested.

Beka mock-scowled. "Hey, low blow."

"Sorry."

"No you're not." Beka grinned again. "Besides, we can't blow Sid up until I've figured out where he's got all his money buried. *Then* you can stuff him into a lifepod and use it for target practice."

"Why waste a lifepod?"

Beka snorted. "You're mean."

"I'm a warship," Rommie said with an elfin grin. "I'm licensed to be bitchy and irritable and willing to blow things up at short notice."

"And people say *I'm* bad-tempered." Beka paused, making an obvious effort to drop the banter and be serious. "So what's going on, anyway?"

Rommie frowned again. "That's just it . . . I don't know. I picked up a couple of anomalous energy readings. I also thought I had Trance on visual for a moment, but she vanished."

Now Beka was starting to look worried. "Anomalous energy readings. I really, really hate it when you say something like that."

"As in there'll be hell to pay?" Rommie said.

"Usually. There are definitely words that come right before major trouble. So . . . anything more specific?"

"Nothing." Rommie frowned in thought. She shut off the self-criticism in a flash. There was no point in fighting it, she supposed. She *was* supposed to be adaptable, after all. "A double blip on my sensors, neither one long enough to give me any concrete readings."

"And Trance in the general area." Beka's expression had become a wide-eyed look of disbelief. "This can't be good."

Rommie shrugged. "I can't make a statement either way until I have more data."

Beka was looking at the deck, frowning. "Well, you *could* start with the blood. . . ."

"Blood?" Rommie echoed.

"I think that was what I said." Beka pointed and Rommie focused. There were a few tiny droplets on the deck. "I think I'm officially worried. Unexplained blood is *never* good." Beka crouched down, tilting her head. "I wonder who it belongs to?"

"Belonged," Rommie said absently.

"Huh?"

"You used the wrong tense. Belonged, not belongs." Rommie tied herself into her main systems. The most formal of her selves took over the sensors. "And the answer is . . ."

"Tyr," Andromeda said, appearing on a flatscreen as Beka looked toward the nearby junction. "DNA match, not to mention a lot of dead nanos."

Beka looked up. "Maybe he cut himself shaving?"

"I doubt that," Rommie said.

"We could always ask him," Andromeda put in.

"Let Dylan know first," Beka said. She stood up. "I hate to say it, I really would like a simple, straightforward, and boring diplomatic mission for a change."

Trance had made it to Machine Shop 17 in record time, managing to make a grand entrance with lots of noise as she ducked around, and sometimes banged into, the piles of parts and gadgets Harper had stacked up. The apparently random mess made no sense to anyone but Harper, and he would have had a major fit if ever the place had been tidied up.

"Harper!" she called out. "Harper, I need you!"

As though by magic, Harper popped up from behind a pile of circuit boards and cases. He was holding a tool in each hand and wearing goggles, and she could have sworn his hair was messier than usual—a difficult achievement for Seamus Harper.

She didn't want to even speculate on the source of the stains on the front of his shirt.

"The boy genius is called," he said cheerfully. He started to push his goggles up, then realized he was about to poke himself in the face with one of his tools. He put both of them down, then pulled off the goggles. He seemed completely oblivious when one of his tools rolled away, clattered through the pile, and vanished from sight. "You know, Trance, I've been waiting *so* long to hear those words. 'Harper, I *need* you!' The part of the universe that is not male but is desired by males displays a vast and frustrating underappreciation of my sheer brilliance, innate talents, and general lovableness."

"Harper—"

"It's freakin' *unfair*. So I'm a little messy, okay, I can understand why some people might have a problem with that. Sometimes I talk a little too much—"

"Harper—"

Now he was pacing around, carried away on the wings of his words. ". . . and some chicks just want the strong silent kinda guy. . . ."

"Harper!"

He swung around and stared at her, a look of shock on his face. "Jeez, Trance, no need to yell at me. I'm givin' you my complete attention here."

She glared at him. "Was there a point?"

"Huh?"

"I came in and said I needed you, and you started complaining about women, the universe, and you."

His eyes seemed to lose focus for a moment. Then he was back again. "Oh. Yeah. It was freaky hearing it come from you. You're, like, my sister. My big sister."

She smiled. "We all take care of each other." She grew completely serious again. "I need you to do something very important for me. It's a lot of work, and it needs to be done really fast."

She held up her hands.

Harper's eyes went wide. "Holy—!" He took a step back and

almost fell over one of his piles. "What the hell happened? You murder someone?"

She looked sadly down at her hands. "No." She looked up at him again. "I can't explain what happened, but I got thrown into the future. I don't know where, I don't know when, but I found Tyr. He was dying."

Silently, Harper handed her a well-handled box of wet wipes. She took out a few and made an effort to clean her hands. The images of the devastated world and its burning moon refused to go away.

"I have to stop this *now*," she said, throwing the used wipes into a nearby bin. "I have to make sure we're ready, or none of us will make it."

Harper waved his hands in the air, looking desperate. "Okay, okay, I'm gettin' *really* confused here. Is this something to do with tesseracting?"

"I don't know," she admitted. "I don't think so, but we don't have time to figure it out right now."

"And you need me to build something?"

"A lot of somethings," she said. "Actually, it's more like *rebuild*."

"Uh, Trance . . . ?" Harper said. His eyes went wide.

There was a prickly feeling at the back of Trance's head. She knew what she was going to see, even before she turned around.

"Seamus?" The light girlish voice was all too familiar. "No, wait. . . ."

Trance turned around. A purple version of her was hanging by her tail from a railing. There was that mutual shock again.

"He's not your Seamus, is he?" Trance said.

"No, he's"—the purple Trance's tail suddenly unwrapped, and she fell, clattering, into one of Harper's unruly piles of stuff; she stood up, looking woozy, and said, affirmatively—"not." With that, she sat down, and added, *"Ow,"* in a distracted sort of way.

Harper looked from one to the other, then back again, then rubbed at his hair first with one hand, then with the other hand. Finally, he said, "Oooookay." He looked at Trance as though he wanted to ask a question, but he didn't know what the question was.

"No, he's not," Trance said in a very matter-of-fact way. She looked at Harper. "She's not *my* younger self."

"Okay," he said, wincing. "If you're going to try and explain this, I'm gonna have to go get drunk, because that's the only way it'll make sense. If it makes sense."

Purple Trance was standing up again. "He *sounds* like my Seamus."

"Just how many of you guys *are* there?" Harper asked.

"I don't know," Trance said, "and I'm not going to try figuring this out yet, I told you that." She gave the purple girl a shrewd look. "As long as you're here, you can help him."

That got a big smile. "I *love* to help," the other Trance said enthusiastically.

The enthusiasm unfortunately manifested in other ways, as the purple girl tried to escape her landing place without giving too much thought to either the effects of gravity or the random nature of the objects she had plummeted into. Consequently she began her effort with a surge, found herself sliding back, tried to get her balance with the aid of her tail, and when that failed, by windmilling her arms.

That didn't work either. She vanished once more beneath the sea of chaos, then reappeared again. "Oops." She looked at the mess around her. "Boy, Seamus, you sure are messy." She looked up at him. "You should tidy up in here."

He didn't answer. He was too busy staring at her, either completely amazed, or simply shocked speechless.

"Just get out of there," Trance said sternly. "We need to get to work."

Dylan arrived at a jog, his force lance in his left hand and a puzzled look on his face. "What's going on?"

Beka pointed at the blood spots on the deck. "That's going on."

Dylan crouched to take a closer look, then looked up at Beka and Rommie. "Somebody's been bleeding without permission."

"It would appear that Tyr is the culprit, Captain," Andromeda said. "It is certainly his blood. I have no idea how it came to be on the deck here."

Dylan stood up, frowning. "I don't recall Tyr having gotten into any fights recently. I think I would have noticed that." He looked at Beka. "You *do* think I would have noticed that, right?"

She tilted her head and gave him an oh-so-patient look that told him she definitely had no patience at the moment. "Dylan, we don't have time for jokes."

He sighed and nodded. "It's never easy." He pressed fingers to the right side of his neck, activating his subdermal comm unit. "Tyr, this is Dylan."

At the sound of Dylan's voice booming over the Command Deck's speakers, Tyr looked up from his fire control panel. He liked to fine-tune the system as much as he could, fitting it to his style and reflexes. Harper was a brilliant engineer, and sometimes quite impressive for a scruffy kludge, but he only built and maintained these systems. Tyr was the one who had to operate them. What worked well for Harper would be disastrous for him.

Rommie's android avatar was the only other person on the Command Deck. Dylan had gone off after Beka's mysterious call.

"Dylan," Tyr drawled. "What can I do for you?"

There was a pause. Then it sounded as though Dylan was taking a deep breath. "Uh, Tyr . . . did anything happen that might have resulted in your bleeding onto my ship?"

Tyr's eyes widened in surprise. "I . . ." He glanced at Rommie, who was studying him intently. Well, she would find no evidence of evasion, he could be certain of that. "My dear Captain Hunt, I have *no* idea what you are talking about."

The flatscreens lit up with the head and shoulders display of Andromeda. "It would appear that someone using your blood was impolite enough to spill a little of it on Deck Fourteen."

The holographic Rommie shimmered into being. "She always gets a bit testy when she has to send in the maid."

"I get a bit testy when we start having mysteries," the android avatar said. Then she smiled brightly. "On the other hand, there's always the chance I'll get to hit something and make myself feel better."

"There are other ways of relieving tension," the holographic avatar said.

"Shooting things helps, too," the ship avatar said.

That brought a scowl from the holographic avatar. "You two are impossible."

The hologram faded away.

"Well," Tyr said, raising his eyebrows and looking at the android, "at least we appear to derive some pleasure from our hobbies."

Dylan slipped his force lance back into its holster. "I guess the solution to this is going to have to wait for a while."

"If there *is* a solution," Beka said. She shook her head. "I used to think my life was crazy before, Dylan, but now I *know* it's crazy."

"Speaking of crazy," the ship avatar said, "I have a location on Trance."

Dylan nodded. "Where is she?"

"That would be the crazy part. Which one?"

Beka and Dylan looked at each other, startled. "Which—" Dylan started.

"Coming through!"

Dylan and Beka turned together, surprised by the shout. Both immediately stepped sideways, getting out of the way of the golden figure racing toward them. Without pause she dashed between them.

Dylan and Beka turned simultaneously again. "Trance—!" Dylan shouted.

Trance turned 180 degrees without pausing, running backward. "I don't have time!" she called back, before turning back. She ran into an intersection and out of sight.

"Well," Beka said, staring at the intersection, "*that* was a White Rabbit moment." Dylan was looking puzzled. "*Alice in Wonderland*."

It didn't help. "Somebody can explain it later," Dylan said. He nodded at the intersection. "Where's she headed?"

"I have no idea," the ship avatar said. "She disappeared as soon as she went past the intersection."

"There's nothing wrong with your sensors?" Beka asked.

"Nothing. Harper's been upgrading me consistently since the tunnelers attacked."

The holographic avatar said, "We've both noticed some curious anomalies, however."

"Unfortunately, I have not managed to analyze them as yet," the ship avatar added. "They occur without warning, and are extremely brief, from the picosecond to microsecond range. They might be spatial anomalies of some kind."

"Could we be passing through a region where this sort of thing can happen?" Beka said.

"Not that I know of," the ship avatar said. "If so, it would be of a type we have never before encountered. Most spatial distortion is a gravitic phenomenon of one kind or another, such as the region around a black hole."

"It's possible that some kind of temporal distortion is involved," the holographic avatar said. "Dimensional distortion is also within the realm of possibility."

"In other words," Dylan said heavily, "we don't know, we can't know, and guessing will just drive us nuts."

"I would say that covers it," the ship avatar said.

Beka had now worked up to her I-don't-believe-this expression. With her full mouth and big eyes, this gave her almost a childlike look. She pushed her hair back with a hand. "I love my job."

"Dylan," the ship avatar went on, "I didn't finish telling you about Trance's location."

"We just *saw* Trance's location," Beka said.

"One of them," Andromeda said. "I also have her on visual in Machine Shop Seventeen."

"For how long?" Dylan said.

"She was there before you were almost run down."

"Alright. Any sign of an anomaly there?"

"One," the holographic avatar said.

"Which might explain the *other* Trance," the ship avatar added.

"Other Trance?" Dylan and Beka echoed together.

"Purple," the ship avatar added.

"I think we'd better go and look," Dylan said.

"I'd say that's the captain-y thing to do, Captain Hunt," Beka said.

"I'd have to agree, Captain Valentine," he responded.

They started off at a quick jog. "Do you think the universe is ready for more than one Trance?"

Beka had her I-don't-believe-it face on again. "I know *I'm* not."

"Harper, this is Dylan. We're on our way down there."

Harper looked up from his workbench, his face twisting into an odd mutation of a frown and a sneer. "Y'know, Trance, I really, really prefer it when the boss stays up on his perch and leaves his favorite boy genius to, well . . ." He thought for a moment, and finished with, ". . . genius. Geniusize?"

The two Trances exchanged a look. With a smile, the purple one said, "I love him anyway."

Harper flicked a row of switches. "Do you mind? You're freakin' me out here."

"I am?" they said simultaneously.

"Harper?" Dylan said over the comm. "Speak to me."

Harper punched a button, then pressed the side of his neck. "Oh, hi, boss. Sorry about that, just got lost in the sheer dazzling light of my own brilliance there. What's up?"

Golden Trance was rolling her eyes, while the purple one snickered. He realized that he had really paid very little attention to the overall change in her personality since the switch. All that had really mattered was that she had been just about his best friend since she had joined the *Eureka Maru* crew.

It was still freaky that this particular version of the purple Trance apparently had a slightly closer relationship with some alternate version of him than plain old best friend. It rattled him even more that she didn't seem to be bothered by the fact that *he* was the alternate version from her viewpoint.

"Is Trance with you?" Dylan said.

The question made him uncomfortable and cautious. He felt as though he'd been caught doing something bad.

"Uh, yeah," he finally said. He glanced at both of them. After a moment, he made up his mind. It wasn't a hard decision, considering that he was feeling more and more guilty with each passing second. "You're gonna ask how many, aren't you?"

The machine-shop door opened. Beka and Dylan walked in, glancing from side to side, and then staring straight at the two Trances.

"I've got two," Harper said. "So how many do you have, boss?"

Dylan and Beka looked at each other, then at Harper. "One," Dylan said.

"Sorta," Beka added. "She disappeared."

The holographic Rommie shimmered into life. "On the other hand, it could be two, as I detected one on Deck Fourteen, just before Beka discovered the blood."

Harper and the golden Trance looked at each other. Finally, Trance said, "It's still only one, then. That was me. The blood, I mean." She frowned. "I guess the other Trance could be me, too. I know I was here when . . ."

She trailed off, looking completely lost.

"That was Tyr's blood," Dylan said.

"I know," Trance said. "I didn't kill him, I promise. Somebody else did."

Beka pushed her hair back with both hands this time. "You know, Trance, sometimes listening to you is cause for a migraine."

"I can't help it!" Trance snapped. "I'm not in control of everything. Something threw me forward in time, and then pulled me back again. I guess there was something I needed to know."

"About Tyr?" Dylan asked.

"About the way things could be." To Harper it seemed that she took on a strange and desperate look. "There are so many places and times that things could go bad. . . . Dylan, I just need you to keep trusting me, that's all."

Dylan seemed about to say something, and then stopped.

"We're still your good-luck charm," the purple Trance said.

Beka and Dylan exchanged looks.

"What I want to know," Harper said, looking back up from his workbench, "is whether that's double the luck, or luck squared. Either way it's ultra-freakin'-cool." He hunched over his workbench again. "Anyway, could you guys take it somewhere else and let the Einstein of the spaceways get his work done?"

"Einstein was a theoretician," the holographic Rommie said, primly.

"Theoretician, shmeoretician," Harper said with a sneer. "Okay, so what? So old Al never picked up a screwdriver or a soldering iron, he was still a pretty damn smart guy, which is the point I'm tryin' to make here, folks, because Mrs. Harper's boy Seamus is *also* real smart, as well as being a practical magician. Y'know, the difficult we do right away, the impossible takes an hour longer?"

"I love it when he babbles," Beka said with a sigh.

"You do?" Dylan answered.

She looked at him. "You sometimes have trouble with irony, don't you?"

"So what do we do about this?"

"Frankly, I don't know." She looked over at the purple version of Trance, who gave her a sunny smile in return. Harper knew neither Beka nor Dylan had a clue what the three of them were working on. Whether Andromeda did was another matter. "Wait and see, I guess. It's always worked out pretty well when it comes to Trance."

"Okay." Dylan turned to Harper. "Well, Mr. Harper, carry on. Just try not to accumulate too many Trances."

"Yeah, really," Harper muttered.

"Dylan?" Tyr's voice boomed tinnily in the scattered confines of the machine shop. "You'd better get back up here."

Dylan pressed the side of his neck. "On my way." He sighed. "It never stops."

He and Beka left.

The holographic Rommie glanced around, then looked straight at Harper. "You really ought to tidy this place up, Harper."

She faded out.

"Everyone's a critic," Harper grumbled. He swung around, tapped on a keyboard for a moment, then stabbed at another button. "Showtime!" He grinned, and then grew serious again as he looked at the two Trances. "This is going to max out our supplies, you know that? Rommie's gonna have to suck down a couple of asteroids to make it up."

"As long as it works," Trance said. "I have to go."

"Where?"

"Command." She frowned. "I think. The way this day is going, it could be anywhere."

With that, she left.

"Y'know," Harper said, leaning back in his chair, "that took a lot less time than it could have. Which is why I'm the genius and so many other folks aren't me." He frowned. "Okay, I think that made sense."

"You've always known what to do," the younger Trance said.

Suddenly she was in his lap, her arms around his neck and her tail wrapped around him. "Ah, jeez!" he exclaimed, standing bolt upright and dumping Trance to the deck.

"Ow?" she said.

"Okay," he said, backing up. "Too freaky. Wayyyy too freaky for me."

She got up, dusting herself off. "Okay." She smiled and went scampering off.

"Freaky," Harper repeated to himself as he sat down again.

In the *Andromeda Ascendant*'s missile construction facility business was proceeding smoothly, but swiftly. Drones sped to and fro with materials while the robotic assembly arms did their work. As each new missile, its warhead firmly in place, was completed it was picked up by a robot crane and deposited carefully in an eight-space rack.

The machines worked with a steady, precise rhythm, disgorging a new missile every two minutes.

Offensive missiles, Andromeda noted, not a single defensive missile among them. That was okay; she was well stocked with those. She was quite intrigued by the payloads, but had already decided not to say anything to Dylan yet.

Still, she had to wonder what Harper and Trance were up to. . . .

"This is not the way I wanted to get my exercise," Dylan complained as he and Beka jogged into the Command Deck. He had his force lance out again, while Beka had drawn her Gauss pistol. Arriving prepared to shoot was always a good idea these days.

Beka didn't answer. No surprise there. He was at a loss for words himself at the moment.

Tyr was standing to his left, at the fire control station. Rommie was standing to his right. Both of them were turning their heads constantly.

"Too weird," Dylan finally said.

"That's what I like, Captain," the android avatar said. "A good objective analysis."

The Command Deck was a chaos of motion and light. Versions of Trance were appearing and disappearing in ghostly, shimmering blurs, often moving around the deck as though in fast-forward. He could recognize Trance in some of the phantoms, but others were little more than moving blurs. None of them seemed aware of the others, or of those on the Command Deck who were watching them.

Dylan turned at the sound of running feet. For a moment he wasn't sure if *this* Trance had any more substance than the others, but her hand on his arm confirmed her as real. Well, apparently real.

"Something, somewhere, is very broken," Beka said, wonderment in her voice.

Trance was staring at the odd ballet. "Oh, no."

"Have you done something we should know about?" Tyr said mildly.

Trance shook her head, not saying anything.

Rommie strode toward them, ignoring the phantoms as she walked through them. "Is there anything you can tell us about this, Trance? Anything at all?"

Trance closed her eyes for a moment, then opened them again. "It isn't happening now."

"Very odd," Tyr said, raising his eyebrows, "considering that it is quite evidently happening now. Unless we are all being deceived in some fashion."

"No, we're not," Rommie said firmly. "It's real."

"That isn't what I mean," Trance said. "I mean it's being triggered somewhere in the future. I just don't know by what. Or when. Or why."

"Let me guess," Rommie said. "You don't know how, either."

Trance shook her head.

Dylan holstered his force lance again. "Whatever this is, it seems to be harmless. So far." One of the phantoms glided up to him, paused for a moment, then moved away again. "On the other hand, it's weird and creepy too."

Trance looked up at him, seemingly dismayed. "You think I'm weird and creepy?"

Beka holstered her Gauss pistol finally. "Trance, some days you *are* weird and creepy, and I think that's exactly what you want."

"Not this time," Trance said. She reached out tentatively as another of her phantom reflections came up. The figure swirled and vanished. "I just want to know what's going on." She looked genuinely lost, Dylan realized. "What it means."

"What it means," Tyr said, leaning against his console, his arms crossed over his muscular chest, "is that we have no doubt had you aboard this vessel for far too long." He turned his head to watch the ghostly figures flickering around him. "I, for one, would prefer my reality to be more stable, less mutable, and free of enigma."

"This sort of thing bothers me, too, Tyr," Rommie said. "I know there's no supernatural aspect to this, but the lack of a concrete explanation is very annoying."

Dylan walked down onto the Command Deck. Rommie smoothly turned and followed him, stopping next to him as he took his command station. After a brief pause, Beka followed, looking a lot less certain.

"Andromeda," Dylan said, looking around, "any idea what's going on here?"

Andromeda's head and shoulders appeared on screens around the bridge. "None. Obviously, these manifestations are nothing like those we saw earlier."

"No kidding," Beka said.

Trance had yet to follow Dylan and Beka. Dylan turned around to look at her. She was staring at the phantoms as they moved around, seemingly hypnotized. One moved up to her, and once again she reached out. As before, the phantom wavered and vanished.

Rommie's holographic avatar shimmered into life. "I believe we're experiencing quantum mechanics in action here. What we're seeing may be occurring in real time, but not in this dimension."

"Something's made the walls between probability lines thin,"

Trance said. "None of this is real, it's just possibilities leaking through."

"The things that could be?" Dylan said. His universe was starting to feel surreal, never a good thing.

"The things that will never be," Trance said. Hesitantly she walked into Command. The phantoms swirled and vanished as she moved through them. "These are the echoes left over after decisions get made."

"I think I will stick with clear decisions, then," Tyr said. He snorted derisively and turned away from her.

Beka said, "Trance, this has got to have something to do with you."

"I know," Trance said. She closed her eyes for a moment. Suddenly the phantoms started to fade away. She opened her eyes and looked at Beka. "It isn't just me, though. I just can't put it all together."

"Looks like you've got it under control," Dylan said, feeling more hopeful than convinced.

"Maybe," Trance said, looking at him. "I don't know if I did that, or it just happened."

Command was clear now. "Well, whoever and whatever, something appears to have worked."

"Unfortunately," Andromeda said, her flatscreen image looking very annoyed, "I am still having a great deal of difficulty locating any energy sources that might be responsible for these various phenomena."

"Does that mean you've got something?" Beka asked.

"Little more than before," Andromeda said. "Picosecond-length trace energy bursts with no immediately identifiable signature."

Dylan sighed. If it wasn't one thing, it was another. He would have tried to complain about the way the universe was treating him, but he knew all too well that a case could be made that he had set himself up in the first place.

"And there's another one," Andromeda added. "Machine Shop Seventeen."

Dylan and Beka started away from their stations, giving each other a weary look.

"Hey, Boss." It was Harper. His head and shoulders appeared on a screen next to Andromeda's image.

Dylan and Beka stopped. "Mr. Harper," Dylan said.

"If you guys picked up anything up there, it's 'cause she just left."

"Left?" Beka said.

"Like, *poof*, left," Harper said, looking and sounding annoyed. "One second she's jumping in my lap and making with the compliments and . . . uh, yeah, anyway . . . then she just vanishes." Dylan and Beka looked at Trance, who gave them an embarrassed shrug in return. "I gotta tell you, this whole experience just about freaked me out, and you know I don't freak that easily anymore."

"Jumping in your lap," Dylan echoed. The image that presented itself made it difficult for him to think.

"An exhibition of frighteningly poor taste," Tyr grumbled. "I am not surprised."

"She wasn't me," Trance said weakly. "That is, she was me, but a different me than me."

"Trance," Rommie said, giving her an almost cross-eyed look, "please don't."

"Oh. Okay."

"This is getting confusing," Beka said.

"Getting?" Dylan responded. "I'm at the point where I can't even think in straight lines anymore." He turned and went back to his station, rubbing at his forehead. "Okay, something is going on here. We don't know what and we don't know why, and we could waste our time running around in circles trying to figure it out."

"Okay," Beka said, giving him a puzzled look. "So what are you saying here, exactly?"

"We proceed as planned," Dylan said firmly.

"Into the valley of death," Tyr said darkly. He tilted his head to look at Dylan. "I am overcome with joy."

"Until we get some clear answers," Dylan said, allowing a commanding edge into his voice, "we might as well go on to Kantar."

To Dylan's surprise, he saw Tyr shiver. It was barely noticeable, but it was there, as though he were reacting to a cold draft. "I am . . . uncomfortable . . . with this."

"Uncomfortable or not, Tyr, it's our job," Dylan said, the edge in his voice growing sharper. He focused, unblinkingly, on Tyr's eyes. "Until we get some answers, and figure out what we need to do about these phenomena, we're going to do that job."

There was a long silent moment as Dylan and Tyr watched each other. There had been a time when this kind of confrontation had held more than its share of danger. Tyr's collection of plots and plans along with his innate sense of self-preservation had made their early relationship an aggressive balancing act.

Finally Tyr nodded. "Very well. I shall acquiesce to your intent, sir, in the hope that this course will prove fruitful rather than dangerous."

"Think of it as a vacation," Dylan said.

"Right," Beka said, giving him a disbelieving look. "A vacation."

A little under two hours later they were ready for the final Slip jump to Kantar. This had not been the simplest of journeys—most of the time a starship could get from one place to another with one or two Slips, with little additional transit time. This journey had taken them four Slips, with one Slipstream portal separated from the next by at least a day of normal-space travel at their highest velocity. It would have taken less time and effort to do a grand tour of the three galaxies.

Dylan, Beka thought, desperately wanted to get away, even if his idea of getting away meant going *somewhere*. As far as Beka had always been concerned, getting away meant *getting away*—no destination, no direction, just running hell for leather away from whatever the major problem was.

She had learned, painfully, that she couldn't outrun herself—and that was exactly what she had been trying to run from. The ever-growing list of failures, weaknesses, and miscalculations that had seemed to plague her life was something she could never escape, no matter how hard she tried.

Years after falling in with Dylan she still had her flaws, her weaknesses. Staying emotionally and mentally afloat sometimes became a battle that left her exhausted.

Dylan was under no illusions about her, she knew that. It didn't seem to matter to him. He had faith in her ability to get the job done.

He had faith in all of them. Having known so many people in her time who would exploit every weakness, every flaw, she had been surprised by Dylan Hunt. Sure, he wanted to exploit her talents as a pilot, just as he wanted to exploit Harper's talents as an engineer, but he had done so in a way that she had never known—bolstering her confidence and putting his trust in her. He respected her, both as a pilot and a person.

She smiled as she reached up and hit the switch that brought the Slipstream console down. There was a full complement on the Command Deck now, Harper having emerged from his playpen—only one Trance, she was happy to see. Tyr, at his console, looked as though he was about to go to sleep but she trusted that about as much as she expected her Uncle Sid to take up the Way.

She made some quick adjustments on her consoles, then grasped the pilot handles firmly, instantly picking up the flow of the *Andromeda Ascendant*.

Still smiling, she increased their velocity by five PSL—five percent of the speed of light. She had always believed that the faster a ship entered a Slipstream portal the easier it was to navigate.

That . . . and she liked to fly fast.

Time.

She let herself flow into the system as she opened the Slipstream runners.

Automatically, she said, "Transiting to Slipstream in five . . . four . . . three . . . two . . . one. . . ."

Light, noise, everything blurring. She hardly noticed, lost in her world. As the ship whipped and spun through the streams, she calmly reached out, making sense of the chaos. She found the threads she needed, aligned the immense craft, and caught the streams in the runners.

Almost done.

Breathing steadily, her focus taken completely by the task at hand, she guided *Andromeda* through the tangled web of Slipstream. This was something only beings with a flesh and blood component could do; synthetic life-forms such as Rommie could not find their way through the Slipstream—*Andromeda* had once been propelled into it after her first encounter with the Magog Worldship; with the entire crew having died at the hands of the Magog she had spent a year lost, unable to find her way out again.

Passable Slipstream pilots could be found everywhere—Dylan, Harper, and Tyr among them. Trance kept pretending to be a klutz, but Beka didn't believe it for a second.

Dylan had told her repeatedly how good she was, how much of a born pilot she was. She accepted that. It helped to define her.

One day it had simply come to her. She wasn't just good. She was the best. Nobody could come close to her.

The streams snapped and whipped. Leaning into the shifts, playing the controls by feel, she kept pace with the changes.

Time.

She played the grips, slipping *Andromeda* from one set of streams to another, then another. A final shift and she brought the ship back out into normal space. *Andromeda* was traveling at close to maximum velocity; Beka intended to trim back to something a little more conservative eventually, but for the moment she wanted the last leg to be over as quickly as possible.

She released the grips, grinning. She reached up and turned the Slipstream hood off, stretching as it rose back to its rest position.

She turned to Dylan, who was standing at his console in parade rest position, something that she always found amusing—he just couldn't shake the years of training and practice.

"Mission accomplished," she said. "We're right on target."

Dylan was about to answer when Andromeda's image suddenly replaced some of the tactical displays. "Captain, we have an incoming transmission."

There was a brief hiss, then a clear metallic voice—a recording, Dylan guessed. ". . . territorial boundary. You are ordered to turn back immediately. If you cross our system border we will take immediate action against you. Unidentified vessel: you are approaching the Kantar System territorial boundary. You are ordered to turn back immediately. . . ."

Dylan looked startled. "Not quite the reception you expected?" Beka asked.

"No," he said. "Kantar never used to be hostile."

"Stop here and try Plan B?" Beka said.

"What's Plan B?" Harper asked. "And why doesn't anybody *ever* tell me about this stuff?"

"Because Plan B, Mr. Harper," Dylan said, "consists of making it up as we go along." He turned to Beka. "Plan B it is. We'll try and contact the Kantar government, and if there's no joy there, we'll go somewhere else."

"Coming to a stop," she said, reaching for her controls.

Andromeda reappeared on the flatscreens. "Captain, the message just changed."

Beka started trimming *Andromeda*'s velocity, bringing the starship to a graceful halt.

"Alright," Dylan said. "Let's hear what they're saying now."

". . . repeat: bring your vessel to a stop immediately and prepare to be boarded. Follow the instructions you are given, or we will destroy you. Respond."

The tactical displays flashed up as Andromeda said, "They seem to be using an advanced stealth technique, and they are very fast. And there's a lot of them."

Dylan stared at the tactical displays. Beka readied herself for Dylan's orders—just giving up wasn't an option.

"Let's give him a response," Dylan said finally. "This is Captain Dylan Hunt of the *Andromeda Ascendant*. Who are you?"

The central display screen cleared. The head and shoulders of a tense-looking middle-aged man appeared. "I know you, Captain Hunt."

Dylan raised his eyebrows. "I don't believe I've had the pleasure."

The man's eyes didn't waver. "I am Colonel Willard Kaczynski. I command the Fourth Battalion of the Kantaran Lighthouse Keepers. Stand down and prepare to be boarded. I will offer no further warning."

FOUR • THE LITTLE THINGS THAT MATTER

In my heart, I have never seen the point of killing when embarrassment will do. Put aside the perfect blow and instead seek a way to break your opponent's belt and buttons, so that he stumbles upon his fallen trousers.

—KORENDO MASTER OF MASTERS SHIAHN,
THE SUBSTANCE OF STYLE,
CY 8233 (3RD REVISION)

Everyone turned to look at Trance. She, in turn, was staring at the central display as the colonel's image vanished and was replaced by one of the tactical displays.

"Oh, no," she whispered.

Before Dylan could say anything, she turned and ran from the Command Deck. He didn't spend any time worrying about her; this wasn't the time.

"Beka," he said, "get us out of here."

"You've got it," she said.

Andromeda appeared on several of the flatscreens. "Captain, they are activating weapons. Firing. We have six incoming missiles."

On the tactical display half a dozen triangles had appeared, converging on *Andromeda.*

"Countermeasures," he ordered. This was just what he needed to complete his day—a battle for absolutely no good reason. "Damn it."

———

Andromeda unfurled her huge electronic countermeasure fans. Glowing a soft violet, the ECM fans were intended to confuse and jam enemy radar and the sensors on incoming missiles. Ship-to-ship warfare was a tricky business, made trickier yet by the certain knowledge that any given opponent might well be equipped with the means to make any kind of countermeasures pointless.

The ECM fans were the gentler part of the equation. Even as they were unfolding, defensive missiles shot from ten of *Andromeda*'s forty launch tubes. A handful of drones followed them into space, ready to provide guidance and communications.

Warfare in space had come a long way from the days when success meant being the one who could hit hardest, fastest, and longest. There was always a bigger ship with more powerful weapons. What counted these days was strategy and sheer cleverness.

Ten defensive missiles shot toward the incoming half dozen. The battle should have been a foregone conclusion.

"Missed?" Dylan said.

"All ten," Rommie said.

"According to the telemetry," Andromeda said, her image appearing on the flatscreens, "they didn't even see the attacking missiles."

"Oh, great," Beka muttered. "Now what?"

"Brace for impact," Andromeda said, in a very matter-of-fact way.

Everyone except for Rommie grabbed a console or the nearest reliable object.

The Command Deck reverberated to the explosions, one after another in rapid succession. The ship vibrated as though she had been picked up and shaken—one of the curses of the antigravity system. On the one hand, the AG field effectively reduced the ship's mass to a few grams, allowing for some impressive maneuvers. On the other hand, when she took a forceful enough hit, it could be a painful experience for the crew. Dylan had once compared it to being inside a giant baby rattle with a very angry baby doing the rattling.

Rommie, staying perfectly balanced, said, "Either their armament is very weak, or they just baby-tapped us as a warning."

"I believe it was a warning," Tyr said. "I'm not too excited by this situation. I suggest we blow them out of the sky."

"That's an option," Dylan said. He took a deep breath, not willing to commit to acts of destruction just yet. "I'm going to hold that in reserve."

"And give them time to destroy us as they have already threatened?" Tyr was definitely unhappy about this course of action, which was too bad. Tyr wasn't the one making the decisions.

"Until I say otherwise, Tyr," Dylan said, "we'll stick with defensive measures only. We don't know just what we're up against here, or the overall strength we're facing. Let them play their hand."

"We're just going to sit here and see what happens?" Beka said, giving him a concerned look.

Dylan shook his head. "Get ready to start backing up on my signal. Slowly, then pick up velocity. Maybe we can get out of here without too much more insanity." He looked back at Tyr. "Tyr, ready on tubes one through forty, defensive only, get ready to lock in a firing solution as soon as they open up . . . *if* they open up. Andromeda, see if you can get Colonel Kaczynski to talk to us."

Tyr gave Dylan a sullen look, then turned his attention to the center screen. Dylan ignored Tyr's studied display of attitude.

"He's answering," Andromeda said.

The center tactical screen cleared to display Colonel Kaczynski's head and shoulders once again. "Well?" the man said brusquely.

"I'm not too impressed by anything except your rudeness," Dylan said, half smiling. He had never been one for displays of contempt, but Tyr had, over time, taught him its value as a tool. The trick was in keeping it subdued enough that it wouldn't provoke an immediate aggressive response. "Now that you've let off some steam, would you mind telling me what the hell is on your mind here?"

Kaczynski was silent for a moment, staring. Dylan had gone from sounding relaxed to wrapping his words in ice and steel.

Finally, the colonel found his voice again. "You are trespassing on sovereign territory. That's what's on my mind. I've already explained the consequences of that."

"Fine," Dylan said, his tone of voice not changing in the slightest.

He was really getting tired of idiotic behavior, whether from individuals or from planetary governments as a whole. "I'll take my ship out of here, and let the Commonwealth know that Kantar is off-limits."

"Oh, *please!*" Kaczynski said contemptuously. Dylan was caught by surprise. "I am not going to be so easily deluded, Hunt."

"What?" Dylan was at a loss now. "Our purpose here was to bring the Commonwealth charter to Kantar. You don't want anything to do with the Commonwealth, fine, we just turn around and go away."

"Oh, yes," Kaczynski said. "Just like the Commonwealth has done with several other sovereign systems." Dylan started to object, then closed his mouth. Since the new Commonwealth had begun to form, there had been quite a bit in the way of underhanded dealing and black ops. He had done his best to stay away from that aspect of the Commonwealth, but it wasn't always possible. "These things eventually come back to bite you on the ass, Captain."

"Alright," Dylan said. "You've no love for the new Commonwealth. But I remember Kantar being a loyal and open member of the old Systems Commonwealth."

"You'll have plenty of time to read our history texts, Captain," Kaczynski said. "Provided that you surrender, of course."

"I'd like to hear a summary anyway," Dylan said. "Humor an old High Guard officer."

Rommie started to correct him. Dylan waved her to silence, leaving her looking baffled.

"Your precious Commonwealth abandoned us, Hunt. *That* is the summary. Nothing to spare for the peripheral worlds, no support during the conflict with the Nietzscheans." The colonel's face was reddening slightly now. "And once all was in disarray, with the High Guard routed, what did our Vedran masters do?"

"Nobody knows what happened to Tarn-Vedra," Dylan said softly.

Kaczynski snorted. "And you believe that?"

"I know that," Dylan said. "Tarn-Vedra is . . . was . . . my homeworld."

Kaczynski seemed taken aback by that. "Then you have made an attempt to reach it?"

Dylan glanced at Beka. She was looking worried now. He turned his attention back to the screen. "We made an attempt. We believe we might have made it about halfway there."

"Somehow," Kaczynski said bitterly, "they broke down the Slipstream routes to Tarn-Vedra. The last reports—"

"Are that Tarn-Vedra itself vanished completely," Dylan said. "I know."

"It wasn't destroyed in the war," Kaczynski said. "We were *abandoned*. Made dependent upon your damned Systems Commonwealth, and then abandoned to bloody insanity. The Vedrans could have stopped what happened, but they chose to run away."

"Maybe," Dylan said. He wasn't going to let himself be drawn by Kaczynski's statements. Dylan had received some answers over time, enough to suggest that the Vedrans had somehow taken their entire system and moved it . . . somewhere else. Where, exactly, was the question. How they had done it was just as big a question to contemplate.

"There is no 'maybe' here, Hunt. The Vedrans ran." He paused for a moment. "The Lighthouse Keepers are the direct result of that. We became a target for raiders and vandals, for Nietzschean pirates looking for easy pickings."

"So you learned to fight back," Dylan said. "And to protect your borders. Not a bad thing if you don't take it too far."

"Don't mistake us for ignorant isolationists, Captain. We maintain our sources."

Dylan signaled to Beka. "I don't mistake you for anything, Colonel."

Beka played her controls, nudging the *Andromeda* into motion. While the ship was subject to all normal laws of physics the thrust from her engines could be aimed in any direction—and given the considerable power generated by those engines and the AG field that reduced her mass, the *Andromeda Ascendant* could carry out flight maneuvers that would have left many other ships spreading parts across a cubic light-second of space.

"You will not find us unkind, Captain," Kaczynski said. He had calmed down now, apparently taking Dylan's willingness to talk as a concession of some kind.

"On the contrary, Colonel," Dylan said sternly. "So far this has been a quite unpleasant encounter." Dylan took a deep breath, well aware that he was committing them all to a potentially disastrous course of action. "I think it's time we called it a day and went our separate ways."

Kaczynski sighed. "That will not be possible, Hunt."

"That remains to be seen."

"You are hardly the first . . ." The colonel trailed off, looking down for a moment, then back up. His face was suddenly a cold, dispassionate mask. "I see. You're a damned fool, Captain Hunt."

The screen blanked, then returned to tactical display.

"No more need to be sneaky," Beka said.

"Best speed to the Slip point," Dylan said, "and then anywhere but here."

"The Kantaran ships are on the move, Captain," Andromeda said.

"Oh, this is good," Harper said. "This is *really* good. As if my day didn't already suck enough."

"You've had worse," Tyr said. He looked calmly down at his fire control panel. "Shall I begin destroying them now?"

"I don't think we need to do that," Dylan said. "Which doesn't mean we shouldn't defend ourselves."

"I think that would be a very good idea," Rommie said. She was glancing from her console to the main screens and back. "I'm detecting multiple missile launches, as well as plasma and particle beam weapons at full charge."

"This Colonel Kaczynski seems determined to piss me off," Dylan grumbled.

"Hey," Harper said from somewhere behind him, "he already succeeded with me. I'm all for giving him an ass-kicking."

"Mr. Harper," Dylan said mildly, "shut the hell up. Tyr, we need a firing solution that'll give us a broad spread."

Tyr's hands were already in motion, but he gave Dylan a dubious look. "Our weapons proved useless last time. Why should—"

"It's a distraction," Beka said, grinning. "We'll get some of the incoming. It's the shotgun approach."

"It's the expensive approach," Rommie said. "We'll have to start getting nasty if this keeps up—our defensive stockpile won't last forever."

"It doesn't have to," Dylan said. He turned to Tyr. "Bring the PDL turrets and AP cannons on-line. Split control with Rommie and Beka." He turned to Beka. "How are we doing?"

"Approaching fifty PSL," she said. "I think that's the fastest I've ever backed up."

"The Kantarans are starting to outpace us," Andromeda said. On the screen a number of fast-moving triangles winked out. "The good news is that we just took out thirty percent of their missiles."

"Keep it up until we run out," Dylan said. "They're not going to stop."

"Then we should demonstrate our seriousness," Tyr said, an edge of anger in his voice. "I say to hell with this game!"

"Oh, great," Harper said. "Just what we need. A mutiny, and guess what, it's our favorite Nietzschean. So what the hell did we expect?"

"Harper," Beka snapped, "shut up."

Dylan didn't move. No threatening gestures, no posturing, nothing to worsen Tyr's attitude. "Mr. Anasazi, this is not a time for arguments. Do your job."

Without answering, Tyr turned back to his console. Forty new triangles sped outward from *Andromeda*'s image on the screens. Almost immediately, another forty followed.

It wasn't going to be enough.

"Time to Slipstream?" he said.

"Thirty seconds," Beka answered.

"Another thirty percent," Andromeda said. "The last volley looks likely to account for fifteen percent of the missiles launched in the past thirty seconds."

Tyr loaded and launched another volley.

"Captain—" Andromeda started.

He had already seen it. Five Kantaran fighters, in formation, had suddenly gained velocity and were outrunning their own missiles.

"Tyr, Beka, Rommie," he said quickly, "target the missiles with the

AP cannons. Get a lock on those fighters and discourage them—close fire only, don't shoot anyone down." Not yet, anyway, he thought.

One by one the missiles were vanishing from the tactical screen.

The Kantaran formation, however, kept coming.

"I cannot get a lock," Tyr snapped. He slapped his console, frustrated.

"Lay down fire anyway," Dylan said. "We just need to cover—"

"Trouble," Rommie said. "There's a line of fighters in our way. We won't be able to go to Slipstream."

The Kantaran formation slowly broke apart, each of the five ships coming in on a different vector.

"Evasive," Dylan snapped.

"Too late," Andromeda said. "Hold on."

Almost immediately a series of loud thuds and bangs resonated through the ship. The deck lurched beneath their feet. Harper lost his balance, coming down heavily. More explosions followed as both fighters and missiles chewed at *Andromeda*'s hull.

Harper ducked and rolled as sparks cascaded from nearby panels. "Jeez, Rommie, did the folks who made you stick fireworks behind all the panels, or what?"

"I'm a sensitive girl, Mr. Harper," the ship replied primly. "We have another formation incoming."

On the tactical screen, another five ships had formed up and were sweeping in. This was getting to be consistently irritating.

"Evasive!" Dylan snapped. There was no indication of course change. Beka should have been whipping the ship through all kinds of unlikely maneuvers by now—even if they couldn't shake these guys, they didn't have to make their job easy. "Beka, you can start anytime now."

He turned angrily, staring at her. Didn't she get it? Her failure to follow his commands endangered his ship. Endangered all of them.

Beka was frozen in place, lost in some kind of panic. Great, after all this time as his XO she had to go to pieces *now*.

Explosions thundered across the hull, and the ship shook. Harper, still on his hands and knees, scuttled out of the way of more cascading sparks. "Y'know, this stuff *really* sucks!" He pushed himself to his feet. "So much for all that great Commonwealth engineering, huh? What a load of junk."

"I will excuse your rudeness, Mr. Harper," Andromeda said. "I need you to start taking care of the more major issues occurring within my power and engine systems."

"What she means, *kludge*," Tyr said in a mocking tone, "is get your worthless carcass out of here and cease being an annoying bug." He turned to Dylan. "What the hell is wrong with her?"

"How the hell should I know?" Dylan snapped. "I'm a ship's captain, not a psychologist." Dylan strode over to Beka's station. "Beka!" She turned her head to look at him, but it was the thousand-meter stare of the lost. "*Captain Valentine!*"

Her mouth worked silently for a moment, then she whispered, "Dylan . . . Dylan, I . . ."

"Oh, the hell with it," Dylan muttered.

He hauled off and slapped her in the face with his right hand, snapping her head back.

"Ooookay, that's it, I'm outta here," Harper said, and with that he raced out of Command.

Beka was suddenly sobbing like a little girl. "Dylan, I can't do it, I can't do it!"

He sighed. More explosions rocked them, spinning the ship. "We're getting killed here," he snarled, glaring at her, "and you're throwing yourself a goddamn pity party? *Not on my ship!*"

He hauled off again to backhand her across the other cheek, seeing her flinch. He never completed the movement—Rommie had moved with blinding speed and grabbed his wrist. She didn't squeeze hard, but it still made him gasp. "Dylan, what do you think you're doing?"

"That's *Captain Hunt*," Dylan growled, glaring at her. "I'm trying to snap her out of whatever state she's in."

"It's what she needs," Tyr said, sounding almost reasonable. He looked up at the ceiling, his eyes tracking the positions of explosions on the outside of the ship.

"What she needs," Rommie echoed, her angry look going from one to the other. "Brutalizing her is what she needs? I don't know what's going on right now, *Dylan*, but if you ever do something like that again, I will immobilize you."

"Don't you threaten me," Dylan snapped. "I'll have you disassembled!"

"We can discuss this later," Rommie said. "Right now we have a battle to fight." She released his wrist and pushed him backward. "Beka, I'll take over."

Beka gave her a pathetically grateful look. "Thanks . . . I just . . . I just can't."

With another angry look at Dylan, Rommie slipped her hands into the controls. "Evasive maneuvers, aye . . . Captain."

"It's about time," the ship avatar said.

Dylan and Tyr both lunged for consoles to anchor themselves, but Rommie, connecting with her ship-self, was too fast for them. As the *Andromeda Ascendant* began full-power maneuvers, both Dylan and Tyr were thrown backward. Both men landed heavily. Dylan, to his regret, landed on his tailbone.

"Sorry," Rommie said with deliberate insincerity. She allowed Dylan a small, sarcastic smile. As he got back to his feet, Dylan noticed that Rommie had reached out and held on to Beka, preventing her from taking a tumble.

"Disassembly," Dylan hissed.

Rommie's smile vanished.

The thunder of explosions diminished, but Dylan knew it was only a matter of time before the Kantarans got a lock on them again.

Tyr had gotten up as well, and he had the darkest, angriest expression Dylan had ever seen on him. Great. More trouble. His hand went to his force lance. Tyr, seeing this, slowly folded his arms over his chest.

"I don't need the two of you growling at each other like angry dogs," Rommie snapped. "If you can't do *something*, get the hell out of Command!"

"I'm *in* command," Dylan growled. "Remember that."

"And I, *sir*," Tyr snarled, "have no desire to work alongside an imbecile who cannot fight a simple battle!"

"Fine!" Dylan yelled. "Fine! Run away, Tyr. You always *were* a problem. Go solve yourself. Go save yourself. We don't need you."

Tyr seemed about to answer, then changed his mind. With a sharp, silent nod, he stalked out of Command.

"Good riddance," Dylan snapped.

"I don't believe what I'm hearing," Rommie said with a look at him, "from any of you."

"Shut up and fly," Dylan growled. "We'll show these bastards what a Commonwealth ship and captain are made of."

"Yes, sir, Captain Ahab," she said, and turned back to her work.

He started to answer, then decided against it. He pressed the side of his neck. "Harper? What are you up to?"

There was a sigh, then Harper's voice. "Listen, I know you're kind of on the stupid side here, boss, and, like, I'm the off-the-scale genius, but even an idiot like you can probably figure out that, hey, golly, the wizard of engineering is probably, well, engineering. As in trying to save our asses, okay?"

"Mr. Harper—" Dylan started, fuming inside at this latest insubordination.

"Listen, Boss, just shove it you-know-where, okay? I've got more important things to do than blow steam with you. Such as, for example"—Harper took a deep breath and screamed—"*saving our asses!* Okay, that should be clear even to you. Hell, even Tyr should understand that one. Now, don't bug me again. Oh, yeah—you can threaten to shove me out of an airlock, but it's your ass if you do. Harper out."

"That little . . ." Dylan grimaced, feeling the muscles in his face and back tighten to the point of pain. Harper had better stay out of his reach or Trance would have to glue all of his teeth back in.

He really, really, wanted to hit something.

Now.

Explosions rippled around the *Andromeda* then, shaking the ship violently. Dylan fell over again, while Rommie held on to Beka.

He didn't waste time getting up. "Full offensive armament, tubes one through forty. Fire at will."

Tyr had stalked out of Command with a specific destination in mind—if the great Captain Dylan Hunt could not bring himself to hit back properly at these people, then he would. He would take a Slipfighter out into the midst of the battle and give the Kantarans a demonstration of the way a true warrior fights.

He was the last of Kodiak Pride. He had fought for his survival all of his life. Even stripped of his bone blades he would continue the fight until—pieces of his enemies' flesh hanging from his bloodied teeth and claws—he was finally brought down like one of those great bears.

His fists clenched as he anticipated the coming struggle. He was Tyr Anasazi, out of Victoria by Barbarossa. He was superior. *Superior!*

Captain Dylan Hunt, that throwback, could never understand.

He started to run. Having the wind at his heels would get him into the fight faster. Faster, better, *superior*.

Suddenly Trance was in front of him. Thrown off balance, he staggered to a halt, almost running into her.

"Trance," he said, baffled by her appearance. "I have no time for your annoyances, child."

"I've no time for your posturing, Tyr," she said.

The sound of missiles and plasma bursts against the hull came through as dull thumps here. In his gut, he could feel the shifts and turns of the continuing evasive maneuvers.

"Very well," Tyr said. "Let us both be on our way."

"This is where I was going," she said softly, her eyes not moving from his.

"Very well," Tyr said patiently, "you are where you wish to be, and I am going to where I wish to be. A positive outcome for us both."

Explosions like drumbeats now.

"Tyr," Trance said, her voice still soft, "I can't let you go out there, no matter how much you think you want to. It would be a mistake. A bad mistake."

"It will be a mistake to attempt to stop me," he said, starting to grow angry. Surely Trance wasn't so stupid as to stand in his way?

"If you go out there in a Slipfighter," Trance said, "you'll get the rest of us killed, and the life you have will be a misery that ends in failure. You'll lose everything you have, everything you hope to gain . . . even your son."

"My—" He stared at her, dumbfounded. What could she know of his son?

"Everything," she said.

He saw that she was holding her force lance.

"You wish to preserve my life by killing me, is that it?" he said. His hand dropped to his Gauss pistol, ready.

"No," she said. She sighed. "I was hoping you'd be reasonable and make this easy, Tyr."

"The reasonable path would not involve threatening me," he snapped, and started to draw his pistol.

She stepped forward, moving inside his guard so smoothly and quickly that he could not change defense tactics. She thumbed a switch on the force lance, and its monomolecular segments expanded and became rigid as magnetic fields repolarized.

The end of the two-meter lance struck him in the chest and shoved him backward as it completed its extension. Before he could get his balance again, Trance was whirling, bringing the lance down across his lower right arm. There was a moment of searing pain, then numbness, and he found that he could neither feel nor control his fingers. The Gauss pistol slipped from his hand, clattering to the floor.

Trance turned and caught the pistol with the end of the lance, sending it flying away.

"I will not yield!" he shouted.

"I know," she replied. "You're Tyr Anazasi, blah blah blah, superior, blah blah blah, etcetera."

Rage welled up now, unreasonable and blinding. Whatever Trance was, she was going to die at his hands—however much effort it took. "I will not be mocked!"

"Oh, blah blah blah," she said, sneering at him. "Blowhard."

He unsheathed his knife, a finely honed piece that could easily cut through steel. He would see what she was made of, oh yes. This was a day that had been due for a long time.

He ran at her, yelling at the top of his lungs.

She stood her ground until the last possible moment. Then she was gone, springing up and over his head with catlike speed and grace.

He turned to see her land on the deck behind him, the force lance held in a ready position.

"You can stop at any time," she said. "I won't mind."

With another howl of rage, he ran at her again. This time he dove at her, intending to tackle her about the waist and bring her down, force lance and all.

It worked. Almost.

As they went down, she folded up, and he felt her feet hit him in the lower stomach. Suddenly he was flying through the air again, helpless. He hit the deck on his back, the thud of impact joining the distant explosions. The breath went out of him for a moment.

He still had his knife, though. He could still—

Trance landed lightly at his right side. Without pause, she stamped down on his right wrist. Pain shot up his arm, and he involuntarily released his grip on the hilt of his knife.

This was not going well for him, he realized. He failed to understand that concept. How could it not go well for him? He was strong, fast, superior. Trance was a little *slip* of a thing who liked plants and riddles and being a good-luck charm.

"Time to stop, Tyr," she said. She lifted her foot and kicked away his knife, sending it after the Gauss pistol. "I don't want to hurt you any more."

He rolled over and came to his feet. "I've wasted enough time with you, girl. I have a job to do."

He turned to make a run for the Slipfighter hangar.

He was barely aware of Trance as she went past him in a flying roll. She was suddenly in the way again.

This was getting tiring.

"I'm sorry, Tyr," she said.

He thought he was ready for her now.

She struck at him with the force lance. He ducked, lunged, and grabbed it firmly, intending to either tear it from her hands or to yank her toward him.

Instead, she pinned the bottom end of the lance against the deck and used it as a pivot. She kicked off, folding up, and kicked out, uncoiling with tremendous speed.

The heels of her boots smashed into his face. His vision and awareness swam. He was aware of Trance landing on the deck nearby, but he seemed to have lost the ability to make his body do anything that he wanted.

He tried to stay on his feet, but he couldn't. He sat down heavily on the deck.

He had to resist the darkness. He had to.

He was going to get up. He could do this.

Superior.

Trance's right boot caught him in the jaw. He felt his jaw break, felt a moment of intense pain, and then nothing more.

"*That* was interesting," Rommie said, shimmering into view and looking down at Tyr's supine form.

"That's one word for it, I suppose," Trance said. She thumbed the force lance switch again. The magnetic fields shifted and the monomolecular segments collapsed. "I had to stop him."

"I'm sure you did," Rommie said, looking up. "Everyone's behaving very oddly, to say the least."

"The Lighthouse Keepers," Trance said. "They're making it happen."

"Whatever you're planning to do, now's the time."

"Good. Beka should get ready to get us out of here on no notice at all." Trance started to jog down the corridor, heading for Command.

"There's a problem there," Rommie said, moving her holographic image to keep pace with Trance. "Beka appears to have lost all self-confidence and has fallen into a state of panic."

"Oh. So Dylan's flying the ship?"

"Dylan's being a martinet." Rommie frowned. "He's insufferable. And violent."

"Oh, no."

"I'm flying myself at the moment," Rommie said, sounding displeased. "Or, at least, my android avatar is doing so while Andromeda keeps track of the tactical situation." Rommie scanned the ceiling and explosions thudded once more across the hull. "We're in serious trouble."

"I think I can help. You already know about the missiles that Harper built."

"Yes," Rommie said. "And I have to say that nanobots are an interesting payload."

"They're the only thing that will save us," Trance said. "Get the magazines ready, and get the first forty set to launch. Wait until I reach Command. I can take over from you there."

"I can fly myself," Rommie said. "It's just—"

"This isn't about you flying yourself," Trance said. "I'd love to leave you to do that, but to make this work I have to be on the flight controls. It's going to be instinct on my part."

"Understood." There was a pause. "Missile tubes one through forty loaded and ready. I've locked Dylan out of fire control."

"Good idea."

Trance broke into a run.

"What strategy do you have in mind?" Rommie asked as Trance ran.

"Bull elephant," Trance said. "It's the only one I can see that works."

"Bull elephant?"

"It's an Earth animal," Trance said, glad to have something to take her mind off of the running and the pounding of explosions. "There are analogues on other worlds, of course. The bull elephant was a gigantic land mammal."

"You're comparing me to a gigantic mammal?" Rommie said, looking confused even as her image, facing Trance, kept pace with her.

"In this instance, yes." Trance rounded an intersection. "Elephants were hunted for their ivory tusks, and one of the methods for hunting them involved setting the hunter's subordinates to harry and exhaust the creature, which the hunter would then kill."

"This sounds promising," Rommie said dryly.

"It's better than you think." She was on the last stretch now. "The bull elephant would fight back, charging its attackers. Sometimes it would crush or gore one or more of them. Sometimes it would kill or injure enough that it could escape."

"I think I see what you intend to do," Rommie said.

"It isn't subtle," Trance admitted, "but we have an advantage. We just have to stay alive long enough."

"We're taking far too many hits," Rommie admitted. "I'm losing power, I've lost weaponry, and I can't guarantee Slipstream capability for more than ten minutes. Harper's doing what he can, but the truth is that it may take weeks to repair the damage that the Kantarans are inflicting."

Trance had reached Command now, and could barely believe her eyes. Dylan was strutting about angrily, red in the face and utterly speechless with rage—that was a relief. The android avatar was at the flight controls, doing her best to minimize the damage being inflicted by the Kantarans. Beka was huddled by her feet, miserable, tears streaming down her face.

She didn't have to see him to know that Harper had been changed in some unpleasant way. As long as he kept holding the *Andromeda Ascendant* together, it didn't matter.

"I have to get us out of this," she said to the android.

"You know," Dylan suddenly yelled, "I am *so* sick of treachery and betrayal! Everybody, and I mean *everybody*, has it in for me!" He strutted toward Trance, his fists clenched. "Especially you, Trance. You've been nothing but trouble. Trouble!"

"Dylan," Trance said mildly, "shut up."

"I will not shut up! *I* command this vessel, not you!"

"You are no longer in command, Captain Hunt," Rommie said formally. "Under High Guard Command Charter article 13302, section two, provisions one through five, which states that in the event that a ship's AI, supported by the ship's chief medical officer, should find the commanding officer unfit for duty, said commanding officer shall be immediately suspended from duty."

"You just made that up!" Dylan yelled.

"She did not," Andromeda said. "The High Guard Command Charter, 727th Amended Edition, can be accessed in your quarters.

The relevant section has been bookmarked for you." Andromeda paused, but Dylan had nothing to say. "Let it be noted that the AI of the *Andromeda Ascendant* finds her present commanding officer unfit for duty. Does the chief medical officer concur with this assessment?"

"I am Trance Gemini, chief medical officer of the *Andromeda Ascendant*," Trance said firmly, "and I concur with the assessment of the ship's AI."

Dylan spluttered helplessly.

"Captain Hunt," Rommie said harshly, "I am requesting that you surrender your weapon, leave Command, and confine yourself to your quarters until further notice. Fail to comply, and I will take such steps as are needed to incarcerate you for the time being."

Dylan seemed about to say something. Then he tensed, as though about to draw his force lance and fire.

"Don't," Rommie said. "I will inevitably break several bones while disarming you."

Angrily Dylan reached down and pulled out his force lance, holding it out to Rommie. She took it. "You'll pay for this," he hissed. "You'll all pay for this."

He turned and stormed out of Command.

"He's going to be so mad," Beka whispered.

Trance looked at Rommie, and the android nodded. Stepping away from the flight station, the android bent down and lifted Beka easily to her feet. "Come on, Beka," she said gently. "I'll take care of you. Trance is going to get us out of here."

If I can, Trance thought. She was on her own here, no help forthcoming from any corner of the universe.

Rommie set Beka down in a corner of Command, then went back to her own station. Trance grasped the flight controls, closing her eyes for a moment, shutting out the sounds of explosions.

"I estimate that we have no more than nine minutes before battle damage becomes critical," Andromeda said. "At that point our artificial gravity field will lose coherence."

Trance was barely listening. She had found the lines of best probability. Her hands played the controls, putting the ship into a wild spinning maneuver. The explosions ceased for a moment.

Another shift, and she was charging a group of Kantaran fighters.

"Fire one through five!" she snapped.

"One through five, aye!" Rommie responded. The missiles appeared on the tactical screen, heading into the Kantaran group, but unable to lock on. That didn't matter, not with these missiles.

"Reload as we go," Trance ordered.

"Reloading, aye." Rommie looked up. "This had better work."

Trance threw the ship into another tight maneuver, rolling over, killing velocity, then applying thrust on a new heading. They were hit again, but only twice.

"Fire six through fifteen!" she said.

"Six through fifteen, aye. Missiles away. Reloading."

Trance sent the huge ship charging toward another group of attackers.

"First salvo has detonated on time," Rommie said.

"Fire sixteen through twenty."

"Sixteen through twenty, aye, second salvo has detonated."

Trance could feel the confusion emanating from parts of the Kantaran fleet. By now they would be starting to realize what had been done to them.

She adjusted their course. "Twenty-one through thirty."

"Twenty-one through thirty, aye, third salvo has detonated," Rommie said.

"I am detecting an increase in Kantaran radio traffic," Andromeda said. "There appears to be a certain amount of agitation."

"Fourth salvo has detonated. All tubes reloaded and ready."

Trance adjusted her course again, charging another group of Kantaran fighters. This group didn't even bother with their weapons. Instead, they tried to get out of her way.

"No doing," she said, her eyes narrowing. "Fire thirty-one through forty."

"Firing thirty-one through forty, aye. Missiles away. Reloading."

"Radio traffic is continuing to increase. Warnings are being issued."

"Too little, too late," Trance said. "They wouldn't let us go, I'm not letting *them* go. Alright, get ready to fire one at a time on my mark."

With that, she put the ship into a wild wobbling spin around its own axis.

"Fire!" she snapped.

"Firing, aye!" Rommie answered.

Missiles hurtled away one after another, each on a different vector.

"Reload and continue firing at will," Trance said. "Empty the magazine."

"I think I'm going to be sick," Beka moaned.

The number of missile traces from *Andromeda* continued to increase. By now, even though Trance had essentially made the ship a sitting target, there were almost no missile impacts and no indication of plasma bursts or particle beam strikes. The tactical screen was still filled with the traces for Kantaran vessels, but now they seemed to be barely moving, all attempts at formation lost.

"The magazines are now empty," Andromeda reported. "All missiles away, and detonating as intended. The Kantaran fleet appears to be in some disarray."

Trance gradually killed the gyroscopic spin, bringing the ship to a level plane at full stop. Her head was spinning a little, but she put that down to having to keep track of so much while simultaneously keeping the best probabilities together in her mind.

"We are holding steady," Rommie reported.

"Can we still make it out of here?"

Rommie tapped away at her consoles and frowned. "Yes, we can, but I would suggest we find a system where I can extract raw materials from an asteroid belt. It will take at least a week to effect even basic repairs. Our Kantaran friends inflicted a surprising amount of damage."

Trance closed her eyes for a moment and sighed. It wasn't just the damage to the ship, either. The psychological changes in the crew could well be permanent, or damaging in some other way. She glanced at Beka, who was still huddled miserably at the other side of Command.

"Let's see how their ships look," Trance said.

The screens cleared to show a panoramic view of a part of the Kantaran fleet. The ships appeared to be drifting aimlessly, and each one seemed, in some way, foreshortened. To one degree or another, each ship had shifting patterns of black moving over it. That would eventually change. Harper had designed these nanobots in a hurry, but he had made sure to build in a time limit as part of their instruction set.

"Alright," Trance said, allowing herself a small smile. "Open a—"

"Open *nothing*!" an all-too-familiar voice grated. Trance sighed. Tyr sometimes didn't have the sense to stay down when it was in his best interests. "I am taking command! This ship is *mine*!"

Tyr was leaning heavily on the entrance to Command. The lower half of his face was swollen and darkening—that was going to take her some time to fix, she thought. His voice was slurred because of the physical damage, but the fire in his eyes was unmistakable—he had his goal, and he was going to achieve it.

"Tyr," Trance said, "you need to get to Medical."

"You," he slurred, "are dead."

"That doesn't work very well," she said calmly.

Tyr raised his right hand, aiming his Gauss pistol at her. His hand was shaking, but his aim remained somewhere in the vicinity of his intent. "I am willing to repeat the attempt as many times as it will take."

Rommie started toward him, and Tyr's aim switched. "I wouldn't do that. I can shoot you two to three times before you reach me."

"After which," Rommie said, sounding quite reasonable, "I will use you as a punching bag until you cease being so troublesome. Tyr, you aren't taking over anything today. You need to get a grip, get to Medical, and *wait*."

"This really isn't you, Tyr," Trance said.

Tyr's aim shifted back to Trance. "Who are you to say?"

He started toward Trance as Rommie said, "Considering the behavior displayed by everyone except for Trance and I, I believe we are."

"I am taking command!" he yelled. His face went gray and droplets of sweat broke out on his forehead. He gritted his teeth and added, "I'll not tolerate argument."

"Oh, tolerate this!" Beka snapped from behind him.

He started to turn. There was a loud, hollow bang, and Tyr stopped. After a moment, the Gauss pistol slipped from his fingers and clattered to the floor.

Slowly, he tilted his head and looked at Trance for a moment, as though baffled. Then his eyes closed and he fell, crashing to the deck with a remarkable lack of grace.

Beka, a piece of broken conduit clutched in both hands, looked up from Tyr, staring at Trance and Rommie as though expecting to be punished at any second. "Did I do the right thing?"

"Yes, you did," Trance said.

"Well, you *could* have shot him," Rommie said.

"I could have . . ." Beka's eyes went wide, and she stared down at her Gauss pistol, snug in its holster, as though she had never seen it before. "Oh, no."

"Oh, yes," Rommie said. "This is better—Trance can fix blunt trauma to Tyr's thick skull quite easily." She looked at Trance, curious. "Just what *did* you do to him, anyway?"

"I won the argument," Trance said softly. She turned back to the pilot console. "Open a channel."

"Opening a channel, aye," Rommie said, and the center screen lit up.

Neither Colonel Kaczynski's look nor mood had improved since the last conversation. Right now he looked quite ill, in fact.

"Colonel Kaczynski," Trance said with a smile. "I suggest taking a few deep breaths and trying to relax. Stress isn't good for you."

"Where the hell is Hunt?" he demanded.

"Captain Hunt is . . . relaxing," Trance said. Rommie turned her head and raised an eyebrow. "I've been delegated to deal with you."

Kaczynski was silent for a moment, apparently fighting an angry outburst. "I see. And you are?"

"Trance Gemini, chief medical officer."

"Chief—!"

"Chief medical officer." Trance smiled again. "Please, Colonel, calm yourself."

"I—" he started. He fell silent again. After a moment he said, "I suppose I'm at your mercy here."

"Yes you are," she said. She had learned a lot from watching Dylan work through these situations. Even when his actions resulted in the humiliation of his opponents, he was somehow able to maintain a disarmingly cheerful air that left them without a clue as to what he had done. He claimed he was no diplomat. She thought he was quite wrong. He just didn't *want* to be a diplomat.

"Very well," Kaczynski said. "If you must gloat, please get it over with quickly."

"I don't intend to gloat," she said. "Actually, I intend to take us out of here as quickly as possible."

"Then why are you even bothering to talk to me?" he said, seeming genuinely puzzled. "Finish us off and be gone."

"No," Trance said. "I'm talking to you because you need to know what I've done."

"I can guess," Kaczsynki said. "Nanobots. And how long do we have until they finish eating our ships?"

"They're not eating your ships," Trance said. "All they've done is remodel them a bit. All of your propulsion and Slipstream capability is gone, along with your weapons. In other words, you're adrift, and you can't shoot at us anymore."

"And we make excellent targets for practice, I'm sure," he said acidly.

With a cheerful smile, Rommie said, "Well, if that's what you'd prefer, I'm sure we could oblige."

"You are attempting to confuse me," Kaczynski growled.

"Apparently, we're succeeding," Rommie said.

"Your life support," Andromeda said, picking up the conversation, "will continue to work—in fact, you will find that its capacity has been expanded, in case your colleagues cannot reach you quickly. In addition, your communications are unimpaired. You will be able to communicate with each other, and with your base, as well as broadcast emergency calls."

"In fact," Rommie said, "emergency beacons should already have been triggered."

Kaczynski's eyes flicked downward for a moment, then he looked up again. "I see." He took a deep breath, sighed, appeared to relax.

"Quite generous, I suppose. So . . . you have won the day. Now what? Return with revenge in mind?"

"No," Trance said. "Now we leave, and we leave you alone. Captain Hunt meant exactly what he said."

"If you need help in the future," Andromeda said, "we will be prepared to provide it. However, you will have to make a formal request."

"We can take care of ourselves," Kaczynski said.

"Then consider the matter closed," Andromeda replied.

"Take care, Colonel," Trance said. "Good-bye."

With no further ado, she put the ship into a broad, looping turn, set the course for the Slip point, and opened the throttles to maximum. Getting out of this system at top velocity seemed like a good idea.

She reached over her head and hit the switches to bring the Slipstream hood down. Concentrating, she fed power to the Slipstream core.

"Transiting to Slipstream . . ." She opened the runners. "Now!"

Existence burst into flares and streaks of white, and they were away.

FIVE • WHERE THE BUSES DON'T RUN

"Have you seen my force lance?"

—HIGH GUARD SPECIAL ATTACHÉ
GORUS EN'KER, THREE SECONDS
BEFORE HIS ASSASSINATION, CY 8336

"This is not good," Trance said.

Plunging into the Slipstream, the *Andromeda Ascendant* was shuddering and shifting. It was taking everything Trance could summon to keep the Slipstream runners locked to any of the streams, and there was no sign of the transition effect abating.

"We have a problem," Andromeda said, her image appearing on the flatscreens.

"No kidding," Trance said.

"Besides the obvious Slipstream issue," Andromeda said, a little testily, "two of the Kantaran ships have either followed us into Slipstream, or have been drawn in behind us. Either way, we will have to find a way to deal with them."

"Do you mind if I worry about them later?" Trance said. She was growing afraid that the ship would shake apart if she tried to stay in the Slipstream.

"I'm detecting multiple problems in the Slipstream core," Rommie said. "Nothing Harper can't fix, but he won't be able to do anything until we transit back to normal space."

"I don't think we can keep this up," Trance said unhappily. At least they would be far away from Kantaran space.

"I am detecting a very minor fluctuation in the AG field," Andromeda said.

Trance's eyes went wide. "That's worse than not good," she said. "Transiting from Slipstream *now*."

The transition was the worst she had ever experienced. *Andromeda* shook wildly, and all manner of creaks and groans came from all corners. Back in normal space, the ship began rolling end-for-end, barely responding to Trance's commands at the pilot station.

"I'm stabilizing," Andromeda said, finally, her eyes and head moving as she appeared to look at readouts—an illusion of course, but it provided a certain humanizing touch. "AG field fluctuations have ceased, thanks to Mr. Harper."

"That was quick," Trance said, feeling relieved.

"Okay," Harper said, his voice booming over the comm system, "who the hell's doing the driving up there?"

"I am," Trance said. She sighed. "One of those desperate times things."

"Huh?"

"Desperate times call for desperate measures," Trance said. "Usually committed by really desperate people."

"Yeah, well," Harper said, "desperate is the word. So where the hell is Beka, anyway?"

Trance glanced around. Tyr was still lying where he had fallen. Beka was sitting down again, her knees pulled up with her arms wrapped around them. Her head was down. Trance wasn't sure if she was crying or not.

"She's . . . not feeling well," Trance said.

There was a pause. "Y'know, Trance, I'm not feeling so freakin' hot myself right now."

The holographic Rommie shimmered into being. "I have a pair of my maintenance androids on the way to get Tyr to the Med Deck."

"What was that about Tyr?" Harper said.

"He isn't feeling too well either," Rommie said as the holographic avatar shimmered out.

"Okay," Harper said. "What the freakin' hell is going on around here? Where's Dylan?"

"Relieved of his duties and confined to his quarters," Andromeda said.

"*What?*"

"Harper," Rommie said, "explanations are going to have to wait."

"Oh, God," Harper moaned. "This is the part where you tell me we're three seconds from blowing up and I'm the only one who can fix everything in time, right?"

"You have more than three seconds, Mr. Harper," Andromeda said. "However, there is considerable work to be done."

"Beginning with the Slipstream core," Rommie said. "It was possible to transit to Slipstream, but was inadvisable to remain there."

Harper's head and shoulders appeared on one of the flatscreens. He looked terrible. His face was smeared with sooty residue, there was a growing bruise on his right cheek, and he seemed to be ready to throw up at any moment. "I fixed the AG field generators already," he said. "Cakewalk. Everything else . . . jeez, guys, it's a freakin' mess."

"You've pulled me through before," Rommie said, smiling. "I have every confidence you'll do it again."

"Yeah, well, that's what this here boy genius does," he said, but without his usual enthusiasm. "Rommie, we're okay for a few more minutes, right? Like, we're not going to blow up or anything?"

Two maintenance androids, ungainly-looking humanoid figures with almost featureless black carapaces, entered Command. One was carrying a stretcher. They carefully loaded Tyr onto the stretcher, picked it up, and left again.

"Not just yet," Rommie said.

"Okay," Harper said. "I gotta go get something before my head blows up. Harper out."

The image blinked off.

Trance looked over at Beka. She still had her arms wrapped around her knees, but now she was looking up. The side of her face that

Dylan had slapped was livid. "I feel lousy. Damn, do I feel lousy." Her head dropped to her knees again. Her voice muffled, she said, "Someone just tell me I wasn't doing Flash again."

Sadness welled up in Trance for a moment. She went over to Beka and knelt by her. "You weren't doing Flash, Beka." Beka looked up at her, silent. "The Kantarans used some kind of weapon that made everybody act weird. That's why you feel sick—we're out of range, and your body is trying to shake it off. I don't know how long it'll take."

"I feel so *miserable*," Beka said. Tears welled up in her eyes and streamed down her cheeks. She reached up and touched the side of her face.

"Dylan slapped you," Trance said. She didn't see the point in avoiding the truth.

Beka started at her in confusion. "He . . . why? Where is he?"

"We threw him out of Command," Trance said.

Beka's eyes went wide. "You threw him out of Command? Oh, no. Oh, no." Suddenly Beka's mouth quirked, and she made a little snorting noise. "Oh, my God."

All of a sudden, Beka buried her face in her knees again, her shoulders shaking. This time, though, she was laughing. Trance smiled. Beka was going to be fine.

With a final snort, Beka's laughter stopped. She looked up at Trance again, her eyes still wide. "This has been a crazy day, hasn't it?"

"Yes," Trance said. She stood up. "I have to go down to Medical. I need to get Tyr patched up."

"What happened to Tyr?" Beka started to get up. She seemed a little shaky.

"Well . . ." Trance tried to figure out a good way to phrase it.

Rommie saved her the trouble. "Trance beat him up when he tried to take a Slipfighter out. And then you knocked him out with a piece of conduit when he tried to take over the ship."

Beka looked from Trance to Rommie and back again. "This is insane."

"I agree," Trance said. "Are you up to staying in Command with Rommie? We've got a couple of crippled Kantarans to bring in."

"I was wondering when we'd get to that," Rommie said.

Beka's eyes narrowed slightly, and she smiled. "Trance, the way my head feels right now, I hope the sons of bitches don't give us any trouble."

"Good," Trance said. "I'll deal with Dylan as well."

Beka was quiet for a moment, then she nodded. "It wasn't him, was it?"

"No," Trance said. "But we have to deal with what the Kantarans did to all of you."

She gave Beka another smile, and started for the exit. Behind her, she heard Beka say, "Rommie, locate our guests, target Bucky cables, and bring 'em in. You don't need to make it a smooth ride."

In his quarters Dylan was stretched out on his bed, his eyes closed tightly. He wasn't sure which was worse—the splitting headache, the churning in his stomach, or the way the room started spinning when he opened his eyes.

Maybe all three.

He tried to remember what had happened. He had no recollection of getting to his quarters, and his last fully coherent memory was of the Kantarans opening fire on the *Andromeda Ascendant*. Everything after that was just a sequence of blurs that he couldn't make sense of—each time he tried to bring them into focus his headache threatened to become a migraine.

He had never had a migraine in his life. He didn't want to start now. He just couldn't summon the strength or the willpower to call for help or get to Medical.

He had to do something.

His stomach churned again, and he rolled onto his side, pulling his knees up, trying to breathe steadily until the spasm passed. He was soaked in sweat, his hair matted to his scalp.

"You look terrible." Rommie's words drove like spikes into his brain.

"Not so loud," he whispered. He relaxed a little. "What the hell happened? I either have the worst hangover I've ever had, or I caught something."

"You could call it a hangover, I suppose," Rommie said. Her voice was much quieter now. He opened his eyes carefully. Rommie's holographic avatar was standing a couple of meters away, her arms folded. "The Kantarans apparently have a weapon that uses an electromagnetic field to disrupt the normal biochemical functions of the brain."

"I think that would explain why my head feels like a Nova Bomb hit it," Dylan said. "Two questions." Tentatively, he started to get himself into a sitting position. The room started spinning again, and Rommie blurred. He felt the cold sweat break out. "How do we block it, and how did I get here?"

"On the first question, we ran away." Rommie gave him an uncertain look, then seemed to steel herself. That wasn't good. It meant that he wasn't going to like what she had to say. "On the second question . . . you were declared incompetent under High Guard rules, ejected from Command, and confined to quarters."

He had made it into a sitting position, finally. He could feel the sweat running down the middle of his back, and he shivered. "This is not good."

"No," she said, "it's not. You were quite the martinet. My physical avatar had to step in to prevent further violence."

"*Further* violence?" Dylan said, his head coming up sharply. It was an unwise move. The pain in his head was so intense that all he saw for a few moments was a sea of white populated by a few rushing stars.

"You struck Beka," Rommie said. He couldn't find the words to respond. What sort of monster had he turned into? "Beka will be fine, fortunately."

"Was it just—" he began.

"No, it wasn't just you," she said. "Harper became more obnoxious than ever, Tyr became irrationally aggressive, and Beka fell apart."

"Trance?" he muttered.

"She remained quite normal . . . or at least she didn't vary from whatever passes for normal for her. She got me into the Slipstream."

"I'm going to try standing up now," Dylan said quietly. "The bathroom seems like a good place to be right now."

"Medical would be better."

"Probably." He reached down for his force lance and found only an empty holster. "Damn it. High Guard protocol. You had to disarm me."

"Yes."

"I'll live with that." Slowly, he got up. At first he staggered like a drunk, but with an effort he managed to get his balance. He had intended to open his force lance to its full extent and use it to help him get to the bathroom, but he could manage without it.

"I will need to keep you under observation, Captain," Rommie said.

"Not—"

"For the moment," she said primly, "that means continuously."

He sighed. "Alright."

She smiled. "It isn't as though you have anything that I haven't seen before, Captain."

There was no sense in arguing. One of her prime concerns was his safety, and there was no way he was going to be able to change her mind. She was going to monitor him whether he liked it or not. Into the bargain, she would be relaying his vital signs to Trance's medical bay.

Instead, he concentrated on getting one foot in front of the other, not lifting his feet too much. He kept his eyes on the deck, trying to maintain equilibrium.

"You'd better fill me in on what happened," he said as he inched along.

She did. He listened silently, hardly able to believe the report. It seemed as though the worst had come out in all of them, except for Trance—and even there they still had a mystery on their hands.

"It would, incidentally," Rommie added, "explain Trance's remarks about 'the plague of lighthouse keepers.' In this instance, however, it is not something that affects the lighthouse keepers."

"It's delivered by them," Dylan said. "Not quite the warm welcome I was expecting."

He had finally made it to the bathroom. His stomach roiled again, more violently this time. He barely managed to reach the sink before he threw up. The spasm was over quickly, but it left him feeling weak and shaky. He quickly cleaned up the mess and rinsed his mouth out.

It seemed to take forever to get his sodden clothes off. He was grateful for the momentary respite from the clammy feeling, but it was short-lived. He turned on the shower, set it as hot as he thought he could stand it, and got in. The water heated quickly, cascading over his head and shoulders, and he had to make an effort to not turn down the heat. It took a couple of minutes, but he began to feel a little better. As the muscles loosened in his neck, shoulders, and back, the remorseless headache diminished a little. The sheer act of washing felt glorious. He hated the idea of turning the shower off and getting out.

Finally, he did. He quickly toweled himself off, glad to have the clammy sensation gone. His equilibrium seemed to be almost back to normal, though he otherwise still felt like death warmed over.

Wrapping the towel around himself, he went to get fresh clothes.

While Dylan was busy pulling himself together, *Andromeda*'s android avatar had left the Command Deck. Beka had seemed to be doing alright, although the readings from the Command biomedical sensors indicated that she was in some physical distress. As long as there were no drastic changes, Rommie felt quite secure in her decision to leave Beka by herself.

Her destination was one of the hangar bays. The two Kantaran ships that had managed to follow them were sitting there, engines and weapons now completely dismantled by the nanobots that had coated them.

As she walked into the hangar, she issued a silent command to stand down the internal defense systems. The Kantaran pilots had already been warned to stay in their vessels until instructed otherwise.

The two Kantaran fighters were a dull yellow in color, with red identification markings. Matte-black splotches showed where the nanobots had clustered. As she walked toward the fighters the splotches were growing smaller—Trance and Harper had deliberately given them a fast reproductive cycle along with a truncated life span once their goal was achieved.

She smiled. It was an elegant solution. Unfortunately, it was unlikely to work twice.

She stopped in front of the two fighters, looking up at them. The craft were utilitarian, lacking any of the grace of her own design.

Even the Nietzscheans included a certain degree of artfulness in their fighter designs. These ships were ugly little brutes.

She unholstered her force lance and activated it. It was more of a precautionary measure than anything else—a gesture to keep the pilots in a polite and pliable mood.

Drones rolled ladders up to the side of the ships, adjusting the heights before locking them in place.

"Alright, gentlemen," she said, her voice echoing over the pilots' cockpit radios, "you can come out."

With loud hisses, the cockpit canopies slid back. The pilots stood up slowly, disconnecting themselves from biosign monitors and life-support equipment. They both wore dark gray flight suits, with insignia at the shoulders and name patches on the right side of the chest. One was male, the other female. Both had close-cropped dark hair. The pallor of their faces suggested that they had not spent any time away from their base or their ships recently.

At first they seemed uncertain of themselves, looking around the huge hangar, and then down at her.

"Come on down," she called. "If you're carrying any weapons, you can either leave them in your spacecraft, or surrender them to me."

The two pilots glanced at each other. "We have no personal weapons," the male said.

Carefully, the two eased out onto the ladders, climbing slowly down. Once they reached the deck, they went to stand together between the two fighters. They had assumed a rigid military stance, their eyes focused past her.

"Welcome to the *Andromeda Ascendant*." She holstered her force lance and walked up to them, looking them over. Her sensors indicated no weapons. Preliminary biosign scans had more worrying news. "Our artificial gravity level is too high for you, isn't it?" she said.

"Ma'am," the woman said, not looking at her, "we are your prisoners. We expect no particular accommodation for our needs."

"Well," Rommie said, folding her arms across her chest, "I wouldn't consider myself a good hostess if I let you suffer." A flash of calculation and a silent exchange with her ship-self was all it took to reset the AG field locally. "That should be more comfortable."

"Thank you, ma'am," the male pilot said.

"You're quite welcome," she replied. "And you may call me Rommie. We generally don't stand much on formality here."

"Understood, ma . . . um." The pilot swallowed nervously.

"I assume we will be interrogated," the woman said.

"As in questions, drugs, torture, deprivation, and general sadistic abuse to derive answers?" Amazingly, they both managed to grow even paler. "No. Well, we *might* ask you a few questions. The rest is neither acceptable nor particularly interesting."

Her holographic avatar shimmered into being at her side. The two pilots glanced at each other again. "Any questions we ask will be solely for the purpose of ensuring your comfort and safe return."

"You can call her Rommie, too," Rommie said. "We are both avatars of the *Andromeda Ascendant*."

"Your temporary quarters have been prepared," the holographic Rommie said. "We will repatriate you as soon as we can."

"Please precede me, and I'll escort you there," Rommie said. The two pilots started to walk stiffly past her. "And, please, *at ease!* You're going to injure yourselves if you're not careful."

"Yes, ma'am!" they said in chorus. Neither one appeared to relax to any appreciable degree.

"And we thought Harper was hopeless," her holographic twin said.

Rommie rolled her eyes and sighed.

Dylan managed to make it to the Med Deck without losing equilibrium again, but by the time he got there he once again felt as though someone had driven a spike into his forehead. Even the normal ship lighting was too painful—he made the last part of his slow, cautious journey with his eyes almost closed.

Trance was still working on Tyr when he walked in and sat down heavily on the nearest chair. The Nietzschean was conscious, but lay prone on one of the beds, staring up at the ceiling.

"Hey, Boss!" Harper said cheerfully. Each of the words seemed to boom inside his skull, generating red flowers of pain. "Geez, you look lousy."

Harper was sitting up on one of the counters. "Thank you for your assessment, Mr. Harper." Dylan closed his eyes as Harper pushed himself from the counter. It did nothing to help him when Harper's shoes smacked into the deck. "I understand you were rather rude and insubordinate."

"Yeah, well," Harper said, "it sounds to me like my usual charming and sweet self, only more so."

"Playing the arrogant worm," Tyr said. He had trouble phrasing the words properly.

"Huh, listen to the Boy Target over there, will ya?" Harper said, grinning. "At least I didn't get myself beat to a bloody pulp."

"Harper," Trance said quietly, "that is completely inappropriate."

"What she said," Dylan muttered.

Trance walked over to Dylan, looking him over. "Tyr's going to be just fine, and Harper's over whatever this was."

"I just need something for the headache," he said. There was a sudden pressure against his left shoulder, followed by a loud hiss. "Hey!"

Trance stepped back, smiling, holding up the hypospray she had used on him. "My special concoction," she said. "Clears headaches, settles stomachs, boosts energy, and makes you regular. Well, actually, I don't know about that last part, but the other three are true."

"I *hate* shots," Dylan grumbled.

"You're gonna love this one, Boss," Harper said, grinning. "I feel like dancing on tables. I could work for a week straight."

Rommie's holographic image shimmered into life between Harper and Trance. "Considering the damage I've sustained, Mr. Harper, one week may not be enough."

Dylan closed his eyes again, and sighed. With any luck, things would improve from this point onward.

Or not.

He stood up carefully. Trance's shot seemed to be working but it would be a while before he felt fully functional. What he really wanted to do was crawl into his bed and sleep for a couple of days.

"Alright, people," he said, "we've got work to do."

———————

Harper's ebullience was gone by the following morning. Dylan had called a breakfast meeting to decide their next few moves. None of them appeared to be too interested in food, he noticed. He, Beka, and Harper were all drinking far more coffee than was good for them. Tyr, looking more dour than usual, was sticking to fruit juice. Trance had a glass of water in front of her, but Dylan suspected that was for the sake of appearances.

"Repairs," Dylan said. "Main priority at this point."

"For which we're currently in a bad position," Rommie said. "While Harper and Trance's idea worked very well—"

"Very well?" Harper blurted. "It worked brilliantly! Boy genius style."

"It was Trance's idea," Dylan said.

Trance smiled.

"I made it work," Harper muttered.

"This isn't a competition, Mr. Harper," Rommie said, giving him a stern look. She looked back at Dylan. "While it took care of the Kantaran fleet, the production of the missiles and their payloads consumed my remaining onboard supplies. Had we restocked before leaving for Kantar, this might not be so pressing a situation."

"So noted," Dylan said. "Mr. Harper?"

Harper shrugged. "We got our asses kicked badly, Boss. I'm running around doing patch jobs with spit and string, but I need parts, and I need raw materials for the machine shop." He sat up straight. He looked worried, something Dylan rarely saw. "The AG field's gonna hold, and I've got the Slipstream core on-line again, but I don't know how long that'll hold."

"The exotic matter pulser is showing signs of potential stress fractures," Rommie said.

"Which means we'll have a rough ride," Beka said.

"Are we near any debris fields?" Dylan said.

"No," Rommie said.

"Andromeda places us about seven thousand light-years outside of the Andromeda galaxy," Beka said.

Dylan stared at her for a moment. "Good throw," he said, finally.

"This wasn't exactly where I meant to go," Trance said apologetically.

"If the Slipstream core holds up," Rommie said, "we should be able to make it back to Commonwealth space in approximately four weeks."

"Four weeks," Dylan echoed. He thought for a moment. "I could take the *Eureka Maru*—" Beka shot him a look. He had tried to apologize to her for his actions, but she had simply brushed it off. She had seemed fretful about her own behavior, however. She couldn't afford to start doubting herself again. "Or Beka could."

"A round-trip transit time of eight weeks, plus layover time, makes that highly impractical, Captain," Rommie said.

"Then what do you suggest we do?" Beka said.

"We first need to get rid of our guests," Tyr said.

"We could throw 'em out of an airlock," Harper said.

"For once," Tyr said, "we think alike."

"Hey! I was kidding."

"Oh." Tyr looked mildly disappointed. "I wasn't."

"We'll send them back where they came from," Dylan said. He sat back and rubbed at his temples. A faint residue of the previous day's headache seemed to be welling up again. He pushed his coffee mug away—all he needed now was caffeine poisoning. Harper, on the other hand, would probably go from guzzling coffee to swilling can after can of Sparky Cola. "It'll cost us a Slipfighter, but I can live with that."

"Do you want them to turn around and come after us again?" Tyr said, astonished. "Along, no doubt, with whatever is left of their defense fleet."

"First of all, Mr. Anasazi, we won't be here," Dylan said patiently. "Secondly, they'll have a difficult time backtracking without a working navigation system, a working Slip drive, or fully functional communications."

"Navigation software and hardware will self-destruct once they transit from the Slipstream," Rommie said. "The Slip drive will likewise be destroyed. Initially, they will only have an emergency beacon and the ability to receive incoming transmissions. Outgoing transmission capability will be enabled after ten minutes."

"I see the potential for a disastrous outcome," Tyr said, looking directly at Dylan. There was no overt challenge in the look. Tyr had an unwavering ability to see the ways in which a given course of action could run counter to his own survival. "If the Slipstream drive should fail, then we will be nothing more than a sitting target."

"Our guests won't be departing before we're ready to leave," Dylan said, sitting back. "By that time Mr. Harper will have the Slipstream drive stable. Correct, Mr. Harper?"

Harper seemed to look inward for a moment, then he shrugged. "Sure."

Tyr turned his gaze on Harper, who shifted uncomfortably. "You seem less than certain."

"It's a Slipstream drive," Harper said, sounding a little testy. "Gimme a break here. It breaks, I fix it. That's why they pay me the big bucks." He glanced at Dylan. "That's *if* they paid me the big bucks."

"Adventure is your reward, Mr. Harper," Rommie said.

"In which case," Beka said, "we're filthy rich. I'm with Harper. I like real money."

"If money talks," Trance said, "what's it saying?"

" 'Spend me, spend me,' " Beka said. She grinned. "That's usually what it says to me."

"Especially after you got away with Sid's credit card," Rommie said.

"Oh, yes," Beka said. "Sid's money has a way of being very loud and insistent."

"Just like Sid himself," Dylan said. "The issue right now isn't money. We need to get to a system where Andromeda can process raw materials. After that we head for the first system we can reach that will take Commonwealth scrip, pick up whatever Andromeda can't manufacture, and get ourselves to a High Guard base so we can drydock to finish any outstanding repairs."

"I like the way you make that sound so easy," Beka said. "We need to make three Slips for the first part of that. Then we're in for a long haul."

"And," Rommie added, "the best-case scenario after *that* is another dozen Slips, with between-Slip periods ranging from two hours to two days."

"Well," Dylan said, shaking his head, "I guess we'll all have to fine-tune our hobbies, won't we?"

"I'm sure Trance has her plants," Tyr said, glowering at her. She met his glare with a sunny smile. Dylan had seen Andromeda's recording of the Trance-Tyr fight. While Tyr had obviously been off his game, making foolish moves, Trance's abilities were frightening. Beka had witnessed the first appearance of this version of Trance and the description she had given him of her fighting skills—dispatching a group of attacking Kalderans—had been no exaggeration. "I have plenty of weapons I wish to clean, overhaul, and adjust. And test."

"Well," Dylan said, "you won't be disturbed in the combat practice range."

"Oh," Tyr said, a bit distantly. "You, sir, are quite right." He had yet to look away from Trance.

"Hey, Tyr," Harper said, "I can improve on those guns of yours. Y'know, give 'em a power-up."

Tyr turned to look at him. "A power-up?"

"Sure." Harper was starting to look excited. "Better batteries, more power . . . hit harder, fire faster. I've got some great ideas for that big multibarreled monster of yours."

Tyr was looking dubious. "I've been satisfied with my weapons so far."

"You can be more satisfied," Harper said.

"I believe he intends to add a barrel that serves soft ice cream," Rommie said.

Both Tyr and Harper turned to look at her. She looked steadily back at them, half smiling.

"On the other hand," she added after a moment, "I wouldn't mind seeing some improvements and enhancements to my own weapons once they're rebuilt. I'm one of those girls who likes *really* big guns."

"I'm not touching that with a ten-meter force lance," Beka said.

"Riiiight," Harper said.

Dylan sighed and looked at Trance. "Everybody's a comedian."

Trance just smiled.

We made room for the variables.
We tweaked all the settings.
We did all we possibly could have
to ensure our success.
But now, in the deepest darkness,
in the deepest darkness we float.
We are becalmed and bereft
in this place without stars.

— FROM THE FREE VERSE CYCLE
STARPILOT'S FATE, BY THAN POET
LAUREATE EXPANSE OF HEART'S-FIRE,
CY 9204

"Harper's not kidding about spit and string, is he?" Beka said.

"No, I don't think he is," Dylan admitted.

She and Dylan had spent a good part of the past three days on a walking inspection of the internal damage to the *Andromeda Ascendant*. It wasn't as bad as it could have been—no one had hit them with a point singularity bomb, unlike their encounter with the Magog Worldship. There were no huge gaping holes right through the ship, just a lot of little holes, sections of hull blown away, and weapon structures smashed. The ECM fans were a mess. Andromeda had broken down the two Kantaran ships for raw materials, but it had only been enough to patch a handful of hull breaches.

Beka and Dylan had talked seriously about cannibalizing some of the other spacecraft kept aboard *Andromeda*—possibly even Tweedle-dee and Tweedledum, the two giant planet-combat mechs. In the end they had decided against it. Neither of them had any intention of giving up anything that could be advantageous in an unexpected battle. It was going to be quite a while before they were in anything approaching good shape, and they could not afford to give up any of the Slipfighters.

"On the other hand," Dylan said, "I just hope Harper's got something more than spit and string in mind for the Slipstream drive."

One of the small junction flatscreens lit up with Andromeda's image. "Judging by the amount of vulgar language Mr. Harper is using, I would say that he is definitely not having an easy time." She paused for a moment. "No spit or string involved, however."

"Well," Dylan said, "that's good." He glanced at Beka. "Isn't it?"

"That depends," Beka said. She had settled for a simple white shirt and black pants for the walk-through, and looked considerably more comfortable than he felt. "Harper burbling and cooing at things, okay. Harper making grandiose proclamations of his own genius, that's okay too."

"Harper swearing," Dylan said, not liking the direction this was going, "is not good."

"Extremely not good," Beka said. She looked as worried as he had ever seen her. "If anybody can get *Andromeda* going, it's Harper. If he's swearing and tearing his hair out—"

"No hair-tearing yet," Andromeda said. "Lots of foot-stamping and tantrum-throwing. I'm having a difficult time restraining myself from spanking him."

"Don't!" Beka blurted. Wide-eyed, she looked at Dylan, and then back at the screen, where Andromeda was patiently waiting. "I mean, don't spank him. Not don't stop yourself from spanking him."

"She means that he might enjoy it," Dylan said with a half smile.

Beka turned her head to look at him again. "Dylan . . ." She paused for a moment. "*Ewwww.*"

"Takes all kinds," Dylan said simply. He looked at the screen. "Restraining yourself is probably a good idea, Andromeda. Just get him to calm down and stay on task. It's nice and quiet out here, but at heart I'm not a country boy."

"I'm not so sure about that," Beka said.

She began walking down the corridor again, her boots crunching on the scattered plastic and metal.

"This is quite depressing," Andromeda said. "I look terrible and feel worse. How can I show up for a battle looking like this?"

Dylan grinned, eliciting a smile from the flatscreen image. "Don't worry," he said, "we'll get your gown ready in time for the ball."

"Just get me some serious upgrades," she said. She smiled at him again, suddenly all elfin innocence. "After all, it's my birthday soon."

"I do not consider this advisable," Tyr said as he and Dylan strode into the brig and stopped. "They are enemy combatants."

Patiently, Dylan said, "Tyr, I don't see an enemy at the moment, and I don't see any combatants. I *do* see altered circumstances, and I plan to roll with them, not fight against them."

Tyr folded his arms across his chest, giving Dylan a skeptical look. "And you somehow believe that this will give your Commonwealth an edge in convincing the Kantaran government of its innate good intentions?"

"Ejecting them out of an airlock," Dylan said, "would certainly make a bold statement in the opposite direction. Very Nietzschean, Tyr, but not particularly Dylan Hunt."

"Granting requests such as these invites surreptitious action," Tyr grumbled. "The viper in the bosom, the dagger in the night, the poison in the cup."

"These are a couple of line fighter pilots," Dylan said, irritated despite knowing that Tyr was doing the right thing by pointing out the negative consequences of what he was about to do. "They're not Nietzschean politicians."

"Merely alien military personnel with homeworld loyalties," Tyr said. "I believe, sir, that you are deluded, and, further, that this will be a grave mistake."

"Well, if so, it wouldn't be the first one I've made," Dylan countered, "and it certainly isn't likely to be the last." He looked Tyr squarely in the eyes. "I recall making a decision to take on a certain Nietzschean mercenary a few years ago."

"Every decision has consequences," Tyr said.

"And as Trance said to me one day, every choice creates its own path." The more he argued this with Tyr, the more certain he became of his choice.

"And you feel secure in homilies uttered by Trance?" Tyr said with a snort. "You would do just as well perusing the shirts and stickers on sale in gewgaw shops on any world or drift."

"Your objections are noted, Mr. Anasazi," Dylan said.

With that, he turned around and walked to the far end of the brig. Tyr followed, adjusting his Gauss pistol holster for a smoother draw. Dylan sighed. It wasn't so much Tyr watching *his* back, but Tyr watching Tyr Anasazi's front, along with every other direction. After the insanity a few days previously, it made him nervous . . . and more than a little irritable.

The two pilots were in facing cells at the end of the brig corridor. That had afforded them eye contact as well as making it easy to talk with each other despite the clear barriers that kept them penned in. They had been promised humane treatment, and that was exactly what they had received. Trance and Rommie had both made regular, if brief, visits to deliver food and observe their guests. Neither of them had shown any sign of wanting to make a break for freedom— if anything, they appeared to be utterly compliant, and willing to toe the line wherever they found it drawn.

Tyr stood next to Dylan and glanced from one captive to the other. "I would venture to say that life aboard the *Andromeda Ascendant* agrees with our prisoners."

Tyr was right. Both pilots had lost their pallor and seemed to have developed a more robust look. They also seemed to have shed some of their rigidity.

"Attention!" Dylan said with quiet force. The pilots were on their feet in a flash. Dylan was certain he heard their boot heels click together.

"Excellent discipline," Tyr said, "for kludges."

Dylan glared at him. Tyr held his glance, but said nothing.

Turning back to the pilots, Dylan lifted a hand and said, "At ease." They assumed a parade rest position that looked uncomfortable. "Trance tells me that you've decided that you don't want to go home."

"Yes, sir," the male pilot—Lieutenant Micah Wright—said. He spoke in a clipped manner that made Dylan wince. He wished some of these people could leave their Academy days behind and cease being cadets.

Dylan turned to the woman, Lieutenant Paula Pogue. "Is this what you want?"

"Sir . . . yes, sir!" She took a deep breath, looking directly at him. She had big brown eyes that were accented by her pale skin and her cropped hair. "We've talked about this for a couple of days, and we realized that it's what we both want."

"We love Kantar," Wright said softly, "but there is more to the universe than our world and its isolationist policies."

"So," Tyr said quietly, "you are in rebellion against your government."

"No!" Wright exclaimed, shocked. "No. We fought to protect our world."

"We simply have no one to go back to," Pogue said. She looked down at the floor for a moment, then back at him again. "Neither of us has any surviving family."

"You have your squadron," Tyr said.

"We wouldn't even have that," Wright said. "At least not right away. If we return in one of your Slipfighters, there will be hell to pay."

"Even if there wasn't that," Pogue said, "we would be grounded for a time, for debriefing. No matter what the truth is, we might well be grounded for life. We would rather our colleagues think us dead or lost, at least for a while."

Dylan held her gaze, silent.

"As we told Miss Gemini, sir," Wright added, "we are formally requesting asylum."

"You can call me Trance," said a familiar voice. Dylan and Tyr turned to see Trance walking down the brig corridor. She gave them a cheerful smile. "'Miss Gemini' sounds silly. It makes me sound like a schoolteacher." She frowned, playing the pixie. "Not that school-teachers are silly, I mean."

Dylan turned back to the pilots. "Once we're in better shape, we can have a courier take a message back to Kantar." He looked at Trance, who nodded, then at Tyr, who gave him a noncommittal shrug. He turned back to the pilots again. "Well, we can use a few extra hands. There are conditions, however."

"Yes, sir!" they chorused.

"First," Dylan said, "you stop doing that."

"I think it's rather charming," Tyr said.

"You would," Dylan said. "There will be restrictions. You'll carry trackers at all times. If you're found in an area of the ship where you don't belong, I'll authorize Mr. Anasazi to shoot you. You will respond immediately to all orders from the Command staff."

"Understood, sir," Wright said quietly.

"You intend to use us as crew members?" Pogue said, nonplussed.

"Absolutely," Dylan said. "You won't have any rank—which is in short supply around here as it is—but you will be part of the crew, at least for the time being. As such, I expect you to carry out all duties assigned to you, and to otherwise spend as much time as you can in educating yourselves." He took a deep breath, let it out slowly. "Once we reach Systems Commonwealth space, you can decide for yourselves whether you want to remain aboard or move on. A High Guard commission might not be out of the question."

"We'll take it one day at a time, sir," Wright said.

"That works for me," Dylan said. He turned to Tyr, nodding. "Mr. Anasazi, if you would be so kind?"

Tyr produced a pair of tiny tracking devices that would allow Andromeda to follow the two pilots anywhere in the ship. They were more for insurance than anything else—the internal surveillance systems could do the job just as well. While the trackers would allow Andromeda to follow their movements in the damaged areas of the ship, the real point was psychological. If Wright and Pogue were planning anything, having the trackers pinned on and being told that Tyr would deal with them if necessary would most likely undermine their self-confidence.

The same reasoning lay behind Tyr applying the tiny devices. Tyr could have the most benign and gentle expression, and he still scared people when he focused his attention on them.

Wright and Pogue seemed uncertain of their grant of freedom, standing just inside their cells and hesitating to step out.

Finally, Dylan said, "Out, both of you. We'll get you settled in your quarters, then draw up a list of your duties for the next few days. Rommie will familiarize you with the bridge. Welcome to the crew, Mr. Wright, Ms. Pogue."

"Thank you, sir!" they choroused, snapping crisp salutes.

Dylan winced again. "First order of business—no salutes, or I'll ask Tyr to hit you. Understood?"

They looked at each other, then at Tyr, then at Dylan. "Yes, sir," Wright said quietly.

"Then we should get along fine," Dylan said. He turned to Trance. "Miss Gemini, if you'll show them to their quarters?"

Trance stuck her tongue out at him, then grinned. "My pleasure . . . *sir*."

Dylan gave the two pilots his long-suffering look. "It's never easy."

Two days later, Harper lay sprawled over a much-abused console in Engineering, trying to patch broken waveguides and reconnect fiber-optic lines that had come loose during the battle. Not only was he finding the job tedious, he was finding it painful. His stomach throbbed, and he was getting a headache.

He was also beginning to feel a little irritated with Dylan. Okay, so he was a miracle worker. It just seemed as though Dylan wanted his miracles *now*, instead of such time as Harper could deliver them. Sometimes Dylan could be as impatient as a Nightsider.

He shifted, trying to get more comfortable. As he did so, his wrist caught a bonding tool. He lunged for it, but missed. It clattered into the console. He reversed his movement instantly, just in time to avoid a shower of sparks as the tool shorted something out inside the console.

"Just. *Freakin'*. Great!" he howled.

Adding injury to insult, he slipped backward from the console and ended up in a rumpled pile on the floor.

The day really wasn't going well, he decided.

"That sounded pretty bad," Paula Pogue said, sitting up from her position behind another console and giving him a concerned look.

Her movement scattered some of the flexis strewn around her, and she hurriedly gathered them together.

"Yeah, it was bad," Harper muttered, stomping back to the console. He lunged over it, and into the cavity he had been working in— why the hell any of these consoles had been built against bulkheads was a mystery to him—and retrieved the bonder. It was blackened, but still working. "Ah, the hell with this crap. I'm gonna see if I can rig a bypass without blowing us to hell."

"You need a break," Pogue said.

"What I need," Harper said, "is to get this freakin' job done so we can get the hell out of here."

"I get that point," Pogue said sharply. She stood up, wiping her hands on her blue coverall. She walked over to him and looked him in the eye, unwavering. "You need a break, Mr. Harper. You've pushed yourself too much."

"Says you," he muttered, uncomfortable with her steady gaze.

"Says me," she echoed. She put her hands on her hips, and suddenly she was glaring at him. "Harper, I haven't been aboard for very long, but it doesn't take very long to get an idea of how you are. It's okay when you're a complete nutball. Right now you just sound exhausted and cranky." She jerked a thumb back at the console he had been trying to fix. "That means mistakes and accidents. We can't afford either of those."

"I'm fine," he insisted.

"My ass you're fine," she snapped. She stepped closer to him. "It's break time. You're going to take an hour off and lie the hell down, or I'll strap you down and have Trance dope you up."

He glared at her. "Where the hell do you get off acting like my mother?"

"I'm your crewmate," she said, putting her left hand on his chest. "Where I come from, you take care of your wingman and your wingman takes care of you." Before he could say anything, she put a finger over his lips. "If we're going to survive, Seamus, we need to look out for each other. I expect you to do the same for me."

He stared at her, speechless. She had a point. He *was* exhausted, and he could make the kind of mistakes that could blow *Andromeda* to hell.

"Well?" she asked, taking her finger from his lips.

"Okay," he said. He blinked, realizing how crusty and sore his eyes felt. His back and shoulders hurt, and he still had the headache. "Maybe two."

"Two it is," she said with a slight smile.

"I bet Trance can come up with something to keep me going after that," he added.

"I'm sure she can. Stay here." Pogue walked across the deck to the cooler that Harper always brought along when he was working in the depths of Engineering. She fished out two cans of Sparky Cola and came back, opening them both. "I figure we can drink on it."

He grinned. "Letting you into my private Sparky Cola stash is looking after my wingman, huh?"

She grinned. "You bet."

"I guess I can live with that," he said, and took a gulp of the cola. She sipped at hers. Trying for a more conversational note, he said, "So, you going to let your hair grow out now?"

She smiled and ran her free hand over her cropped hair. "Absolutely. Maybe not to any great length, but it'll be a relief to be done with the regulation haircut. I may even start wearing makeup and decent clothes."

He took another gulp of cola. "Yeah, well, you're gonna have to ask Beka or Trance about that. Rommie's got a thing going with the hair, but she's kinda one-note with her outfits."

"Like someone else I know," she said. "You planning to ever comb your hair and wear decent shirts?"

"Hell, no," he said, giving her a mixture of a grin and a sneer. "It's a mark of genius, looking like this."

"It's a nerd beacon," she said with a laugh. He frowned at her, and she laughed again. "It's okay. I'm just teasing."

He gulped down the rest of the cola. "Yeah, well, that's what they all say." He crumpled the can and tossed it over his shoulder. It landed squarely in the recycling bin, making a tinny rattle as it hit the other cans. He regarded her sleepily. "Okay, I guess it's time to go lie down for a couple of hours."

She smiled. "Yes, it is. Rommie, will you wake him up in a couple of hours?"

Rommie shimmered into view, looking a bit stern. "I'm a warship, not an alarm clock." Pogue frowned at the hologram. "Of course, it does mean tormenting Harper, so I'll be happy to do so. I have a wonderful recording of a full bagpipe band playing the 'March of the High Guard' that should do the trick."

"Oh, joy," Harper said.

"Well," Rommie said, "*I* think so."

"Good night, Mr. Harper," Pogue said.

"Yeah, g'night," Harper muttered, shuffling toward the exit.

Behind him, he heard Pogue quietly counting backward from five. Just as she reached zero, he felt the familiar pressure that came with drinking Sparky Cola too fast. The result was an enormous belch—he was impressed with himself; it was a real blue-ribbon effort.

Grinning hugely, he left Engineering.

Once Harper had left, Pogue and Rommie turned to look at each other. "Before you ask," Pogue said, grinning, "it's a barracks trick I learned years ago. The timing depends on whether it's beer or a soft drink. But if they gulp, they're going to belch."

Rommie stared at her, looking befuddled. "You must have been fun at parties." Pogue laughed. "On the other hand, I used to have four thousand High Guard lancers aboard."

"That's potentially a lot of noise."

"To say the least." Suddenly Rommie's face took on an expression of deep sadness. "I miss them sometimes. Losing my crew left an ache that's never quite gone away." She sighed. "Someday I'd like to have a full crew again."

Pogue regarded her seriously. "You've told Captain Hunt about this, of course?"

"Oh, yes. There's supposed to be something in the works, but the wheels of bureaucracy turn slowly. It could take a year or two before anyone is assigned to us." Rommie regarded her steadily. "In the meantime, you and your colleague are a start, at least for the moment. It's your choice in the end, of course."

"I think I'm going to stay," Pogue said with a smile. "I could get spoiled here."

"Just don't betray us," Rommie said, her expression deadly serious. "I've had enough of it. We all have. Keep in mind that I'm a warship, and I *will* kill you if I think it's in our best interests."

"I think that point has gotten across very well," Pogue said ruefully. "While the idea seems not to have occurred to Mr. Harper yet, Mr. Anasazi made his opinion very clear without saying a word. He's a beautiful man, but quite terrifying."

"Yes, he is," Rommie said, smiling again. "I'm satisfied about the intentions you and Mr. Wright have, but I'm afraid that you'll have to endure the Sword of Damocles for a little longer when it comes to my crew." Pogue frowned, missing the reference. "Large pointy object hanging by a thread over your head. A wrong move, and it's all over."

Pogue nodded. "Understood. More mythology for me to learn. I'm still in the middle of the Greeks." She made a moue. "I have to say I empathize with the labors of Hercules—fixing you seems like an impossible task."

Rommie smiled. "It's been done before, Ms. Pogue, and I've never needed Hercules to help out. Literally, in fact, as *The Labors of Herakles* was a High Guard long-range cargo hauler with a lughead of an AI. Great personality, mind you."

With that, Rommie shimmered out. Pogue stood in thought for a moment, then went back to the console she had been working on.

A few days later, Harper's manic energy was back in full force as he made his final round of checks and tweaks—*several* final rounds, as it turned out, because he apparently didn't want to accept that there was no more fine-tuning to be done on those things he was able to fix right now.

His nervous energy was beginning to put everyone else on edge—at least that was the assumption. Even Trance, who had managed to be the model of decorum during the enforced pause in their journey, was getting twitchy around Harper.

At least the job was getting done. They were finally going to be able to get out of the doldrums and, albeit slowly, get somewhere. Maybe then everyone would be less edgy and frustrated.

———

Beka couldn't seem to get comfortable at the pilot station, no matter how she shifted or balanced herself. She felt oddly unsettled and more than a little uncertain of what she was doing. Hardly a surprise, though—after all, nobody knew if the *Andromeda Ascendant* was going to hold up, even after Harper's work. They needed too much in the way of parts and supplies to be really secure.

It suddenly occurred to her that Dylan was going to be really, really ticked at her if things went wrong and they blew up in Slipstream. He would probably hold a grudge against Harper as well.

She had to suppress a giggle. Rommie glanced at her, curious. Beka waved a hand at her, unwilling to explain the goofy thought she had just had.

Four weeks ahead of them, just to get back to Commonwealth-friendly space. It promised to be an exhausting journey, even with Dylan, Harper, and Trance taking over some of the Slipstream flying. Still, Slipstream was a strange environment—just as they had been thrown this far out when things went wrong, it might be possible for her to shorten their coming journey by playing the streams once they made the transition to Slipstream. She had done this before, but never on the scale that she was contemplating now. She would have to be as close to perfect as she could manage, though—one slip, and they would probably be worse off than they were now. She had no desire to explain to Dylan that she had tried for a shortcut and ended up in even deeper woods.

She sighed, suddenly feeling weary. It would be a snap to get them out of this if she could just mix up a batch of Flash, just enough to . . .

Her head began to pound, and she felt her strength pour away like water. She grabbed the sides of the console in front of her, feeling desperately sick and ashamed. *What the hell am I thinking?*

"Beka?" She hadn't noticed Rommie coming to her side. The android laid a gentle hand on her arm, giving her a concerned look. "What's wrong?"

Beka stared at her, unable to form words for a moment. Finally, she mumbled, "Flash. I was thinking about Flash. About it helping me get us home faster."

"Beka . . ." Rommie started.

"I'm having crazy thoughts," Beka said. She closed her eyes and took a deep breath, trying to bring herself under conscious control. At this rate she wasn't going to be able to fly. "I'm scared, Rommie. I'm afraid that I'm going to screw up getting us out of here."

"You won't," Rommie said. She squeezed Beka's arm slightly. "I trust you completely. We all do."

"I don't," Beka muttered.

Rommie was silent for a moment, looking at her. Finally, she said, "My guess is that there's some kind of residual effect from the Kantaran attack. I've noticed that everybody except Trance is exhibiting unusual responses to the stress we're under. Trance is, well, Trance."

"Good for her," Beka said, almost managing a smile.

"You need to go and talk to her," Rommie said firmly. "She can probably find something to help you."

"God, I hope so," Beka muttered. "I feel miserable right now. I can't believe I was thinking about Flash."

"You thought about it, and you talked about it, and you dealt with the temptation," Rommie said, releasing her arm. "I don't see an issue. Now get to the medical bay. We need you ready to fly us out of here."

Trance didn't seem surprised to see Beka. To Beka's surprise, however, Micah Wright was stretched out on a diagnostic table, looking pale and drawn.

"Migraine," he said, when he saw Beka. He started to sit up, but stopped, wincing, shutting his eyes. Droplets of sweat broke out on his forehead.

Trance, who was filling a hypospray, turned around and frowned at him. Without argument he laid back down. She stepped over to him, pressed the hypospray to his neck, and pulled the trigger. There was a low hiss. After a moment he relaxed a little, and his face began to regain some of its normal color—not that there was much to regain, as far as Beka was concerned.

Trance turned to Beka, smiling. "All I need now is Tyr."

"You've seen everybody else?" Beka said, startled. "Today?"

"Today," Trance confirmed. "Migraines, headaches, upset stomachs . . . I'm seeing all kinds of things right now."

"Stress sucks," Beka said. At least she seemed to be feeling better than Micah. After a moment, she decided it was apples and oranges—while she had a physical problem, her biggest issue seemed to be psychological. "Count me in on the headache list." She hesitated for a moment, then added, "I'm kind of . . . weak in the knees right now, too."

Trance frowned and looked down at Beka's legs. "Did you bump into something?"

Beka stared at Trance for a moment, uncertain whether this moment of cluelessness was the real thing or not. "Let's just say that with everything that's going on, I'm having a few confidence issues."

"Oh," Trance said. She put the hypospray into a holder, picked up another, and snapped an ampule into place. "Rest and relaxation would probably be better, but this should help give your body and brain a boost. That should help your state of mind too. Other than that, I think we could all use a week on a nice warm beach with absolutely nothing to do but be lazy."

"That sounds like a plan," Beka said. Trance pressed the hypospray to her shoulder and pulled the trigger. "I hope you've got plenty of that stuff handy. It's going to be a long trip."

Trance's concoction had helped a lot. Beka's headache had vanished within a few minutes, and she had felt a surge of energy that had driven back the shadows. She wasn't about to start doing back flips down the corridors, but she could at least face her appointed task.

Back at the pilot station, she ran through some final checks. While she was doing so, Dylan walked into Command. His movements seemed leaden, and he looked as though he wasn't quite focusing on his surroundings.

"Dylan?" she said, concerned.

Slowly, he turned his head to look at her. "Yes?"

"You okay?"

He seemed to think about this for a few moments. Finally, he said,

"Yes." He smiled. "Trance had to play doctor with me." He frowned and shook his head. "Wait. We weren't playing doctor."

He stopped, looking baffled.

"You were feeling lousy in some way," Beka said, trying to stifle a chuckle at the lost look on Dylan's face. "She had to fix you up."

"Right," he said. "I feel a hell of a lot better." He stopped to think again. "You ever feel better in slow motion?"

Beka opened her mouth to try to answer the question, and then realized that she didn't *have* an answer. Whatever Trance had given Dylan, it had left him amazingly mellow. It was a good thing they didn't need Dylan to be in the same time zone right now.

"I was getting cranky," Dylan said. "Sick from the stomach on down, too."

"Dylan," she said, "I think you're probably about to give me too much information."

"Probably," he said mildly. "Captain's privilege."

"That plays two ways," Beka said, smiling. "I'm exercising mine to tell you to stop right there, mister."

"Right," he said. "But it's *my* ship."

"Not if she shoots you and takes over command," Rommie said. Both Dylan and Beka turned to look at her. She was giving them a half smile. "Not that I could possibly advocate mutiny, of course, as I'm an android and I'm designed to protect the interests of the Commonwealth at all times."

"There's a big fat loophole in there, isn't there?" Beka said. "I can tell. I grew up around people who never said anything that didn't have a loophole built into it."

"Are you suggesting that I'm a conniving person?" Rommie said.

"I've known you for several years, Rommie."

"Moving on," Rommie said, without changing expression as she avoided offering a riposte to Beka's comment, "are you ready to take us out of here?"

"Just what I was going to ask," Dylan said sleepily. "It's time to go."

Beka turned her head to look at him. "I think I got the idea at some point, Dylan. Next time Trance gives you a shot, make sure she doesn't overdo it. You're just too weird right now."

"She said I needed it," Dylan said. "I'll snap out of it if I need to. Trance says so."

"Trance says a lot of things," Rommie said.

"And a lot of what she says is right," Dylan responded. "Okay, so a lot of what she says isn't quite right either. Plus there's all the weird stuff." He frowned. "I think I need coffee."

Beka shook her head. "I think you need to hang on to something." She reached overhead and tapped the switches that activated the Slipstream hood. She opened a shipwide commlink and said, "Heads up, folks, I'm about to take us out of here. I need everybody on station now. Mr. Harper, are we good to go?"

"We've been good to go for hours, Boss," Harper said. He sounded irritable. "Just get our collective asses out of here before I go completely nuts, okay?"

"Spoken like a scholar and gentleman, as always," Rommie said, looking rueful.

"Yeah, right," Harper snapped. "Whatever. Harper out."

Rommie and Beka exchanged a look. "Overworked and underpaid," Beka said.

"Whatever it is," Dylan said, "he sounds pissed."

Beka didn't answer. She was too busy concentrating on her work. Normally she would simply have opened the throttle and made a high-speed run for the Slipstream portal, but caution was the watchword for the moment. It really didn't matter how fast they were moving in normal-space terms when the portal was opened—an entirely different set of rules came into force at the moment of transition.

Carefully, she increased their forward velocity. "One more rabbit hole," she muttered. Opening shipwide again, she said, "Transitioning to Slipstream in five . . . four . . . three . . . two . . . one . . . *now!*"

The portal burst into life ahead of them, the runners caught hold, and the universe went white and shook furiously as the *Andromeda Ascendant* drove on into the Slipstream.

She keyed the shipwide again. "Ladies and gentlemen, we are on our way."

SEVEN · THE PRICE OF A BROKEN HEART

Just as you get comfortable with the universe, the bitch
hits you smack in the teeth . . . with a hammer.

—ADMIRAL KADYMAE KELLER,
AT THE DELPHIC
CONFLAGRATION, CY 8733

Beka's palms were sweating as she brought the *Andromeda Ascendant*
back into normal space from the first Slip jump. So far so good. She
quickly scanned her instruments, then reached up to shut off the Slipstream hood. As it rose she clenched and unclenched her hands, trying to get her fears under control.

She knew she could do this. She knew it.

The next jump was going to be a short one, but at least the next
Slip point wasn't too far from their present position. She was beginning to map out their Slipstream journey in her head now, which, for
her, was always the key to getting where she wanted to go. Some Slipstream pilots, such as Dylan, were content simply to open a portal and
plod along, unable to see even a couple of jumps ahead. Her ability
went far beyond that, and she was sure she would start finding short-
cuts within the next few jumps. If she could find one Slip point soon
that showed even the slightest sign of regular travel, then she could

almost guarantee that their travel-time estimate could be tossed out—Slipstream travel had its own peculiar set of rules. The more often a route was used, the more direct, swift, and reliable it became.

Andromeda just had to hold together long enough. They were all hoping for a miracle at this point—a debris field would be a godsend, even if it meant being at a standstill for a few more days while *Andromeda* took care of repairs and rearming.

Beka scanned her instruments again. Nothing. They hadn't even reached the outer edge of the galactic rim yet. It gave her the creeps to realize there was almost nothing out here but infinitesimal amounts of hydrogen. If something happened now, they could still use the *Eureka Maru* to find their way back—but it would mean abandoning *Andromeda*, possibly forever. She didn't think she could leave the *Andromeda Ascendant* to die alone in the deep dark.

She took a deep breath, trying to get hold of her more depressing thoughts. They were going to be okay. Nobody was going to abandon *Andromeda*. There was always a solution—Dylan and Rommie had demonstrated that time and again, while Harper was an absolute master at pulling life-saving solutions out of nowhere in time to stave off calamity.

The fear just wouldn't go away.

She opened a comm channel to Engineering. "Harper, how's it going down there?" She was startled at how loud and abrupt she sounded.

"Jeez, Boss," Harper snapped. She couldn't blame him for being annoyed with her tone. "You could at least wait until I screw up before you bite my damn head off."

"Sorry," she said. She tried to relax, but it just wasn't happening. "I just wanted to check, that's all. Trying to stay on top of everything here."

"You're gonna give yourself an ulcer," Harper muttered. "Hell, you're gonna give *me* an ulcer."

"*Harper,*" Beka snapped. Silence. She noticed Rommie looking at her again. "All I wanted to do was find out if we're holding together, okay?"

"We're holding together," Harper answered petulantly. "End of report, Harper out."

"He's a little testy, isn't he?" Rommie said.

"Probably got out of the wrong side of bed," Beka answered.

"I doubt he got in either side of his bed recently." Rommie turned back to her instruments. "Everyone needs to be very conscious of exhaustion, Beka, with the exception of Trance."

Beka gave Rommie an unhappy glance. "Yes, Mom."

"Beka," Rommie said sharply, "understand something here. If anything happens, *my* life is on the line. I've survived the loss of my crew before, but I was pretty much whole at the time. Right now I'm in very bad shape, and I'm depending completely on you and the others to get me through this. I don't need any of your grandstanding, Beka. You don't need to prove anything to me."

"I can do this," Beka said stubbornly. She realized that she sounded almost childishly petulant, but she didn't know how to stop it. She increased their forward velocity slightly, alert for any warning signs.

"I know you can," Rommie said. "Let's just say that I'm nervous."

"Understood," Beka said. "I just need to do my job. It keeps me calm." Beka was silent for a moment, staring down at her console. "Hell, it keeps Dylan calm."

"Something else to keep in mind, I suppose," Rommie said, turning back to her own console.

"I suppose," Beka said.

She closed her eyes for a moment, wishing that the wait before the next Slip point was over. More than that: she wished this swirl of feelings would just go away.

As always, however, she was having no luck with wishing.

Trance had been relieved that their first Slip had gone well, but there was still much that was nagging at the back of her mind, including the vision she had had of a frozen world. There was a direct path from where things were now to that place she had seen, but she had yet to be able to put it all together. For all she knew they would only encounter that world years in their future.

For the moment, she was content to spend some time in the hydroponics gardens, moving through her plants, spraying here, trimming there, moving around those living in pots and planters. Working with living things, nurturing and nursing them as needed, brought her great joy.

She looked up and around, suddenly aware of a new presence. Not an alternate version of herself this time, though, but the android Rommie, standing at the end of the main path.

Trance smiled beatifically. "Hello. Do you like plants and trees?"

Rommie raised her eyebrows, looking around at the garden as though trying to fathom exactly what it was. "In terms of my programmed aesthetics, yes." She looked directly back at Trance. "That, however, is in terms of my programming."

"Rommie-in-the-box," Trance said.

"Rommie-in-the-box," the android agreed. She walked up to Trance, then knelt down, pressing the fingers of her right hand into the loam. "I can feel the electrical impulses in the soil and use my sensors to map the things that lie beneath it."

"But then the organic response is missing," Trance said gently. Rommie turned her head to look up at Trance. "The appreciation. It's one thing to be able to scan something, analyze the scent by applying forensic methods, and match it against a database to find out what it is. It's another thing entirely to just take in something like this without analysis. You allow yourself to be subjective rather than objective."

Rommie looked back down at the loam, pinching a piece of it between her fingers and holding it up to her nose. "That's one of the things I'm working on. That's the thing about being an artificial intelligence, Trance. We're like any other sentient—we can learn and grow. I like being what I am, but I don't have to play Rommie-in-the-box to do that." She dropped the crumbled loam and dusted her hands together. "You can thank Mr. Harper for some of my ability to stretch myself . . . although I still haven't made up my mind whether giving me the ability to be hormonal is a good or bad thing."

Trance shook her head. "I wouldn't know, but as long as you can turn it off . . ."

Rommie grinned. "It's a function I prefer not to access." She stood up, suddenly serious. "I didn't come by to talk about sentience and aesthetics."

"I didn't think you did," Trance said. She had a good idea of what was on Rommie's mind—and why the android had come to her rather than anyone else in the crew. "I can be fun company, but I don't think now's the time for that."

"Now is definitely not the time for that," Rommie said. "Trance, I'm practical. I'm a warship. My philosophy centers on one thing—load up my armory and point me at a target. In the past few weeks I've encountered exactly one thing I could shoot at, and that almost got me killed."

"Everything else disturbs you," Trance said.

"Putting it mildly," Rommie answered. She sounded frustrated, almost angry. "We're in the middle of nowhere, trying to get *somewhere*, I look like a decade-old High Guard practice drone, I have no supplies, no nanos, no missiles, and a total of one working cannon. I can be thankful, I suppose, that I have functioning Slipfighters and some ancillary ships."

"We still have Tweedledee and Tweedledum," Trance said.

"I don't know how much help they'd be in space," Rommie grumbled.

"They did a great job with the Magog swarmships that attacked us."

"They were sitting ducks attached to my hull," Rommie protested. "Of course they did a great job. They couldn't miss."

"So," Trance said, not looking away from Rommie, "we're vulnerable. One or two more Slips and you can start fixing that."

"It's still scary," Rommie said. "I'm not used to being afraid, Trance."

"It's okay to be scared sometimes," Trance said sweetly. She immediately regretted allowing herself to sound so perky. "I bet even Tyr sometimes gets scared. Think of it as being part of that growing process you were talking about. It's very healthy."

Rommie gave her a half smile. "That isn't all of it, Trance."

"I know." Trance picked up a spray bottle and handed it to the android. "I've still got stuff to do, so you can help me while you talk, okay?"

They started down the path. Trance suddenly turned to the right, stepping onto a barely visible access path as Rommie followed.

"That's a nutrient mix," Trance said without looking back. "Whenever you see a plant that looks like it needs it, just go ahead and spray away."

Rommie found a candidate immediately, and gave it several precise squirts from the bottle.

Trance had stepped into a group of tall plants, and was barely visible. She turned, assessing the growths she was looking at. Taking out her shears, she made several quick cuts, pleased with the way the plants seemed to brighten. She scattered the off-cuts around so that they could decay and feed back to the plants around her. The chemistry-set method was all well and good, especially the way that the Commonwealth had implemented it, but she believed strongly in adding the natural component as well.

She looked back at Rommie, who was diligently spraying plants. Trance crossed over the path to Rommie and took the spray bottle from her, adjusting the nozzle. "This isn't a battle, Rommie. They'll take the nutrients just as well if you mist them."

Rommie took the bottle back and began carefully misting the plants. "I came down here to talk about you."

Trance smiled slightly. "Not about me," she said. "About what's been happening around me, or to me, or however you want to put it."

"Yes." Rommie looked at Trance for a moment. "I'd like to talk *about* you too, but that always leads nowhere."

"Rommie, it isn't about who I am or what I am," Trance said softly. "I'm just a tiny, tiny part of things."

"You have a propensity for being in the middle of things, Trance." Rommie's eyes crossed as she focused on a flying insect that was trying to land on her nose. "Right now, though, I'm a lot less concerned about you generally than the things happening around you. I've said it before—I get very cranky when I can't quantify things. I haven't been able to quantify many of the events that occurred just prior to our battle with the Lighthouse Keepers. I'd like to know what's going on, Trance, and I'd like an honest answer."

Trance started back to the main path, and Rommie followed. "Rommie, I wish there were some way you could tell that I was telling the truth, but my body doesn't work the way you need."

"I know that the truth with you is fluid," Rommie said, sounding severe.

"My whole existence is fluid," Trance said. Not smiling, she looked directly at Rommie. "It's also hard to know what to do and what not to do. Everybody has this idea that I'm cunning and devious and somehow I secretly know all the answers. Well, I don't. There are times when I'm really, truly, terrified. I can't fail, Rommie." She closed her eyes for a moment, but all it did was allow old images to surge up. "I've seen what happens if I do."

"Which is your contention," Rommie said, "but we have no way to confirm anything, do we? What about these recent events?"

"Believe me," Trance said, "I wish I knew. Things just started happening. I'm sure there's a reason behind it, but . . ." She shook her head. "When there's another one of me around, I usually *expect* it."

"Do you mean that this happens to you a lot, Trance?"

Trance sighed. "No, that's not what I mean. What I mean is that these were all pretty rude surprises."

"Could the Kantarans' mind weapon have had any effect on you?"

Trance shook her head. "Even if it had, it wouldn't result in what happened. Reality was having small fits. Anyway, it seems to have stopped now."

"For the time being," Rommie said. She frowned. "I still don't have answers, do I?"

"Sorry," Trance said. She turned to the right and started down another access path. "Let's get these plants down here. They get crotchety if they're left alone too long."

Tyr was standing in the darkness of the observation lounge when Dylan walked in. The tall Nietzschean was looking out at the distant points of light that were all the illumination they had this far out in deep space. One more Slip, however, and they would be somewhere a lot less foreboding. He was grateful for that fact.

"Hello, Dylan," Tyr said. He sounded contemplative. "I find myself restless. I had hoped to center myself here, but it seems that it will not work."

Dylan stopped next to Tyr. "I had the same idea, Tyr. Unfortunately, I don't think there's any way to not be on edge until we get out of this situation."

"If." Tyr's voice was solemn.

"When," Dylan countered firmly. "*When*. It's a matter of time, that's all."

"Ever the optimist, sir." Tyr didn't look away from the dark vista before them.

"We always find a way," Dylan said.

"Not always." Tyr finally looked at Dylan. "Need I remind you why we began this doomed voyage in the first place?"

Dylan sighed. "Would you like me to find an albatross and wear it around my neck?"

"An . . . a what?"

"*The Rime of the Ancient Mariner,*" Dylan said, smiling. "A long poem about lost seafarers in ancient times. One of them shoots an albatross—a kind of bird—and dooms the entire crew. His punishment is to wear the dead bird around his neck. He's the one left to tell the tale."

Tyr was silent for a moment, then he said, "Dylan, there are times when I truly am afraid for your sanity." He turned away from the window. "Good night."

"Good night, Tyr," Dylan said affably.

A moment later he heard Tyr say, "Good night, Rommie, and no, you cannot move quietly enough to evade my senses."

"Good night, Tyr," Rommie said seriously. She walked up to Dylan's side. "Sometimes he carries that superiority business a little too far."

"I try to ignore it," Dylan said. "He's turned out to be worth tolerating for the most part."

"We could say the same for Trance," Rommie said.

"We could," Dylan said. "Which leads to the next point—did Trance have any answers?"

"She taught me how to feed and trim plants," Rommie said, frowning. "I believe she also attempted to explain aesthetics, the nature of fear, and why chocolate is good. She did not, however, have any explanation for the phenomena affecting her several weeks ago."

"Should we be worried?"

"Unanswered questions are always cause for worry, Captain."

"A simple 'yes' would have done," Dylan said, amused.

"I'm more concerned about the fact that multiple types of phenomena were involved, not just one. We have Trance's assertion that she traveled forward in time on what would now be an alternate timeline. We have at least one alternate Trance—and Trance believes that each of the alternates actually came from different timelines. Finally, we have the ghosting on the Command Deck. The first few might seem extremely important, but they aren't as important as the last."

"Why?"

Rommie had her most serious expression now. "While the images we saw appear to have no tangible existence, that's not true—we were seeing across the boundaries of multiple realities. At best, this is harmless. At worst, it would indicate that reality is somehow breaking down."

"Bad," Dylan said.

"Very," Rommie added. "If those boundaries give way, we won't have time to ask why."

"How likely?"

"Not very. Which, considering our past history, doesn't mean much."

"It's these moments of reassurance that I treasure, Rommie."

"I do my best," she said.

Wright was in the medical bay again, with another migraine. This time it was accompanied by a sudden nosebleed that had left the front of his uniform sticky with blood. At first Trance had thought he had some kind of accident while working in the damaged corridors.

She had quickly gotten the nosebleed under control and his nose packed with cotton. The migraine took a couple of minutes longer while one of her special medical concoctions did its work.

"I hate this," Wright muttered. "Haven't had a nosebleed like that since Jenblossom broke my nose at the Academy. First it was like someone was pumping my head full of air, then out it comes, and the migraine kicks in." He carefully touched the bridge of his nose.

Trace looked at her readouts. "It looks like something elevated your blood pressure and did so very quickly. It's almost down to normal now, and you seem to be okay."

"I don't feel okay," he mumbled. "It's better than having a migraine, though."

"That's the way," she said, smiling brightly. "Focus on the positive."

He tried to smile back, but it was a weak effort. "Listen, I'd try to be a flirt here, Trance," he said, "but I'm having too many problems, and so is Pogue."

"Everybody seems to be," Trance said.

"I thought we'd been hit by our own weapon," he said. He swung his legs over the side of the diagnostic table and sat up. "I still think that's pretty much the case, except we've been thinking of the wrong weapon. I need to talk to Dylan."

"It's nicknamed 'the mind torpedo,'" Pogue said. She, Wright, and the crew were sitting in the commissary, drinking coffee.

"The full-scale weapon basically unleashes a torrent of energy at its target, achieving results very quickly—you've seen this for yourselves." Wright took a sip of coffee. "The torpedo works on a much smaller scale. It's designed as a fallback device if a ship manages to escape."

"The torpedo detonates close to the hull of the target vessel," Pogue went on, "scattering thousands of microscopic transmitters that stick in place. Each individual transmitter is essentially harmless."

"It's the accumulation that does the trick," Rommie said. "Given time, the effects on the crew cause a breakdown, with potentially disastrous consequences."

"Like making stupid mistakes," Harper muttered.

"Or Micah's migraines," Trance said. "The physiological side effects are dangerous. This time he had a massive nosebleed. Next time it could be a stroke. I'm keeping him on medication that should help with the migraines and keep his blood pressure down, but I don't know how long that'll last." She looked around the table, displaying her worry. "I keep having to give you medication, and that could be very dangerous."

"I've seen it cut Dylan's reaction time down," Beka said, giving Dylan a concerned look. "You're creepy on that stuff."

"Better that than having me running around ranting about who ate my strawberries, or whatever," Dylan said.

Harper looked confused. "Huh? Strawberries?"

Dylan held up a hand. Harper sat back looking at Trance, who smiled and shrugged.

"So," Dylan said, sitting up, "we find out where they hit, scrape them off, and start having normal lives again."

"It isn't quite that easy, Captain," Pogue said. "Begging Andromeda's pardon, it was a bit like shooting at the broad side of a barn. More than likely you were hit by several torpedoes. By now they'll have networked."

"Then you tell us what to do," Tyr said, glowering. Pogue glowered right back, silently. The sight amused Dylan. Tyr hadn't met his match, but Pogue wasn't going to be intimidated.

"We'll need to disrupt them somehow," Wright said. "Once the transmitters have been shut down, they can be scraped off the hull en masse. Before that, if anything gets close enough to cause damage, they'll defend themselves."

"Then I suggest we make that solution the first order of business after this next Slip," Rommie said. "I'm very much looking forward to this one. A prime selection of raw materials will improve my day greatly."

Beka stood up, smiling. "Time to *really* get this show on the road, folks."

Harper and Pogue headed down to Engineering—Harper was justifiably nervous about the state of the Slipstream core, never mind everything else. There had been some noncritical problems since the first Slip, but those had represented little more than tidying up for Harper.

While the rest of the crew headed for Command to wait out the time before the next Slip, Trance headed back to the medical bay to pick up her hypospray and a medical kit with her various concoctions. Even Dylan was accepting the shots as routine now.

She had just reached the medical bay when the universe twisted around her. She was caught so completely unawares that she stumbled and fell headlong, catching herself at the last moment.

"Welcome aboard the *Perseus Triumphant*," a woman said. Slowly, Trance looked up to see a tall middle-aged woman with close-cropped blond hair and emerald-green eyes looking down at her. She was wearing what appeared to be a modified black High Guard uniform, and had a Gauss pistol in her left hand, although it was no design that Trance had ever seen before. "I am Captain Diana Hunt, hereditary shipmaster."

"Nice to meet you," Trance said. "Sorry about the undignified arrival."

Captain Hunt regarded her steadily. "You may stand, slowly." She turned to a bronze-skinned man standing next to her. "Perseus, relieve her of that . . . whatever it is."

"It's a force lance," Trance said, standing up slowly. She smiled at Perseus as he took it from its holster. "Be careful with it. Force lances are individually keyed, and you'll be zapped if you try to fire it or open it."

"Open it?" the android said.

"It opens out into a quarterstaff," Trance said. "It's a pretty useful weapon."

"I imagine," Hunt said. "So."

There was a moment of silence, then Perseus said, "It's her."

That statement startled Trance. "What?"

"Trance Gemini," Captain Hunt said. She smiled slightly. "It's been a while since I saw you last, Trance, but the years haven't done you any harm."

"You don't have questions about how I just appeared out of thin air right in front of you?" Trance said, confused.

"It's quite a trick," Perseus said, "although the landing needs a little work."

Oh, this is going to get complicated. "I'm, uh, not your Trance," she said. Hunt and Perseus looked at each other. "That's why I arrived the way I did. I'm from another timeline, and I have the feeling I'm a long way from home."

"You always were one for surprises," Hunt said. Smiling, she reached out with her free hand and squeezed Trance's shoulder. "You chose a great moment to arrive, however."

"I'm under attack," Perseus said. "There's a swarming pestilence called the Doeia. Our support group got bogged down and my defenses were overwhelmed. We finally scraped them off of my hull, but there are some stragglers on board."

"Not for long, though," Hunt said.

Perseus handed Trance's force lance back. "We learned early on not to attempt a dialogue with the Doeia. They're utterly amoral."

"What do they—"

There was a loud chittering and scraping behind her, and she turned in one swift movement.

"Like that," Perseus said.

Facing her was a spidery creature, about her height. It was wearing some kind of plastic armor that covered its thorax and its eight jointed limbs; it was walking on four of the limbs, while the other four functioned as arms. A plastic mask covered what appeared to be the head. Under the mask she could see a mouth filled with rows of tiny teeth. Sixteen unblinking eyes arranged in rows of two stared at them.

The Doeia lifted a long slender weapon, but it was too slow. Hunt and Perseus were firing to either side of her; her own shots came instinctively. The Doeia staggered backward, its armor and mask ripping apart and its weapon flying out of its thin hands. For a moment it tried to get its balance using three legs, two undamaged arms frantically snatching at other weapons. Then the barrage took its toll, and it fell, kicked twice, and lay still.

The three of them holstered their weapons. Perseus looked momentarily lost in thought, then said, "That seems to have been the last of them, Captain."

"About time," Hunt grumbled. She turned to Trance. "Why are you here?"

"I don't know," Trance said honestly. "It just happened. One second—"

The universe twisted again, and she was suddenly back in her familiar medical bay.

She definitely needed answers, and soon, but she didn't have the slightest clue where to look.

She had never felt so helpless.

"I wish I had a better idea," Trance said as Rommie pinned a tracker to her collar. She gave the android a despairing look. "At least you'll have an idea *when* something happens, if not what's going on."

"I'm hoping for a little more data than that," Rommie said. She stepped back slightly, frowning. "Well, there you are. Or it is."

"For right now," Trance said, "wherever it is, I am."

"Wherever you go, there you are?" Rommie suggested, her right eyebrow raised.

Trance grimaced. "There are times when I'd like to take a vacation from myself. You're lucky. You can."

"Only one of me," Rommie said.

The holographic Rommie shimmered into life. "Patently untrue. I can schedule rest cycles for myself, as can Andromeda."

"How long do those last?" Trance said. "Microseconds?"

"Picoseconds, usually," the holographic Rommie said. "Not quite long enough to get bored."

"Right now," Trance said, "I wouldn't mind being a little bored. Everything's getting too exciting lately."

"I'm heading back to Command," Rommie said as her holographic counterpart faded out.

"I'll be there in a minute," Trance said. "I just need to gather some things."

"Good enough."

Rommie left. Trance went to her workbench and gathered together the small kit she needed. For the moment Beka and Dylan were her main concern, so she could keep the kit to a minimum.

Ready, she left the medical bay. She hadn't taken more than three steps before she lost track of reality altogether and felt herself—no, not herself this time, just her perceptions—thrust into the future. They were racing toward catastrophe, and from there forward all she could see was an ever more tangled morass of timelines until darkness drowned them all.

Suddenly shipwide was on. "Ladies and gentlemen, hang on to your hats, here we go again. Slipstream in five . . . four . . . three . . . two . . . one—"

"Beka!" Trance yelled. "Don't!"

"—transiting to Slipstream now," Beka concluded.

Trance started running as the *Andromeda Ascendant* jumped to Slipstream.

EIGHT • A PAINTED SHIP UPON A PAINTED OCEAN

It isn't "ghost ship," it's "ghost ships," plural. A few go in every month and they never come back—bad Slips, bad maintenance, who knows? Sometimes they go in and a long, long time later they come out again. You don't want to know about those. Slipstreaming is about skill . . . and it's about luck.

—HIGH GUARD ACADEMY SLIPSTREAM
INSTRUCTOR MARDI GIACOMO,
CY 8823

Her sense of dread increasing with each step, Trance raced toward Command. She had been unable to open a channel to Command, and now she was convinced that their only hope was for her to get there on foot. The rapid cycle of probability lines running through her mind didn't help—she could barely focus on the lengths of corridor she was racing down.

Not far now.

The universe twisted again.

Oh, no, not now.

She almost stopped, but the corridor had remained familiar. This was still the *Andromeda Ascendant*—and it was *her* version of the ship. All she had to do now was figure out *when* she was.

Voices in the corridor, around an intersection. She turned the corner and saw Dylan and Beka together.

She knew the location, too. It was the point at which she had returned from her inadvertent future jaunt to witness Tyr's death. They had been discussing the mysterious blood drops, and . . .

Trance almost laughed.

"Coming through!" she shouted, not slowing her pace. Startled, Beka and Dylan stepped aside, letting her through. Any moment now . . .

"Trance!" Dylan called.

She turned around, running backward. "I don't have time!"

She turned and sprinted down another corridor, wondering if she could have used this time to try to prevent the things that were going to happen. The possibilities played out instantly in her mind. She found nothing but disaster if they changed course now.

No pain, no gain . . . that's stupid. The universe twisted again, as she had hoped, and she knew immediately that she was back in the right time and place.

Well, almost the right place. She let out an inadvertent squeak as she stumbled and almost fell into Beka. Where she had expected to be and where she was were quite a few meters apart.

She was in the right place, however. Frantically, she grabbed Beka's arm. "Beka, trust me, you've got to get us out of Slipstream *now!*"

Dylan, Rommie, Tyr, and Wright were gathering around them now, staring at Trance.

"That was quite a jump," Rommie said.

"In more ways than one," Trance said. "We need to get out of Slipstream right now, or something very bad is going to happen."

Andromeda appeared on several of the flatscreens. "As in making-my-life-worse bad?"

"As in it'll-only-hurt-for-a-second bad," Trance said. "Trust me!"

Dylan nodded at Beka. "Do it."

Beka gave Dylan a helpless look. "Dylan, if we exit Slipstream now, we—"

"Where there's a portal out, there's a portal in," Trance said.

"Gotcha," Beka said. She reached for her controls.

"Hey, Boss!" Harper's voice almost boomed over the comm system— more urgency.

"Harper," Beka said, "I'm busy."

"Gonna be a hell of a lot busier if—oh, *jeez!*"

" 'Oh, jeez' is definitely not good," Dylan said.

"It's worse than not good," Beka said. She had suddenly become very pale. "Dylan, half of my systems are down and the other half are freezing."

"Harper," Dylan said, "we've got problems up here."

"There's worse freakin' problems down here, Boss," Harper responded. There was the sound of snapping and fizzing somewhere in the background. "I dunno what we're about to lose, but it's gonna really freakin' *hurt*." Somewhere in the background Pogue yelped.

"I'll see if I can help," Tyr said. Dylan nodded and the Nietzschean left Command at a sprint.

"I'm losing the core," Harper yelled. "I don't know what the hell happened but the exotic matter lens started to fracture and that screwed up the pulser. I'm trying to keep everything together, but I've got other stuff going down as well. Cascade *ow goddamnit!* failures."

"We've got systems down or locking out up here," Dylan said.

"I need some kind of emergency bypass," Beka said frantically. "I can't get us out of Slipstream otherwise."

"I'll see what I can do, Boss, but you gotta remember, I'm just a genius, not a miracle worker."

"That wasn't what you said last week, you liar," Trance said.

"Hey, golden girl," Harper answered. He sounded a bit more cheerful, which was what she had wanted. "Miracles comin' up. Harper out."

Dylan looked around at Beka. "Keep trying."

"What do you think I'm *doing* here, Dylan?" Beka snapped.

Dylan's expression started to darken. In a flash, Trance had her hypospray out, loaded, and against Dylan's neck. There was a brief hiss, and Dylan's expression relaxed.

Suddenly the ship began to shudder violently.

"Trouble," Rommie said.

"One of the runners is starting to lose cohesion with the strings," Beka said. "If the other one goes as well, we're dead."

Andromeda appeared on the flatscreens again. "I'm attempting to hold on as long as I can."

The ship shuddered even more violently this time.

"Of course," Andromeda added, "that may not be long enough to help us."

"Still nothing," Beka said. "This is goddamn frustrating!"

"*Ow!*" Andromeda said, sounding and looking piqued. Everyone stared at the main flatscreen, startled. "Mr. Harper did something extremely off-specification."

Trance saw Beka's control console change.

"It's gonna be tricky," Harper called over the comm, "but I can get us out of here. I think."

"I'm ready," Beka said. "I don't have full control yet."

"That's the tricky, Boss."

Trance was almost blinded by the probability lines again, but she managed to focus on the one they needed. "Harper, let me call the timing, okay?"

There was a pause. Then he said, sounding uncertain, "For my golden goddess, sure, babe."

The ship began shuddering violently. This time the vibration didn't stop.

"Starboard runner is now completely disengaged," Andromeda said.

"The portside runner is losing cohesion," Beka said. "Trance, we can't wait. Trance?"

"I'm completely losing the core!" Harper yelled.

Trance held up her right hand and counted off three. "Now, Beka!"

Beka initiated the Slipstream transition commands.

"I'm losing the portside runner," Andromeda said.

The shuddering increased in violence. *Andromeda* was going to come apart if this kept up. Just a little longer . . .

"Now, Harper!" Trance yelled.

"Portside runner is now completely disengaged," Andromeda said calmly, as though she wasn't being shaken to pieces.

There was a tremendous bang as they were hurled out of Slipstream.

———

"This is going to *so* screw up my record," Harper was complaining.

"I doubt it," Tyr said flatly.

While Beka had set up the Slipstream exit, he had set the core from its control station on the catwalk that overlooked the immense engine. On Trance's mark, he had shut the core down—just pulling the plug, in short. It had worked, even though it wasn't the way anybody wanted to exit Slipstream. In the process the exotic matter lens had shattered and the pulser had taken enough of a pounding to put it beyond the hope of repair.

"One thing's for sure," Harper muttered, looking down into the now-quiet core pit, "we aren't going anywhere for a while."

"As Dylan keeps insisting," Tyr said, "some things are only a matter of time."

"Oh, surrre," Harper said, throwing his arms up—which was the point at which the lighting and the artificial gravity field shut off. "Oh, freakin' great! *Now* what?"

Red emergency lighting came on, giving the cavernous area a hideous look. At first Harper was focused on fixing *this* problem . . . until he realized that he was floating in midair over the Slipstream core pit, and if the artificial gravity field came back on now, he had a long scream ahead of him.

"Don't move!" Tyr's order seemed to come from right behind his feet.

Naturally, Harper moved, trying to see where Tyr was. The action sent him drifting farther.

"Mr. Harper," Tyr said patiently, "if you don't pay attention, I am going shoot you, do you understand?"

"Got it," was what Harper meant to say. "*Eep!*" was the sound that actually came out.

He felt Tyr's hands grip his ankles. Slowly, he was drawn backward until Tyr was able to grab the waistband of his pants and swing him around. Tyr had swung over the railings of the catwalk, locking himself into place by crossing his ankles.

Tyr got Harper to the railing and let go of him as soon as the engineer had gotten onto the catwalk. With a single graceful movement, Tyr drew himself back and swung himself to the catwalk, looking for all the world as though he operated in microgravity day in and day out. Harper could barely remember how to move in microgravity—his body wanted to do all the wrong things. Feeling sick, he clung to the railing. That was the inner ear, he remembered, trying to get him balanced. *Great, now I get to upchuck.*

He turned his head and opened his mouth, then closed it again when Tyr said, "Don't waste time with thanking me, Mr. Harper. Fix the ship."

"Comm system is down," Rommie said, "but there may be a workaround for that. We can patch through the *Eureka Maru* and other vehicles, and both Dylan and Harper have their subcutaneous transmitters."

"For now," Dylan said, "we're not going anywhere. Which means we do it the hard way, using the *Maru* there and back." Dylan started to turn, as did Beka.

The lights went out.

"I'm not sure which circuit that was," Rommie said. "And the AG failed at the same time."

"I know," Beka and Dylan chorused.

Emergency lighting came on, bathing everything in a dull red. Dylan and Beka were in midair, floating slowly toward the ceiling. Dylan, looking aggravated, muttered, "It's never *ever* easy, is it?"

Beka, on the other hand, looked quite comfortable. "Hey, you added a word."

"Both of you may add another at any time," Rommie said. "That being 'ouch' right after your keisters hit the deck when Harper gets the AG working again." Rommie turned her head to look over at Micah Wright. "Mr. Wright?"

"I'm fine," he answered. "I was holding on to my station."

"We could leave them up there," Trance said helpfully. Both she and Rommie had managed to stay on the deck. Rommie had clutched the edge of a console. There was no telling how Trance was managing it.

"Hey!" Beka said, looking startled.

"What she said," Dylan added.

Rommie looked at Trance. "I think they want to come down."

"I think so too," Trance said. "We could wait until they bounce from the ceiling."

"Might be too late," Rommie said. "Seriously. You know how fast Harper works."

"*Very* fast," Beka said. She had drifted over Trance's head. "I like my butt the way it is, thanks."

"Are you helping?" Rommie asked Trance.

"Why not?" Trance said cheerfully.

They kicked off simultaneously, Rommie aiming for Dylan and Trance heading for Beka. They caught their respective targets around the waist, slowing from the added mass—Rommie slowed slightly more than Trance, thanks to Dylan's greater mass.

Both used their free arms to cushion their arrival at the ceiling, killing their momentum.

"Free ride's over," Trance said, releasing Beka.

"Thanks," Beka said, floating against the ceiling. "I think." She looked down. "You know, it doesn't look *that* far up from down there. Looks like a *long* way down from up here."

"See you down there," Trance said.

She pushed off again and went floating feetfirst toward the deck. Beka drifted past her. Rommie, still holding Dylan, had just hit the deck and was going into a crouch to kill her momentum.

Straightening up, the android looked up at them. "Everything okay up there?"

"Perfect," Beka said.

"I think you can let Dylan go now, Rommie," Trance said.

"Oh. Of course." She released Dylan, looking at him. "Sorry, Captain."

Beka and Trance touched down, and Trance had to grab Beka's shoulder to stop her from bouncing up again. Beka looked at her and started to ask a question, but Trance said, "Don't ask."

Dylan was carefully settling himself at a console. Beka carefully pushed off, angling herself toward the pilot station, catching hold and using it to swing herself around and into place. Her boots made a clumping noise on the deck. Trance followed, a little more delicately.

"Well," Dylan said, taking a deep breath, "that was a fun interlude between disasters." He looked at Rommie. "Can we do something with the emergency lighting?"

Rommie tapped at her console. "Blue-shifting the lighting in Command," she said as the lighting became cooler and brighter. "I'm reluctant to do that all over the ship, especially in Engineering."

"Understood," Dylan said.

"We're dead in the water," Beka said. "I've got nothing here."

"'A painted ship on a painted ocean,'" Dylan said.

The Rime of the Ancient Mariner," Rommie said, "by Samuel Taylor Coleridge."

"Albatross," Dylan said absently.

"What?" Wright said from behind them.

Dylan carefully turned his head to look at the pilot. "Coleridge's poem tells the story of an old sailing ship that ventures out farther than any ship has ever been. When they get stuck, an albatross—a seabird—turns up to guide them. For some reason, the mariner shoots it, everything goes to hell, and his shipmates make him wear the corpse." Dylan paused for a moment. "Albatross. Portending winnowing doom."

"It sounds . . . charming," Wright said. He didn't look too thrilled.

"It's quite the epic," Rommie said seriously. "One thing after—"

"Rommie," Trance interrupted, "what's the *positive* part of the story?"

"The positive part," Tyr said from the entrance to Command, "is that he survives to tell his tale. As shall we." He glided into Command, grabbing his console and swinging around it to a stop. "Mr. Harper believes we can route comms through the *Eureka Maru*."

"We came to that conclusion as well," Dylan said. "How is Mr. Harper doing?"

Tyr raised an eyebrow, which gave him quite a disingenuous look. "Quite well, once I retrieved him from his inadvertent dive into the core pit."

Beka raised both eyebrows, making a moue of surprise but saying nothing.

"Miss Pogue," Tyr added, "is helping a great deal."

"We have a lot of microgravity and low-gravity experience," Wright said.

"Then," Dylan said, "you'd better get down to Engineering and see what you can do to help Mr. Harper. Tyr, get him there, and let Mr. Harper know that we're setting up the comm solution."

"On my way," Tyr said, turning himself around and pushing off. Wright followed him, moving almost as easily.

"I'd better get out to the *Maru*," Beka said.

"At this rate," Rommie said, "I'm going to end up as a crazy-quilt tramp steamer."

"You'll never fall that low," Dylan said. "Beka, do it as fast as you can." Beka kicked off and sailed out of Command. Microgravity had some advantages—at least until someone turned the gravity back on, or a wall got in the way and provided a reminder about basic laws of physics. "Rommie, I need some kind of status report."

Rommie was looking worried. "Bad, bad, and worse," she said. She looked at Dylan. "Dylan, my core AI isn't responding. Neither is my holographic avatar."

Dylan closed his eyes and gritted his teeth. "Damn it."

Trance moved up to Rommie, putting a hand on the android's shoulder. "They'll be okay."

"If they're not," Dylan said, "we could be in even worse trouble. Let's hope Harper's up to his usual standard."

Rommie stared down at her console, looking as though she was about to cry.

"Harper, can you hear me?" It was Beka's voice, echoing in his head.

Grunting slightly as he worked his way along an access tube to a panel that was burned on the inside, Harper said, "Loud and clear, Boss. Hey, Dylan, you catchin' this station too?"

"Mr. Harper," Dylan responded.

"So speaks Mr. Excitement," Harper answered. He pulled the panel off and shone a flashlight inside, wincing as he saw the damage.

"I'm not feeling particularly lighthearted at the moment," Dylan said. "We've lost both the core AI and the holographic avatar."

"Yeah," Harper said, "I figured that'd happen." He realized he sounded annoyed, which annoyed him even further. He shone the flashlight farther down the access tube. More visible damage. Pogue would be able to figure out some of the problems where she was, but both Tyr and Wright were pretty useless when it came to doing this—neither one was trained for the job. "I've got redundant back-ups and Rommie can help update."

"It's that easy?" Beka said, sounding surprised.

"Nope," he said. He hauled himself uncomfortably around to a new position. "It's all gonna depend on the hardware. I'm finding stuff screwed up here that I've *never* seen screwed up before, and that's saying something on this ship." He fished in his pockets, finally turning up his wire. He snapped one connector into the jack at the side of his neck, unraveled the cord quickly, and plugged the connector on the other end into a nearby diagnostic socket. "Okay, boys and girls, shut the hell up while I get right under the hood here and work some Seamus Harper magic."

In an instant he was connected with the cybernetic landscape of the *Andromeda Ascendant*. Not everything in here was driven by the AI—there were plenty of autonomic systems for him to look at on his way to the heart of things. He passed defenses, some of which he had added himself, scattering passwords and ciphers as he went by.

It was always a rush going into the system.

Suddenly he was there. The cybernetic heart of the *Andromeda Ascendant* rose about him like a glowing city. There were stories in those buildings and once you learned to read them you could be set for life.

He looked up, scanning the sparkling and glowing images around him, immediately finding some of the problems. Some he could fix in here. Others needed work in the real world.

"Hey, Andromeda!" he called. "You awake, gorgeous?"

She was suddenly there, a sparkling, semitransparent image. "Don't yell," she said. She seemed unsteady. After a moment, she sat down. "Harper, I have a hell of a headache." She looked up at him. "AIs don't get headaches."

"I'm just glad you're pretty much okay," Harper said, relieved. "It's turning into bypass city out there."

"Can you get me out of here? I hate being deaf and blind and I'm dying of boredom."

Harper scanned the cyberscape again. "It's gonna take a while, babe. I think there's some reconfiguring you can do in here that'll help." He pointed to several different areas. "Try those to start with. I've gotta get back out into the real world before Tyr decides to break something."

"Okay." Andromeda stood up, looking up and around. "See you soon, I hope."

"Count on it," Harper said, jacking out again. It took him a moment to readjust to reality. He plucked the flashlight from where it floated and tapped the side of his neck to activate his subcutaneous transmitter. "Found Andromeda, guys. She's got a headache, she says, but she seems okay otherwise."

"Any ideas on how to get her back into operation?" Dylan asked.

"Some," Harper said. He started inching along the access tube again. "She's gonna have to do some work herself, and once she's done I can put together a bypass that'll get her on-line. If I can do that, I can get holo-Rommie out as well."

"As fast as you can," Dylan said. "What about AG and main power?"

"Working on the AG right now," Harper said. Carefully, he pulled off a panel. "I'm not gonna get it back all the way right now," he added, "so don't go taking any big steps. Main power'll come when I see which main relays and breakers got toasted." Harper shone his flashlight into the circuitry. "I'm gonna have to shut down lots of the ship, Boss."

"Just as long as it's nothing critical," Dylan said.

"No problem." Something fizzed and snapped, stinging Harper's hand. "Jeez! Yeah, anyway, the regular drive did an emergency shutdown when we kicked out of Slipstream. I haven't had time to really check it, but it looks okay, so once I get AG and main power back, we'll be able to move."

"We don't know where we are," Beka said.

"Take the *Maru* out," Harper said. "The astronav isn't as good as the one *Andromeda* has, but it'll give us a rough idea of where we are."

"What about communications?" Dylan said.

Harper did a quick calculation in his head. "We're good up to a thousand meters," he said, "and you don't need to get that far out to get a reading."

"Okay," Dylan said, "do it. Go out about two hundred and fifty meters."

"We could be anywhere," Beka said. "That was a hell of an exit."

"No kidding," Harper said, quickly splicing broken and burned lines. He knew he was making a mess as he went along, but he didn't have a choice. "Look on the bright side, huh? We don't have to clean out a ship full of dead Magog."

"I so didn't need to remember that," Beka said. She was quickly running through the preflight checklist and feeding power to the engines. "I'm good to go."

"Captain Valentine," Dylan said formally, "permission granted to leave the *Andromeda Ascendant*."

Beka grinned. "It's just a drive around the block," she said. "Hey, at least it gets me out of the house so Mom and Dad can have some fun."

Carefully, Beka engaged the thrusters, moving the *Eureka Maru* forward toward the docking bay entrance. It was a frustratingly delicate task—normally she would just activate the AG field, power up, and go, full-tilt.

Reversing thrusters, she came to a full stop just past the 250-meter mark. Looking through the freighter's front windows, she was relieved to see darkness peppered by unblinking stars.

She turned to the astronavigation computer, requesting a positional analysis, waiting impatiently as it went through its observations and calculations. The *Andromeda Ascendant* could finish this in a hundredth of the time, maybe even faster, but the big ship had far more data to work with, as well as far faster systems—a dedicated neural network.

Finally, the computer produced a result. Beka stared at it for a few moments, then opened a comm channel. "I've got a result."

"Where are we?" Dylan asked.

"In the middle of nowhere," Beka said heavily. She grimaced. "There's nothing for parsecs in any direction." She felt like crying, but pushed it aside—that was Kantaran weaponry speaking, not her own emotions. "It looks like we managed to actually come out inside the Andromeda galaxy. I guess that's progress."

"That's progress," Dylan said firmly. "There are more complications than we expected, but it's all just a matter of time."

"Right," Beka said. Suddenly she felt exhausted. More and more seemed to be going wrong, and it was just getting to be too much. She had never had this much trouble before Dylan came along.

Not true, a smaller inner voice insisted. She closed her eyes and tried to will the negative feelings away, focusing on the positive. Dylan had come along and put an end to her scrabbling for a living. Now she helped to make a difference. She still encountered lowlifes and scum, but now they were in politics—criminals with respectable faces.

"On the good news side of things," Harper said, "your in-house boy wonder and neighborhood genius has just fixed the AG and is now turning it back on."

"Still miles to go, as they say, Mr. Harper," Dylan said.

"Or parsecs," Beka added quietly. "*Lots* of parsecs."

Sighing, she activated the thrusters and turned the *Maru* around.

NINE • PIONEERS OVER C

> Reality shifts beneath our feet on a constant basis. It's nothing more than the universe making little adjustments to keep things in line, which is why most are not aware of it. Those who are aware of it, however, usually go quite mad as a side effect. We sometimes call these people "prophets."
>
> —REMNIMAAT, PERSEID PHILOSOPHER,
> CY 6422

Harper was flitting about the Command Deck, referring periodically to a stack of flexis clutched in one hand and punching at controls with the other. Pogue was still down in Engineering, dealing with assorted little problems—this apparently including gathering up a collection of tools that Harper had left in his wake like a trail of bread crumbs.

There had been some desultory talk of getting the *Eureka Maru* ready for its long haul. They were going to come back with the cargo pod stuffed, supplies shoved into every spare corner, and probably things strapped to the exterior by the time they were done. As far as Harper was concerned, however, just acquiring a replacement lens and pulser wasn't enough—the *Andromeda Ascendant* might not survive another jump into Slipstream. They couldn't even risk trying to tow her.

Dylan was unwilling to leave her right now, even with Harper and Rommie still aboard. Harper had managed to fix the AG, bring back main power, and check out the normal-space engines, which were down to fifty percent of their capability, but getting the core AI back was proving to be a monumental task. Harper had been jacking in and out of the ship's cybernetics system on what seemed to be a half-hourly basis for the past three days.

He sipped gingerly at the glass of cavenga juice Trance had handed him when she arrived in Command just after Harper had charged into . . . what *was* he doing, anyway? He was all over the place. Trance had sworn that the juice was just what Dylan needed. Maybe it was meant to help him concentrate? Give him stamina?

Maybe the idea was to burn his taste buds out—she hadn't said anything about the taste. It tasted as though someone had started with some kind of fruit, managed to make it bitter, and then poured in sugar to try to cover the bitterness.

He turned his head to look at Trance, who smiled back from a console where she was entering data from a flexi Harper had shoved at her on his way past. Dylan smiled weakly back.

Beka, who was wearing one of her more impractical black dresses, sidled over to him. Ducking her head and lowering her voice to a whisper, she said, "You don't look too happy with that stuff."

"It's . . . no." Dylan looked down at the glass. He had barely touched it. "It's not my taste."

"Well," Beka said, "maybe it's something I'd like." She reached for the glass.

"Beka," Dylan said, alarmed, "I wouldn't—"

She had the glass, however, and there was no stopping her. Beka Valentine, fearless guardian of the universe, was going to check this out. She took a sip.

Beka Valentine, fearless guardian of the universe, managed to stop herself from spitting the juice onto Dylan's maroon shirt. It was a close call.

"Oh, God," she spluttered, her face screwed up and reddening. She put the back of her free hand to her mouth and gave Dylan a wide-eyed helpless look. "This stuff is supposed to *help* you?"

"That's what she says," Dylan replied nonchalantly. "She's my doctor, you know."

"Oh, right," Beka said hoarsely. "*Always* trust doctors, sure, yep." She swung around, holding the glass away from her, frowning at Trance. "Trance, what the hell is—"

Suddenly Harper darted by them. Just as suddenly he darted back, plucked the glass from Beka's hand, and said, "Thanks, Boss, cool!"

"—this stuff," Beka finished weakly, turning to watch Harper with a mixture of horror and fascination—exactly what Dylan was feeling right now. He had a vision of his engineer taking up residence in a bathroom for the next two days.

"Harper—" Dylan started.

Harper wasn't even halfway across Command before he'd tilted back his head, upended the glass, and swallowed the entire contents in one gulp.

"Oh, no," Beka said.

Harper doubled back and put the glass back in Beka's hand. "That's some great stuff, what a *rush*!" He turned around yet again and resumed his original course.

Beka and Dylan looked down at the empty glass, then up at each other, then over at Trance, who grinned and gave them a little wave. Beka and Dylan looked back at each other. Quietly Beka said, "I hate it when she does that sort of stuff."

"If it works," Dylan said, "I'm all for it. Even Harper can't keep going forever."

"Ladies and gentlemen, boys and girls," Harper suddenly announced, whirling around and flinging the stack of flexis into the air, "all-around boy wonder and heroic stud of the century Seamus Zelazny Harper has done it again! No, not inflated my ego to monstrous proportions, being the modest guy that I am. I've tunneled Andromeda out from under the debris." He turned to the main flatscreen. "Babe, come on up and show your gorgeous face!"

The screen flickered to life, displaying Andromeda's head and shoulders. She looked down at them, then smiled. "It's good to be back, even in this state."

"And we also have—*ta-da*—holo-babe Rommie!" The hologram

flickered into life, looking very confused, glancing around at the crew. "I was going to do the swimsuit edition," Harper added, attempting to be nonchalant, "but I figured now wasn't the time for that."

"Oh," said holo-Rommie. "I think I might have liked that." She looked down at herself. "Some other time, I guess. I seem to have some corrupted data in here." She turned to look at Harper. "Good job, Mr. Harper."

Holo-Rommie flickered out.

Andromeda squinted slightly and looked in Harper's direction. "I'm working on the corrupted data side of things. I *still* have a headache."

"Probably needs a hardware fix," Harper said absently, already focusing on something else. He tapped rapidly at some keys. "Wait-asec. That should help."

Andromeda gave a rapid shake of her head, as though clearing out morning cobwebs. Her hair promptly turned several shades of gold.

"Oh," Rommie said, watching this unexpected adjustment.

Holo-Rommie reappeared, looking at the screen. She also said, "Oh." Then she too shook her head. Her hair turned shining gold.

All heads turned to Rommie, who gave them a bemused smile. "I think I prefer my present look," she said.

"Well," said Andromeda, "at least my headache's gone. We can fix the image issue later."

"If we want to," said holo-Rommie.

"I think *you* need to go and read a trashy fleximag until Harper gets you fixed," Andromeda said sternly. "I'm a warship, not a fashion model."

"Hey!" holo-Rommie said. "Anyway, how'd you know about the fleximags?"

"Lucky guess," Rommie said, folding her arms and giving Harper a dirty look.

"Oh."

Holo-Rommie vanished.

"Okay," Harper said, spreading his arms and making an effort not to look horribly embarrassed, "maybe I was a little *too* quick on the draw with holo-Rommie." He looked at Rommie and swallowed, hard. "Hey, I only get 'em for the articles."

"She's a total space cadet," Beka said, glaring at him, "and I don't mean that in a nice way, either."

"Oh," Harper said. "Yeah, I guess she's coming across that way. Could be worse, though."

"Could it?" Dylan asked.

Beka started to cut Harper off, but it was too late. "There was this pink-haired chick a while before we ran into you guys."

"Haruko," Beka said sourly. "We had her as a passenger. Picked her up at Mamimi Drift."

"Yeah," Harper said with a lopsided grin. "I thought she was really into me—"

"Desperation speaking of course," Beka said.

"*Anyway*, that was until she whacked me in the head with a guitar and started yapping about robots." Harper rubbed his forehead absently. "Trance patched me up."

"She paid good money," Beka said defensively. "We didn't find out until later that nobody else would take her, and for lots of good reasons, too."

"I'll keep this in mind if we encounter any pink-haired women carrying guitars," Dylan said patiently.

"She really was kinda cute, though," Harper said.

"Desperation," Beka said, making a face.

"Hey!" Harper objected.

"Okay, people," Dylan said, wanting to cut the exchange off and get down to business, "we need a game plan here."

"I've got an idea," Harper said.

"Mr. Harper?"

"Beka takes the *Maru* out, hits the nearest debris field, and brings back a chunk of rock for the *Andromeda* to work on."

"I'd need to find an asteroid the *Maru* can carry," Beka said, looking at Harper. She glanced at Dylan. "I'm not too worried about mass in normal space—the AG field will handle that. It's in Slipstream that I'm worried about."

"Break it up," Harper said. "You could load the cargo pod."

"That'll take too long," Beka said.

"Not if you give it a little bit of momentum first," Dylan said. "Objects in motion tend to stay in motion, right? Break it up on the right vector and the work gets done for you."

Beka shook her head. "Not a good call. First, some of that stuff could punch through the pod. Second, even if I made that work, the pod's only going to carry a couple of hundred tons of rock that way."

"That's barely enough raw material to patch up a couple of holes," Rommie said, "and that's only if I can find the right elements. We don't have the time for multiple trips, and the risk versus benefit analysis is not good."

"So," Dylan said heavily, "we'd better figure out where Beka's going and how long it's going to take—"

"I don't think she needs to go anywhere," Andromeda interrupted.

Everyone turned to look at the flatscreen, where Andromeda was looking at them. Beka blinked, obviously surprised. "I don't?"

"Dylan has to go," Andromeda said. Beka and Dylan looked at each other, then back at Andromeda. "I've been searching my astro-navigation databases, and I've found something interesting. It's called Waystation and we're practically in the neighborhood."

Thirty minutes later the entire crew, including Pogue and Wright, were gathered in one of the briefing rooms. Flatscreens were alive with images, including Andromeda's head and shoulders.

"When Slipstream theory was first worked out," Andromeda said, "and practical experiments began, nobody had any idea how long a Slipstream field could be maintained, or how long a ship could stay in Slipstream."

"It took hundreds of years to get any sort of real understanding," Dylan said admiringly. "Every jump was a risk."

"In the first century of Slipstream travel," Andromeda said, "more than two hundred vessels were lost—out of two hundred and twenty."

"The point being that these people were pioneers," Dylan said. "Pioneers push the limits, whether it's settlers looking for new lands, someone trying to break a speed record, or the first-generation ships. In this case they were pioneers over the speed of light."

"Is this the High Guard history lecture, then?" Tyr drawled.

"Consider it the setup, Tyr," Andromeda said.

"Basically," Beka said, "they found out they could get from point A to point B faster than light."

"Wasn't that easy," Harper said.

"Harper's right," Andromeda said. She pointed toward one of the flatscreens and it obligingly lit up with an image of the Andromeda galaxy, overlaid by a schematic. The image rotated, showing the twin black holes at the center of the galaxy. Short lines were drawn on the image. "Slipstream jumps were generally very short, and exploration was confined to a relatively small area."

"However," Dylan said, leaning forward and resting his elbows on the table, "the itch to explore more and go farther out each time never goes away. Someone always wants to go off the map."

Andromeda gestured again. A number of bright red points appeared on the map. Lines connected to them, and new lines threaded out from them. "As exploration moved farther out, supply lines were created. Depots were built on or in orbit around a number of planets scattered across the Andromeda galaxy. These stations expanded the frontier, allowing much of the galaxy to be mapped, explored, and exploited."

"And then," Dylan said, "they hit the rim. Next stop, the outer dark."

"Naturally," Beka said, "they'd gotten that far, so they didn't want to stop."

Tyr was inspecting his fingernails, looking bored.

"They were about to go right off the map," Dylan said.

"Bunny-hopping to the next galaxy over," Harper said. "Except they were doing bigger hops."

"The explorers didn't confine themselves to a single direction," Andromeda said. She gestured and the galactic image rotated, blue lines branching from it in a number of directions. "They also didn't leave without preparation."

This time the scattering of dots was yellow, some on the rim, some toward the upper and lower edges of the galactic center.

"This was the Long Jump," Dylan said, looking in turn at the screen, and then at his crew. "The only galaxies explorers ever returned from were the Milky Way and Triangulum, which is why efforts eventually focused on them."

"The supply stations on the rim were a necessity," Andromeda said. "Ships returning from missions usually returned with supplies and fuel exhausted, often damaged. Reaching anywhere beyond a supply station would be impossible."

"As the millennia passed," Dylan said, "life ceased to be about frontiers and exploration and started to be about the Systems Commonwealth. Slipstream travel had become an uneventful reality."

"So," Andromeda said, gesturing again, "the supply stations were taken over by the High Guard and converted into High Guard bases." Images flashed onto the screens now, both still and moving, showing a series of High Guard bases. "Over time a number of these bases were closed or automated. A few of the rim bases were closed down entirely." Several images flashed up onto the screens and remained there.

"Waystation?" Beka asked. "Just a guess."

"Waystation," Andromeda said.

"Waystation was automated in CY 9206," Rommie said. "It was considered a good idea to have at least some stations in operation on the rim. Eventually, however, a combination of underuse and adverse conditions led to it being scheduled for decommissioning. It would have been shut down approximately two years after the Commonwealth fell."

"It looks quite inhospitable," Tyr said.

"It is," Andromeda said. "However, the base was designed to cope with the environment. The complex lies mostly underground; the surface portion is to allow entrance and exit. Provided that everything works as it should, the *Eureka Maru* can be flown directly into the base."

"How can we be certain that anything of use is to be found there?" Tyr said. "We all know how many High Guard bases were raided or destroyed after the Fall."

"Risk versus benefit," Rommie said. "Not to mention the difficulty factor. Waystation was to be closed because nobody ever came out this way—there are no inhabited planets in this region and there are more easily exploitable resources in far more accessible locations."

"Waystation," Andromeda added, "was exactly that—the last stop for the outbound explorers and the first stop for the inbound. I'm really not sure why it was kept active for this amount of time."

"Nostalgia," said Tyr.

"For a place *that* frozen?" Beka said. "I think some bureaucrat managed to lose the paperwork a couple of thousand years back."

Dylan was quiet, looking at the images on the screens. There seemed to be nothing but ice, with no evidence of life anywhere. The High Guard base consisted of a surface dome, under which the main complex lay—five chambers, three levels each, extending for a kilometer out from a central access area. Each level was ten meters deep. If worst came to worst, Dylan thought, and there was nothing there but the base, they could try cutting up whatever was left and bringing it back to the *Andromeda Ascendant* before going to Plan B.

"This is the planet I saw," Trance said. The others looked blankly at her. "It was a while back."

"Anything to say about it, Trance?" Dylan asked her.

Trance looked at the flatscreens for a few moments, then shook her head. "Nothing."

"I've got somethin'," Harper said loudly, staring at the screens. "Frostbite in my shorts just lookin' at this freakin' place. Good thing I wasn't countin' on snowboarding practice here. You guys have fun, huh? I'll be here on the nice warm *Andromeda Ascendant*—" His rush of words, which had been emerging a little high-pitched because of his suddenly obvious nervousness, rattled to a stop. Dylan was gazing evenly at him, half smiling. As the truth dawned on Harper he began to look horrified. "No. No no no. *Ohhhhh* no! No!" Wide-eyed, he looked around at the people seated around the table, looking for help. "No. I can't go anywhere I'm needed here what if something happens besides I gotta fix holo-Rommie and there's the engines Boss what if—"

"Shut up, boy," Tyr said in an affable tone that was nevertheless loud enough to cut right into Harper's unpunctuated and breathless spray of words. The engineer stopped talking instantly, staring at Tyr as though the Nietzschean had shot his cat. "Mr. Harper," Tyr went on, less affably, "you are without question a fine engineer. I also know full well that while you hardly have the heart of a lion, as they say, you are far from being a coward. You are demeaning yourself with this hideous display." He leaned forward, glaring. "You are also annoying me."

Harper flinched back. "Yeah, I got it, I really won't like you when you're annoyed."

Beka looked around at Tyr. "'Grow up, Harper' would have been shorter."

"Or 'Shut up, Harper,'" Trance said, smiling. "That was our favorite on the *Maru*."

Tyr looked evenly from one to the other and said, "I'm a Nietzschean," as though that explained everything—which it very probably did.

"Well, Mr. Harper," Dylan said, starting to get up, "it looks like some of us are getting an early winter vacation."

"Vacation," Harper said, his voice hollow. He turned his head to stare at the screens. "Vacation."

Rommie smiled at him as she got up. "Looks like great skiing weather to me."

Harper couldn't even muster a reply.

One of the more pleasant things about having a gigantic starship occupied by only a handful of crew was that no matter what recreational activity any of them might engage in, there was always bound to be room or equipment available for it.

In some instances, of course, the lack of personnel could be a problem—as with Dylan's preoccupation with basketball. Rommie could, of course, be counted on to obediently participate. Harper might have been interested had there been hoverboards, skateboards, rollerblades, or seminaked women (or any combination of those) involved, but as it was a mere unassisted game of skill and stamina he gave it a pass. Beka had tried it three times, and on the third had gotten so exasperated that she shot the ball. Trance had run rings around

Dylan and then announced that she probably wasn't going to be very good at the game.

Which left Tyr . . . and Tyr's flagrant disregard for the rules of the game when it was a matter of advantage. The memory of surprising Dylan and knocking him flat never failed to make Tyr grin. Dylan had learned instantly from that encounter, and while their play remained friendly it also remained a battle of both wits and force.

Tyr had changed during his time with Dylan. His arrogance, the attitude of "mine by right or conquest," had been replaced. Dylan had been his challenge, and to meet it he had made a fundamental change: he had made himself willing to learn from Dylan and from others he might never have considered equals. In doing so, he had taken note of his own flaws, and the failures of the prides.

He had been a dangerous man the day he met Dylan. He was infinitely more dangerous now.

Jogging toward the gym, where he had his own personal corner set up, Tyr shook his head, trying to clear the overly grandiose thoughts. Right now, he reminded himself, he was no threat to anybody—

"Nietzschean!"

He was at a junction, just about to turn, when the shout came. Startled, he turned to his left. Trance's voice—

Without being conscious of his reaction, he was diving into the adjoining corridor and drawing his Gauss pistol. He rolled and came up, his back against the corridor wall as he listened for sounds of movement.

Trance's voice, but she had been shouting angrily. The way she had pronounced "Nietzschean" had given it the sound of an intended racial slur.

Not our Trance Gemini, then. "Andromeda," he whispered as he edged toward the flatscreen at the junction, "do *not* speak. Monitor this area, and get Dylan and Trance down here. And be ready to assist me. Acknowledge."

The flatscreen had lit as he was talking. Andromeda nodded to acknowledge what he had said.

He stilled his breathing, listening. There was a cautious footstep. Another.

On the flatscreen, Andromeda made a chopping gesture with two fingers toward her left shoulder, then downward—right hand side of the corridor. A slight clockwise gesture—slow forward movement. Then a thumb and forefinger gesture—she has a gun.

"Nietzschean," the newest Trance said, sounding far more reasonable now, "I am willing to accept your surrender."

Andromeda gestured again, but Tyr had already placed the position of this latest version of Trance. He stepped into the junction, turned to his right, and took a quick, long step. The muzzle of his Gauss pistol hit the new Trance squarely in the middle of her chest, pushing her back against the corridor wall. With his left hand he pinned her gun hand against the wall.

"You're signing your death warrant," Trance hissed, glaring at him.

He looked her over, curious. In her looks she seemed more like the purple version of Trance than the gold one, but her skin shaded almost to an azure tone. Burnished gold hair had been carefully arranged, military fashion. The most surprising thing, however, was her clothes—at first he thought she was wearing an adaptation of a High Guard uniform. With a start, he realized it wasn't an adaptation at all.

Trance, a military officer? The thought actually shocked him.

"Listen to me," he said urgently, emphasizing the order by pressing the pistol into her chest. He was in unknown territory here—he doubted that he could present enough of a threat to be effective. Still, he was committed now. "You are not where you think you are."

She stared at him. "I listen to nothing that comes out of the mouth of a *filthy lying Nietzschean!*"

Terrible anger swelled up in him then, and in a flash he had smashed the barrel of the Gauss gun across her face, snapping her head back. He jammed the muzzle back into her chest again, harder this time. She gave no indication that she was feeling pain.

"I know I can't kill you," he growled, staring into her eyes. "I doubt I can hurt you. I do know, however, that a smart bullet to the chest will make things uncomfortable for you for a little while." He took a deep breath. "You are not where you think you are, and I am not who you think I am. Look at my wrists, girl!"

Her eyes shifted as she looked at his left wrist, and then his right. "No . . . no bone blades?"

"That's right," he said. "If you seek Tyr Anasazi, then I am not the incarnation you are hunting."

"It's a lie," Trance mumbled, "a lie."

A flatscreen lit up behind Tyr. "He isn't lying."

Trance's head jerked up. "Andromeda?"

"You seem surprised."

"You were . . . they erased you. . . ." Trance's eyes flicked from Andromeda to Tyr. "You Nietzscheans have been destroying and despoiling the Known Worlds Confederation for centuries. We're finally eradicating you bastards."

Tyr raised his eyebrows. "I do believe that's the first time I've heard that word issue from your mouth, Trance."

"That you've—"

"Tyr is a member of my crew, Trance," Andromeda said gently.

"He can't—no." Trance was staring at him, horrified. "You and your crew attacked us and took over the ship. Andromeda was erased and Captain Valentine murdered."

"And you've been taking the ship back," Tyr said.

"Killing Nietzschean scum all the way," Trance snarled.

Running footsteps. Dylan, force lance out, arriving at a run. Tyr, Trance, and Andromeda looked toward him.

"All heads turn as the Hunt goes by," Dylan quipped, seeing their looks. He stopped in the junction. "Trance, Tyr's speaking the truth, and if you were talking about Captain Rebecca Valentine, ours is alive and well and up on *our* Command Deck. Oh, and I'm Captain Dylan Hunt, commodore of the new Systems Commonwealth High Guard fleet. The old Commonwealth fell down and broke three centuries ago."

Trance was silent.

"Hello," said a familiar voice from just behind Dylan. The customary golden Trance stepped forward. She smiled. "I'm one of the major reasons everyone knows you're in the wrong place."

"It's an illusion!" the other Trance screamed suddenly. She wrenched her gun hand free of Tyr's grip and tried to knee him in the groin. Adroitly he stepped back and shot her three times in the chest, the charges in the smart bullets sending out a shower of sparks.

"Ow!" their Trance said, wincing as her counterpart fell back against the corridor wall and slid down.

Keeping a watchful eye on the apparently dead woman, Tyr picked up her Gauss pistol and hurled it down the corridor away from them. Stepping back, he said, "I'm assuming that when she returns to where she belongs, so will her weapon."

"Probably," Trance said. She stepped closer to the body slumped against the wall and crouched down. "She's so *different*. So angry."

"Sounds like she has cause," Dylan said. He hadn't holstered his force lance yet.

"It does leave me uncomfortable to discover that I have a counterpart who is apparently considered to be no more than an animal," Tyr said. "She's stirring."

"Don't try to get up," Trance said to her as she tried to get to her feet. "Tyr's likely to shoot you again."

"I don't . . . I don't understand," the other woman said.

"You're in the wrong timeline," Trance said. "I don't know why, but you're not the first. Here." She grasped her counterpart's left hand with her right.

Tyr wasn't sure what was happening. A ripple of golden light appeared to wash over both of them and both appeared to suddenly focus on a distant point.

Trance released her counterpart's hand. The other woman stared at her for a moment, then said, "We were hunting down the last of the Nietzscheans. I did feel something, but the AG was damaged in the battle. I had no idea . . ."

"Now you do," Tyr said brusquely. "Be polite from now on and I will refrain from shooting you."

"Alright," the second Trance said.

Tyr jogged up the corridor and retrieved her weapon, throwing it to her. "Put it away. I'm told that it will return with you. You might well need it immediately."

She seemed momentarily hesitant to holster the pistol. Dylan's force lance lifted slightly, aimed just to one side of her. Jamming the Gauss pistol into its holster, she nodded toward Dylan's hand. "Interesting weapon. Unorthodox design."

"Standard High Guard side arm issue for millennia," Andromeda said. "Another indicator."

"So," Dylan said, "you don't have any idea why this is happening, either."

The other Trance looked at him for a moment, then shook her head. "Aside from the recent battles, things have been very quiet."

Dylan nodded, then looked at their Trance. "I'd say I didn't like the way this adds up, Trance—"

"But none of it adds up," she said hurriedly. "I know. It's making me crazy too."

The other Trance sighed, prodding unhappily at the burned holes in her uniform. "Well, that's it for this tunic." She looked up at Tyr. "The quartermaster'll be furious."

"Would you like me to write you an explanatory note?" Tyr asked, seeming for all the world as though the concept of a ship's quartermaster baffled him. Wondering if they were going to have to stand in this corridor for the rest of the day, Tyr looked at the golden Trance. "Is there any obvious time limit on these phenomena?"

Trance shook her head. "As short as a few seconds to as long as a few hours when I got thrown forward in time."

Tyr looked back at the other Trance, weighing his options. "Very well. I have a fitness regimen to observe, one that *you* interrupted my progress toward. I am going to continue on my way now." He paused, glowering at her. "You will not give me reason to return."

She glared back at him, but said nothing.

Tyr nodded at Dylan and Trance. "Dylan, Trance?"

Dylan nodded back. "We can take it from here. Enjoy the gym."

Tyr resumed his jogging pace along the corridor, grinning as he heard Andromeda ask Dylan, "By the way, Captain, when did you say you were resuming your full exercise schedule?"

"Nag," Dylan muttered under his breath. Both Trances grinned as Andromeda frowned.

"Captain, there is nothing wrong with my auditory capabilities," Andromeda said stuffily. "I heard that."

"I've got more on my mind than exercise right now," Dylan snapped, regretting his tone immediately. He put his fingers to his temples as his head throbbed. "Damn it. The next time we go by Kantar, remind me to drop a Nova Bomb on the bastards."

He regretted saying that, too.

Trance's counterpart looked at her and said, "That doesn't sound good."

"It isn't," Dylan answered before Trance could say anything. His head throbbed again.

"We were in a battle recently," Andromeda said. "Unfortunately, rather than being boarded by anything we could hunt down, my hull was sprayed with devices that affects crew psychology."

"I turn into an evil-tempered martinet if I don't watch it," Dylan said.

"Isn't there something you can do?" the second Trance asked him.

"We have a skeleton crew," Dylan said, "and all of our resources are tied up in trying to keep the *Andromeda* together."

"Oh."

Trance stepped over to Dylan, her hypospray in hand. She gave him a shot, and the throbbing in his head went away, replaced by a dull ache and a degree of fuzziness. He was looking forward to spending some time away from the Kantarian devices.

"I think we'd better get up to Command," he said. He gestured at the two Trances. "Lead the way."

With a look at each other, they did. Dylan didn't see any reason to worry about their unexpected visitor now—whatever Trance had done, it had obviously reset her counterpart's perspective.

They soon reached Command, where Harper was making a last-minute attempt to bring the holographic version of Rommie up to something approaching specification. She was gradually improving in terms of comprehensibility, but she had become impressively vain for some reason. The parade of costume changes and virtual makeovers had been amusing for about five minutes, and even Harper had quickly grown bored.

The new Trance looked around Command, apparently fascinated. "This looks nothing like our bridge. We have our pilot station . . . right . . . there."

She was staring at Harper.

Beka picked up on this immediately. Cheerfully she said, "That's just Seamus, our pet monkey."

"Hey!" Harper said, looking up. "That's pet *supergenius* monkey. Make that pet supergenius monkey popsicle. And, by the way, Dylan, old pal o' mine, there's still time to reconsider risking your biggest asset."

"No way out, Harper," Dylan said. "I need you."

"Why is it that everybody who says that to me needs me for everything except romance and pleasure?" Harper complained. "Oh, yeah, hi, Trance. Hi, Trance." He frowned. "Oh, wait . . . oh, no."

"Commander Harper," the new Trance said. She turned her head and looked at Beka. "And Captain Valentine."

"*Commander?*" Harper said in disbelief. "As in spit, polish, and black leather high-tops?"

The new Trance stepped toward him. "Commander Seamus Zelazny Harper, master engineer." She looked at him sadly. "It was against protocol, but we had a relationship. We always looked out for each other, always were there for each other when something needed to be done."

Harper started to say something, then stopped, looking strangely at her. "Waitasec, babe, that sounds awfully past tense to me."

"Your counterpart was killed six months ago," she said softly. "During a battle. There was nothing anyone could do. I miss him terribly. I'll miss Rebecca almost as much."

"Son of a bitch," Harper said softly, looking shocked.

"Well," Beka said, in the tone of someone trying to brighten up a graveyard full of mourners, "neither of us is past tense here."

"Feelings are feelings," Trance said glumly.

"Got it," Beka said, "party hats away, champagne back in the fridge."

"Sorry," the other Trance said.

There was an awkward silence.

Suddenly holo-Rommie flickered to life. She was wearing an ornate gown, a feather boa, and a huge floppy hat with a gigantic plume sticking out of it. "I think we're finally getting the data issues under control," she said. "I also believe that my characterization problems are finally getting ironed out."

Beka shook her head, sighing. "Not with that hat, they aren't."

The alternate Trance vanished without preamble a little over an hour later, with only a tiny snapping sound marking her passage—air filling the vacuum she left behind.

Harper had continued working on holo-Rommie, apparently in the hope that his increasing success would persuade Dylan that his resident genius was better off remaining aboard the *Andromeda Ascendant*. Dylan listened politely to Harper's protestations . . . and ignored them completely. No one else came to Harper's aid, either.

On the bright side, holo-Rommie seemed to be coherent, finally, and stable—except for the fact that she now had the blue-haired look that the android Rommie had abandoned several months ago. However, given that she seemed content to remain with a single look for more than five minutes, no one was willing to tinker further.

That left Harper nowhere to go with his protests. Instead, he settled for a sullenly irritable attitude as final departure preparations were made. To his relief, part of those preparations involved checking out the *Eureka Maru* from stem to stern, making sure that the to-specification parts were in good order and that his many lash-ups weren't going to fail in the middle of a Slipstream jump.

Once he had pronounced the battered salvage ship and its cargo pod free of anything immediately life-threatening, Dylan and Rommie brought equipment aboard, loading it into the forward storage area.

Harper stared as boxes were stacked and outfits hung up. "Wait-asec, I thought we were gonna fly straight in, Boss. What's *that* for?"

Dylan hung up another arctic outfit. "We won't know until we get there if we can do that. If we have to land outside, it's likely to be bad."

"I keep hearing that," Harper said, his face screwing up. "Why d'you think I don't want to go? I'm nuts, but I'm not crazy."

Dylan picked up another outfit. This one was made of a rich black material, with white piping. Magnetic clasps were arrayed in a row down the left side of the tunic.

"Uh, Dylan? You said you weren't gonna wear that anymore," Harper said, nodding at the uniform as Dylan hung it up.

"That's what I was planning," Dylan said. He smoothed the material.

"It's a measure for our security and safety," Rommie said. "There is a mesh woven into the material, consisting of microcircuitry. High Guard installations recognize the signals as part of a security protocol."

"We might be able to get away without it," Dylan said, "but it's always possible that this will be the only thing that the security system recognizes as a command presence on-site."

"Being shot full of holes can really ruin a person's day," Rommie said with a rueful look. "Something I know all too well, I'm afraid."

"Right," Harper said weakly. "So, okay, seeing as you don't need me any—"

"Mr. Harper," Tyr said, actually sounding cheerful. He had come up quietly behind Harper. The engineer jumped, half turning. "One more complaint, and I will make certain that you make the journey inside the cargo pod."

"Right," Harper said. He turned to Dylan and Rommie. "You got a spare uniform for a scared supergenius?"

Dylan smiled. "Rommie, see what you can do for the man."

"On my way," Rommie said with a beatific smile at Harper, who seemed taken aback by this willingness to hand him a High Guard uniform.

Tyr raised his eyebrows. "Seamus Harper wearing a uniform? I find myself at a loss for words."

"Funny," Harper said, glaring at him. "You sound like you're still talking."

"Pure momentum," Tyr said.

"Mr. Harper wants to look the part," Dylan said. "I'll have him polishing his boots yet."

"Yeah, right," Harper said with a snort.

"Mr. Wright is on his way," Tyr said. "I've issued him a personal weapon. It might be needless, but stepping unprepared into a possibly insecure situation is not something I recommend."

"Yeah," Harper said. "You tend to go with the philosophy of 'nuke 'em 'til they glow in the dark and then shoot at them from orbit.' "

Tyr smiled at him. "I see I have actually taught you something."

Harper gave him a disgusted look and walked away, toward the aft end of the ship.

"We should be back inside two weeks," Dylan said. "If we aren't, there's a problem, probably a bad one. I'll leave it up to you and Beka whether you come and look for us, or head for known territory."

"We could do both," Tyr said. "The good Captain Valentine is hardly likely to give up her ship without a fight."

"Good point," Dylan said. "Either way, someone will need to get to the Commonwealth and get a retrieval mission started."

"You seem fatalistic," Tyr said.

"Realistic," Dylan said. "I just don't have a choice in this."

"Understood," Tyr said.

Rommie returned, carrying a uniform on a hanger. "This should fit Mr. Harper quite nicely, and I do believe he'll look quite handsome in it." She glanced around. "Well. I flatter him for a change, and he's hiding in the back of the ship. Hmph."

She hung the uniform next to Dylan's.

Micah Wright was the next to arrive, a force lance holstered at his hip. He made to remove it, but Dylan held up a hand. "Keep it with you at all times. Standard protocol."

"Yes, sir," Wright said, forgetting himself and saluting. "Err, sorry, Captain."

"We'll get that discipline trained out of you yet," Rommie said. She glanced at Dylan. "Do you think Mr. Harper can provide a course in remedial slovenliness?"

"This," Tyr announced gravely, "is more than I can handle. I'll bid you farewell, then, and a swift and safe journey. I've no wish to travel for weeks in a Slipfighter, or even one of the transports."

Tyr left.

"Mr. Wright seems to have a thing about proper discipline," Dylan said.

"I think so," Rommie said. "Who's doing the driving, you or Harper?"

"I'll take the first leg," Dylan said. "After that I don't see any reason why all four of us can't take turns."

"We can start at any time," Rommie said. "Everything we need is aboard."

"Then we'd better get going," Dylan said. He pressed the side of his neck. "Mr. Harper, we're ready to go. Time to get up front. Oh, and your uniform is here."

"Wow," Harper replied unenthusiastically.

Rommie and Wright followed Dylan through the ship to the cluttered cockpit. Dylan sat down in the big, worn captain's chair, strapping himself in. Rommie took the astronavigation station. Harper arrived a few moments later, to take his place at the forward engineering station.

Dylan quickly ran through the preflight checklist, then turned to Harper and said, "Mr. Harper, are we good to go?"

"Except for me having to come along," Harper said, "yeah, we're good to go."

Dylan flipped switches, tapped buttons, and brought main power up, adjusting the AG field to reduce the effective mass of the *Maru* to a few grams.

He activated the subdermal communicator again, and said, "*Andromeda Ascendant*, this is the *Eureka Maru*. We are good to go."

"Bon voyage," Beka said. "Take care of my ship, and bring our favorite engineer back toasty warm, not as a popsicle."

"I'll do my best," Dylan said.

"*Eureka Maru*, you are cleared to depart," Beka said formally.

"Good luck, Captain," Andromeda broke in.

"Thank you, Andromeda." Dylan activated thrusters, lifting the

Maru from the docking bay deck. Carefully, he eased the ship into forward motion. "We are on our way."

"Fasten your seat belts, make sure your tray table and seat back are in the upright position," Harper said, "and keep all luggage stored in the overhead bins or under the seat in front of you." He frowned. "Hey, do we get in-flight flexis and peanuts or even a movie on this trip?"

They were out of the docking bay now. Dylan started to open the throttle, increasing the *Maru*'s velocity. "I don't know about the peanuts, Mr. Harper, but I'm sure you know where to find the flexis and the movies on this ship."

"Oh," Harper said, looking as though this idea was coming as a surprise to him. "Yeah. I probably do."

Wright lifted a flexi. "Already found one down here."

Harper tilted his head to look, started to grin, noticed Rommie looking at him, and said, "Oh, yeah, there's some great . . . articles . . . in there."

"I don't believe that's the term they use in the anatomy books, Mr. Harper," Rommie said primly.

Wright chuckled and tossed the flexi to Harper, who hurriedly put it away.

"One minute to the nearest Slip point," Rommie said.

"I think we can shorten that time a little," Dylan said, opening the throttles all the way. The *Maru* surged forward as he activated the Slipstream drive system. "Let's bring it."

The Slipstream drive came to life and the oscillating white and blue shape of a portal burst into life ahead of them. The *Eureka Maru* drove straight into the center of it and vanished from normal space.

TEN • FROST AND FIRE

You know what's wrong with winter sports?
Nobody ever does them in a tropical climate.

> —CAPTAIN IAN QUINN, SHIPMASTER OF
> THE FREE TRADE ALLIANCE FRIGATE
> *STEFFI37,* 222 AFC

"Exiting Slipstream *now*," Wright said, and the coruscating superstring universe visible through the cockpit windows gave way to a blaze of light and the star-studded black of normal space. Wright shut down the Slipstream controls and turned his attention to piloting in normal space. "Vectoring to new course . . . new course locked in, velocity is fifteen PSL and holding."

"We should make orbit within twenty minutes, Captain," Rommie announced, looking up from her instruments.

"Thank you, Rommie," Dylan said, getting up and moving forward to look through the cockpit windows. "And thank you, Mr. Wright, good work."

"Thank you, sir," Wright said. "She looks like hell, but she handles like a dream."

"Courtesy of your resident High Guard-flavored supergenius-popsicle-to-be," Harper said sourly.

"But you'll look *so* attractive when the inevitable end comes, Harper," Rommie said, giving him a big smile and a wide-eyed innocent look. "Just think—most people have to pay to be put into cryonic storage."

"Thanks so much," Harper said. "I feel so much better now."

"You're welcome," Rommie said, turning back to the astronavigation station.

"Would you like to take over, Captain?" Wright said, gesturing at the piloting station.

"Apple polisher," Harper muttered, not quite under his breath.

Wright stared at him. "Y'know, I have to wonder why Pogue hasn't whacked you with a spanner yet."

"She's female," Rommie said. "Different rules apply."

"Hey!" Harper snapped. "She does good work."

"And different rules apply," Rommie repeated.

"*Anyway,*" Dylan said in his best I'm-in-command-so-shut-up tone of voice, "the center seat remains yours for now, Mr. Wright. We'll see who does what when we make orbit."

"Which we could do if we were going faster," Harper said. "I'm gonna see if we have a couple of oars aboard so I can help row."

"Point to Mr. Harper," Dylan said. He gestured vaguely toward the cockpit window. "Pick up her heels a bit."

"Aye, Captain," Wright said, his fingers playing over the controls. "Velocity increasing to twenty PSL . . . and holding."

"I'm going back," Harper said, jerking a thumb toward the aft end of the ship. He got up and left.

After a few moments, Dylan followed him. As it turned out, Harper hadn't gone far. He was in the storage area where their gear had been stowed, looking at the uniform that Rommie had brought for him.

"Alright," Dylan said, startling Harper, "I'm going to make a guess that it isn't just Waystation that's on your mind."

Harper was silent, his left hand on the tunic. Dylan was beginning to think that Harper was going to be stubborn and refuse to answer when the engineer bowed his head for a moment and said, "Yeah, it isn't just that." He looked around at Dylan, his expression forlorn.

"That other Trance . . . this . . . I mean, I hear it from *her* that in some other universe I'm a freakin' officer, not just some smart guy who got lucky. All the way up to commander, pretty freakin' good for a guy my age, right?" He looked back at the uniform again. "Except that other me's dead, and that feels *weird*. Freaky. Then there's the Trance in the machine shop." He looked back at Dylan. "It's like the universe is tryin' to get a balance or something. Like making a circuit work, trying different things until it clicks."

"And in the here and now?" Dylan asked, leaning back against the bulkhead.

"In the here and now . . ." Harper was silent for a moment, thinking. "In the here and now I think it clicked, I think it's right. It's like we were best friends right from the start, and that's exactly how it's meant to be."

"And you don't want anything more than this?" Dylan said.

"From Trance?" Harper said. "Hell, no. That's what made it so freaky." He looked at the uniform again. "Besides, one me is confusing enough. Thinking about other Seamus Harpers in other realities is quick head-explodey time. I mean, name, rank, serial number . . . wearing a uniform like this every day . . . maybe coming from an Earth that wasn't overrun by Magog and Nietzscheans . . ."

He turned away from the uniform.

"I just try to ignore it," Dylan said. "As far as I'm concerned, there's here, there's now, there's this reality, and everything else is a dream."

"Or a nightmare," Harper said.

"Sometimes." Dylan was silent for a moment, watching Harper. The younger man seemed haunted, and the less-serious, self-possessed side of him seemed to have vanished completely. "Sometimes you have to accept the nightmares and keep going anyway."

"Or be a gutless wonder like me," Harper muttered, not looking at Dylan.

"As gutless as you were when you helped me hunt down the pieces of the Rimini Vase," Dylan said calmly. Harper looked up, meeting his eyes. "Or as gutless as you were fighting back to back with Tyr when the Magog were overrunning the *Andromeda*. I don't think you have *any* idea just how much respect that won you from Tyr."

"I guess not," Harper mumbled, looking away.

"There's nothing wrong with fear. Fear's good because it can help to keep you alive." Dylan paused for a moment, watching Harper. Harper was focused on him. Good. "What kills people is paralysis. No ability to make choices, no ability to move forward."

"Yeah, well, I get scared enough, and real fast," Harper said.

"As I said, not a bad thing," Dylan replied. "There's no such thing as a man without fear—think about it. What would happen?"

Harper thought about it for a second, then he started to grin. "Live fast, die young, don't stay swimming in the gene pool."

"In one," Dylan said, smiling. "Real courage isn't about charging into the teeth of the enemy with guns blazing. It's about being scared to death and getting the job done anyway."

"Hey, you know how I was acting," Harper said, his grin fading. "Dylan, I didn't wanna come here. Seeing those pictures really gave me the creeps."

"Well," Dylan said, "I didn't want to come here either, but I like the alternative even less. I'm also betting that if we get the *Andromeda* Slip-capable again and we bring her out this way that Beka can find us a faster route home."

"Jeez," Harper said, "that's an idea I like. Gotta catch up on all my fleximags, plus I think my *Anti-Proton Engineer* swimsuit calendar's due."

"Sounds good to me," Dylan said.

"Don't be so sure," Harper said. "The last calendar I got was from the *Slipstream Journal*." He curled his lip. "It was the Centennial All-Than Edition. Oh, man."

"I'd guess the Than liked it," Dylan said. "Come on, let's go forward before Rommie starts thinking we fell out of an airlock."

Trance stood on the darkened Observation Deck, looking out through the huge window and feeling miserable. The *Eureka Maru* had been gone for a little more than two days, but that wasn't the source of her unhappiness.

She was sure now that she was somehow the focal point of a tesseract effect. Space, time, and dimensions were all folding, converging on her, and she was helpless to stop it. She couldn't even place the crux of the effect—it had to have started somewhere, and she was certain that this time it had nothing to do with Harper's machine.

This was something that could eventually tear down dimensional walls, rupturing the barriers that kept everything safe, and she was completely helpless to stop it.

Holo-Rommie flickered into life next to her. The holographic avatar had managed to retain the blue-haired look and showed no signs of pulling a sudden makeover anytime soon.

"This sucks," Trance said, sounding as miserable as she felt.

"No answers?" Rommie said, folding her arms.

"The quantum twists of fate," Trance said, and sighed. "I'm on my own, Rommie." She turned away from the window. "I've got all kinds of answers for all kinds of things, but not for this, not yet."

"You're doing your best to figure it out, right?" Rommie said.

"Yes, I am," Trance said. "But until I do get it figured out maybe I should leave the ship. I can take a Slipfighter or a transport and jump somewhere. Anywhere. If I'm the focus of a tesseract effect, anything could come through."

"It looks to me," Rommie said reasonably, "as though *you're* the only thing coming through. Repeatedly, I admit, but not really dangerous."

"Except for nearly getting Tyr shot."

"Someone wanting to shoot Tyr is hardly a new thing," Rommie said. "Anyway, I don't think you should go anywhere right now. You don't know what could happen if you leave me. It could make things worse."

"Maybe." Trance turned back to the big window, looking out at the stars. "I just wish someone could help. Not even explain it, just turn it off." She bowed her head. "I don't think that's going to happen."

"No," Rommie said, "I don't think it is. You're going to have to ride this one out."

"Captain," Rommie said, "I've got something strange."

Wright had settled the *Eureka Maru* into a head-down parking orbit around Waystation, keeping them three thousand kilometers above the surface. Once contact was achieved with the base, they could go straight down. If they failed to achieve contact, Dylan planned to take the ship down for a quick investigation. He would decide what to do from there.

"Define strange," Dylan said.

"There is another vessel in orbit around Waystation," Rommie said. "It's in an orbit higher than ours."

"That isn't strange," Harper said, "that's scary."

"Let's go take a look," Dylan said. "Give Mr. Wright the details. Mr. Wright, take us in, and try to make it cautious."

"Aye, Captain," Wright said, "taking us in."

He applied power to the thrusters, rolled the ship over, and put them on a heading for the other ship.

"According to sensor data," Rommie said, "what we're approaching is a High Guard *Azure Harmony*–class light transport."

Dylan frowned. "That wasn't a class that was active at the time we were serving, was it?"

"No, it wasn't," Rommie said. "According to my database, the last of the *Azure Harmony* transports was decommissioned in CY 9660, when the design was replaced by the *Golden Dawn* class."

"It could have been left here after it was decommissioned," Wright said.

"Unlikely," Rommie said. "Either the craft would have been scrapped and the matériel recycled, or it would have been parked in one of the High Guard storage locations."

Harper was looking at the scans now. "I'm guessing it's been here awhile, guys. Lots of the kind of micrometeorite pitting you'd get if you stuck a ship in orbit for, oh, a couple or three hundred years. And that's one cold, dead ship."

"We're coming up on her," Wright said. Dylan looked out of the cockpit window to see a distant, gracefully bulbous craft. "I'll bring us alongside."

"Uh, guys," Harper said nervously, "just don't start talking about going aboard, okay? The deader and colder an abandoned ship is, the more likely it's gonna have something nasty aboard that, like, wants to stick its tongue down your throat and leave an egg behind." He turned paler than usual, his face screwing up. "Jeez, I had to remind myself, didn't I?"

"Don't worry, Mr. Harper," Dylan said. He turned his head to look at the engineer, smiling. "Maybe you should stop watching cheap horror vids and stick with Than comedies."

"Those *are* cheap horror vids," Harper said. "Anyway, you didn't grow up on Earth hearing about stuff like the cockroach that ate Cincinnati."

Wright reduced the forward velocity of the *Maru* to a slow drift as they came alongside the transport. A little more than 500 meters long, 200 meters tall, and 250 meters across at its widest point, the ship hinted at practicality beneath its graceful curves. Command and Observation Decks were set forward, while crew quarters occupied the top section of the vessel. The rest consisted of engines and cargo space.

"I'm trying to identify the vessel," Rommie said, "but with all of the systems cold, it's difficult—the transponders are down. It looks almost as though it was put into permanent shutdown." She frowned. "All I'm getting from the dermal encoding is a High Guard ship registry number, but it's showing up as invalid. The dermal encoding should also include a name, but it doesn't."

"Maybe this predates full dermal encoding?" Dylan suggested.

"No," Rommie said. "Full dermal identification protocols were introduced more than fifteen hundred years before this class of vessel entered service."

"No known registry number, and no name," Dylan said, frowning. "And here I'd fooled myself into thinking this was going to be easy. What else?"

"It looks as though the antiproton tanks were emptied, and some of the ship stripped." Rommie turned her chair around. "This isn't just a cold ship, Captain, it's a hulk."

Dylan thought for a moment, then said, "I'd guess we can tow it. Can we haul it through Slipstream? Hook it up with Bucky cables and pull?"

Harper snorted. "Boss, that's what this ship was designed to do. Beka's got a point about flying an asteroid, but the *Maru*'s meant to haul wrecks around. That's why we were the ones pulling you out of the black hole."

Rommie frowned at him. "I am *not* a wreck."

"Didn't say you were, Rom-doll, just sayin' what this ship was meant for."

"'Rom-doll'?" Rommie echoed, an eyebrow raised. "It seems you're feeling a bit better, Mr. Harper."

"Jeez," Harper muttered, "is everyone playing shrink with me today?"

"The only way I shrink things, Harper," Rommie said, "is by blowing them up."

"I'll pass," Harper said. "Anyway, yeah, we can tow it."

"Good," Dylan said. "Rommie, can you dismantle and process whatever's left of this ship?"

"Much more easily than the average asteroid," she said. She turned to look at her station. "There's plenty of mass, and the initial quick analysis does indicate that there's quite a bit that will only need cutting up and recycling."

"Some of it's gonna be unusable," Harper said. "If this baby was in use for hundreds of years and parked for a few more hundred, there's gonna be stress fractures and decomposition issues."

"We can worry about that when we get it back and Andromeda starts taking it apart. Is there anything else showing up that we can use?"

"Deep scanning now, Captain," Rommie said.

"Slipstream drive's gone," Harper said.

"The antiproton drive is still in place," Rommie said, "but at the moment I can't tell if it's functional."

Dylan frowned. "No Slip drive."

"Coulda been towed here," Harper said.

"The question is," Dylan said quietly, "why. It makes sense that the drive would be gone if it was decommissioned, but why pull it out of mothballs and tow it *here* and then abandon it?"

"More curious is the lack of identification," Rommie said.

"Black operations," Wright said. They all turned to him. "Look, everybody knows that organizations of this kind exist—it's not a matter of paranoia. There's always a need for organizations that don't exist. They're funded through back channels, do the really dirty work, and are never acknowledged."

"A good theory," Dylan said, "but that leaves a couple of points. First of all, while the High Guard had secret ops and special ops divisions in the Argosy Service—I served in both before being put onto the command track—the High Guard never had a black operations division. I doubt the Vedrans would have tolerated even the idea of it."

"That's the thing," Wright said. "The point of a black ops division is to remain invisible. If it comes out that there is such an organization, then the information should be made to turn into an urban legend or a running joke."

"I'd tell you, but then I'd have to kill you?" Harper said.

"Right. With an organization the size of the High Guard, a black ops division would just vanish from sight."

Dylan was starting to feel a coldness now in the pit of his stomach, and he seemed to be having difficulty mustering an argument against Wright's suggestion. The new Commonwealth had, for whatever reason, an active black ops division, albeit one that didn't cover its tracks as well as it should have.

"There were rumors and whispers about this among various members of the crews who served aboard me," Rommie said. She turned to look straight at Dylan. "At one point I was programmed to gather statistical data regarding mentions, casual or otherwise, of secret divisions within the High Guard."

"Sounds like somebody was trying to plug a hole or something," Harper said.

"I had no idea about this," Dylan said softly.

"It was before you became captain," Rommie said. "It wasn't a matter of applying information to individual records. The final analysis of my data did indicate a belief in something more than Argosy Service operations. There was no indication that any of the crew members that I monitored had any concrete knowledge of such operations, however."

Dylan was watching through the cockpit window as they drifted past the huge transport. "Friend of a friend of a friend?"

"Fish stories," Wright said. "They always get bigger every time they're passed on. Again, that's how they cover up."

"That's all well and good," Dylan said, "but it doesn't answer the questions." Coming to a decision, he thumped the top of the captain's chair.

"We're going aboard, aren't we?" Harper said unhappily. "You always act like that when you decide something like that."

"*I'm* going aboard," Dylan said. "Rommie's coming with me. You and Mr. Wright will stay on the *Maru*, so there's no need to worry about egg-spitting slime creatures."

"Yeah, right," Harper said.

"There are aft cargo bay doors open," Rommie said, looking at her instruments. "We should be able to enter the main part of the vessel through any of them."

"Is this an advisable course of action, sir?" Wright asked. "I'm with Harper insofar as ghost ships worry me. I'm not worried about malevolent creatures or evil spirits—I'm concerned about the possibility of booby traps."

"Rommie?" Dylan said.

"Absolutely nothing active," she said. "I can't guarantee that the ship is one hundred percent clean, of course, but all of the more obvious traps can be eliminated."

"It's the ones where you get aboard, the thing lights up, somebody says 'gotcha!' and it sets its controls for the heart of a sun," Harper muttered.

"No fuel," Dylan said.

"This will cut into out primary mission time," Rommie pointed out. "We could investigate this later, when we've returned with the hulk."

"We could," Dylan said quietly, "but we need to make an attempt to find answers here before we go any farther. This shouldn't take us long."

"Uh, Dylan," Harper said, "maybe you oughta say somethin' like 'This could take a while, guys, keep a light on but don't wait up, have a cup of cocoa and get your cuddly toys and go to bed when you're supposed to because Mom and Dad could be out partyin' pretty late.'"

"I could do that," Dylan said, grinning, "but I don't talk as much as you do."

"Besides, Harper," Rommie said, "if we do run into trouble, I have complete faith in the fact that you'll come heroically dashing to my rescue."

"So I'd have to depend on Mr. Wright?" Dylan said, raising his eyebrows.

"Different rules apply again, Captain," Rommie said with a happy smile, "but this time it's because Harper didn't build you."

"I'm not even goin' there," Harper said.

"Good," Dylan said, turning to look at the hulk. "But we're going there. Mr. Wright, pick your spot and take us in."

"Aye, Captain," Wright said, "initiating docking maneuvers." He touched the thruster controls and the *Eureka Maru* began to slowly change course, heading for the aft end of the dead ship.

Harper shook his head, looking down at his console, but said nothing more.

Andromeda's head and shoulders appeared on the main screen and on screens around the Command Deck. "I believe we have the correct mix of counterfrequencies to combat the mind torpedoes."

Beka was the only one on the Command Deck. She regarded Andromeda steadily for a moment, then said, "Do you think this'll work? It'd be nice to not have to get shots every few hours."

"As far as I can tell, it will work," Andromeda said. "I've run multiple simulations and the final frequency mix tests out every time. Some of the signals will be jammed, others blanked completely. The result should be nothing more than a pattern of static."

"Okay," Beka said. "How do we deliver this?"

"Ms. Pogue was originally going to modify several electromagnetic field generators, but my estimate was that this would take too long."

"So?"

"The best solution, in my opinion, is to use the ECM fans. I can program the system to produce a continuous low-power output rather than the usual high-power signals." She turned her head, looking toward the screen next to hers. A schematic cross section of the

Andromeda Ascendant appeared and rotated, showing the fans out. Two of the six were darkened. "Even with only four of the fans in operation, this should be quite effective."

"Alternatives?" Beka asked. She didn't really want alternatives, but she had to ask. What she really wanted was for this part of the nightmare to be over and done with.

"Other than raking me stem to stern with plasma bursts—and I've had quite enough of that—the one other viable solution would be electromagnetic pulse. We have EMP generators on hand."

Beka shook her head. "I don't see that as a good choice, Andromeda. Too much potential for damage."

"It would require a full shutdown," Andromeda said. "However, I am a warship, and I do have hardened systems."

"So, one way or another, we get rid of these things?"

"It may take a little time, but yes," Andromeda said.

"Just as long as I don't have to go out there with a butter knife and scrape them off," Beka said.

"That," Andromeda said with a slight frown, "should not be necessary."

"I hope not." Beka considered for a moment, then said, "Well, I'm in charge, so I guess . . . let's do it."

"Aye, Captain," Andromeda said, "doing it."

"Let me know when everything's ready," Beka said. "I'm going to get a bite to eat."

Dylan had very little experience with boarding and inspecting dead ships, and it wasn't too long after he and Rommie had boarded the mystery ship that he began to understand Harper's nervousness.

Getting the *Maru* into one of the aft cargo docks had been no problem at all. From that point on, however, everything required an effort. With no ship power available, he and Rommie were forced to move slowly, using a device Harper had retrieved from somewhere inside the *Maru* to open each of the bulkhead doors. If any air had remained in the vessel after its abandonment, it had long since frozen.

"Looks deader'n dead to me, Boss," Harper said, his voice echoing in Dylan's head.

"I think our prospects of finding a party are minimal at best," Rommie observed. While she didn't need air, even to communicate, and could easily survive for some time in open space, she had suited up as well. There was no need to put additional strain on her systems.

Dylan turned, shining the powerful beam of his spotlight down a corridor that angled off from the junction they were in. He had no difficulty telling that the ship was of a much older design than the vessels he was familiar with—there was an oddly ornate style to the corridors, and the flatscreens were set firmly into the bulkheads, rather than hanging from supports at the junctions.

"This way, Captain," Rommie said, gesturing with her spotlight. She turned and kicked off from the wall, floating serenely along the corridor. Dylan, a little more ungainly, followed.

"Hey, Dylan," Harper said, "that electronic mega-key of mine opens damn near everything."

"It's good to know that, Mr. Harper," Dylan said. "I take it that there are some limitations?"

"Yeah. It doesn't open anything Tyr wants opened."

Dylan chuckled. "Very good, Mr. Harper."

A few minutes later, they were at the Command Deck. Dylan and Rommie looked around in silence. A pilot's chair still sat at the center of the deck, but the Slipstream hood was gone, leaving a mounting bracket and a few fiber-optic lines. Consoles had been removed, and one of the big flatscreens had a crack across its surface.

"I'm having horrible visions of my future," Rommie said as she looked around. "This is sad."

"No argument there," Dylan said. "I'm not seeing anything useful. How about you?"

"Not yet," Rommie said.

"Mr. Harper? Anything showing up on your monitors?" Harper was monitoring cameras mounted on his and Rommie's suits. His display systems could enhance the images, and between those and Rommie's systems it was unlikely that they would overlook anything.

"Just a sec . . ." Harper said, sounding thoughtful. "Go right." Dylan turned slightly and eased forward. "There. Looks like flexis in some kind of pocket."

"I see them," Rommie said. She kicked lightly at the deck and went floating over to the find. She pulled them out and riffled through the small stack. She tapped experimentally at the top one and was rewarded by having it light up. "Well, at least one still works."

She pushed off and floated to Dylan, handing him the one she had activated. He looked at it, frowning. "Paperwork. Looks like bureaucratese to me." He tapped at the paging controls, stepping through page after page. "It's a decommissioning report for the *Azure Harmony*-class vessel *Dark Fire*."

He handed it to Rommie, who looked at it and stepped through several more pages. "The registry number is the same, so I would say that we are standing on—or floating inside—the *Dark Fire*. That seems an odd naming protocol for a class of cargo vessel." She tapped again, calling up further pages. "Placed into secure storage at the Kelkoso Facility . . . which I've never heard of."

Dylan took another of the flexis and turned it on. "More bureaucratese. Memos listing parts and sections removed, authorizations from various names. Division Forty-seven engineering, Division Fifteen supply control." He looked up. "Much more of this stuff and my eyes are going to reach down and strangle me."

Rommie had turned another flexi on. "Captain, this is a reactivation order, dated CY 9766. It authorizes the use of the *Dark Fire* for the specific purpose of acting as a cargo barge, cargo and destination not specified."

"Well," Dylan said, "we know where it ended up."

"It's over the signature of General Janus Altmann," Rommie added. She tapped the paging control. "There's nothing after that on this one."

"Janus Altmann," Dylan said, thinking. "Right, I know who he was. Rear echelon flexi-sorter on the supply chain. . . ."

"Not to be obvious or anything," Harper said, "but I can see where this is heading. Just the right guy to know all about Waystation, right?"

"Right," Dylan said.

"I just can't see the point," Rommie said. "The Commonwealth was in serious trouble by that point, so what was the point of coming all the way out here with this ship?"

"Maybe he loaded up all the Vedran silverware and fine china," Harper said, "switched ships out here, and went off and bootlegged it somewhere else."

"Too complicated," Rommie said, "not to mention highly unlikely."

"It could have been a meeting point," Dylan said. "Harper's idea isn't all that crazy."

"But why not just go to the final destination directly?" Rommie said.

"Blastin' out of Slipstream towing a mothballed ship full of stuff kinda attracts attention," Harper said. "Better if you go somewhere quiet, offload the goods onto another ship, and then go wherever you're going looking normal."

"Plausible, I suppose," Rommie said.

"Sometimes thinking like a scoundrel has its pluses," Dylan said. "One of the many things Mr. Harper's good at."

"Gee, thanks, Boss." He paused for a moment. "I think I just got complimented and insulted in one go there."

"Complimented only, Mr. Harper," Dylan said. "We'll spend a few more minutes looking around and then head back. I suspect this is it, though."

He was right.

"I'm opening the ECM fans now," Andromeda announced. She turned to look toward the screen on her right side, where a ship schematic was being displayed. "The two sections that are out of commission should not affect the countermeasure mix."

Beka stepped around her piloting station and walked toward the screens. "You're going to full power right away?"

"No," Andromeda said, looking toward her. "I will gradually increase the gain. That will give me an opportunity to assess the effectiveness of this approach. I will also be able to judge whether or not there are any adverse effects." She looked to the right again. "ECM fans are locked."

"Then," said Tyr, who was standing at his usual station, "should we not begin?" He turned slightly and inclined his head toward Pogue, who was at Rommie's station. "Is there anything else that occurs to you before the switch is thrown?"

Pogue thought for a moment, then said, "Nothing. We've told you everything we know."

"Very well, then," Tyr said, looking back to the screens.

"Where's Trance?" Beka asked.

"On her way here from the medical bay," Andromeda said. "She should be here shortly."

"Okay," Beka said, "she can join the party late, I guess." She took a deep breath and let it out slowly. "Let's do it."

"Doing it, aye," Andromeda said. "Feeding minimum power to the ECM transmitters. I will increase power by ten percent per minute until I reach maximum output."

Beka took another deep breath, trying to maintain her focus. She glanced at Pogue, and saw the tension in the pilot's face. Tyr, on the other hand, seemed completely composed, standing casually at his station.

"ECM output is now at twenty percent," Andromeda said.

"I'm starting to feel better already," Beka said.

"Imagination, and hopefulness," Tyr said, looking at her. "You will not benefit from the effects for a while. Brain chemistry must first return to normal."

Beka sighed, frowning at him. "So it's psychosomatic. So what? Leave me a crutch here."

"Very well," he said, "if you wish me to see you as lamed."

Beka gritted her teeth and refused to respond.

"ECM power at thirty percent," Andromeda said. "I'm beginning to see signs of an interference pattern."

"Keep going," Beka said. "We're going to break this thing."

Trance swung out onto a between-decks ladder and quickly climbed down, dropping into the corridor that led to the Command Deck.

She froze as she felt a ripple of energy pass through her. She turned.

A ghostly version of herself was walking away up the corridor. The phantom Trance was wearing an ornate gown, and her dense fall of hair was interwoven with glittering jewels that looked like tiny stars.

Trance started in pursuit, but the phantom faded away before she could catch up.

She turned back. "Andromeda?" There was no answer. "Andromeda? Rommie?" She glanced back along the corridor. She was starting to feel afraid now. "Beka? Tyr? Paula?"

Only silence.

"Andromeda?" She turned around. If she ran, she could make it to Command. "Rommie?"

She started to run. Another ripple of energy passed through her, and she stumbled, sprawling on the deck. She got to her hands and knees, but she couldn't seem to get farther than that.

I shouldn't be this weak, it's not possible.

She managed to turn around, getting her back against the corridor wall. She felt weak and dizzy, and her hands were shaking.

Phantoms swirled in front of her. Several turned and looked in her direction. There was a flurry of motion.

They can see me.

The phantoms faded away. Trance closed her eyes.

It's almost here. It's happening.

"Andromeda," she whispered. "I know. I know."

She opened her eyes and looked at her hands. They were blurring, seeming out of focus. She tried to force herself back into focus, but she no longer had the energy.

"I'm not the only one," she whispered. "Andromeda, I can't stop it."

All she could do now was wait.

"Everyone to your positions, please," Dylan said as he sat down in the captain's chair. Wright had taken the *Maru* back out and back to their original orbit while Dylan and Rommie had shed their EVA suits. Now it was Dylan's show. "Let's see if anything's alive down there."

"Oh, yeah," Harper said, his expression cynical, "that's a real comforting way to put it."

Dylan grinned. "Just stay strapped in, Mr. Harper. This is likely to be a bumpy ride."

"Yeah, well," Harper muttered, "that's how they all seem lately."

Dylan tapped at the controls, and the *Maru* broke orbit, heading for the surface.

"ECM power at ninety percent," Andromeda said. "I am now seeing a pattern of static, as predicted."

Beka turned around to look at the entrance to Command. "Where the hell is Trance?"

Andromeda looked distracted for a moment, then frowned. "I've lost her signal. It isn't because of the ECM signals, either. Other trackers are working to specification."

"Great time for this stuff to happen again," Beka muttered.

"Where was she when you last had a signal?" Tyr asked.

"Fifty meters from Medical, on a ladder to the next deck."

"I'll see if there is any sign of her along her intended route, then," he said.

"Sounds good to me," Beka said. She managed a nervous smile. "At least some things seem to be going right."

Tyr left, moving swiftly but not running.

"ECM power to maximum," Andromeda said. She looked pleased with herself. "I detect nothing but a hash of static."

"Yay," Beka said. "Now we figure out how to scrape those barnacles off the boat."

Andromeda smiled.

That was the moment in which the first of the pulses hit.

Waves of energy poured through Trance, and she screamed in agony.

Desperately, she fought to keep herself together, but it was too hard a task, and she didn't have anything left in her for it.

She screamed again, and shattered, her mind scattering in all directions.

Convergence.

As swiftly as she had shattered, she came back together. There was no time to protect herself, however. Now she couldn't even scream as her once-possible pasts and presents swept over and into her.

Her body blurred, shimmering with color and light. Her eyes flickered with fire for a moment, and then were normal again. Changes came rapidly at first, and then slowed down. Finally, they stopped. She looked almost normal now—except for the odd out-of-focus appearance she had attained.

Her eyes closed for a moment, and then opened again.

Her name was Trance Gemini.

Their name.

Legion.

She began to slowly push herself to her feet.

There was a long, high scream from somewhere down the corridor, the wail of a soul about to be lost to terrible things.

The sound chilled Tyr.

"Andromeda!" he shouted as he started running. "Activate automated defenses."

"Automated internal defenses are active," she replied.

"Trance—" he started, and then his brain filled with a terrible white fire.

As he plunged helplessly forward to the deck, he heard Andromeda's anguished voice saying, "Code Blue, officers down!"

White turned to red and then to black, and Tyr lay very still, very silent, on the deck.

On the Command Deck, Andromeda's voice was repeating the Code Blue alert, although there was little point to it—no one was left to hear it. When the first pulse had hit, both Beka and Pogue had fallen, screaming briefly.

Now they were sprawled on the deck, unmoving, and to all appearances dead. Andromeda was relieved to find that her scans proved otherwise. She shut down the automated alert.

She shut down the ECM fans and felt the static fade away.

Her holographic avatar flickered into life, forming a direct link. There was no reason to waste time by talking in the nonvirtual world. "A booby trap."

"I feel like a complete idiot," Andromeda said. "I'm not used to that."

"Don't be so hard on yourself." Rommie folded her arms. "Nobody had any idea that these things could do this. I smell an upgrade that Micah and Paula hadn't heard about."

Andromeda nodded. "Agreed."

"There's something else," Rommie said.

"Trance."

"Something's happened. I think it's whatever she was expecting . . . whatever she was dreading." Rommie was looking scared now. "Andromeda, we're going to lose her, aren't we?"

"I don't know," Andromeda said unhappily. "I don't have any idea what might happen."

Beka was conscious again, trying to push herself up and making quiet little sobs as she did so. Blood was dripping from her nose and mouth.

Silently Andromeda put out a call for maintenance androids.

How did I ever become so incapable? she wondered.

"We didn't," Rommie said firmly. "The challenges just got a hell of a lot tougher."

ELEVEN • THE RAINBOW AT THE END OF THE GOLD

> Remember that old saw about "It is not my place to judge; that is for God. My job is to arrange the meeting"? Well, it would be nice if someone would return my calls so we could get on with this. I never see this sort of thing happening to social secretaries!
>
> —FIELD MARSHAL OMALLEY HARRIS AT THE
> ACHILLEAN SUICIDER UPRISING, CY 8501

The *Eureka Maru* was five hundred kilometers above the surface when Rommie said, "We have an incoming communication."

"Let's hear it," Dylan said. He tapped at controls, and the ship's attitude changed as it moved into a stable orbit. "No sense in running around while we negotiate with the gatekeeper."

Wright and Harper were watching Dylan intently. Rommie, meanwhile, seemed completely unconcerned. "Bringing the signal up now, Captain," she said.

The cabin speakers hissed slightly. "—Guard outpost Waystation to unidentified vessel. Please transmit identification or leave this area."

"This is the *Eureka Maru*, seconded to the *Andromeda Ascendant*, Captain Dylan Hunt commanding," Dylan said. He nodded to Rommie. "Transmitting identification and clearance codes now."

Rommie tapped at several keys. "Transmitting. Done."

"Stand by," Waystation responded.

"Friendly," Harper said.

"Let's hope they decide we're okay," Dylan said.

"What happens if they don't?" Harper asked nervously.

"They shoot us down," Rommie said.

Harper made a strangled noise.

"Identification, command, and clearance codes accepted," Waystation said. "You are cleared for approach and landing. Transmitting flight path information."

"Well," Rommie said with a smile, "they aren't going to shoot us down yet."

"Oh, yeah, that really makes me feel better," Harper said.

"Good," Dylan said. He was grinning as he turned to the pilot controls. "Now all we need to worry about is the weather."

"Right," Harper said. "Weather."

"Well," Rommie said, the picture of innocence, "it *is* much milder at the base's actual location. The planners chose to locate it in the more temperate zone at the equator."

"Oh, thanks," Harper snorted. "You could have told me this before."

"More temperate, Mr. Harper," Dylan said, "means it's only minus fifty Celsius and the winds only get up to two hundred kilometers an hour."

Dylan fired the thrusters again, taking the *Maru* out of orbit. With Waystation's flight plan locked in, there really wasn't much for him to do until they came in for a landing.

"Okay," Harper admitted, "maybe I *didn't* want to know that."

Tyr struggled back from darkness to find himself sprawled uncomfortably on the deck, his head throbbing. His nose had bled at some point, but the bleeding had stopped, leaving him with the uncomfortable sensation of blood drying in his thin beard.

He rolled over and sat up, trying to focus. The effort made his head throb all the more, but he resolutely ignored it.

He had been looking for Trance. Then something had all but torn his mind apart. It wasn't difficult to guess what had happened—

Andromeda's efforts to counteract the mind torpedo had obviously triggered some kind of high-powered counter-attack.

"Andromeda?" he said, his voice sounding hoarse. "Status?"

Holo-Rommie flickered into life a couple of meters from him. "To hell in a handbasket," she said. "You look worse for wear."

"Yes, well," he muttered, "having my brain torn apart from the inside certainly has not improved my day."

"Beka and Ms. Pogue are in bad shape," Rommie said. "I'm getting them to Medical now. Can you make it there, or do you need assistance?"

He got to his feet, slowly and shakily, steadying his breathing. "I've been in worse shape than this." He looked along the corridor, but there was nothing to see. "What of Trance?"

"Don't worry about her right now," Rommie said, frowning. "There's something very strange happening, but I need you in Medical at the moment. You need to patch yourself up and then take care of Beka and Pogue."

"Then I am on my way," he said heavily.

Slowly he started in the direction of the medical bay.

Her entire body was wracked with pain—so much so that she felt as though she were afire from head to foot. Vertigo assailed her, her head spinning with such force that she felt as though she might black out at any moment.

She couldn't give in now, not while the ship was threatened.

Trance leaned against the corridor wall for a moment, trying to pull herself together and focus on what needed to be done.

She straightened up again and resumed her labored walk. Each step was a fresh agony, but she forced herself to disregard the pain. She was going to take this fight all the way to Kalderash if she had to. The Kalderans were a violent and pestilent breed, and their actions kept interfering with her plans.

Now a Kalderan raiding party had boarded the Andromeda Ascendant. *In the all-too-typical Kalderan manner they were doing their best to lay waste to large chunks of the ship as they went.*

She stopped as she heard the hum and snap of Kalderan rifles, followed by the thudding sounds of explosive rounds hitting their marks.

Sixty meters past the junction, off to her right. She drew her force lance from its holster and thumbed it on. Pressing back against the corridor wall, she eased slowly toward the junction.

Kalderan voices, high-pitched and urgent.

She stopped, waiting.

The first of them stepped into the junction, looking up the corridor away from her. A two-meter-tall gray-skinned reptilian creature clad in brown fatigues, the Kalderan was armed with a large rifle.

A second Kalderan stepped into the junction, glancing down toward her. It let out a cry of alarm as it swung its rifle to aim at her.

She was faster by far. She shot the second Kalderan twice in the head, shifted her aim in a blur of motion as the first tried to dodge the falling body of his compatriot. She fired twice more, and the Kalderan fell backward as the effectors hit him in the head and chest.

There was no more time for subtlety. Ignoring the pain in her body and forcing herself to remain coherent despite the vertigo, she ran into the junction, spinning around and diving, firing down the corridor as she arced toward the deck.

She hit the deck, sliding a little. She rolled to her left, finishing up in a prone firing position. Three visible targets, too close together for their own good, their reactions confused. She shot all three and was in motion again even as the third hit the deck.

She ran along the corridor, following the incline. High-pitched chattering ahead, sounding frantic. Two more.

She ran toward the wall and jumped, letting her momentum carry her into a short loping run that ended as she kicked hard. She cartwheeled through the air at an angle, firing, hitting the other wall feetfirst, and continuing her brief run. She landed on the deck, going into a crouch, looking for targets. The two Kalderans lay sprawled on the deck, dead.

"Andromeda, give me an update," she said as she scooped up one of the Kalderan rifles.

Andromeda appeared on one of the junction screens. "Tyr is down. Beka and Dylan are holding their own on the Command Deck, and Harper is locked safely in Engineering. My android avatar is using a couple of lengths of steel pipe to make the Kalderans regret coming aboard."

"Need help?" Trance asked.

"Not really. I will try and reach Tyr. I suggest you head for Command to help Dylan and Beka."

"On my way," she said.

She ran down the corridor, climbing the first ladder she reached. Swinging onto the next deck up, she sprinted along the corridor and into a junction, going to her right.

Two more Kalderans. Startled, they swung their rifles up. She aimed her force lance and fired. One of the Kalderans spun and fell, his chest blazing.

The other staggered back, screeching, one shoulder blazing. She aimed and fired again, but she wasn't quite fast enough. The Kalderan opened fire just before she did. He only managed a single shot, but it was enough. The round slammed into her chest and exploded, throwing her backward even as her shot finished the Kalderan.

She wanted to scream her frustration, but there wasn't time.

She landed facedown on the deck. A small trail of smoke rose lazily from her.

"*Now* what?" Tyr said, halting. Holo-Rommie flickered into being. "That's a force lance. Why would anyone be firing a force lance?"

"A question you might wish to ask Trance," Rommie said. "She's the one firing it."

"At what?" Tyr couldn't believe what he was hearing—it sounded like one-half of a pitched battle going on somewhere in the near distance.

"A good question. Unfortunately, at me for the moment, as her effectors have to go somewhere." Rommie frowned, then scowled angrily. "Damn it. Command circuitry for my internal defenses in that area has gone down."

"You're planning to shoot her?" Tyr said, astounded.

"It's unlikely to be permanent," Rommie said, sounding utterly reasonable. "I have no idea what's behind this, but having someone running around being randomly and inexplicably homicidal is not something I really want."

"Understood," he said. "I think it prudent to stay out of her way for the time being."

"That might not be an option," Rommie said. "She's heading in your direction."

Tyr looked around quickly, but there was no cover immediately available. There was only one choice—go back the way he had come and find the nearest interdeck ladder.

He ran, entered a junction, and bore right.

Running footsteps behind him. He drew his Gauss pistol, turning and running backward.

Trance was racing toward him, her force lance out and aimed in his direction. In her left arm she was cradling a rifle that looked Kalderan in design, although he didn't know the model.

He threw himself to the deck and rolled toward the wall as she skidded to a stop and started firing. Effectors hit the corridor walls and flared.

He blinked, surprised. For a moment he thought he had seen ghostly figures appear.

He couldn't allow this to continue. Even as Trance aimed at something unseen, he brought his pistol up, aimed, and fired once. The bullet hit Trance in the chest, and she fell back, hitting the wall and sliding down. The rifle clattered to the deck, sliding toward Tyr.

"This seems to be turning into a habit," he said.

"I'd like to know what she thought she was shooting at," Rommie said.

Tyr stood up, then bent down to retrieve the Kalderan rifle. "I would like to know where she obtained this," he said.

"Out of thin air, apparently," Rommie said. "I'm detecting odd energy fluxes and surges, and I suspect Trance has a great deal to do with them."

"Medical," Tyr said. He sighed, then, without releasing the Kalderan rifle, bent down again to pick Trance up, slinging her over his shoulder. She felt unusually warm, and she was surprisingly heavy for someone so slight. "I hope I won't have to shoot her again before I get there."

Rommie sighed. "The day is young."

———

The *Maru* bucked and then slid to port as Dylan fought to keep the ungainly ship steady in the buffeting winds. They were five hundred meters from the surface now, and the wind had become even more of a nemesis than the cold. Waystation was not a forgiving place.

"See?" Harper said. "This is why I don't come to planets like this. Does anyone ever listen to me? Nobody *ever* listens to me. Why? I'm just the engineering monkey, that's why. This—"

"Shut up, Harper," Rommie snapped.

Harper fell silent, just in time for the *Maru* to roll slightly and slide to port once more. Dylan righted the ship and got it back on course.

"The cargo pod's the source of the problems," he said, finally. "The wind's getting in between the *Maru* and the pod. The airflow around the struts is causing most of the problems."

"We could have left the freakin' thing in orbit," Harper said. "It's designed for that."

"Do you really want to make multiple trips to and from the surface, Mr. Harper?" Rommie said. "That is what we would have to do."

"Never mind," Harper muttered.

"One trip down is enough for me," Wright said. He was looking pale again. "I don't want to see the inside of a galley for a while."

Dylan made some quick adjustments to the AG field as the ship tried to roll to starboard. They leveled out for a moment, then dropped like a stone.

"I'm so glad I'm not prone to motion sickness," Rommie said, sounding annoyingly cheerful.

"I'm too busy for it," Dylan said. His hands flew over the controls again, and the ship rose slightly. He dipped the nose and fired the rear thrusters for a moment. "I'm used to just flying in and putting down."

The *Maru* shot toward the surface. Dylan pulled the nose up again, and adjusted the AG field, firing the landing thrusters as he did so. Somehow, the ship stayed level.

Cautiously he brought the *Maru* down to a hundred meters, then to seventy-five.

"There it is," Rommie said.

Dylan had seen it too—not through the cockpit windows, but on one of the cockpit monitors. There was little to see through the forward windows other than a white glare. The enhanced image from one of the forward cameras showed the surface dome of the base as a distinct shape against the icy backdrop. They were right on course for the main landing bay.

"*Eureka Maru*, this is Waystation Control." The radio voice was nondescript, male, but lacking proper inflection.

"Go ahead, Waystation," Dylan said.

"We show you on course for landing," Waystation responded. "However, there is a problem here."

"Explain."

"We are unable to open the landing bay doors to admit you." There was a pause. "There are two options open to you. Return to orbit while my maintenance drones attempt to deal with the issue, or execute a platform landing outside and enter through one of the cargo locks."

Harper was looking stricken. "No," he said. "No, no, no—"

"Shut up, Harper," Wright said.

"Considering the ride down, Waystation," Dylan said, "I'll take the second choice. We'll bring the *Maru* inside as soon as the doors get fixed."

"Acknowledged, Captain Hunt." There was a pause. "Transmitting revised landing instructions."

Dylan glanced at a monitor. "Instructions received, Waystation. *Eureka Maru* out."

There was silence as Dylan maneuvered the ship closer and closer to the dome, looking for the landing platform. They would need to get the main doors open as soon as possible—trying to move what they needed to the *Maru* via a cargo lock would be arduous and dangerous work.

The landing platform appeared on the navigation monitors, and he brought the ship down carefully, easing forward a few meters above it. Moving slowly over the platform, he fired the landing thrusters several times, blasting away accumulated snow and ice.

"Harper," he said, "ready Bucky cables and scan for good anchor points. We're going to need to hold on to something if we want a ship to come back to."

Harper didn't waste time sounding off. "Bucky cables are ready to go, Boss. Scanning for anchors."

"Alright," Dylan said. He took a deep breath and eased the ship the last few meters over the platform.

"I've got anchor points," Harper said.

"Good work, Mr. Harper. Everyone hold on to something; this is going to be bumpy."

"The rest of the ride wasn't?" Harper said.

Dylan didn't answer. He adjusted the AG again, and simultaneously fired the thrusters. The *Maru* responded to this tactic by ferociously shuddering. Dylan could hear things being shaken loose in the back of the ship. There were several loud snapping noises somewhere behind him, and the acrid smell of shorted circuits.

"Ready on those Bucky cables," Dylan said.

He cut back the power on the landing thrusters. The *Maru* didn't usually touch down heavily, but in this instance there was little choice.

The ship boomed as the landing legs hit the platform. Shock absorbers took up some of the impact, but not all of it, and the *Maru* momentarily threatened to tilt sideways.

"Now!" Dylan snapped.

Harper fired the cables.

"On target," Rommie reported.

The winches whined into life. The icy world outside came level again, and the ship settled into a low vibration from the wind. Between the Bucky cables and the AG field, the *Maru* would stay put.

Dylan unbuckled himself and stood, stretching, trying to ease kinks out of his muscles. "I suggest we have a good meal—"

"Sadist," Wright muttered. Dylan glanced at him. "Sir," Wright added.

Dylan grinned. "I'm sure there's something aboard to settle your stomach, Mr. Wright," Dylan said. "Either way, you'll eat before we go outside." Dylan started to make his way aft. "Let's hope that the cargo lock isn't stuck as well."

"Some days, Dylan," Rommie said, "you're just a paragon of hopefulness."

"I do my best," Dylan said, grinning.

———————

In the medical bay, Tyr deposited Trance on a diagnostic bed with about as much attention as he would have paid to putting down a sack of potatoes. When Rommie flickered into life, looking disapprovingly at him, he glared back and said, "What?"

One of the flatscreens lit. Andromeda looked down at him. "I think she's hinting that you should treat Trance with a little more respect."

"Trance is to all intents and purposes quite dead," Tyr said with more patience than he felt, "I very much doubt that Trance, for the moment, cares. My concern is with the *living* members of the crew."

There was a groan from Trance's direction. Rommie and Tyr turned to look. "Then again . . ." Rommie said. The sentence went unfinished.

Trance let out another moan. Tyr noted with mild interest that her skin had developed a pinkish cast. After a moment she rolled onto her side, groaned again, and rolled off of the bed.

There was a flat thud as she hit the floor.

Rommie and Tyr looked at each other.

"I think that woke her up," Andromeda said.

Tyr turned to look back at the bed. Trance had gotten to her knees and was peering over the bed at him, looking rather woozy. "Oh, boy, that was bad, wasn't it?" Using the side of the bed, she got shakily to her feet.

"You could say it was . . . bad," Tyr said.

Trance stared at him blankly. After a moment, something seemed to occur to her and she looked down at her outfit. She prodded hesitantly at the charred parts, wrinkling her nose as some of it crumbled away. She frowned, then gave her chest an experimental poke with a thumb. She winced. "I got myself shot again, didn't I?"

"An astute observation," Tyr said.

She sighed. "I really hate these backwoods drifts," Trance said unhappily. "Somebody always starts trouble, then somebody pulls out a gun. . . ."

Tyr and Rommie looked at each other. "This," Tyr said, "is making less sense than usual."

Rommie looked back at Trance. "I suggest lying down for a time, Trance."

"Didn't I just do that?" Trance said. She looked down at her outfit again, frowning. "I think I need to get changed. At least Harper didn't throw up on me this time."

Tyr bowed his head and touched the fingertips of his right hand to his forehead. "Go. Change. Rest."

Trance nodded, then, delicately, turned around and walked out of the medical bay. Tyr noticed that she seemed quite unsteady.

As soon as she was gone, he looked at Rommie and said, "I have seen Trance drink alcoholic beverages. I have seen her give every appearance of being drunk. I do not recall her ever exhibiting symptoms of a hangover afterward."

"For all we know," Andromeda said, "she might have experienced hangovers prior to joining my crew."

"She might," Rommie said.

"I have to wonder," Tyr said, "if that was a hangover at all."

Rommie folded her arms. "All things considered, I have to wonder the same thing. In the meantime, you need to attend to yourself and see to Beka and Pogue."

Trance wandered, lost in a haze. She had the vague idea that she was supposed to be going somewhere, but the destination somehow escaped her. She didn't know where she was going, she didn't know where she had started from, and the space in between was a fog that refused to lift.

She tried standing still and leaning against a wall, but that only made the fog worse—it became violent, something that shifted and swirled around her, trying to pass through the space she inhabited.

For a few moments she was blind. Her existence echoed in an infinite number of ways through the quantum multiverse, and it was too much. Too much of her. Too much of everything. There were too many branches on the tree, and she couldn't pick out the one that represented her.

"I'm going to have to get bigger shears," she said, and giggled because it sounded silly, especially in that faraway voice.

She stood upright, then frowned. There had been a flicker of coherent thought, but it had been washed away by a rush of other thoughts, none of which seemed to be her own.

The sound of tinkling bells . . .

She frowned again. The sound seemed to be coming from somewhere close to her.

No . . . the bells seemed to be around her. Part of her.

There was a quiet snapping sound as she vanished.

"Your Highness," said the Guardian at the Command Deck entrance. He politely bowed his head, but his stance didn't change in the slightest.

"Guardian Ataturk," she replied with a polite nod. "How goes the watch?"

"Quiet, Highness," he said, smiling. "All the same, I stand vigilant."

"Not to mention poised for promotion," said a deep voice behind her.

Ataturk came to full attention, saluting crisply. "Yes, sir, Captain Anasazi. I could not call myself a Nietzschean if I lacked ambition."

"A commendable answer," said Captain Tyr Anasazi.

Trance turned her head to smile at him, making the tiny bells woven into her long fall of hair chime softly. "Alas," she said, "such ambition will someday cost me an excellent captain."

"Then let us hope, Highness," Captain Anasazi said, "that it eventually provides you with an even better admiral."

She laughed. "Indeed."

She turned, her ornate robes rustling, and walked onto the Command Deck of the Andromeda Ascendant. *There was a quick flurry of crew members snapping to attention and saluting.*

Andromeda appeared on the central screen. Soon after Trance had taken over the Andromeda Ascendant *as her personal ship, Andromeda had altered her image, although her core AI had replaced the bells with a weave of tiny jewels—far less distracting when trying to communicate information. The holographic and android avatars had distinct but subtle variations of their own. The least subtle variation came with the android, who wore a close-fitting uniform that allowed for ease of movement—part of her purpose was to serve as a bodyguard. Trance found this more than a little amusing— she had been adopted into the Vedran royal family many years before, and there was a tendency to treat her as a delicate little creature.*

She did a little dance, her bare feet soundless on the deck, and went over to the android avatar. "One of these days, Andromeda, dear, I ought to borrow one of those leather jumpsuits of yours and go out on the town for a night of revels. I'd be delighted to have you join me."

Andromeda bowed slightly, but she had the unblinking look that Trance associated with the android's disapproval. "Whatever you wish, Your Highness."

Trance gazed at her with a serious expression. "There's that protocol again."

"Protocol, Highness?"

"'Whatever you wish' tends to mean 'not on your life' when you say it." She pouted slightly. "Don't forget that the late Empress adopted me into the royal family because of my public appeal."

"A princess for the people," Andromeda said, with no change whatsoever in her expression.

"Not to mention this apparent tendency you have," Captain Anasazi said, "to survive assassination attempts unscathed."

Andromeda raised an eyebrow. "It's hell on the royal wardrobe budget, however." She raised the other eyebrow and pursed her lips for a moment. "The People's Princess or not, Your Highness, you must consider those around you."

"Alas," Trance said, "too true." She turned toward the front of the Command Deck, where the main AI was waiting patiently. "Are we on schedule?"

"To the second," Andromeda said. "The Than and Ogami contingents should be here momentarily."

"In fact, I'm detecting Slipstream events as we speak," the android said. She frowned suddenly. "Courier vessels, three of them."

"Incoming message," the main AI said. "On screen."

The face of a young woman flashed up onto the screen. "Princess Trance, Captain Anasazi, the Admiralty is ordering you to withdraw the Andromeda Ascendant *from this area. You are about to be ambushed by a Than-led fleet."*

Tyr wasted no time in discussion. He turned to face the pilot station.

Bright Morning's Dream, their Than pilot, was facing him, her force lance aimed at his chest. He was hurling himself aside before she could fire, drawing his own force lance. Andromeda already had hers out and aimed.

Trance ducked her hands into the voluminous sleeves of her robe, coming out with a matching pair of miniature gold-plated force lances.

There was no way to tell who fired the first shot. Bright Morning's Dream fired only once, the effector striking a bulkhead at the back of the

Command Deck. Tyr, Andromeda, and Trance all fired raking bursts that cut into the Than's insectoid body, sending the pilot backward in bursts of fire and trails of smoke.

"Get the Princess to safety!" Tyr shouted as he rose from the floor. "Andromeda, get those couriers aboard and stand by all weapons. Destroy anything that emerges from Slipstream."

"Acknowledged, Captain," the main AI replied.

"We're trapped in here," Trance said quietly.

Tyr spun around to face her. "Your Highness?"

"There are other Than aboard this ship, Captain Anasazi," Trance said. "There is no reason to assume that any of them are innocent in this plot."

"The second and third courier vessels are carrying accounts of Than-led attacks on various worlds, including Tarn-Vedra," *said the holographic Andromeda as she appeared.* "Other Than crew members aboard this vessel are indeed on the move."

"Activate internal defenses," *Tyr snapped.*

"Acknowledged," *said the main AI.* "How is this to be played?"

"Kill them all," *Tyr said.*

There was the sound of force lances firing, a body falling, and a high-pitched chittering from the entrance to Command. Several Than had arrived, weapons in hand; Ataturk would no longer achieve any of his ambitions. Now everyone on the Command Deck had their force lances out.

Chaos ensued as Than and crew members alike opened fire.

One of the Than twisted the end of an egg-shaped object and rolled it into the Command Deck. In a blur of motion, Andromeda was upon it, sweeping it up and hurling it past the Than and out of the Command Deck.

There was a loud blast, and the Than were blown forward by a concussion wave.

"Multiple Slipstream events," *the main AI announced.* "Targeting. Finding firing solutions."

"Fire at will," *Tyr snapped.*

"Firing cannons. Launching a full offensive spread from missile tubes one through forty. . . ." *Trance ignored further entries in the list.*

More Than in the entrance. She fired bursts from both lances.

"I suggest we get out of here," *Andromeda said.* "Captain, can you reach the pilot station?"

Effectors raked toward Tyr's position, forcing him to roll and duck behind another station for cover. The Than fire was answered by shots from the crew.

It was only a matter of time before they ran out of ammunition. She could only hope that they would manage to beat the Than back before that happened.

"I'll do it," she said, and before anyone could object, she was up and sprinting for the pilot station, firing as she went. All she needed to do was get them into Slipstream.

On one of the main flatscreens, Than ships were bursting into pyrotechnic flowers.

Trance settled herself at the pilot station, reaching up to bring the Slipstream hood down over her head. It felt strange to be taking over as pilot while dressed as ornately as she was, but she really had no choice.

There was more commotion from the entrance to Command. Ship's security had arrived, striking at the rear of the Than contingent.

Trance fed power to the engines amd turned the ship toward the Slip point. Than ships pursued, only to encounter the ferocious barrage being laid down by Andromeda.

She opened the Slipstream runners. As a portal bloomed ahead of the ship, she pushed the real-space engines to their maximum capabilities. The Andromeda Ascendant *plunged into Slipstream at full forward velocity.*

She smiled. They were going to be fine. The Than insurrection would be put down and the Vedran Empire could get on with business as usual.

Andromeda shouted, "Princess!"

Startled, Trance released the controls and turned.

A Than, clacking its mandibles and chittering angrily, had made a dash into Command, a force lance aimed at her.

"That won't work," she said. "Give up, and you'll live."

The Than chittered again, and opened fire. The effectors drove her back into the pilot station. Smoke trailed up from the front of her gown, and the tiny bells in her hair tinkled softly.

She sank slowly toward the deck as the Than was cut to pieces by lance fire from several directions. Her last thought before the temporary darkness came upon her was that she had really liked that gown.

Harper felt as though he had turned into a small species of polar bear. Getting into the High Guard uniform had been bad enough—he felt constricted by it, and the boots were driving him crazy—but adding the cold weather suit over the top of it left him on the verge of claustrophobia. Dylan and Wright seemed to be completely unaffected by being so bundled up, while Rommie was smiling cheerfully.

"Everybody ready?" Dylan asked.

"No," Harper said.

Rommie stepped up to him and looked him over, front and back. "Your caution is admirable, Harper, but you're more than ready."

"Did I mention that I don't wanna go out there?" Harper said unhappily.

"Too many times to keep count," Wright said wearily. "Hell, *I* don't want to go out there."

"None of us do," Dylan added.

"Oh," Rommie said cheerfully, "I'm looking forward to it myself." The three men turned to stare at her. She beamed at them. "Kidding."

Harper shook his head. "Boss, I swear I didn't build that sense of humor into her."

"Imagine that, Harper," Rommie said. "I have a self-upgrading humor subroutine. I'm positively full of wit these days."

"I didn't hear that," Harper muttered. "C'mon, no competition for the bad pun awards here, okay? Leave me somethin', already."

"Rommie," Dylan said, "I think it's an adorable part of your character."

"I'm glad to see *someone* appreciates that side of me." Nose in the air, she brushed past Harper as she moved to the main airlock.

"Thanks for the backup, Dylan," Harper grumbled.

"Anytime, Harper," Dylan replied. He gestured for Harper and Wright to precede him. "Just keep in mind that she can make my life a lot more miserable than you can."

"Right," Harper said after a moment. "She's got the edge over all of us, huh?"

"Never forget it."

Rommie was resolutely ignoring their comments as she stood by the airlock. "The docking tube has deployed properly, and is locked in place. So far it's standing up to the wind, but I'm not sure how long we can expect that to last."

"A long time, babe," Harper said, feeling momentarily self-important. "Don't find too many this tough and well built, but I'm not only the kid supergenius, I got a good eye for stuff like this. *And* I installed this baby myself."

"And if you screwed up," Wright said, "you'll be stuck right along with us."

Harper deflated slightly. "Yeah, well, I didn't screw this up."

"Then let's put it to the test," Dylan said. He hit the airlock release with the heel of his palm. There was a hiss, and the big double door opened smoothly. He pressed the release for the outer door.

Harper winced as the sound of the wind against the docking tube poured in. The tube boomed, vibrating. "Y'know, Boss, whoever decided to stick this place down *here* was nuts, and in a very bad way."

"It's a good thing that they were, Harper," Rommie said. "The orbital stations were the first on the closure list."

With that, she stepped out into the docking tube, striding toward the entrance twenty meters away. Dylan, looking like an immense snow creature, followed her, ducking his head slightly at the threshold.

Harper looked at Wright, who shrugged. Not willing to be the last in line, Harper stepped into the tube. He winced again as the booming and howling surrounded him; he could feel the sound in his gut, and he was glad that his ears were partly covered.

He was also glad for the arctic suit. The docking tube was unfortunately semitransparent, and his imagination was quite capable of providing anything he was missing from the direct picture he was getting of the world they had landed on. He immediately felt as though his body temperature had dropped twenty degrees, and he shivered. He doubted he could have made even this short trip without the protection of the tube. He would have thought himself to death before they were halfway to the entrance.

All of a sudden, he was at the far end of the docking tube. He looked back toward the *Eureka Maru*. It seemed to be a long way away from him.

They were gathered together at the entrance. He relaxed a little. This was the easy part, he figured. Open the door, turn on the lights, make hot chocolate by the liter.

"That's a negative, Waystation," Dylan said suddenly, and Harper tensed again.

"Oh, jeez," Harper said. He felt desperation rising. "Not another problem?"

"The door's supposed to open once we reach it," Dylan said. He had the sort of determined look that he got when he was about to deal with a problem head-on. "Waystation, I repeat, that's a negative. We are tied down and will not be returning to orbit at this time. We can't wait for you to get around to fixing this problem." Dylan turned to Harper. "Look for anything that seems like it could be an engineering access, get jacked in, and see what you can do."

"Oh, that's nice and specific." Harper flapped his arms experimentally, trying to figure out how to get inside his suit. He hadn't thought that he would need the wire until they got inside, which was his mistake. "Uh, Boss . . . ?"

Rommie's hand was suddenly in front of his face, with a wire across her palm. "It may not be your regular wire, Harper," she said, "but it'll work just as well." He stared at her, flabbergasted. "I'd say I know you pretty well by now."

"Yeah," he said, taking the wire. "I'd say that too."

Finding the access panel wasn't difficult, but getting it open proved a little more difficult. In the finish Rommie had to slip off one of her thermal gloves and pry it open.

Harper managed to fumble his way to the jack on his neck without doing himself any damage. He plugged the other end into the access jack.

"Here goes," he said.

He took a deep breath, closed his eyes, and jumped the mental boundary that separated the real world from the virtual. A tunnel of light swept up around his consciousness, and he allowed himself to fall. He took note of the data around him, but made no attempt to get close enough to cause a commotion. First he had to get used to this system—he didn't want to find himself being tossed out or, worse, being hit with defensive feedback.

Suddenly he was all the way in, standing in the virtual representation of the main system. He glanced around, looking for the pathway that he needed. Unless he was seriously mistaken, he just needed to find a way to reroute power to the entrance so that they could get the door open.

There.

He frowned. Not a power issue, at least not completely. He could see where the control subroutines should have been, but either they hadn't loaded or they had been deleted.

His face screwing up in concentration, Harper traced out where the subroutines should have been. That triggered another thought, and he looked more deeply into the control systems. It didn't take long to find another hole.

"So that's why you can't open the freakin' main doors," he muttered. "Great, like I don't have enough freakin' work."

He took a startled step backward as a figure sparkled into life in front of him. It appeared to be a male Vedran, but the imaging of the centaurlike being was crude. Harper guessed that no one had found a reason to update the internal avatar for the place.

"I am Waystation," the Vedran image said. "Who are you?"

"Uh . . . Seamus Harper." Harper hesitated for a moment, then added, "I'm the master engineer for the *Andromeda Ascendant* and the *Eureka Maru*."

"I have no rank on record that matches 'master engineer.'"

"Yeah, well," Harper said ruefully, "things have kinda changed. It's that thing about time and tide and stuff."

The virtual Vedran gave no indication of understanding this. "Why are you connecting with my systems?"

"Well, we're kinda stuck outside where it's real cold and windy," Harper said as he continued to trace out the second missing subroutine, "and we figure I could help with whatever problem it is you're having."

"I have maintenance systems to take care of operational issues," Waystation said. "I do not see what you will be able to achieve that I cannot."

"Yeah, well," Harper said, "that's where you, the basic artificial and sorta chunky-Vedran-looking AI, and me, Mrs. Harper's handsome boy genius, see things differently." Harper pointed up and to his left. "Like the missing software stuff over there, and more missing software stuff over here, and there's probably some other stuff as well, but that's gonna wait 'til we're inside and I'm warming up again."

The Vedran image turned its head to look where Harper had pointed. "Those subroutines were removed in my last upgrade, I believe. According to the notes, they were discarded as redundant."

"Yeah, well," Harper said, "somebody screwed up, 'cause they weren't." He concentrated again. "I'm betting you've got backups around here, and I can restore from those, at least get one door open. When was this upgrade done? Helps me find the backups."

"Commonwealth Year 9765," the AI said promptly.

"Okay," Harper said absently. Then it struck him. "9765? You sure about that? Yeah, of course you're sure about that."

The AI didn't answer. Instead, it just watched him patiently.

Harper quickly dug into the AI's data storage, sorting through the files as quickly as he could. *There.* He opened the compressed backup files, code-scanning for the sections he needed—no need to restore everything. Right now he just wanted that door open. The main doors he could take care of when they were settled inside and really needed them open.

He smirked silently at the thought of Dylan having to go back out to bring the *Maru* in.

He slotted the code block into place, looked it over, and gave it a few tweaks to tighten it up. Once he was sure it was clean enough, he booted it.

"Interesting," Waystation commented. "My diagnostic reveals no duplication. Obviously there was an error."

"Yeah," Harper said, watching as power was routed into the proper circuits. "Somebody screwed up." He looked down at the Vedran image. "Get that door open, pal. I'll be back later to do the rest."

The AI didn't have time to answer before he was back down the rabbit hole into the real world. He unplugged the wire and turned to Dylan. "We're in."

"Good work, Mr. Harper," Dylan said, clapping a hand on the engineer's shoulder.

There was a boom from the direction of the door, and it slid open somewhat reluctantly. The four of them hurried inside, and the door slid shut again. The sudden quiet startled Harper.

Several lights flickered on, revealing a curving stairway and an elevator.

"Stairs," Dylan said. "We can use the elevator once we've checked everything out and confirmed that it's working properly."

"Dylan," Harper said as they started down the stairs. A few of the lights had failed, leaving patches of darkness that spooked Harper more than a little. There was something about this place that seemed wrong, but he couldn't figure out just what was bothering him—except for one thing. "The AI said his last upgrade was in CY 9765."

Dylan, who was on point, stopped so suddenly and turned that the rest of them almost piled into him. "That's impossible."

"Technically," Rommie said, "it isn't impossible, but it is extremely improbable."

"Yeah," Harper said, "that's what I'd say too, except for the fact that the AI's software just happened to be missing subroutines that control the entrances into this place. The AI said they'd been deleted in the upgrade because they were redundant."

"I take it," said Rommie, "that this wasn't true."

"You got it, doll," Harper said nervously. "I went into a backup and restored the code. The AI did a diagnostic afterward, and he says there's no visible redundancy."

"This sounds creepy," Wright said.

"This *is* creepy," Harper said. "It's bad enough seeing an AI with a Vedran avatar created in the dark ages of AI imaging."

"Now *that*," Dylan said, "is a relic. And, yes, that sounds like something we need to look into. In the meantime, let's get going."

Dylan started down the stairs again, this time at a noticeably faster pace. After a moment, the others started after him.

TWELVE • BLACK THIRTEEN

Ethics. A strange concept in our business, certainly, but it's our business that makes ethical behavior so necessary. Secrets, lies, and evasions are what we're about here—we are thus always in a state of dilemma, as we're also about new ways to blow up entire solar systems. Without an ethical touchstone, we would likely sow catastrophe and reap disaster.

—GENERAL JANUS ALTMANN,
UNHEADED MEMO,
CY 9763

"Whatever it is that is happening to Trance," Andromeda said, "it isn't the result of spatial or dimensional tesseracting as she was starting to believe."

Beka, Pogue, and Tyr had made themselves comfortable in the officers mess. Tyr, following Andromeda's instructions, had given all three of them injections that had helped ease the symptoms they had suffered from the retaliatory pulses.

Now it was time for food and strategy . . . and to figure out how to deal with Trance, who seemed to have gone on several different flavors of rampage.

"Then what the hell *is* happening to her?" Beka said. She sipped at coffee and made a face. "I'm used to Trance behaving in every weird way I can think of, but this is definitely way out there."

"Not to mention extremely dangerous," Tyr said. He sounded

calm, and was eating heartily, but Beka knew this situation was bothering him.

"It isn't exactly helping the *Andromeda Ascendant* to have her running around shooting at phantoms," Pogue said. "Isn't there some way to stop her?"

"Trance suggested taking a Slipfighter or a transport and leaving the ship," Rommie said.

"A good idea," Tyr said. "I would have found that quite acceptable."

"It wouldn't have worked," Andromeda said flatly.

"Why not?" Beka asked, frowning.

"Because," Rommie said, appearing unusually severe in her seriousness, "I don't believe we're seeing a single Trance here."

"Okay," Beka said, shaking her head, "now I know my brain's really fried. You've lost me."

"None of us as yet has a real understanding of just what Trance is," Andromeda said, "or what she's capable of. What we *do* know is that she has an ability to see probabilities. She has demonstrated the ability, as absurd as this seems to me, to time-travel on at least one occasion, and there may be other instances. She may be able to alter the outcome of events."

"Look at this," Rommie said, and she nodded toward the center of the table. Holographic images flashed into life.

Beka watched as one image of Trance was replaced by another, then another, and more in sequence. "Wait a second . . ."

"That's crazy," Pogue said, staring.

"That's a lot of different Trances," Rommie said. She nodded again, and more images flashed by. "From what we can tell, she's involved in a wide variety of circumstances, and is playing a variety of roles."

"And a hell of a lot of different looks," Pogue said.

Beka pointed at one of the images. Trance was curled up in bed, a sheet pulled up to her chin, one bare arm lying across a pillow. In a dismayed voice, she said, "Don't tell me that's . . ." She trailed off, unable to finish the sentence.

"Dylan's quarters," Rommie said flatly. "Yes. To say anything further would come under the heading of 'too much information,' I think."

"I appreciate your sparing us the details," Tyr said. "Where is she now?"

Andromeda looked off into space for a moment. "Deck Nine, and she appears to have your favorite gun."

Tyr sat stock still for a moment. "She does?"

"I don't know how, but yes," Andromeda said. "She wasn't in your quarters, or in the armory."

"I had better take care of this," Tyr said after a moment. "I will stop in at my quarters first, however."

He got up and left at a run. Beka found Tyr's anxiety understandable—that huge multibarreled monster could do a tremendous amount of damage, especially in plasma burst mode.

"Okay," Beka said. "So what *is* happening to Trance?"

"You could call it possession," Rommie said, looking more than a little dubious.

"Oh, great," Beka said. "Where the hell do we find an exorcist?"

Rommie didn't look amused.

"You're saying that Trance is being possessed . . . by herself?" Pogue asked.

"Judging by what we are seeing, yes," Andromeda said. "Trance is experiencing parts of lives that she might have had. Some of those realities are dependent only on one or two alternate choices having been made. Others seem more outlandish. For example, this one."

Another image appeared in the middle of the table. Trance, in an ornate gown, her red hair woven together with tiny bells and jewels; the fall of hair reached all the way to her waist.

"Interesting look," Beka said.

"She looks like a fairy-tale princess," Pogue said. "She looks gorgeous this way."

"There are subtle differences in her physiognomy and her apparent physiology," Andromeda said. "Her hair is the most obvious element, of course. Less obvious from the image alone is her height—she is fourteen centimeters taller." The image shifted as Andromeda stepped through the recording. The recording stopped on a frame of Trance standing in firing position with two undersized, golden force lances in her hands. "Obviously, something unpleasant took place at this point. Equally as obviously, it did not end well for Trance."

The holographic recording stepped forward again. This time it stopped with an image of Trance slumped on the deck, the gown ruined by still-smoldering damage from effectors.

"Somebody shot her," Beka said, staring at the image.

"Somebody," said Rommie, "who definitely wasn't one of us—in fact, somebody who wasn't even present on this ship."

"This is crazy," Pogue said.

"This is Trance," Beka responded. "I'm just glad Dylan wasn't here." She hesitated for a moment. She looked momentarily thunderstruck. "Rommie, she hasn't—"

Neither Rommie nor Andromeda said anything. Pogue and Beka looked at each other. Beka didn't know which way to take the silence from the two avatars.

Finally, Rommie said, "No. She hasn't. Yet."

"Yet," Beka said. "Well, *that's* a relief."

"We have no idea just how many possible variations there are," Andromeda said.

The image stepped forward again, then went into real time. Trance seemed to blur as she lay on the deck, and Beka could see what appeared to be phantom versions of Trance cycling around the prone woman.

Suddenly Trance was gone again.

"I counted a total of three hundred and seventy-two Trances before she vanished," Andromeda said.

"There may have been more," Rommie added, "but too subtle for my sensors to catch. There seems to be no particular order here, aside from each variant representing a path not taken. The more divergent the manifestation, the further back the decision points run."

"In this case," Andromeda said, "at least several hundred years."

"Several hundred?" Pogue echoed. "How do you know?"

The image flickered and they were looking at an earlier point in the recording. "While her form remains humanoid, the mode of dress and key accessories, such as this lineal brooch"—the image zoomed in—"indicate that Trance, in this iteration, is at least a member of the Vedran royal court, if not a member of the royal family itself, presumably by adoption if so."

Beka was openmouthed, staring at the image. She closed her mouth, shook her head, and said, "How do we fix this?"

"I don't know," Rommie said. "I'm not certain how it was triggered in the first place. It may stop of its own accord eventually. Or not. It's impossible to estimate how many different alternates there might be. The reason why one alternate manifests so completely while others barely appear is another thing I don't understand."

"Great," Beka said. "I guess we didn't have enough problems."

"Look on the bright side," Rommie said, "she's not actually shooting at any of you, which makes it less likely that she'll actually manage to hit you when she's in a gunslinging state of existence."

"That's so reassuring," Pogue said.

"The universe is a dangerous place," Andromeda said.

"And we still need to get the transmitters off of the hull," Pogue said. The pilot looked extremely unhappy. "Dylan's right. It's never easy."

Tyr might well have agreed with Pogue. He had stopped in at his quarters to pick up his huge multibarreled gun, and then had set out, with Andromeda giving him directions, to go after Trance. Under normal circumstances it would have been very clear who was stalking who.

Right now, he wasn't the least bit certain, and it made him extremely uncomfortable—putting himself in this sort of uncontrolled situation ran completely counter to all of his instincts and training as a Nietzschean. Nietzscheans simply didn't place themselves in situations that were contrary to survival.

Except that he did so regularly.

Thank you, Captain Hunt, sir.

"One hundred meters," Andromeda said quietly, "next ladder, go up to Deck Seven, then go to your right."

Tyr nodded silently, and went into a fast trot. Reaching the ladder, he jumped, caught the side, and had his right foot already on the third rung. He climbed quickly, cautiously looked out onto the deck in all directions, climbed the rest of the way, and stepped onto the deck. Going to his right he slowed to a fast walk.

Trance was directly ahead of him.

Although he knew by now that Trance was manifesting a range of different appearances, he was still startled when he encountered one that was so divergent that he had difficulty matching it with the Trance he knew. This variant was wearing tan coveralls, the legs tucked into heavy combat boots. Her hair was close-cropped and white, and her skin was the color of polished mahogany.

Trance was indeed carrying a multigun like the one he had. She also seemed to be on the hunt for something—in fact, he thought, she looked as though she were acting as the point for a military team.

He hesitated for a moment, then made a decision. He sped up, catching up to Trance as she continued, apparently oblivious to his presence, along the corridor.

Coming up behind her, he said, "Trance!" There was no response from her. "Hey!"

Cradling his gun with his right arm, he reached out and clapped his left hand onto her right shoulder. Panic rose momentarily in him as soon as his hand made contact. First he felt as though he had clapped his hand onto something made of steel. He had no time to consider this, however, as his sense of reality twisted and he lost all comprehension of which way was up. Reason told him one thing; what his senses told him was something else entirely.

He pushed the panic aside. Rationality in an irrational situation, then. Dispassionately, he looked at the situation. First of all, Trance seemed to have no idea that he was there. Secondly, he seemed now to be trailing along in her wake. Third, there were obvious visual phenomena occurring—his left arm seemed foreshortened, and the walls around seemed to be rippling slightly. Fourth, gravity seemed to be acting strangely at the moment—he had no sense of his feet touching the deck, and Trance appeared to be towing him along like a balloon.

Rommie flickered into being ahead of them. "That's quite a trick, Tyr."

"It's quite disturbing," Tyr said. "I'm at a loss as to how to handle this situation."

"You could take the standard approach and shoot her," Rommie suggested, an eyebrow lifting.

"I don't see that as a good approach," Tyr said, his voice filled with frustration. "I have enough on my hands—"

"No pun intended," Rommie said.

"—without risking this situation worsening. Accidentally opening a dimensional portal is not an end I wish to achieve."

Rommie nodded. "Considering that this is some kind of gravitational phenomenon, albeit one that does rude things to our laws of physics in some respects, that sort of side effect is certainly possible." As they were about to pass her image, Rommie moved to get ahead of them again. "According to my sensors, you're presently stuck to a mass that's equivalent to a small star."

"That can't be possible!" Tyr said.

"I agree," Rommie said, "for obvious reasons. However, there is an extra twist here—while my sensors are detecting that mass, analysis indicates, to one hundred percent probability, that said mass is dimensionally offset. It would appear that some very minor effects are somehow being filtered through Trance."

Tyr raised his eyebrows. "I'm glad for that, at least."

"You should be able to extricate yourself relatively easily," Rommie said. "You will be passing a ladder momentarily. Take hold of it. Be warned that normal conditions will reassert themselves instantly."

Trance and Tyr passed into a junction. As Trance stopped to check in all directions, Tyr dropped his multigun and reached out for the ladder, grasping it firmly. As Trance started to move again, he pulled against the ladder. It felt as though he were trying to extract his hand from congealing mud.

Suddenly reality gave another massive twist, and he found himself executing an unintended flip. He crashed to the deck on his back.

"I did warn you," Rommie said.

"I believe that was unavoidable," he said, getting to his feet and sweeping up his multigun. "It seems that greatly increased caution is called for here."

He resumed his pursuit of Trance, maintaining his distance and keeping his gun ready. The slow chase continued for another quarter of an hour without incident.

Suddenly Trance swung around, leading with the multigun, and yelled, "Down!"

Tyr didn't need the instruction—he was already on the deck and rolling over to the wall.

Trance opened fire on full auto, all of the projectile barrels spitting smart bullets in rapid sequence. Whatever her target was, she was determined to kill it.

Suddenly she reached down and flipped a selector switch just above the trigger guard.

"Damn," he muttered. That was the last thing he had wanted to see—she had just switched the multigun to plasma burst mode.

Before she could fire the first burst, he brought his own multigun to bear and, flicking the selector to full automatic, fired a burst. The bullets hit Trance, who staggered backward, sparks and smoke erupting from her chest.

He came to his feet quickly.

Instead of falling down as she should have, Trance regained her balance. She gave her head a quick shake, then looked around.

Suddenly she looked directly at him, swinging her multigun up. "Where did you come from, and what happened to my team?"

"This might be a little difficult to explain," he said quietly.

"Try," she said. "Drop the gun."

"Very well." He held the huge gun out to his right and let it go. It hit the deck with a thud. "As for the rest—"

Without warning he went as limp as a rag doll, dropping down and rolling sideways, drawing his Gauss pistol. He managed to fire three shots before he hit the wall, and a fourth immediately afterward.

There was a yelp from Trance, and then the twin thuds of her multigun and her body hitting the deck. Tyr stood up, carefully.

The alternate Trance blurred and faded, replaced by something resembling their Trance. As he watched, she seemed to lose definition.

"How did you know?" Rommie asked.

"I didn't," Tyr said quietly. "Obviously, I guessed correctly." He sighed. "This has to be stopped, and soon."

It seemed to take forever to make the descent into the heart of Waystation, and by that time all three humans were more than glad that they hadn't had to climb *up* those long, cold flights of stairs. Dylan wasn't about to give himself over to relief completely yet—while Harper had confirmed that Waystation's core AI was still functional, there was no way of telling yet if anything else still worked.

If worst came to worst, he thought, he could make it back up. He had climbed greater distances at far sharper inclines in inclement weather on heavy-gravity worlds.

Of course, I did that when I was a lot younger, too.

"Let's see what's behind door number one, shall we?" he said cheerfully.

Harper was winded from the long walk down. Fitfully, he said, "Jeez, Boss, gimme a minute here. I think I'm dyin'."

"Nonsense, Mr. Harper," Rommie said sternly. "You only feel that way."

"Besides," Dylan said, "you don't have my permission to die."

Harper snorted. "Yeah, right." He reached out and tentatively pressed the door activation panel. The door hissed open. "Whaddya know, it works! There's life, there's hope, hell, where there's hope there's probably even more hope. Which means there's hope for me yet."

"After you, Mr. Harper," Dylan said, amused. Harper gave him a worried glance, but said nothing. Instead, he stepped into the gloom of the lock. Immediately the interior of the lock lit up. Dylan squinted. "Bright."

"Not really," Rommie said. "It's actually no brighter than normal ship illumination. You've just gotten used to the lack of light on the way down."

"Andromeda," Dylan said in his best I'm-being-patient manner.

"You knew that already?" she said innocently.

"There are times when you can be picayune beyond belief," Dylan said.

"In a way," Rommie said, "that's a compliment."

She stepped into the lock ahead of Dylan.

"Don't bother going head to head with her, Dylan," Harper advised, giving him a weary look. "She's devious . . . and I didn't even make her that way."

Dylan and Wright followed Rommie and Harper into the lock. Dylan closed the outer door. Harper pressed the release for the inner door. The cold air in the lock blew out into the warmer air of the arrival area, resulting in a momentary mist.

They stepped out of the lock. Harper closed the door behind them. "Hey, at least it's warmer in here."

Rommie removed her face mask and folded the hood of her arctic suit back. "Don't celebrate yet, Mr. Harper. It's better down here, but it's still only six degrees Celsius at the moment."

"Yeah, well, I'm betting I can change that in a hurry," Harper said, "even with all the old junk around here."

"Lights first," Dylan ordered.

"Yes, sir, Boss, sir, Captain," Harper muttered. "Jeez, gimme a sec here, okay?"

"Considering that he's in uniform," Rommie said, "we could keel-haul him for insubordination."

"That's a little impractical on a starship," Wright said. Rommie fixed him with a too-serious look. "Well, I suppose you could *try*."

"After I have him walk the plank," Dylan said.

"Very funny, ha ha, you guys," Harper grumbled. "Let the smart guy here do his thing, okay, and if you're gonna treat this like the monkey cage at least throw me a banana."

"Shutting up as ordered," Rommie said.

"Wow, I can do that?" Harper said, surprised.

"No, but I wanted to be polite," Rommie responded.

"Alright," Dylan said, "you two put it on ice for now. That was a bad choice of words, wasn't it?"

Nobody replied.

"Got it," Harper announced. He played his gloved fingers over a faintly glowing panel. "Better squint."

Dylan narrowed his eyes to slits as the lights came up. "What about heat?"

"That's on too." Harper turned around. "Probably won't get too toasty around here, but it'll get better. Which is good, 'cause there's a lot of stuff I can't do with these gloves on, and it'll really piss me off if I freeze to something and tear off my fingerprints. Which I've done. Lemme tell you, Boss, that hurts even worse than picking a soldering iron up by the business end."

"Mr. Harper," Dylan said, "you're absolutely overflowing with information that I don't think *anyone* really wanted to know."

"How the hell do you make the mistake of picking up a soldering iron by the wrong end?" Wright asked.

"Comes with being the house wunderkind," Harper said. "Just don't always pick up on the details."

"In that case," Wright said, "I'll stick to being a bit above average. At least I'll keep my fingertips."

"And I'll have all the fun," Harper said. Now he seemed to be getting excited. "Let's go take a look at what we've got here."

The lock area was an enclosed space, with the elevator shaft to their right. With Harper in the lead, they walked out onto a broad walkway—more of a gallery, Dylan thought, as it was enclosed by thick windows of hardened plastic.

The view from where they stood was breathtaking. The enclosed area surrounded a landing pad and cargo area that could easily have handled the *Eureka Maru* and several more just like it with space to spare. Looking up, he could see the indistinct outline of the ship lock distantly overhead; it was a way of allowing ships in and keeping the environment out. If all went well, one of them would be flying the *Maru* through it shortly.

He looked back down again. They were in the top level, with four more below them. Dylan looked around, seeing High Guard logos along the walls, along with Vedran royal seals. He found it fascinating that each design change seemed to have a place—a little bit of Systems Commonwealth history presented in an understated manner. He wondered what other pieces of history might be stored here.

"I don't think this will be the last time this place is visited," he said. "I'm betting that this base is an accidental museum."

"Better hope it isn't *just* a museum, Dylan," Harper said. "We're gonna need some pretty recent stuff—well, pretty recent for your day and age, anyway."

"I'm impressed," Wright said. He had moved to the edge of the walkway and was looking out over the landing pad. "I can imagine a place like this under manned conditions, with ships coming and going. That'd be a hell of a place to be."

"It sounds to me as though you're setting yourself up for a career change," Rommie said. "Well, we can always use more people in the shipyards and on Mobius."

"Let's get there first," Wright said. Suddenly he straightened up, his eyes narrowing. "What the hell is that?" Dylan, Rommie, and Harper turned to look as he pointed toward a spot two levels down and not quite opposite them. "I thought I saw something moving, but I lost it. Damn."

Dylan glanced at Rommie, who was frowning. She said, "According to the information I downloaded before we left, there should be nothing active here. Even the machinery should be inactive until we need to utilize loaders and haulers and the like."

"I guess it could be my mind playing tricks," Wright said as Dylan turned to him. "I'm pretty whacked right now."

"I like the mind playing tricks choice a lot better than the other one," Harper said, his excitement replaced by nervousness. "The other one involves a lot of icky, painful stuff that usually gets dumped on me first because I'm the universe's favorite putz."

"That's one way of putting it, I suppose," Rommie said.

"Let's take it as a trick of the light," Dylan said, "and get to work. Mr. Harper, we need to find somewhere for you and Rommie to get plugged in so we can get some idea of what is and what isn't."

"That's it, Boss," Harper said, starting to regain some of his positive mood, "hit me with those technical terms." He turned to Rommie, who was grinning at him. "You're the one with all the plans and blueprints in her head, so lead on, Rom-doll." She remained where she was, her expression becoming neutral—apart from her raised right eyebrow. "Please?"

She inclined her head with deliberate graciousness. "My pleasure, Mr. Harper," she said, starting along the walkway. "I'm always happy to assist a well-mannered High Guard officer."

"Shee," Harper sighed. "And people say *I* lay it on thick."

It was the end of the line, she knew that all too well. They had been living on borrowed time, and the bigger surprise was that their pursuers hadn't caught up with them months ago. Perhaps there was less determination among them now, with the assassination of Warner Ellis, the corrupt head of the Planetary Alliance. The Alliance had risen from the ashes of the fallen Commonwealth not long after the Andromeda Ascendant *had been trapped at the edge of a black hole during the Battle of Witchhead. The ship had been freed after three hundred years, its captain and crew forced to come to terms with the fact that their lives had been completely and irrevocably changed.*

Captain Dylan Hunt was an optimist, however. He had chosen to pitch in and do his part in support of the changed universe. She had become part of his crew not long after he made this decision. She had been there when he discovered the rot at the heart of the Planetary Alliance. A case could be made, indeed, that she had quietly guided him in his discoveries.

The Andromeda Ascendant *became a rogue ship. Before long they were the symbol for the rebellion that was growing against the Alliance, and against Warner Ellis. She knew that there was more to the situation than was apparent; as much as she desired it, this was no matter to be simply resolved. Dylan's assassination of Ellis was a moot point—there would be someone as bad, or worse, ready to step in; there always was.*

For the moment, it didn't matter. This was the end of the road. They were surrounded by Alliance hunter ships and there was no way out. They had put up a tremendous fight, but the missile magazines were empty and their guns destroyed.

The ship boomed.

"They hit us with a Slipstream anchor," Andromeda said. "We're not going anywhere."

"Do you have regrets about what we did?" Trance asked the AI.

Andromeda smiled. "None. I would have taken measures to stop Dylan if I had thought he was wrong." The smile faded. "I regret only those we have lost along the way."

There were several quieter booms.

"We're being boarded," Dylan said quietly. He had been sitting silently in the pilot's chair ever since they had been declawed and crippled. She had first known him as a vibrant man, someone who loved life and adventure. Now he was drawn and gray, emotionally drained.

"You don't intend to stop fighting, do you?" she said to him, smiling slightly.

"Never," he replied. "Not while I have breath left in my body."

She ached at his words, knowing where this path would soon end. There were so many different choices she could have made, right from the start. This should never have been the result.

"Shipwide," he said softly. Standing up, he took a deep breath, composing himself, then said, "Ladies and gentlemen, this is the captain. As you are well aware, we have come to the end of the line. As of today, our war is over. I am proud of each and every one of you, and it has been my honor and privilege to serve with you. I believe our cause is just. The Planetary Alliance obviously disagrees with me.

"As you are no doubt aware, we have been trapped by a Slipstream anchor and Alliance agents are in the process of boarding us. At this point, if you decide that you are done with the fight and it is time to lay down your arms, let it be known that there is no dishonor in this. If you choose to continue the fight here and now, there is no dishonor in that either.

"Our war is done, but the struggle will continue. Dylan Hunt, out."

He bowed his head, eyes closed. She went to him and put her right hand on his left arm, looking up at him.

"I was so naive," he said. "A fool."

"Never," she said. "Wrong choices were made, that is all. Few of those were yours."

"Too many," he said.

"It's too late for self-recrimination," Trance said. "I will not hear it from you now."

"I'm just sorry I'll never have time to figure you out," Dylan said, opening his eyes.

"That's alright." She put her arms around his waist, and placed her head against his chest. After a moment, he put his arms around her as well. She listened to his heart beating. "You'll always be with me, and I will always be with you. Know that."

"*I know it,*" *he said.*

"*Good.*"

"*Alliance agents are dispersing throughout the ship,*" *Andromeda said.* "*The crew is fighting, but they stand little chance.*"

"*How long before they get to Command?*" *Dylan said.*

"*One point three minutes,*" *Andromeda said. She paused for a moment, then added,* "*The Alliance commander is Colonel Rebecca Valentine.*"

Dylan was silent for a moment. Then he said, "*Up close and personal, just the colonel's style. This could get messy.*"

There was time only for a quick kiss, and then they parted, drew their force lances, and waited. They didn't have long to wait.

The Alliance agents wasted no time on subtlety. A pair of egg-shaped objects arced into the Command Deck, and everyone dove for cover behind consoles.

There were two blinding flashes, accompanied by enormous bangs—flash grenades. They meant to take someone alive after all, then; most likely Dylan.

"*That was your one chance to surrender!*" *The amplified voice was female and familiar—Colonel Valentine. She and Dylan had once been friends, but where Dylan had rejected the corruption of the Planetary Alliance, she had embraced it.*

A few silent moments passed.

"*Time's up, boys and girls.*" *There was a click as Valentine's suit amplifier was turned off.*

Four more eggs arced into the Command Deck. They exploded in midair, spraying shrapnel. Somebody screamed.

Alliance agents, clad in black armor, poured in through the entrance to the Command Deck and the battle began in earnest. The atmosphere in Command was soon hazy from the exchange of fire.

There were too many Alliance agents. As one fell, two others ran onto the deck, firing at any potential target. One by one, as Trance and Dylan fought on, the Command crew died. It was becoming quite obvious that the Alliance agents were under orders to avoid killing Dylan, if at all possible.

Suddenly Command was quiet, and she realized that both she and Dylan had used up all of their effectors.

Colonel Rebecca Valentine walked down into Command, giving Dylan a sickly smile. "*You and your bitch-queen here should have surrendered,*"

Hunt." She kept walking toward him, then stopped a couple of meters away. She looked around, her face taking on the expression of a happy psychotic as she surveyed the destruction and death around them. "You've racked up a hell of a cost in blood and money."

"Somebody's always gotta pay," Dylan said. "My crew, your people, your sorry ass someday."

"Yeah, well," Valentine said, "we're saving a few guilders here and there by skipping the trial part of the equation. Speaking of which—"

Valentine snapped her right arm up, dropping a force lance out of a wrist holster and shooting Dylan in the chest. He fell like a rock, crashing to the deck.

"Nooo!" Trance screamed. She went to her knees next to him.

"Oh, yes," Valentine said. "That's his sorry ass."

Trance lifted Dylan's head and shoulders, cradling him. He was still alive, but she could tell that his life was slipping away. There was nothing she could do to stop it.

"Trance," he whispered. She heard blood bubbling in his throat.

"I know," she said, "I know." Despite her best intentions, she was starting to cry.

He reached up and touched her face. "I didn't know you could do that."

"There's so many things . . ." She stopped, beginning to ache again because he never would come to know those things.

"I love you," he said.

"I love you too, Dylan Hunt," she said softly. She placed her free hand on his chest. "Just as my heart is yours, so is my light, for they are one and the same. Wish upon a star, and I will be there, always."

Golden light spread from her hand, across Dylan's chest. As it suffused his body, she felt his life fade away.

One of the Alliance agents swore quietly. Another made a shushing noise at him.

She laid Dylan down again, and looked up.

"How touching," Valentine sneered. "The little girl likes to play Star Mother."

Trance stood up, not facing the colonel. "There was no need to shoot him like that."

"I thought there was," Valentine responded. "What are you going to do about it? Kick my ass? Give me a light show?"

"Something like that," Trance said, her grief turning to cold anger.

She spun around. She had a force lance in each hand—she had never dropped hers, and she had picked up Dylan's; it had been trapped beneath his body.

She leapt, flying into the air. The unexpected action caught the agents flat-footed, and their awareness that the lances had run out of effectors made them careless.

She had already flipped the selectors. As she flipped over in the air, she fired. Each of the lances could fire three plasma bursts.

Six men fell. She landed next to one of them, snatched up a fallen rifle as confused agents tried to draw a bead on her. She fired several times, clearing the remainder.

She swung toward Valentine, who had her force lance aimed at Trance's head.

"This may be futile," Valentine snarled, "but if I throw you into space after I shoot you, I wonder just how you'll do."

"You would be surprised," Trance said, walking toward the colonel, who backed up slowly. "You said something about a light show, didn't you? By the way, that thing is even more useless than ever."

Trance grabbed the barrel of the force lance. Valentine shrieked and dropped the lance. Her gloved hand was smoldering. "What the hell did you do?"

"A tiny version of this," Trance said, and she suddenly flared with golden light, lunging toward the colonel. Trance threw her arms around the other woman, looking into her eyes. "Congratulations on your Pyrrhic victory."

The golden flare was replaced by fire. Valentine didn't even have time to scream.

The fire was gone as quickly as it had arrived. There was no sign of Colonel Valentine bar a very light ash floating in the air.

"That was new and interesting," Andromeda said. "What now?"

"Are any of our crew still alive?" Trance asked.

"No," Andromeda said. "It was a slaughter."

"I need to go," Trance said. "You know—"

"That you can't help me now?" Andromeda said. "Yes, I know. Whatever happens, I will die. I'd rather decide for myself."

"Give me ten minutes to get clear, then," Trance said.

"What are you going to do?"

"Think of the Phoenix, Andromeda," Trance said. "Rebirth. A chance to try again. I could probably explain what I am, but there's no time anymore."

"Get going," Andromeda said. "Trance, it's been good to have you with me."

Trance smiled. "It was good to be here. I'm sorry it didn't work out better."

"Keep trying."

"I will, I promise."

Trance left the Command Deck at a run, knocking down agents when she encountered them. Five minutes later she was in a Slipfighter and weaving her way through the net of Alliance ships.

Ten minutes.

A few minutes later the light made by the Andromeda Ascendant *as she blew up reached her.*

Now it was her time.

She closed her eyes. A moment later, she was gone.

Once they had found the operations center, Dylan made a spur-of-the-moment decision to leave Harper and Rommie to play with the equipment and databases while he and Wright went exploring to see what else the base had to offer.

The plan was very simple—split up, Dylan going to the top level and Wright going to the lowest. Dylan would follow the gallery in a clockwise direction, while Wright would go counterclockwise. Eventually they would meet up again somewhere in the middle of level three.

If all else failed, they had radio communication.

Wright made his way down to level one, overwhelmed by the scale of the place. It was hard not to just stand and gawk—this one facility alone was bigger than a regular Lighthouse Keeper station.

He kept moving, trying to avoid being overcome by fascination. It would be possible to spend hours exploring down here. Or days. At least it seemed unlikely that anyone could get lost.

Still, being here alone also made him feel more than a little uneasy. He was unused to flying a solo patrol these days, and he missed the support of a wingman right now. Having someone watch your back could be a lifesaver.

He put those thoughts aside again as he continued looking around and making mental notes. There was a commissary on this level, and he went in to look around. It was completely self-service and, despite likely long disuse, in full working order. He found food stores in stasis cabinets against the far wall—items catering to dietary needs for species from Vedran to human to Perseid. He figured they would find more of the same in the main storage area.

He was contemplating the idea of making something to eat when he heard a noise behind him. It sounded like rustling cloth. He turned around, startled.

A shadow flitted across his field of vision.

He jerked the force lance out of its holster, thumbing it on.

The commissary lights shut off without warning, leaving only a mild glow coming from the gallery outside. He closed his eyes for a moment, then opened them again, trying to will his night vision to start working again.

Somewhere to his right there was a deep hiss, followed by a low growl. The hair rose on the back of his neck and along his arms.

This is definitely not good.

There was another hiss to his left, and the sound of movement. He swung that way and fired high. The flare of the shot revealed the source of the hissing—a dark-furred creature crouched a few meters away, its narrow red eyes fixed on him. Its mouth was drawn back in a silent snarl, revealing a horrifying double row of sharply pointed teeth.

Another hiss behind him.

What were they waiting for? They could only perceive his action as hostile, yet they were waiting.

Maybe these creatures only wanted to warn him. . . . He almost laughed at that idea. They were waiting for him to panic, that was all.

Where the hell had they come from?

He started to edge toward the glow from the gallery.

All three of them growled. The growling increased when he tried to take out his radio to call Dylan.

"It's going to have to be the hard play, huh?" he said. The growling subsided. Did they understand him? "Okay, look, I'm going to move nice and slowly, and I'll get out of your way. . . ."

The growling returned, even more forcefully—and a lot closer.

Alright, now was the time. Making a quick judgment as to where each of the creatures was, he made a dash for the gallery. He didn't get very far before his right foot snagged a chair leg. He crashed into a table, bounced off, and landed on the floor on his back. The impact knocked the wind out of him.

He heard one of the creatures leap, and tried to roll out of the way. A second one dropped down into his shoulders.

He tried to aim and fire the force lance, but the position was awkward. The effector clipped one of the creatures, and it howled. He could smell burning hair, but he didn't think it had done any real damage.

It did cause the creature on his shoulder to roar angrily. Suddenly his right arm was being grasped by huge paws and bent awkwardly.

He heard the bones in his forearm break, and then the pain hit, washing everything in a red haze.

Distantly he heard a low voice say, in Common, "You damned fool! The Guardian wanted him unharmed!"

"What does it matter?" another low voice said. "They are a threat. This has always been clear. We should take them and leave them to the winds."

"Do yourself a favor, Reinken," the first speaker said, "and shut up."

There was a sound like an exhalation of breath, and a light mist touched Wright's face. The red haze began to fade . . . as did everything else.

Harper was pleased with himself. He could usually count on being fast when it came to inputting data and working at control consoles, but he had outdone himself getting their list of needed supplies into the Waystation network. With that done, they could start compiling a list of what was available.

So far, it was looking good.

He jacked out and grinned at Rommie, who watched him with a neutral expression. "So far so good," he said. "Now all we have to do is get the *Maru* loaded up and get back home. Oh, yeah, and pretty much rebuild the Slipstream core from scratch, but that's what they made maintenance androids and boy geniuses for, right?"

"Among other things," Rommie said.

"Okay," he said, stretching and trying to get some kinks out of his back. "I'm starvin' here, so I'm gonna go find somethin' to eat."

Rommie held up a hand. "Not so fast, Mr. Harper."

"Huh?"

"I'm not needed here at the moment," she said. "You, however, are. We need to get the ship lock working, which is your job."

"Right," he said. "Better make it quick. I think I'm gettin' a low blood sugar attack."

"I'll be sure to hurry," she said, and left.

Released back to the lure of technology, Harper got back to work. After a little while he tapped at a panel and said, "Hey, Waystation, this is Harper."

A screen lit up to his left. "Master Engineer Harper," the Vedran AI said. "How can I be of service?"

Harper raised his eyebrows. "An avatar being polite to me," he said. "Now *that's* different."

"I do not understand."

"Don't worry about it." He held up his wire. "I'm gonna jack in so we can get those subroutines back in place for the big doors. We need to bring the *Maru* inside."

"Understood, Master Engineer," the AI said. "I will be waiting."

The screen blanked. Harper shook his head and grinned, then plugged himself into the interface console. A moment later he was inside the cyber environment and looking around. Waystation shimmered into being next to him.

"This one's a piece of cake," he told the AI. "We already got the backup, and we got the files ready. So all it takes is"—he waved his hands—"the magic word, which is *'restore!'* and we're done."

The AI got a momentary look of distraction, then said, "Interesting. The ship lock is now operating as it should."

"Yeah, well," Harper said, "I'd like to know what that was all about."

"I have no information on the matter," the AI said.

"I figured as much," Harper said. He looked around, trying to figure out where to go next. Waystation was networked, with some systems being older than others. He figured it wouldn't hurt to tweak a few things here and there. Smoother running, increased efficiency, the Harper magic at work. "I'm going to take a look around."

"Very well," the AI said. "I will be here, of course, if you have any need for me."

That thing's unreal, he thought as he picked a virtual direction and went farther into the system. He made adjustments as he went, tightening pieces of code here and there, but not finding any real bugs. As much fun as it might have been to do some real fixing, he was glad he wasn't finding anything—they really didn't have time for that. What they needed most of all was a structure for getting the supplies together and getting them loaded into the *Maru*. That was something he could set up with one brain lobe tied behind his back.

He was startled when he found himself in a brighter, faster area of the system—both newer hardware and software than he had been dealing with until now. Curious, he picked a direction and moved to investigate.

Suddenly there was a tall human male standing in front of him, a hand held out with the palm toward Harper's virtual self. The avatar was dressed in a black High Guard uniform. There was little that was immediately distinctive about the avatar's facial features, although the sandy, thinning hair was an unusual touch.

"Okay," Harper said, regarding the new arrival dubiously. "So who the hell are you?"

"I am Black Thirteen," the avatar said. It spoke in a clipped manner—this was a basic AI, serving a very limited function.

"Gotcha," Harper said. "Okay, Black, what am I looking at here?"

"This is a classified level," Black Thirteen said. "Ultra Red classification, quadruple encryption."

"Oh, great," Harper said. "That sounds like 'destroy before reading.'"

"You are not authorized for entry," the avatar said. "Present authorization or leave. Failure to do either will result in protective action."

"Just say you'll fry my brain," Harper said. "Jeez. Okay, I'll go, but I'll be back, and then you'll be opening right up, just wait."

The avatar didn't answer. Harper backed out of the area, stopped for a moment, then decided he was done. He exited the Waystation system and dropped back into the real world. As he unplugged his wire, the lights went out.

"Oh, just great," he said. "Now I gotta go back in."

There was a low growl from somewhere nearby. He went cold. Slowly he turned his head, trying to locate the source of the sound. Carefully, he reached down to his pistol, getting ready to draw and fire.

Another snarl.

"Uh, Waystation," he said, "what's goin' on?" There was no response.

He reached up and pressed the side of his neck. "Uh, Dylan?" Silence. "Rommie?" More silence. "Micah?"

Something rustled to his right, and he turned, trying to draw his Gauss pistol. Something hard slammed across his wrist, and his hand went numb.

The front of his shirt was gathered up and he was pulled forward, helpless. He had a dim flash of a big face full of fur and teeth.

"Not again," he said. "Not the Magog again."

Before he could completely panic at the thought of being reinfested with Magog larvae, there was a light hiss and he found his thoughts fading away.

Darkness.

This was not what Trance had expected. While the *Andromeda Ascendant* had taken her own life by choice, Trance herself had taken the option of discorporation and a subsequent rebirth.

She should not have found herself trapped in darkness like this. Wherever she was, it was a cold place, somewhere vast, something abyssal.

Fear almost took hold of her then. With a massive effort, she pushed the fear down, closing her eyes, stilling her senses for a moment.

Calm again, she opened her eyes. Carefully, she exposed her mind to the darkness, reaching out. When nothing attacked, she shifted her senses to the greater part of her body, building a sensory net that she allowed to expand outwards from her.

There!

She turned, and as she did so she realized that she had no point of reference in a physical sense—she was there, yet she seemed not to be there; Trance Gemini the person was there, but she lacked substance and weight. It was an eerie feeling. No matter which state she chose to be in, she could count on having mass—it was a subconscious anchor for her. Whatever this place was, she couldn't count on many of her abilities.

For a moment a terrible black weight of loneliness settled upon her, followed by sadness at the losses she had so recently endured and then confusion as her mind was flooded with inconsistent memories.

At the end she tried to focus. At the end, Dylan and *Andromeda* were gone, but there was no time for heartbreak. She had taken a Slipfighter, but not to escape, just to make the final step easier.

She had calmed herself, and begun the discorporation process, but before she could blaze to life in her natural state she had been unceremoniously yanked from that universe to this black one where the rules of her existence seemed to have changed.

She gasped, realizing where she must be. She had somehow been drawn into the foundation of the universe—of *all* the universes that she had the power to cross. This was the place where particles danced with cosmic strings, where strong and weak forces met, the place of first existence, from which all things had originally flowed.

She had come to the wellspring of her life. She had not been born in this place, but without it she would never have come into existence. *Nothing* would have come into existence.

She held up her hands. They were filled with tiny glowing bands that shimmered and gyrated. She watched, smiling, as the strings she held traversed the dimensions of time and space and shifted around the additional dimensional sets. Those additional dimensions made it possible for her people to do the things they could do.

They made it possible.

She looked up from her hands, her momentary playfulness gone. The strings faded away.

Slowly, she turned around. Fear was once again rising within her.

Light seemed to be coming from somewhere overhead. It was enough to illuminate an ornate cherry wood side-table, a design she recognized as Terran, although she could not place the time period. It would have been enough of an oddity by itself, but the incongruity was compounded by the presence of a fine china teapot, matching cups and saucers, and small containers of milk and sugar. To her senses, all these were undeniably real.

She walked slowly forward, curious. As she did so, she saw that there was also a heavy ashtray on the table. A curved tobacco pipe, a wisp of smoke rising from the bowl, had been carefully placed in the ashtray.

Closer yet, and she saw a tall wing-back armchair, covered in maroon leather. It was at an angle to her, but facing in just the right direction to obscure its occupant. Growing less and less fearful, and ever more curious, she increased her pace.

As she came level with the chair, an arm reached out and long, bony fingers swept the pipe from the ashtray. The owner of the pipe leaned forward, turning his head to peer owlishly at her. He looked to all intents and purposes like an elderly human. His shock of white hair was swept backward in a proudly leonine manner that helped to give him an air of insufferable arrogance. His hawk nose only added to this effect. He wore black trousers, a white shirt with a cravat, and a black frock coat.

She was certain that this was an illusion, just as the place where she was standing was an illusion—it was all relative, all a matter of perspective.

"Who are you?" she asked the old man.

Without smiling, he replied, "I am who I am, Trance Gemini." With a shock, she realized that he had spoken the language of her people. He had said her true name, not the Common-language name she had translated it to. "Welcome, Granddaughter."

"I am not your granddaughter," she responded absently, distracted by the emanations she was beginning to pick up.

"Then consider it a figure of speech!" the old man snapped. Abruptly, he came to his feet. "Never mind that it's accurate!"

"After all," a second man said from the darkness, "you exist because we came before you and set down the foundation."

The second man moved into a patch of light. He was smaller and younger. He was dressed shabbily and his hair was an unruly black mop. He gave her a bemused smile, and she smiled in return.

"There's something wrong," she said. "Something really bad is happening."

The older man hooked his thumbs into the lapels of his frock coat. "Indeed there is," he said imperiously. "Something very bad indeed."

"Where am I?" Trance asked.

"Somewhere safe," the second man said.

A third man was walking toward her. This one seemed almost as arrogant as the first. He was wearing a maroon velvet jacket, and she could see lace cuffs at his wrists. His white hair was artfully unruly. "We prefer to observe," he said. "We only act when there is no other option left to us."

"What are you?" she asked the third man.

"We are an avatar of Order," a fourth man said, as he walked toward her. This one seemed almost as tall as Dylan. He wore a long coat. His floppy fedora seemed to barely contain a riot of long curly hair that fell almost to his shoulders. He seemed amused at something. "This is the point, actually. You've been very naughty, you know. You've become terribly disorderly."

A fifth man, sandy-haired and dressed in a cream blazer and slacks, emerged from the shadows. "This is why we had to bring you to us," he said. "If we had let the situation continue, there would have been a breakdown in reality. This would have been quite intolerable."

"I don't understand," Trance said.

A sixth man now came forward. He was burly, and his hair was an unruly explosion of curls. "It's quite simple, really. The *Andromeda Ascendant* was attacked by devices that emitted electromagnetic radiation which, for the most part, affected your fellow crew members, but essentially didn't affect you. That changed when those same devices went into full defensive mode."

With an effort, she tried to remember. Something had happened.

"You succumbed to powerful forces that sent you out of balance," a seventh man said as he walked forward. He was small, dressed in a rumpled white suit. In one hand, he carried a cane and a white fedora. With a flourish, he put the hat on. "An unhinged quantum being is a terribly dangerous thing."

"I could have corrupted the main timestream?"

"Exactly." An eighth man came forward. "One timeline after another would fall toward the mainstream."

"Pieces of each reality would struggle for a place." This from a ninth man. "Reality would cease to make sense. Chaos would reign."

"Eventually, everything would fall to the Abyss," Trance whispered.

A tenth man approached her, a bluff, shaggy fellow in a corduroy shirt and jeans. "That is so. We heard your calls for help when no one else did but at first we did not understand."

"I didn't either." Trance said. "I'm not sure I understand even *now*."

"From the precipitating incident you send shock waves throughout the quantum foundation of the universe." This came from an eleventh man, one Trance could not see clearly. "In turn this filtered down to the primal foundation—here."

A twelfth man appeared. "We acted."

"Who are you?" Trance asked once again. "How many of you are there?"

A thirteenth man walked toward her. He was a stern looking man, his black hair cropped close to his scalp. His clothes were black, as deep as the darkness she had first encountered.

"We are the beginning," he said. "We are the end. We are one; I am many. We are known to your people; I am found in the heart of your deepest ancestral memories. You know us without knowing; you are part of me."

Trance turned her attention inward and sank deep into her memory but the ocean of her history yielded nothing. If these beings—these avatars—were indeed part of her deep ancestral memory she could not find a way to access the knowledge.

"Do not doubt me, Granddaughter," the first of the men said, giving her an imperious look. "We are there; I am the root, not the branch."

"You have called for help, Trance Gemini," the thirteenth man said.

Trance's mind suddenly filled with flashes, images, possibilities. "Dylan . . ." she said. "Dylan is in danger." She frowned, confused. "Dylan's dead . . . or is he?"

She felt panic rising. One timeline seemed as real as the next. She realized that she was starting to slip again, to become another Trance. It was time to be healed.

"A last question, out of curiosity. Why did you appear to me in this form?"

"Why do you take the appearance you have?" the third said.

"A frame of reference," she said. "A familiar look to disguise something less comprehensible."

"Precisely so," the old man said.

"You cannot help Dylan Hunt," the thirteenth man said. "You have only one choice: to help yourself."

The old man walked toward them. The others faded silently.

"Please," Trance said. "Please heal me."

The two remaining men flowed together. Finally, only the old man remained.

"Very well," he said briskly. He reached out and touched her forehead. "You must be remade as you were, Trance Gemini."

"I understand," she replied nervously.

"Very good." He paused for a moment, then recited, "I am the beginning. We are the end. We are one. I am many. I am the circle. We are the line. I live in you as you live in us."

The old man flared with white light, his form vanishing beneath the glare.

The light swept over Trance. She didn't even have to scream as she was torn apart.

THIRTEEN • "HERE THERE BE DRAGONS"

The inventive approach. A wonderful thing, that, finding solutions to problems and cooking up bright new things. Unfortunately, there is the other side of it as well—the fit of invention that results in a demolished laboratory, for example. Or, worse, the spasm of brilliance that results in the inventor, sometime later, asking himself, "Why did I do that?"

—VEDRAN SCIENCE COMMENTATOR PHENARII III,
CY 4399

"Harper?"

There was no answer from the engineer. Rommie frowned, suddenly concerned. She had come back to the operations center with food and drink for Harper—who she was certain would be grateful for it, even if she was enforcing a positive diet—only to find the place apparently deserted.

"Harper?" she said again, a little more loudly.

Still no answer.

She put the tray she was carrying onto the nearest flat surface, then went to surveillance mode. Almost immediately she found Harper's gun lying on the floor, halfway beneath a console. That was definitely not a good sign.

She bent down and retrieved it.

She opened a radio channel and tried again. "Mr. Harper?" Nothing but silence. She shifted frequencies. "Dylan?"

"Go ahead, Rommie." She was relieved to hear his voice.

"We've got a problem. Harper's vanished." She looked down at the Gauss pistol in her hand. It hadn't been fired recently. "He left his gun lying on the floor, however, so I very much doubt he went in search of a bathroom."

"We may have two problems," Dylan said. "Micah's supposed to be searching the lower levels while I scout around in the upper levels. He just missed a radio check, and he isn't responding to my signal."

"I don't know what this is adding up to," Rommie said, "but I really don't like it."

"Same here," Dylan said. "I'm coming straight back to the ops center. Wait for me there."

"I'll see if Waystation has any information," Rommie said.

"Just be careful. Dylan out."

She certainly had no intention of being reckless, considering the circumstances. She thought briefly about Wright's comment that he had seen something at the other side of the base; it might have some bearing on this mystery. What if the base had somehow been occupied by squatters since the fall of the Commonwealth?

That seemed a bit of a stretch, however. There would be more evidence of occupation, and the base seemed to be in fairly pristine condition.

There was one place to start. She placed her hand over an open access port and connected herself to the system—unlike Harper she had no need to use a wire. Come to think of it, there was no real reason why Harper needed to use a wire either—it seemed to be one of those organic affectations that she sometimes found herself at a loss to explain.

Inside Waystation's virtual cityscape, she quickly looked around, seeking Harper. There was no sign of him, which meant that he hadn't jacked into the system from another location.

"Waystation," she said, "locate Lieutenant Seamus Harper."

Waystation shimmered into existence. "I am unable to locate Master Engineer Harper, Andromeda."

Master Engineer? "The last time Mr. Harper was here, did he enter and exit normally?"

"Yes," the Vedran avatar said. "He made a series of adjustments that I have logged. He then went to investigate some retrofitted systems."

"Copy the log to me," Rommie ordered. The file appeared immediately in her safe storage area. She looked at it, and found nothing out of the ordinary. "What about the retrofitted systems?"

"Here is the trace log," the Vedran said politely, sending her a copy of the file.

She looked through it, following Harper's virtual movements. "Interesting. These seem like very recent additions." She frowned—virtually—as she looked at the end of Harper's progress through the newer systems. "What do you know about this Black Thirteen?"

"Nothing," Waystation said. "It is not an anomalous program, however."

"An advanced firewall," Rommie mused. "It appears that Harper decided to resist the challenge of cracking it." She paused for a moment. "I'm going to see for myself. Maybe I can get him to talk, avatar to avatar, even if he does seem a bit simpleminded."

She dove farther into the system, following Harper's trail and admiring the work he had done simply on the fly. Very quickly, she found herself being confronted by a new avatar.

"Black Thirteen?" she said. "I am Andromeda, of the *Andromeda Ascendant*."

"I am Black Thirteen," the avatar said.

Rommie stared at the avatar for a moment before saying anything else. Then she said, "You're modeled on General Janus Altmann, aren't you?"

The AI seemed slightly surprised. "Yes, I am."

Rommie couldn't put the pieces together yet. "What can you tell me?"

"Nothing," Black Thirteen said, "unless you present proper authorization. I am fully authorized to take punitive measures as required."

"In other words, you'll fry me if I try to break the encryption," Rommie said. "I get the point."

She withdrew swiftly, while the other AI remained neutral. She didn't bother with Waystation on her way out.

She disconnected from the system, lifting her hand from the access port. As she did so, there was a noise behind her.

"Harper?" she said, turning, and then, shocked, "Herakles?"

"Hello, Andromeda." The android avatar of *The Labors of Herakles* was patterned after a human male, tall, powerful-looking with bronze skin, dark hair, and brown eyes. He was smiling. "I see you finally decided to join the android world."

She smiled, trying to put this latest twist into some kind of perspective and assess the threat level. "Blame my chief engineer. What are *you* doing here?"

"I have the same question," he said. "As for me, I live and work here now. There'll be time to exchange notes later."

"Why not now?" she said urgently.

"This," he said, pointing a tiny black tube at her.

She tried to draw her force lance, but she was too slow. There was an electrical snap, and she shut down.

Trance was coalescing. Her consciousness had a slow-moving, airy feel to it, but it was definitely a single mind, not a multitude of variations vying for dominance.

No pain. Another relief.

She continued to come together, like a new star forming from a nebula, particles spinning together faster and faster as she gained cohesion.

She found both the process and the sensations utterly fascinating. Whatever Black had done to fix the problem had the side effect of making her feel very good indeed.

Faster and faster . . .

All of a sudden, she was assailed by doubt. Had she imagined Black? Why would an entity—or entities—capable of healing rips in reality bother with fixing her? It would have been far easier to simply erase her completely and cure the problem that way.

She vaguely recalled a voice: *The cause that you serve is one higher than even you know. The struggle will begin in earnest before long, Trance Gemini.*

Faster and faster . . .

You will soon forget this encounter. Serve your cause well, Trance Gemini.

The memory was becoming more and more distant, ghosting away.

Coalescing, Trance fell through darkness. Eventually she drifted into a dreamless sleep.

"She's got to be somewhere on board," Beka said, feeling panic starting to rise again.

"If she is," Andromeda said, "I can't locate her. The last time I saw her, she was heading for the Slipfighter hangar at a run. Just before she got there, she vanished."

"Damn it," Beka muttered. She was pacing back and forth across the front section of the Command Deck. She looked up toward the fire control station, where Tyr was lounging.

"It's fruitless to worry about Trance." He shrugged. "There is absolutely no telling what she will manifest next. We might get her off of the ship, only to have her change again and pop right back here."

"Tyr has a good point in this," Andromeda said. "We are also running out of time. The mind torpedo transmitters are increasing their output."

"The EMP generators are in place," Pogue said. "We need to do this *now*, Beka. We've waited as long as we can."

Beka started to issue a rebuke, but stopped. Pogue was only voicing the same thing that she herself knew in her gut. "We don't know what high-powered electromagnetic pulses could do to Trance, especially when she's in this kind of condition."

"She's resilient," Rommie said. "I'm more worried about me."

"Point taken," Beka said.

"If we're all in agreement, then," Tyr said, "I suggest we repair to the Slipfighter hangar and get ourselves ready to go."

Beka looked around, and nodded. "Andromeda, are you sure you're going to be okay?"

"Life holds few constants and fewer certainties," Andromeda said. "I'm very sure that shutdown will proceed very smoothly. Restarting is where the questions come in . . . and I wish Harper were here to answer those."

"Yeah," Beka said. "Me too."

"Initiating shutdown procedure in five minutes," Andromeda said. She gave them a smile. "I'll see the three of you very shortly, I hope."

"Indeed you will," Tyr said.

The three of them left Command at a fast walk.

"Rommie?" Nothing but silence. "Andromeda, come in. Harper?" Still nothing. "Mr. Wright?"

He stood in the fourth-level gallery, looking out over the landing area. Nothing seemed to be moving anywhere. That was both good and bad news.

He had no doubt that something had taken the other three down. He just didn't have a clue as to what he could be facing. There certainly wasn't anything to indicate that the Magog had taken over the base. Nietzscheans would have stripped the place and blown up the shell. There were other possibilities, but unless someone had recently dropped off a crew and taken off again, none of them bore scrutiny.

Just the same, the idea of something living in the place for an extended length of time seemed outlandish.

Something's taken Rommie down. What the hell could do that?

"Waystation," he said.

"Yes, Captain Hunt?" the AI replied.

"I seem to be missing three members of my crew. Can you locate them for me?"

There was a pause, then: "My sensors detect no sign of Mr. Wright, Andromeda, or Master Engineer Harper."

Master engineer? Dylan had to suppress a grin; Harper was trying to get his self-esteem out of the gravity well it so often fell into.

"Could they perhaps have returned to the *Eureka Maru*?" Waystation asked politely.

"No," Dylan said. "Not without telling me."

He increased his pace, heading for the operations center. The sense that something was badly wrong was accompanied now by a distinct prickling unease that had him constantly checking his surroundings. He wished he knew what he was looking out for.

Here there be dragons. What if something got left behind hundreds of years ago? If some kind of life-form had been living and breeding on the base, it would have the advantage.

He reached the operations center. Force lance at the ready, he swung in through the doorway, ducking down, moving cautiously into the room. He had it cleared in a matter of moments.

Nothing.

He found Harper's Gauss pistol on a console, and guessed that Rommie had left it there. On the other hand, he doubted that Rommie had intentionally left her force lance lying on the floor between two consoles. He bent down and picked it up, inspecting it. It was still fully loaded and charged—either she hadn't found reason to use it, or hadn't had the opportunity; the latter seemed more likely.

He put Rommie's force lance on the console; he wouldn't be able to use it. Harper's Gauss pistol, on the other hand, might come in handy. He looked it over, then opened his jacket and shoved the pistol into his belt. On quick reflection, he decided to take Rommie's force lance along as well. He slipped it into his holster.

He felt uncomfortable carrying so many weapons, but if he should find Harper and Rommie anytime soon, he was sure they would want to be armed.

He started for the doorway.

The lights went out.

He stopped, listening, the hairs on the back of his neck rising. He caught a musky scent, then a tinge of something burned—singed hair.

There was a growl to his left.

Without hesitation, he turned and fired at the sound. The effector struck the side of a console, causing an eruption of sparks and flame. At the same time there was a guttural yelp and Dylan caught sight of something large and furry stumbling back.

There was a roar behind him, and a deep, rough voice cried out, "Reinken! *No!*"

Dylan turned and dropped to one knee, firing almost overhead. In the flare of the effector and the subsequent hit, Dylan saw a monstrous visage lunging toward him, all teeth, blazing eyes, and fur. He rolled aside as the creature came down. It howled as it slammed to the floor.

Dylan came to his feet, trying to get a sense of where he was, and how many attackers there were. *Sentient* attackers, he realized, as the one he had shot started to get up, snarling. "The bastard *shot* me!"

Dylan turned and fired in the direction of the sound, aiming low. There was a crash as the creature—Reinken—threw itself backward.

"Good work, Reinken," said another. "I'm sure you'll delight the Guardian for the *second* time today."

"The other one will mend," Reinken muttered. "Are we here to debate, or to bring him in? He's going to get away, you idiots!"

That's the plan, boys. Dylan had the doorway placed now, as his night vision returned. He edged toward it, triggering his force lance to full extension.

He took a deep breath, letting it out slowly as he prepared himself. Without warning, he sprinted for the entrance. The dark silhouette of one of the creatures loomed up in front of him. Dylan brought the two-meter lance under and around, knocking the feet out from his would-be assailant. Up, over, and down; there was a crack and the lance slammed into the creature's head.

He swung the lance up again and hit the trigger twice. Effectors spat out. Most of the doors vanished in an eruption of fire and smoke.

He ducked and dodged through the opening he had made, and came out onto the third-level gallery. He went to his left, running.

There were several roars and howls behind him, catching up. He turned, lance ready.

"Damn," he muttered.

The creatures coming toward him were humanoid, but they bore some resemblance to Magog—they were covered in fur, and he could see way too many teeth for his comfort. In this light, though, their eyes had a disturbingly human quality.

He swung the lance over, aiming at the oncoming group. He fired twice over their heads, and they stopped, glaring at him.

"The next time I fire," Dylan said darkly, "I'll be shooting to kill."

The creatures exchanged glances, then one of them—Reinken, he guessed, going by the wound in his upper left arm—said, "You can't get us all before we take you down."

"Guess again," Dylan said, sounding a lot more confident than he felt.

More glances.

Dylan started to back away. "You fellows just stay here and behave yourselves." The one called Reinken started to advance toward Dylan. One of the others growled and pulled him back. "I'll shoot anyone who comes after me. I don't like threats, and I don't like being chased."

Reinken started to edge forward again. Once more he was stopped. The one holding him back growled, "It's alright."

"I don't believe that," Reinken said. "They're destroyers."

"What the hell *are* you?" Dylan demanded.

The one holding Reinken back said, "We're one of the mistakes that the Commonwealth buried. One of the many dirty little secrets of the Systems Commonwealth."

Dylan started backing away again, trying to understand what he was being told. He collapsed the lance again, then turned around and ran.

"Yo ho ho, this is the life for me," Beka sang. Then, sounding resigned to the vagaries of fate, she said, "This is what I always wanted to do, sit in a Slipfighter and float pointlessly in space for a few hours."

"There must be a point to it," Tyr said, sounding bored. "It seems to be providing you with an excuse to entertain yourself."

"And everyone else," Pogue added.

They were in individual Slipfighters, sitting a kilometer off the *Andromeda Ascendant*'s starboard bow. Beka's displays showed two of the three EMP generators that were now floating around the ship. She also had a close view of a section of the ship where the mind torpedo transmitters had taken hold. Tyr and Pogue would have similar displays.

"Hurry up and wait," Beka grumbled.

"Are you going to start yo-ho-ho'ing again?" Pogue asked.

"I don't think so," Beka said. Her temples throbbed. "I'm annoying my headache."

"You're annoying mine, too," Pogue replied.

"What's a headache?" Tyr said, his tone overflowing with mock innocence.

"It's like a pain in the ass, only higher up," Beka said. Her temples throbbed again. "My headache doesn't even like my lousy attempts at humor."

"Attention." The radio voice was male, neutral in tone, and devoid of expression. "Final phase of *Andromeda Ascendant* shutdown commencing now." There was a long pause. "Concluding in five . . . four . . . three . . . two . . . one."

Silence.

"Confirming final systems shutdown," Pogue said. "The *Andromeda Ascendant* is now off-line."

Beka scanned her own displays. "Yes she is, and let's hope like hell that we can bring her back when this is over." She took a deep breath and let it out slowly. "Alright, let's do this. Fire up the generators and start frying 'em, Paula."

"Firing up and frying, aye, Captain Valentine," Pogue replied.

"Hey, I like the way you say 'Captain Valentine.'" Her jovial comment did nothing to alleviate the tension she was feeling. "Makes it sound as though it means something."

"That's the sort of thing you learn in the military," Pogue said.

"There's a technical term for that, isn't there?" Beka said.

"Yeah," Pogue said, chuckling. "'Sucking up.'" There was a pause. More seriously, she said, "I have a full charge. Firing."

Beka's instruments registered the burst quite clearly, even though they were out of the way of the pulses.

On *Andromeda*'s hull numerous transmitters lit up as they burned out.

"So far so good," Pogue said.

"My instruments indicate some forty percent destroyed," Tyr said.

"Confirmed," Beka said. "Tough little buggers, aren't they?"

"Solid Kantaran workmanship," Pogue said.

"Nasty Kantaran weapon," Beka said.

"A good weapon to have at hand," Tyr said.

"I should have known you'd like it," Beka responded.

"I didn't say I liked it," Tyr replied. "I am simply acknowledging its usefulness."

"Gotcha." Beka scanned her instruments. "Time for the second shot. Maybe we can be up and running again by dinner."

"Charging the generators," Pogue said. "Firing."

Little flowers of light grew and died on the hull.

"Well," Beka said, watching, "they sure do look purdy when they do that, yup." She sighed and shook her head. "I know exactly how bored I am when I start talking like that."

Trance woke up slowly, feeling comfortable in the darkness. She no longer felt as though she were falling. She felt whole, and rested.

Something wasn't quite right. Several things, in fact. She knew she was on the bed in her quarters, but she wasn't entirely sure how she had come to be there. There were hints at the back of her mind, suggestions of memory, but something had been lost.

She was naked. Not entirely a surprise, and something easily remedied.

The most worrying thing involved her sense of the ship. There was something drastically wrong there—the ship felt cold, lifeless. Everything seemed to be shut down—the AI, life support, the AG field.

She got up carefully and went to her closet. She dressed quickly. The darkness and lack of gravity were no problem—she had her own ways of coping. Life support wasn't a problem, either, at least not for her.

She made her way to the Observation Deck, and stood at the huge window, reaching out with her senses.

There.

There were three Slipfighters less than a kilometer out, heading back toward the ship. She deduced that drastic measures had been required to deal with the mind torpedoes. She knew that something had gone wrong with Andromeda's countermeasures; whatever had happened had affected her in some way.

Perhaps something had been done that had brought her back and restored her? She couldn't tell.

Abandoning that line of thought, she ran down to Command. Everything was dead there, too. She went over to Rommie's console and tapped at a key. The console lit up, taking a moment to reinitialize.

"Time to wake you up," Trance said. She tapped out a sequence of commands. The remainder of the Command consoles lit up, and the main lights came on. "Come on, sleepyhead."

A neutral male voice intoned, "Initializing. Restart sequence has begun."

"Well," Trance said, "I guess I'd better go meet up with the others." She left Command.

Dylan continued moving down through the complex, looking for clues and finding nothing. In the level-one commissary he found indications of a fight, but nothing else. At least he now had an idea of where Micah had been brought down by these creatures.

He was baffled still. This was something that should have been clear-cut. Strange beings roaming around, his crew vanishing without a trace . . .

One of the many dirty little secrets of the Systems Commonwealth.

They looked like offshoots of the Magog; moved like them, too. Yet their eyes seemed human, and they spoke Common. Magog slaughtered everything that got in their way. These creatures . . . these *people* . . . had shown restraint.

Even so, his crew was still missing, and he had been attacked.

We're one of the mistakes that the Commonwealth buried.

"One of the Commonwealth's dirty little secrets," he said softly. "My God. Micah, you were right, weren't you?"

An organization existing off the books and off the record, a law unto itself, funded through convoluted secret channels and sheathed in a layer of ridiculous legend. An organization that could conduct the deepest, most destructive covert operations anywhere in the three galaxies, complete with its own fleet of ships. The same organization could as easily develop new and deadlier weapons, new breeds of spacecraft . . .

New forms of life.

One of the many dirty little secrets . . .

His head spun. How the hell could they justify making monsters? The Vedrans would never have approved of such a program.

. . . the Commonwealth buried.

He ran his fingers through his hair, trying to get a mental balance. He knew that he was wrong about this. The Vedrans would have known—a very small number in the government and in the royal court.

He knew no life beyond his work as one of the High Guard—he had always seen the High Guard, and the Home Guard, as something glorious and ideal. No matter where corruption might have sprung forth within the political structure of the Commonwealth, the High Guard was inviolate. He would never have expected perfection; that would be flawed thinking. He did, however, see the High Guard as representing truth and justice, something powerful yet compassionate because of the diversity of its members—thousands of species from a million worlds, millions of sentient beings working in harmony with hundreds of thousands of AIs of all kinds.

It had been his ideal. His spiritual home.

His truth.

It had brought him Sara, his long-lost fiancée; he had met her during a mission. She had unwittingly saved both his life and that of *Andromeda* during a failed attempt to retrieve the ship from the black hole that had trapped them. It was the High Guard that had been kept alive as Sara led the settlement and development of Terazed as a monument to the fallen Commonwealth and an expression of the ideal he represented.

. . . dirty little secrets . . .

He felt the strength draining out of his mind and body. The Nietzschean betrayal had been bad enough, but he could understand their reasoning, even though he could never agree with it.

This was a betrayal that went far deeper, and was far more personal. He had always believed in getting the job done, but the codicil to that had always been "in the best possible manner," not "by any means necessary."

. . . buried . . .

The pieces were fitting together neatly—the derelict in orbit, the problems getting into the base in the first place, the oddities that had turned up. They had walked into a trap, he guessed, one set hundreds of years previously.

These beings had been down here for centuries, yet there was no indication of their existence in the main complex. Even more confusing was the fact that these beings appeared to have at least a basic education, going by their command of Common.

He had tried like hell to hold on to his ideals, to his belief in the High Guard and the Commonwealth, to the notions of honor and service.

How can I do that any longer? How can I lie to people any longer about the things the Commonwealth and the High Guard represent?

He heard footsteps behind him, and swung around, bringing his force lance up.

It was Reinken. He held his hands up. His mouth quirked slightly, and he managed a crooked smile. "Don't shoot me yet, Captain Hunt."

Dylan's eyes narrowed. "You know who I am."

"Oh, yes," Reinken said. Still holding his hands in the air, he sat down cross-legged on the floor. "It is why I wanted to apologize for acting as I did. I am known for my temper, alas. This can be dangerous with us." He flexed his hands, and claws slid out from the tips of his fingers. "The reason should be obvious."

"Why did you attack me?" Dylan demanded. "And where is my crew?"

"Believe it or not," Reinken answered, "the idea was to reduce the possibility to conflict. We needed to establish that you were who you claimed to be. We were afraid that there would be a battle."

"And there was," Dylan said angrily. "I could have killed any or all of you."

Reinken looked over toward the gallery windows. "I know. We all know that." He looked back toward Dylan. "You arrived in a ship that's hardly High Guard standard issue."

"It's a damn good cargo hauler," Dylan snapped. "Are my people okay?"

"More or less." Reinken looked away again, and Dylan could have sworn he detected a note of embarrassment in the action. "The android and the loudmouthed little one are in perfect shape, aside from the fact that the little one has a hysterical fear of us, it seems."

"If you knew his past history, you'd understand," Dylan said. "What about Mr. Wright?"

"The third one." Reinken hesitated for a moment. "He's alive and in good shape. Unfortunately, I managed to lose my temper when we were trying to capture him. I broke his arm."

Dylan was silent. All of this was beginning to seem surreal.

Reinken looked back at Dylan. "I suspect I know too much history, Dylan Hunt. The knowledge leaves me afraid, and the fear leaves me with anger."

"Understanding that," Dylan said, glad to have something reasonably sensible to cling to, "is good. Can you take me to my crew?"

"I can," Reinken said. "It would be better if you went with the Guardian, however."

Dylan turned too quickly, almost losing his footing. A strong hand caught his arm, steadying him.

He found himself facing a tall, bronze-skinned, dark-haired man wearing a black High Guard uniform like his. No, not a man. An android—an avatar.

"I am the one they refer to as the Guardian," the android said. "I am Herakles, avatar of *The Labors of Herakles*. I am pleased to meet you, Captain Hunt."

The android held out a hand. After some hesitation, Dylan reached out and shook it. "At the moment, Herakles, the pleasure's all yours. I want some explanations, and I want my crew."

"Very well. Come with me." Herakles started to turn. "Explanations first, and then your crew."

Dylan didn't move. "Wrong way around, Herakles." The android turned back. "They're my crew. As far as I'm concerned, whatever you show me, you can show to them at the same time."

Herakles regarded him silently for a few moments. "Both your engineer and your support crewman are potential security risks. Andromeda is, of course, secure."

"I trust both of them," Dylan said. "It's what's important to *me*, not *you*."

"These matters—"

"These matters," Dylan snapped, "involve a deeply buried, long-standing black bag operation that created beings like Reinken here." Dylan took a deep breath. "Do you have *any* idea how this hits me?"

"You have served in covert High Guard units yourself," Herakles said.

"The units I served with," Dylan said, "didn't play genetic mix-and-match." He nodded back at Reinken, who was still sitting, although he now had his hands down. "Does he know? Do his people know?"

"Yes," Reinken said. He stood up. "We know what we are, where we came from, why we were made . . . that we failed our purpose. We know why we were brought here."

"Why?" Dylan asked. "Why were you brought here?"

"Mercy," said Herakles. "Or weakness. It doesn't really matter."

"There's a big difference between the two," Dylan said.

"Let them all see it," Reinken said. "He will tell everything to them anyway. No matter how we shake his faith now, Guardian, this one's an idealist."

"Not anymore," Dylan said. "Not after this."

"You'll get over it," Reinken said, walking past Dylan. Standing upright, he was several centimeters taller than Dylan. "I imagine my ancestors were none too thrilled about many things, but they carried on regardless."

"Follow me," Herakles said, turning around again and walking along the gallery. They had gone no more than two hundred meters before he stopped and pointed to the entrance to what appeared to be a service tunnel. "Down here."

They walked along the tunnel in silence for another two hundred meters, following a downward incline. Dylan didn't recall seeing any indication of something like this on the plans of the base.

Herakles stopped at a smooth, silvery door. He reached out and touched a panel. There was a hiss, and the door slid open smoothly.

Dylan stopped, staring past the doorway. "It's a ship? They buried a ship here?"

Herakles looked at him. "Yes. Specifically, they buried me here."

"This just gets stranger and stranger," Dylan said. "You're *comfortable* with being buried?"

"I serve a purpose," Herakles said. "I'm as comfortable underground as I was in space."

"Programming?"

"Adjustment," Herakles said. "An advantage of being an AI, I suppose—being able to make a drastic choice like that without undue difficulty or the slightest regret. Going from cargo hauler to caretaker could be considered a promotion." Herakles turned and walked through the doorway. "Welcome to *The Labors of Herakles*, Captain Hunt."

"I really don't get you," Beka said, shaking her head. Trance smiled at her in response. "Yeah, I know, so what else is new?"

They were sitting in the officers lounge, along with Tyr and Pogue. The *Andromeda Ascendant* hadn't completed her restart yet—the process had been slowed down by the overall state of the ship. The main systems were back on-line, finally, but neither Andromeda nor Rommie had showed up yet.

Tyr was silent, watching Trance as though he expected her to revert to her previous condition at any moment. Trance could hardly blame him for his uncertainty. She was sure the problem no longer existed in any form, but the others were going to have to see that for themselves.

"Well," Trance said, "it was just . . . one of those things."

"That sounds weak," Pogue said.

"That sounds like Trance," Beka said with a look of resignation.

"Beka's right," Trance said. She turned her smile on Pogue.

"Explanations only make the confusion worse. It's sometimes better to just accept things as they are and go on."

There was a brilliant shimmer to one side of the table, and Rommie appeared, smiling at them. It was immediately apparent that something had gone wrong with her imaging system—she was wearing a summer frock and a floppy hat.

Tyr raised his eyebrows as he looked at her. "There is obviously a tea party somewhere. Are we invited?"

"If there was, Tyr," Rommie said, "everyone would be on the guest list. Well, everyone here, anyway, including Princess Trance over there."

"Princess . . . ?" Trance said, dumbfounded.

"We haven't gotten to that one yet," Beka said.

Rommie nodded toward the middle of their table, and an image of Trance in full finery appeared.

"Oh," Trance said.

"A Vedran Princess," Beka said, shaking her head. "Trance, I'm jealous. Even if the Vedrans were still around, I couldn't get 'em to adopt me at gunpoint."

"It doesn't seem to have been the most secure life, however," Rommie said. "Someone was apparently attempting to kill you."

"It's all about choice," Trance said softly. "Many choices, not all of them mine. The road not taken is not such a simple thing as it sounds, you see." She looked at Tyr, who was watching her, his expression as neutral as he could make it. "This is one of the reasons why some of the things I say are such a riddle, or seem so enigmatic. I am not playing a game."

"How are we to know that?" Tyr said. "You seem to know more than you will share, you are overflowing with dark secrets, and you manipulate those around you."

Trance shook her head. "Tyr, I promise you that I don't. I can guide, I can suggest, I can offer whatever I perceive, even if I do not understand it myself." She looked at Beka, then at Pogue. "I cannot make choices for anyone, I cannot steer your lives or the lives of anyone else in the way that you may think I do. No matter what, you choose for yourselves." She looked at the image again. "Whether it is the road taken or the road not taken, it is never simple. Dylan often asks me to simplify things, to be direct. . . ." She was silent for a moment. "The universe is synergistic, you see. Every element influences other elements. Everything works together, for good or bad. It is the same with the choices we make—they work together. My choices affect others; their choices affect others still."

"And the choices others make can come back to you in some form or other," Pogue said.

" 'The worms go in, the worms go out, the worms play pinochle on your snout,' " Beka said in a singsong voice. The others looked at her as though she'd gone crazy. She grinned. "It's an ancient kids' rhyme that Harper taught me years ago. It's one of those silly gruesome things kids like, but it's really about the cycle of life—how everything feeds into everything else."

"The nail," Tyr said abruptly.

"Oh, yes," Trance said, recalling her meeting with her purple-skinned alternate in the hydroponics gardens.

"Come again?" Pogue said.

Tyr gave her a patient look. "It is also quite ancient," he said. "There are versions to be found in the literature of many species. It is a story of influences and consequences. There were two ancient kingdoms that went to war, and while the foot soldiers walked, the officers rode creatures called horses. These horses required shoes—horseshoes is the proper term; these were three-quarter round open metal hoops that were nailed to the horse's hooves."

"Sounds barbaric," Pogue said with a shudder.

"Not at all," Tyr said. "If the procedure was done correctly, the horse felt no pain, and it was protected from many potential problems that could lame or topple it—and if a horse was lamed, it had to be destroyed; the injuries would often be terrible." He sat back. "Anyway, as the story had it, in brief, before going to battle, the most important general in one kingdom took his horse to be reshod. As always, the blacksmith did a splendid job—not knowing that one of the nails he used was faulty. On the battlefield, the nail broke and the chain of consequences began. 'For want of a nail, the shoe was lost; for want of a shoe, the horse was lost; for want of a horse, the general was lost; for want of the general, the battle was lost' . . . and, finally, the war, the king, and the kingdom."

"All this and more," Trance said, continuing to speak quietly. "All of this on a cosmic scale, and the only thing I can do is hope that the choices I make are the right ones. At least I've had a second chance."

"Are things getting better?" Beka asked.

Trance shrugged. "I don't know. I think so, at least in some ways." She paused for a moment, listening inwardly. "There is much to do, though, and it will not be easy. At times it may seem almost impossible to overcome the things we face."

"Oh, joy," Beka said.

"There's something else," Trance said. "It's no longer urgent . . . I had a strong feeling that Dylan was in danger at Waystation. Also, does the name 'Black Thirteen' mean anything?"

"Nothing here," Rommie said.

"No," Pogue said.

Tyr shrugged and shook his head.

Beka didn't answer immediately. She seemed to be thinking about something. Finally, she said, "What I remember is that Black Thirteen was supposed to be this supersecret Vedran dirty operations outfit. Nobody has ever been able to turn up proof that they existed. You can find lots of stories about stuff they supposedly did. If there was really a Black Thirteen, they vanished when the Vedrans did."

Abruptly Tyr stood up. "I'm going to Waystation," he said. "I'll take a Slipfighter . . . unless Trance has another reason to try and stop me?"

Trance smiled at him, refusing to take the bait. "None."

"He's just stir-crazy, being stuck on the ship all this time," Beka said to Trance. "Especially with three wild women."

"Four," Rommie said.

"Five," Andromeda said as flatscreens lit up around the lounge.

"Hey, it's about time you showed up," Beka said. "You're getting to sleep in way more than you should."

"It will certainly be a pleasure," Tyr said dourly, "to be by myself for a time."

As Tyr was leaving, Rommie turned and said, "By the way, if Dylan can spare him, please bring Mr. Harper back. That was one of the most unpleasant full restarts I've ever experienced."

"Lying down on the job, Andromeda?" Dylan said.

Rommie's eyes moved as she focused on him. "I apologize for not springing up in welcome, Captain, but it seems that Herakles thinks a little restraint was called for."

Rommie had been laid out on a table in one of *The Labors of Herakles*'s machine shops and kept in place with restraining bands. The one that went around her forehead was the important one—it shut down her main motor functions. She could move her eyes, but was otherwise paralyzed.

Dylan bent over her and released the restraints while Herakles stood a couple of meters away, watching. Reinken stood farther away, by the door. "How do you feel?"

"Like punching Herakles very hard," she said, sitting up and taking her force lance as Dylan held it out. She glared at the other android. He tilted his head and raised his right eyebrow. "Several times."

"She's rather aggressive, isn't she?" Herakles said.

"I'm a warship, you idiot, what do you expect?" Rommie snapped. "Besides, you sucker-zapped me."

Dylan gave Herakles a questioning look. Herakles reached into a pocket and took out a small black tube. "Designed to instantly shut any android down," he said. "The alternative would have been to shoot her, which I didn't want to do."

"That was no way to treat an old friend," Rommie muttered as she stood up.

"I'm sorry about it," Herakles said, "but the situation was very difficult. People were very scared by your arrival, not to mention the fact that you got into the base." He looked at Dylan. "We knew you had been suspended in time, but we had to be sure that it was really you and not some marauder looking to raid the base."

"We tend to be a little on the paranoid side," Reinken said.

"I noticed," Dylan said. He looked at Rommie. "There are explanations for all of this, apparently."

"I hope so," she said. "Mysteries can be quite irritating."

"Let's go get Mr. Harper and Mr. Wright," Dylan said. "I gather Mr. Harper is a little upset."

Harper and Wright were being kept in the small brig area of the ship. Harper was pacing nervously back and forth in his cell, while Wright was stretched out on his bunk, his arms on his chest—the broken one was in a cast and sling, so the pilot had obviously been taken care of immediately.

"Mr. Harper, Mr. Wright," Dylan said as he stopped between the two cells. "This is no time to be slacking off."

Harper stopped in midstep, turning so fast that he almost fell over. "Boss? They got you too?" His eyes widened even farther as he saw Reinken, and he took a step backward. "Ah, jeez."

Dylan glanced at Reinken, who had held up a hand and was waggling the fingers at Harper. "Don't do that. He thinks you're some kind of Magog, and he has a bad history with Magog."

"Sorry," Reinken said, lowering his hand.

"A *very* bad history," Harper muttered. He looked at Dylan, puzzled. "Wait. They're not Magog?"

"They're not Magog," Dylan said.

"No larvae?"

"Not a one," said Reinken.

"Okay," Harper said. "This is where you shoot all the bad guys and get us all out, right, Boss?"

"Not today, Mr. Harper," Dylan said. He reached out and tapped the door release. The door hissed open.

"Huh." Harper looked out of the cell, but was reluctant to come out. "You're not, like, brainwashed or anything, right?"

"Mr. Harper," Rommie said impatiently, "get your skinny butt out of there." She turned and opened Wright's cell. "You too, Mr. Wright. Injury is no excuse for shirking."

Wright got up slowly. "Boy, I thought my old job was tough."

"It's an Andromeda thing," Dylan said, sounding more cheerful than he felt. "Death does not release you, and all that."

Rommie pouted. "I wanted a cat-o'-nine-tails for my next birthday, but Dylan says I can't."

"So now what?" Harper asked, taking his Gauss pistol as Dylan held it out by the barrel. He looked it over, then holstered it.

"Now," Dylan said, "we hear the truth." He looked at Herakles. "I hope."

The android nodded. "Follow me."

Herakles led them to the recreation deck of *The Labors of Herakles*. Several dozen of Reinken's species were there—Harper recoiled, and then got as close as he could to Rommie—playing games, reading flexis, watching movies, and more. Every head turned as the four newcomers entered with Herakles and Reinken, and there was a sudden undercurrent of whispering.

"Most of them had no idea you were here," Herakles said. "When Waystation notified the watch of your arrival, I was awakened—I spend much of my time suspended, you see, to extend my service life. That applies to all of us."

"All of you?" Rommie said.

Herakles pointed to a large table to one side. There were three figures waiting there—a black-skinned female human, a Perseid, and the blue-skinned centauroid figure of a Vedran.

Dylan stared, shocked into silence.

Rommie looked at them for a moment, then said, "They're all androids. The Vedran is the avatar for the *Empress Sucharitkul III*, a ship of my class. I don't recognize the other two."

As they approached the table, Herakles said, "The human avatar is Star, from the *Dark Star*. The Perseid is Herine, from the *Dark Thought*."

"I am named," Herine said in the peculiarly cadenced manner common to Perseids, "after the most renowned code breaker to ever have lived."

"Give him a chance," Star said, "and he'll ramble on forever."

"Pooh!" Herine said, sticking his beak of a nose in the air, which caused his long gray chin to point at Dylan.

"No dignity, these Black Thirteen types," Sucharitkul III said. "Hello, Andromeda. We knew you had survived the Commonwealth by ending up frozen for three centuries, but I don't think any of us expected to actually encounter you. After all, we are rather out of the way."

"That was sort of the point, Empress," Star said.

They all sat, with the exception of Sucharitkul III, whose form didn't lend itself to ordinary seating.

"There's four of you?" Dylan asked. "There's *four* ships buried here?"

"Five," Herine said. "The other is a decommissioned vessel, no avatar, android or otherwise. Originally used for cargo, now for homes."

"There's a derelict in orbit," Rommie said.

"That was towed here, loaded with cargo," Herakles said. He smiled. "My trailer, in fact. The cargo was shuttled down."

Harper was looking from one android to another, gaping. "You buried five ships?"

"Correct," Sucharitkul III said.

"That's gotta be a hell of an engineering project." Harper seemed to have forgotten his terror. "You got anything on this? Flexis, holos, any kind of records?"

"I think we can oblige." The Vedran avatar's eyes fixed on Harper's, her expression intense. "Understand me, young human—all of this is knowledge that must be protected."

"It will be," Dylan said. "I'll be happy to share our information with you as well. It should help to fill you in on the last three hundred years or so."

"There's a new Commonwealth now," Harper said. "You can thank Dylan for that."

"We can talk about that later," Dylan said. "Right now, I want some answers."

"Indeed," the Vedran avatar said. She had all of the commanding tone and bearing Dylan remembered from the few encounters he had

had with members of the Vedran royal court's upper echelon. She made an elegant gesture toward the center of the table. "Then we must begin here, near the end."

A hologram shimmered into life—an image of a pale human with unmemorable features and sandy hair. He was sitting in a large, comfortable chair behind a big polished dark wood desk. He seemed perfectly at ease, but his eyes had an intensity to them.

"General Janus Altmann," Dylan said softly. "Son of a bitch."

"I am Janus Altmann, and I am a general in the now-defunct High Guard. This message is for Captain Dylan Hunt of the *Andromeda Ascendant*, and though I am recording it at a distant High Guard base it will be copied and distributed to a number of safe locations. I hope that it will someday reach its intended recipient.

"Greetings, Captain Hunt. As you are no doubt beginning to realize, I am not the rear echelon flexi-shuffler that I am made out to be." Altmann smiled, then grew serious again. "This is Commonwealth Year 9770. The Commonwealth is finished, Empress Sucharitkul IV is dead, Tarn-Vedra itself seems to have vanished, and the High Guard and Home Guard are memories.

"I am the head of Black Thirteen, Captain." Altmann stood and walked around his desk, the image adjusting to keep him in focus. "Black Thirteen is the black operations division that is neither discussed nor acknowledged. Where there are hints of our existence, the very idea is treated as a fantasy of conspiracy theorists. This is how it should be.

"By the time you see this message, you may well know of the existence of Terazed, a project begun by your fiancée, Sara Riley. This is a massive undertaking and, as of now, I could not say whether or not it will succeed. I hope so. I am turning many of our resources toward this end, both to help build this dream, and to protect it. We have done many terrible things in the name of the Vedran Empire, built terrifying weapons and created monsters. Now we will turn our skills to something positive.

"Black Thirteen will not cease to exist, Captain Hunt. While some of us will certainly be quietly absorbed into the social fabric of Terazed, others will continue the organization. You intend to bring about a reborn Commonwealth. I want to have Black Thirteen acting in support of your efforts—quietly, and invisibly, of course.

"There is always more to say . . . fortunately, there is already much that has been said." Altmann's mouth quirked into a smile. "Certain details have been left out, of course. The important details are there.

"Good-bye, Captain Hunt, and good luck in your quest."

Altmann saluted crisply, and the image faded out.

Dylan was silent, trying to take it all in.

"That," Harper said, a bit too loudly, "is freakin' . . . freaky."

"I was right, wasn't I?" Wright said quietly.

Dylan nodded slowly. "Yes, Micah, you were." He sighed and sat back. "I'm an idealist, I always have been. It's my answer to the universe—Trance wants her perfect possible future, I want an ideal universe. There wouldn't be a place for an organization like Black Thirteen."

Micah shrugged. "Dylan, what they did was for the defense of the Commonwealth."

"And a lot of what they did," Dylan countered, "was for the sake of keeping control of conquered territories. The Vedran Empire wasn't built in a day, and it wasn't built on the back of diplomacy, not in the beginning." Dylan sighed. "Something like this poisons the dream. Poisons *my* dream."

"Then you're making a mistake," Rommie said, intensely focused on Dylan. "Why allow this knowledge to bring you down, Dylan? This isn't about you, it's about Black Thirteen, the old Commonwealth, and the Vedrans."

"Allowing yourself to be so affected is impractical," said the Vedran avatar. "You must ask yourself a single question, Captain Hunt. *'How can I use what I have learned today?'* "

"Look around you, Captain Hunt," Herakles said. "Does this suggest poison? Or does it suggest a journey toward an ideal?"

"It will be a long, long journey!" Herine said. He smiled with the manic cheerfulness that the Perseids seemed able to summon up at a nanosecond's notice.

"In other words," Star said, elbowing the Perseid avatar before he could say anything else, "there's no true ideal, just as the perfect possible future your Trance strives for is unreachable."

"The effort is no less worthwhile, however," the Vedran said. "In the end, the only thing that truly counts is choice, good or bad."

He looked at Rommie. She was watching him intently, her expression concerned. "This was something buried, Dylan. It doesn't put the lie to what you are and who you are, not unless you decide that it should. That much is about you."

Dylan turned to the Vedran avatar. "Where is Black Thirteen based now?"

She shook her head. "I do not know. We have heard nothing since General Altmann and the others left. I would think they will be difficult to find, if the organization still exists at all."

Dylan looked at Rommie. "We'll find them. Someday." He looked back at the Vedran avatar. "I don't want to admit this, but we may need them."

"The Magog Worldship is coming, isn't it?" Star said. "Yes, we know about that, and about *Andromeda Ascendant*'s encounter."

"First encounter," Rommie said.

Silence.

Dylan closed his eyes for a moment, then opened them again. "What about Reinken . . . his people? What was done here?"

"General Altmann was responsible for creating us," Reinken said. "We were intended to fight the Magog on their terms, and to act as troops against the Nietzscheans when their coup finally came. In the records we are Project One Four Oh Six Six. We call ourselves Altmann's People."

Others were gathering around the table now, curious and interested.

"I am Evern," said a taller male at the front. "You will see this in the records, in more detailed form, but our basic genetic structure is human. Nietzschean technology was used to alter and enhance that structure, and to add elements from the Magog. We were created to be fierce, unstoppable warriors."

"Project Fourteen Zero Six Six, File Nine," the Vedran avatar said. A flat image appeared, floating in the air.

This was a much younger Janus Altmann, a brigadier, going by his rank insignia. He was saying, ". . . have finally achieved a positive result, with every expectation that the first embryo will come to term. I am authorizing three embryos a month until the first births. At that point we will know if we really are successful, or if we must start from scratch once again."

"Same project, File Twenty-one," the Vedran said.

"Now that we are certain that the births will go as planned," Altmann was saying, "we find ourselves hurrying to create an environment for them, as well as safeguards for us."

"File Forty-seven."

A being covered in light gray fur looked toward the camera. Its eyes were bright, and all too human.

"What is your name?" Altmann said from somewhere offscreen.

The child was silent for a moment. Then it said, "My name is Sammo."

The image vanished.

"Sammo was the beginning," the Vedran said. "Altmann saw the Commonwealth threatened by monsters in the form of the Magog—"

"So he set out to create monsters of his own to send at them," Dylan said, hearing the bitter tone in his voice. "Fighting fire with fire."

"Fighting fire with high explosives," Star said. "Altmann's People were designed to be stronger, faster, and tougher in all regards, as well as being smarter than most humans."

"File Two Hundred and Ninety-three," the Vedran avatar said. "Twenty-three years later, the first real field test."

Dylan and the others watched silently as the recording played, following the mission from the loading of the transport ships, to the dropships landing on the Magog-infested Brandenburg Tor, to the unleashing of the People. At first there was chaos as the People and the Magog plunged into battle. The People carried weapons, while the Magog had none; the battle should have gone against the Magog.

Suddenly the People began to retreat back to the dropships. It was an orderly retreat, but seemed, to Dylan, to come out of nowhere.

On one of the dropships, the field leader—Dylan realized that this was the adult Sammo—ordered the pilots to take them back to the transports.

The image faded.

"Sammo and his teams had the revelation that the battle was pointless," Sucharitkul III said. "They also realized that while they had been bred for warfare, their natures were far from violent. Something had gone wrong. General Altmann had intended to breed warriors, but he got something else entirely."

"One of the many mistakes buried by the Commonwealth, one of you said earlier." Dylan looked around, looking at the intent faces, the multitude of fur colors and patterns. "Why here? Why this?"

"File Three Hundred and Seventeen," Sucharitkul III said.

Altmann, alone at his desk. "The days of the Commonwealth are drawing to a close. This project should have been closed, with full termination protocols, but I cannot justify the requirement to destroy them. Just as I will preserve Black Thirteen, I will preserve this species. I accept the responsibility for their creation. I cannot accept the need for their destruction. I will find them a home, or make one, whatever it takes.

"These are my children."

The image faded.

"Where are your ideals now?" Sucharitkul III asked Dylan.

He looked at her, uncertain. "Shaken," he said. "Very badly shaken."

"Will your spirit recover from this, do you think?"

He looked around at the gathered People, and he had to wonder what kind of accident of fate could tilt the balance. It could have been anything; the universe was both a dangerous and a magical place.

Finally, he said, "I think it will. It's my choice to heal."

"Yeah, well," Harper said, looking around at the People who were gazing at him with open curiosity, "I'm choosing to find something to eat, because I am freakin' hungry!" He looked at Rommie. "Nobody thought about giving me anything after I woke up."

"You have discovered something special here, Dylan Hunt," Sucharitkul III said as Harper followed Evern and Reinken in search of food. "Absolutism is a fool's path. Only a fool thinks of black and white, good and evil, when there are so many shades, so many colors to choose from."

"There is true evil," Dylan said softly. "I will always fight against that."

"That," she said, "is a decision that only you can make."

"Yes," he said. "Yes, it is."

On the *Andromeda Ascendant*, two days away by Slipstream, Trance Gemini sat amid a mass of plants in the middle of the hydroponics gardens. In her lap, she had a pot with a bonsai tree in it. She had been gazing intently at it for a little while, following the intricacies of its form.

She looked up, as though listening to something, and after a moment she smiled, pure and radiant.

She looked back down at the bonsai. "All is well," she said softly. She looked up again, growing more serious. "At least for now."

There would always be something else.

ABOUT THE AUTHOR

Steven E. McDonald was born on the edge of Sherwood Forest, in Nottinghamshire, England, and has never quite recovered. He has written for print, television, film, and the stage and has composed a large body of music. His published works include the SF thriller *The James Syndrome*. He currently lives in Tucson, Arizona.

Visit him at http://www.sanityassassins.org/~papabear

24.95

FIC   McDonald, Steven E.
Mcdonald
           Waystation.

WITHDRAWN

DATE